2016 JSC FD 34.84

THE ADMISSIONS

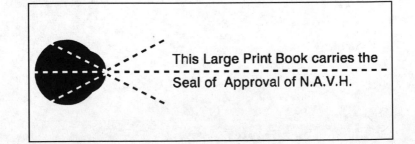

This Large Print Book carries the
Seal of Approval of N.A.V.H.

THE ADMISSIONS

MEG MITCHELL MOORE

WHEELER PUBLISHING
A part of Gale, Cengage Learning

GALE
CENGAGE Learning·

Farmington Hills, Mich • San Francisco • New York • Waterville, Maine
Meriden, Conn • Mason, Ohio • Chicago

GALE
CENGAGE Learning·

Wheeler Publishing Large Print Hardcover.
The text of this Large Print edition is unabridged.
Other aspects of the book may vary from the original edition.
Set in 16 pt. Plantin.

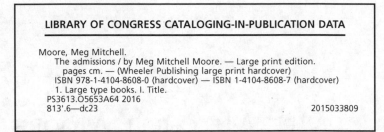

LIBRARY OF CONGRESS CATALOGING-IN-PUBLICATION DATA

Moore, Meg Mitchell.
    The admissions / by Meg Mitchell Moore. — Large print edition.
      pages cm. — (Wheeler Publishing large print hardcover)
      ISBN 978-1-4104-8608-0 (hardcover) — ISBN 1-4104-8608-7 (hardcover)
      1. Large type books. I. Title.
    PS3613.O5653A64 2016
    813'.6—dc23   2015033809

Published in 2016 by arrangement with Doubleday, a division of
Penguin Random House LLC

Printed in Mexico
1 2 3 4 5 6 7 20 19 18 17 16

For my parents

December
The phone.

Nora was trying not to worry. But she'd been a mother for nearly eighteen years now. She was going to worry.

It was a beautiful early-winter day in the Bay Area, which meant that it was sixty-five degrees and sunny, or would be until the fog rolled in later in the afternoon. No need for so much as a mitten. Christmas was nine days away.

She was reaching for her cell when the home phone rang.

Nobody ever called the home number. She'd threatened to have it disconnected so many times that it was now a standing joke in the Hawthorne family. Because she never had time to do anything she threatened to do, until now.

Mrs. Hawthorne?

Yes. Her hand shaking as she cradled the

7

receiver.

A man's voice, unfamiliar.

Nora hadn't thought her heart could climb any farther up her throat than it had in recent weeks. But it could, it turned out, it could.

When Nora and her sister, Marianne, were young, growing up in Narragansett, Rhode Island, they used to play a game. One of them would say to the other: A genie grants you three wishes. What would you wish for?

They would say things like: I wish all the appliances in the house would turn to chocolate. Or: I wish I could have the gift of flight for twenty-four hours. Or: I wish we had pizza for dinner every night for three weeks. When they got older, they might say: I wish Jennifer Johnson would get a really bad perm that lasted for the rest of the school year. Or: I wish my breasts would grow (Nora) or stop growing (Marianne).

Mrs. Hawthorne?

Yes.

My name is Sergeant Stephen Campbell, California State Highway Patrol.

Stephen. Such an ordinary name, Nora would think later, for such an extraordinary phone call.

8

Three wishes, Genie, rapid-fire.

One. Say what you have to say, quickly.

Two. Tell me it's going to be okay.

Three. Let me go back to the beginning and start over.

Mrs. Hawthorne. I'm in the security office at the Golden Gate Bridge.

The *what*?

Do you know how to get here, Mrs. Hawthorne?

She couldn't say another thing. The room was whirling. She sat down on one of the kitchen stools.

Listen carefully, please. I'm going to tell you how to get here, and I want you to come right away. Do you understand me? We're on the south side of the bridge. From where you are you have to cross the bridge to get to us.

She swallowed, tried to breathe. She watched a hand that didn't seem like hers grasp at the edge of the counter. She watched the fingers try and fail to grip the edge. There was a sharp sound all around her, a high-pitched noise three octaves beyond glass breaking.

Mrs. Hawthorne?

Mmmmmmph. The only sound she could manage.

■ ■ ■ ■

Later Nora would figure that it all started with her job. If she hadn't been a working mother. If the situation with the Watkins home hadn't happened, and then the horror show at the Millers' house. If she'd been more available, more aware. If she'd been better. *If if if.*

CHAPTER 1
ANGELA

Three months earlier . . .
In the front of the house the rest of the family went about their business. It was early September, a shade past Labor Day. If Angela Hawthorne had to put the situation into words that her AP English teacher, Ms. Simmons, would appreciate, she might say that *the moon was picking its way across the sky.* The school year was *still a virgin: barely touched, unsullied.*

Above Angela's desk, tacked to the colossal bulletin board, was a calendar. Circled with a red marker snatched from Maya's room (seven-year-olds had a lot of markers) was the date. November first, fewer than eight weeks away. Her mother had added the rest for Angela with a black ballpoint in her neat, Catholic-girl-school hand, using exactly the words on the website: *deadline for all early-action application materials.*

Eight weeks. Seven and a half, really. So

11

much to do. Five AP classes this year: European History. English Literature and Composition. Chemistry. Statistics. Studio Art. ("Studio Art can be an AP class?" her father had asked. "That seems bogus." Angela, in tacit agreement, said nothing.)

The battle for class rank was a bloody one. Its victims were laid out all across the campus of Oakville High and across much of Marin County. Figuratively, of course. Ms. Simmons might appreciate that metaphor. Sammy Marshall, felled by an ill-timed bout of mono the previous spring. ("Not his fault," said Angela's mother. "The poor thing." Was she smiling when she said that?) Porter Webb, the school's foremost scholar-athlete, already being scouted by the minors. Lots of time on the baseball diamond. ("Too much athlete, not enough scholar," said Angela's father ruefully, though it seemed to Angela that part of the rue was manufactured.)

At the moment Angela was first. Valedictorian. *But the wolves were nipping at her heels.* (Did this count as a cliché?)

The wolves were snapping at her feet. Better? Better.

One of the wolves was Maria Ortiz, poetess extraordinaire, already published in several journals, only some of them obscure, fluent in four languages. (Angela's father: "Technically, are we counting the Spanish as a foreign language? Because she *did* grow up speaking it at home . . .") Henrietta Faulkner (no relation, though if you didn't ask, Henrietta didn't offer), Angela's erstwhile best friend. *Erstwhile.* SAT word.

Angela, are the class rankings out yet?

Ask Angela. Angela will know the answer. Angela knows everything.

Angela, did you do your homework?

Angela, did you practice?

And already, in the first week of school, a paper due in AP English Lit, as though the two novels Angela read in August for summer course work weren't enough. It didn't seem fair. "But I also have to say, for the umpty-umpth time, that life isn't fair. It's just fairer than death, that's all," said Cecily over dinner — an aphorism she'd picked up from *The Princess Bride,* which she'd spent countless hours of the summer watching with her best friend, Pinkie. At ten years old, Cecily and Pinkie seemed to have an unlimited supply of leisure time with which to watch movies and ride scooters and twist each other's hair into unnatural shapes to see how long they held.

Where was Angela's leisure time? Gone, vanished. *Taken from her in the night by an invisible thief.* Wait, a thief couldn't actually be invisible.

Stolen in the night by an unknown assailant. Corny. Overwritten. And assailants didn't necessarily steal, they might just attack.

Purloined. Better. Simple and elegant. SAT word.

Or, more likely, if memory served, Angela's free time had never truly existed. Perhaps, eons ago, when she was an infant, reclining in the Moses basket that her mother kept in the attic, the only remaining relic of Angela's and Cecily's and Maya's babyhoods. Maybe then Angela had had leisure time, though a foggy memory persisted of a swinging ball of red and black and white, something she was meant to study and perhaps learn from. "I'm saving it," said Angela's mother (about the Moses basket). "For one of you. For when you have your own." And Angela nodded, absorbing this sentiment, while in truth she couldn't imagine ever marrying or becoming a mother. Where, on earth, would she find the time?

They were expected to read all of *Beloved* and write a paper on its central theme. By tomorrow. Angela hadn't begun the book yet, never mind the paper. Cross-country practice after school, the first meet only two

14

weeks away, six-by-one-mile repeats through the woods and over the river.

Over the river and through the woods, to grandmother's house . . . Angela's only living grandmother was her mother's mother; she lived in Rhode Island, nowhere accessible by horse-drawn sleigh. (Was anywhere?)

Eight thirty. *The fatigue was pulling at her eyelids.* (Good? *The fatigue was like a blanket* . . . No. Too much. Pulling at the eyelids was better.) Again Angela looked at the calendar: November first. Not so long now, not so long.

Should she?

She never had before, hadn't wanted to, hadn't needed to, though she kept them at the ready. They all did — for emergencies, or not, as the case may be. Angela had gotten hers from Henrietta Faulkner, who had gotten them God-knows-where. A harmless little study aid, no big deal. A few of them secreted inside an Advil bottle, the bottle tucked inside her desk drawer, behind the pencil sharpener, the old iPod, no longer working, long since replaced, the odd collection of shoelaces.

Angela pulled out the bottle and shook the capsule out into her hand. Five milligrams, not so much. Other kids used

15

more. Lots more. Five was nothing, a baby dose. A warm-up, an appetizer.

She reached for the glass of water at the edge of her desk. Hydration was super-important after a workout like the one they'd had today. Were the varsity cross-country teams at Novato and Redwood and all across the county working as hard as they were, as hard as the mighty Warriors? It was difficult to say. They would find out when they went head to head in November, at the regional meet. Foot to foot.

She lifted the glass, drank. The capsule was so small she scarcely noticed it going down. It was a blip, a hiccup.

She waited. Nothing. She waited some more. And more. And longer.

There it was. Her head cleared. It all faded to the background: the *screech-scritch* of Cecily's bow across the strings ("Practice makes perfect," Cecily said cheerfully, though there was little evidence that Angela could find to confirm the *veracity* of that statement, at least in Cecily's case. Although those same words had been repeated to Angela ad nauseam for the past seventeen years), the sounds of the television, the neighbor's dog barking at the back door to be let in or out.

There it was. Tunnel focus, that's what

they called it. And for good reason. Angela Hawthorne, valedictorian, was staring down a tunnel, no stopping, no sleep until Cambridge.

You get there, and then you can rest. Then you can rest.

But not yet, not now. Now she would work until it was done, and then she would *sleep under a crimson moon.*

CHAPTER 2
NORA

4:44 a.m.

Dear Marianne:
Do you know I thought about seeing a therapist? There: I said it. I haven't told a single soul, not even Gabe. Don't tell Mom, okay? Seriously.

I was going to go because of *stress* and *sleeplessness*. I thought, what have I got to lose?

I looked into it, and I even wrote down some numbers and checked with my insurance. Which didn't cover any of it, of course. Though Elpis is ridiculously proud of its insurance. And then I looked at my schedule, and I thought: Ha.

17

When? It turned out that what I had to lose was time I don't have.

I changed my mind. I didn't call. I decided you can be my therapist instead. So pardon, in advance, the long emails.

Insomnia is new to me, and on the one hand upsetting, but on the other hand I'm finding that I can really be productive when I put my mind to it. Just before I began this email to you I sent three requests for prices for the booths for the Spring Fling for the elementary school. I got the booth job again, ha, look at that, the first time I typed "booth" it autocorrected to "boob." (I wish.) I drafted some language for the ad for my next open house and I made a list of all the appointments everyone in the house needs in the next six months: teeth, flu shots, general physicals, etc. Maya needs to see an ophthalmologist even though she's only seven. Cecily has to go to the orthodontist. I need a mammogram. For healthy people, Marianne, we're alarmingly busy just taking care of our bodies.

Lucky you, Dr. Sister! You're hired, and you never even applied for the job.

Two showings in Sausalito went late, but

then one in Belvedere was canceled, so Nora arrived home not so long after she'd told the sitter, Maddie, she'd be there. Unfortunately, the showing that was canceled was the only one Nora wanted *not* to be canceled: the Watkins property, which had been a thorn in Nora's side all summer — a thorn that showed no signs of being removed. The property was priced too high, in Nora's opinion. But the sellers were firm, and they were difficult, and because they wouldn't budge Nora knew that all sorts of potential buyers were walking right by and not asking for a showing.

You wouldn't think, maybe, that two girls with a seventeen-year-old sister would need an after-school babysitter, but not only was Angela supremely busy every day after school but so were her friends and the friends of her friends. They had glee club and band practice and varsity sports. They had recycling club (true story) and Best Buddies (partnering up with kids with disabilities) and French Club or Spanish Club, or sometimes both, and if they weren't acting in the school plays they were directing them or painting scenery for them or sewing costumes for them. They were preparing for Mock Trial or Speech and Debate; they were applying to be pages at the state

General Assembly. They were organizing their twenty-five hours of community service for the National Honor Society. And when they weren't doing all of that, they were doing homework, homework, homework.

All of the high school students Nora knew were so busy, in fact, that when Nora had gone back to work two years ago she'd had to cast the net far and wide to find someone to shuffle Cecily from school and to her Irish dancing lessons and back home after. Maya, in second grade, traveled along for the rides like a barnacle tucked into a car seat.

Currently Nora shelled out twenty dollars an hour to a USF junior from Wisconsin named Maddie who spent most of the afternoon on her iPhone.

The first thing Nora did when she arrived home was to open the shutters. Maddie had an unfortunate habit of closing them against the afternoon light; she claimed some sort of diagnosed sun sensitivity but Nora suspected (and Cecily confirmed) that the problem was actually that the light made it more difficult to see the screen of her iPhone or iPad. When Nora had time (unlikely) she was going to look into finding Maddie's replacement, someone who would read with or to Maya, maybe take her through some of the classics Nora had loved when she was young, the irrepressible Anne of *Green Gables* fame. Betsy, Tacy, and Tib. Nora had been an avid reader of the *Betsy-Tacy* books as a child; when Angela was in kindergarten Nora had trotted out her dog-eared, licorice-stained copies and read them to her. Angela easily could have read them to herself, of course, she could practically take herself through Tolstoy at that age, but Nora loved spending all that extra time in Deep Valley, Minnesota, in the early nineteen hundreds. She had neglected to do the same for Cecily, and probably by now Cecily had outgrown the books. But Maya still loved to cuddle, still loved to be read to. Plus she couldn't read to herself. Don't think about that now, Nora. Her private rule (never enforced): one worry at a time. Okay, that was impossible. One major worry at a time.

The afternoon light flooded the living room. The shutters were partly a reaction to Nora's growing up in a house where curtains reigned supreme: in the bathroom, curtains with yellow and pink flowers; in the kitchen, red-and-white-checked country curtains; and in hers and Marianne's room, curtains depicting little flying fairies —

these remained far too long, until Nora went off to the University of Rhode Island at age eighteen. When they'd bought this house Nora had had plantation shutters installed, not because she liked them — though in fact she did — but because they were neutral and expensive and generally acceptable and because Nora, as much as she professed not to be, was just as influenced as the next guy by that ultimate driver, that unseen hand: resale value.

"Mom!" said Cecily, propelling herself toward Nora and then wrapping her skinny arms around Nora's waist. Cecily ate and ate, she ate everything in sight, and still she retained the half-starved look of an old-fashioned orphan: pointy elbows, hollow cheekbones. She didn't care. She did a bit where she sucked her stomach in as far as it would go and put each and every rib on display, offering them for counting. ("Wait until she hits puberty," said Angela darkly. "I used to be skinny too." Angela, at 108 pounds, barely registered on the digital precision pet scale Nora had purchased from Frontgate when Frankie, their beloved, deceased Newfoundland, had flirted with an overeating problem.)

"Where's Maya?" asked Nora.

"Playdate," said Maddie. "Penelope's. I

texted you."

"Right." For a fraction of an instant Nora allowed herself to plant her face in Cecily's hair, which smelled like strawberry shampoo, and to drink in her unadulterated affection.

"Ava broke her toe and can't dance and my hard shoes got too small over the summer and I need new ones *before* the *feis,* which means they won't be broken in but look I got that last part of my solo *perfectly,* you have to see this, I don't have any music but just watch."

Maddie roused herself from the couch, more slowly than Nora thought was necessary for a twenty-year-old. Nora tried not to think about how much she was paying Maddie. She tried not to think about the fact that the Watkins listing was due to expire in November and that, when it did, Mr. and Mrs. Watkins were going to take the home off the market for the holiday season and list it in the new year with a different agency. (Arthur Sutton, her boss, did not know this, and it was Nora's mission in life to sell the home before he found out.) She tried not to think about the fact that she didn't have ingredients for dinner, and the fact that she should have picked Maya up at Penelope's on the way home, and she tried not to think about the three loads of laundry waiting for her, which she had forgotten to mention to Maddie and which, if she had, Maddie would have ignored anyway.

For now, she and Maddie stood in solidarity, watching Cecily dance. Cecily was a gorgeous dancer, absolutely gorgeous, and Nora took a moment to appreciate this, that this child who had come from her, from Nora (a woman who possessed no musicality, no dance talent, a woman who could not even learn the Electric Slide properly when it was being played at everyone's weddings), had become this magnificent creature with long, lean leg muscles and a smile that could break your heart. Nora allowed herself to be transported to the Old Country, home of her ancestors; she imagined standing on a hilltop one hundred years ago or in a darkened pub on a Sunday afternoon, where she sipped from a pint of stout while a musical trio in the corner struck up a tune.

"Beautiful, Cecily," she said, when Cecily had finished dancing and given the requisite toe-point-out bow, and that smile, that *smile* that the judges ate right up. Very few girls smiled at the Irish dance competitions. They were too busy girding themselves against vomiting onstage, a phenomenon of nerves

24

that was, unfortunately, more common than you might think. "I would totally give you a first," said Nora. Then, in a poor imitation of Cecily's dance instructor, Seamus O'Malley, she offered up an Irish-accented "Well done, lass." Cecily rolled her eyes, but in a good-natured way that Nora appreciated. Nora knew, having been through it once before, that the good-naturedness departed around age twelve or thirteen and returned — when? She didn't know. She hadn't found out yet. Nora paused. Deep breath. "Where's Her Majesty?" she asked.

Cecily shrugged. "Not home from cross-country practice yet, I guess. Haven't seen her."

Just then the front door opened to reveal a sweat-soaked girl wearing running shorts and a crimson T-shirt that said HARVARD across it in proud silver letters. Angela had her sights set on her father's alma mater, and had fixed them there long ago and never wavered. (Though it was hard to say, sometimes, if Angela had set them there or if Gabe had set them there for her.)

Angela must have run home, her chest was still heaving, though how she did that with the backpack Nora didn't know. She didn't even want to know. Maybe someone had dropped her off, another mother, a nonworking mother who had time to attend not only all of the meets but all of the practices as well.

"Hey," Angela said, surveying the scene, smiling, but only, if you looked closely, with her mouth. Not her eyes. She let her gaze roam over the room, over Cecily, over Maddie, settling finally on her mother. "I am absolutely starving," she said. "And I have hours of homework."

Nora Hawthorne took a deep breath, opened her arms, and folded her oldest daughter into them. Angela: her angel, for so many years the one and only. This was the girl who had frantically sucked her own fingers to get herself to sleep, necessitating early and expensive intervention by one of Marin's most reputable orthodontists. This was the girl who read a chapter book long before she turned four and spoke an entire sentence in perfectly accented Spanish at age two. This was the girl who had, as a kindergartner, accompanied her father on a trip to Cambridge, Massachusetts, where they had taken in the Harvard–Yale game on a crisp November afternoon, and who had allowed herself to be photographed wearing every sort of crimson paraphernalia that money could buy and some that it couldn't. The photograph, enlarged, framed, now hung over the desk in Gabe's home office, a sanctum rarely used for its stated purpose but nevertheless extravagantly decorated with all manner of collegiate memorabilia.

"Mom," said Angela. She tried to pull back from Nora but Nora wouldn't allow it; she didn't care if Angela was sweating or unwilling. She was Nora's for only a little while longer. Nora hugged the heck out of her anyway.

Twelve months from now Angela would be gone from them, launched into the particulars of her almost-adult life, dependent on her parents to buttress her bank account and occasionally her emotions, but really, truly, for all intents and purposes, *gone.*

"Mom," said Angela again. "Let me go. Please? Mom?" But Nora felt her lean in before she pushed away, and all through that fall (was *fateful* too strong a word to describe it?) she held on to that fraction of a second, that clue that Angela was still a part of them.

"Mom. I'm all sweaty. I'm gross."

Maddie had gone back to tapping on the screen of her iPhone, almost as though the person who handed her a sizable check each week wasn't in the same room. Cecily was performing a set of elaborate stretching exercises that involved extending her leg over the couch, lowering it, then lifting it again. Nora's phone buzzed: probably Penelope's mother, wondering when Nora might be by to fetch Maya.

Nora released her oldest daughter. Earlier that week she had written seven important words on Angela's wall calendar: *deadline for all early-action application materials.* November first.

Here it was. It had arrived. The most important period of Angela Hawthorne's young life was beginning. Brace yourself, thought Nora. Batten down the hatches. Here we go.

CHAPTER 3
GABE

Gabe was early to the appointment with the college counselor, which was fine, except he had taken a half day off for this so in truth it really wasn't fine for him to have to wait — things at Elpis were busy busy, always busy, the wheels of industry and commerce turning.

It was harder to get an appointment with the college counselor than it was to get a reservation at the French Laundry, and so

Nora had sent him several emails and a text the day before reminding him about it. Two p.m., she said. We need to be there together, to support Angela. Gabe checked in at the main office, where a young woman with dramatic red highlights in her hair pointed toward a closed door with a light wooden bench outside of it. "Wait there," she said. "Ms. Vogel will be with you shortly." In fact he didn't consider this appointment to be necessary anyway; this was Nora's doing. Gabe did not, as they say, have a dog in this fight. Or, more accurately, he had only one dog, and he didn't consider it a fight. Angela was going to Harvard. Ergo, the meeting with the college counselor was a formality.

He waited five minutes, then ten. Three minutes to two now. How unlike Nora to be late for something like this. He checked his phone and there it was: a text, lacking in punctuation (he blamed Siri) but not clarity: *Meet without me have to show the watkins house just came up sorry*

The Watkins house, all four bedrooms and six and a half bathrooms of it. Breathtaking views of the Golden Gate Bridge. Every freaking listing in Belvedere offered breathtaking views of the bridge; if Realtor.com was to be believed, none of the town's two thousand citizens had taken a full breath in decades. Every home in Belvedere also had more bathrooms than it had bedrooms, which seemed to be a phenomenon of the very wealthy, one that Nora couldn't explain away, though Gabe had asked. This listing was not the most expensive in Belvedere, but it was the biggest property that Sutton and Wainwright had been offered this year, and the listing had gone to Nora. A very big deal. Four bedrooms on a quarter-acre lot. (*"Seriously?"* said Gabe, who, though he now considered himself a Californian, and though he loved it here in his adopted state, could still not believe what your money did not get you. The whole state of Wyoming, where Gabe had grown up, would probably sell for less than eight million dollars. "Eight *million*?" And Nora had said, "Eight point eight. But it's a *Cooper Sudecki.*" This last said quietly, reverently, as though no elaboration were needed.)

Once, before kids, they had had fantastic sex on the kitchen floor of Nora's first listing, a two-bedroom condo in Sausalito. The home was unoccupied — in general, not just at the time, though that too, of course — which made the act seem a little more acceptable, but Nora freaked out after: What if there were security cameras? What if she lost her job? Her license? What if she disappointed the unflappable, undisappointable Arthur Sutton, who doted so thoroughly on Nora?

A murmuring at the office desk, and here, at last, came Angela. She sat down beside Gabe and released an enormous backpack from her shoulders. (Why so big? Hadn't everything gone digital?) Her eyes were the same blue as Nora's, though bigger, rounder.

"Hey," she said. "Hi, Daddy."

Angela looked tired. "You okay, sweetie?"

"Of course," she said. Angela and Maya had inherited from Nora the blondish-red hair, the Irish skin, while Cecily, the Irish dancer, looked more like a Syrian refugee — a throwback, maybe, to some Native American blood Gabe's family had never acknowledged, some kind of skip-a-few-generations gene pool situation. He noted that Angela's nails were bitten to the quick — a new habit? He couldn't say — and that they were nonetheless painted a deep purplish black. Angela said, "Where's Mom?" and went at one of the fingernails, though what was left to chew Gabe couldn't imagine.

Seventeen years old, and still Angela called him Daddy. He loved that, didn't want it ever to change. He wanted all of his girls to call him Daddy forever. He wanted Angela to call him Daddy when he walked her down the aisle (many years hence, he hoped) and he wanted her to call him Daddy when she introduced him to his first grandchild.

He held up his phone. "Just got a text. She has to show the Watkins house."

Angela — if this was possible — opened her eyes even wider than she already had. Those eyes, so big and round that each was like an individual moon set into her face, considered his. "Yeah? That's great. Let's hope these people are The Ones." She knew — as everyone but Arthur Sutton knew — that the Watkins listing was going to expire at the end of November. Five percent of $8.8 million, $440,000. Then, divide that by two, half to the buyers' realtor and half to Sutton and Wainwright, that was $220,000. Even after Arthur Sutton had taken his cut (and Gabe was never quite sure about what that cut was), it would be a considerable sum for the Hawthornes, coming at just the right time, before the first tuition payments came due. "Still," continued Angela, "I wish she could be here. She set this whole thing up. I met with the counselor last year. And I'm missing AP English. We're talking about our college application essays."

Gabe grew up on a real working ranch outside of Laramie, where the sky was obscenely big and the closest McDonald's was forty-five minutes away. When he applied to college his personal essay was about birthing a stillborn calf in the middle of a blizzard. True story! It was harrowing, and when he stood next to Nora in the delivery room for the births of all three of their daughters he couldn't shake certain images from his mind: the blood, the way the mother cow's eyes rolled back in their sockets, the smell of birth and death "intermingling in the black of a midwinter's night," the way he'd written it in the essay. He'd always had a way with words: this helped him enormously in his job at Elpis. He also had a way with people.

He wondered what Angela was going to write about. Had he and Nora done a disservice by not putting her in front of a childbearing cow? He thought they'd given her every advantage, starting with the early days at Little Nugget Montessori. Who was the kid she'd pushed from the top of the slide? Timothy Maloney. (*We understand that you and the Maloney family have come to a suitable agreement regarding Timothy's medical bills, and we are ready to move*

33

forward and enjoy the rest of an enriching year here at Little Nugget, said the letter home. "I just wanted to be *first,*" a tearful Angela had said.) Then there were the swimming lessons, the flute, the dancing, the skiing, the running, French, Italian. But they'd forgotten about the cow. Nobody in his family lived anywhere near a ranch now, his parents had both passed and his two brothers lived in Vancouver and South Carolina, of all places. Everyone was craving water after years of being landlocked. "The essay!" he said. "That's the best part of the application. What are you thinking about —"

Just then the door beside them opened, and out stepped a mop-haired boy followed by his parents; the man was an older, wearier, tidier version of the son, and the woman was an even wearier version of the man. The tension released from the office was thick thick thick; Gabe would have whispered to Angela that you could practically cut it with a knife, but he knew that was a cliché, and he knew that clichés were *verboten* at Oakville High, especially in the top fifth of the class.

"That's Jacob Boyd," whispered Angela as the backs of the three disappeared around the corner. "He's, like, fifteenth. Not bad. He'll probably go somewhere like Occidental."

Gabe knew that if Nora were there she'd say something cheery and accepting about Jacob Boyd, like, "Occidental is a wonderful school!"

But Nora was not there, she was showing the $8.8 million in Belvedere, and anyway, hard-to-schedule Ms. Vogel was waiting for them. She had a deeply tanned, deeply wrinkled face and wiry gray hair sticking out all over and she wore a sweater that was almost certainly hand-knit. She shook Gabe's hand with a grip that was limper than Gabe would have liked and said, "Come in, both of you. Mr. Hawthorne. Angela. My next appointment is at two twenty and I know we've got a lot of ground to cover here. Mr. Hawthorne? You look a little deer-in-the-headlights. Please don't worry. I haven't bitten any parents since second semester of last year."

CHAPTER 4
CECILY

"You are *so* lucky," said Cecily. "I wish my dad worked for Apple." She held Pinkie's iPhone 5s reverently, the same way she held Pinkie's dwarf hamster, Mouse, although she preferred holding the iPhone 5s because

Mouse always pooped on Cecily's shirt.

They were lounging on Pinkie's queen bed, avoiding their homework. Pinkie's room was enormous, with its own marble bathroom (*en suite,* Cecily's mother would have said) and a shower with four separate shower heads that you could turn on at the same time if you wanted to. Pinkie was an only child. Cecily shared a room with Maya and a bathroom with both of her sisters, which was fine, but Maya always forgot to rinse the sink after she spit out her toothpaste, so every time Cecily went to take her turn she found herself staring at a dried riverbed of pink. Angela, though she represented only a third of the Hawthorne girls, took up way more than half the bathroom — she had even installed a *padlock* on her *cabinet* — and every time Cecily lodged a complaint her mother said something vague and unsatisfactory about Angela going through a hard time right now and couldn't they all be a little bit patient.

First they tried a slow-motion video. Cecily did part of her Irish dance solo, and Pinkie did a handstand.

"I'm glad you got the gold phone," said Cecily when they repaired to the bed to look over the video. "I totally would have gotten the gold too."

They sat in respectful silence for a moment, admiring the 5s. Cecily's father worked for a management consulting company, which meant that there was nothing he could bring home to Cecily. When she was younger Cecily had asked once what he made at work and he had said, "Ideas." Yawn.

"We could invent our own Rainbow Loom bracelet," said Pinkie. "And make a video, and put it up on YouTube."

"Yeah," said Cecily, thinking of the triple starburst girls, now YouTube famous for their bracelet. "But I didn't bring my loom."

Instead they did accents. Pinkie could do British, but Cecily was much better at Irish because she spent so much time with Seamus O'Malley. They could both do Australian from watching *Mako Mermaids* on Netflix, but Pinkie's was a little more authentic. Probably because she'd actually been to Australia.

"Okay," instructed Cecily. "Record me. Guess who I am."

She took a deep breath and closed her eyes and said, "Time for dinner, everyone!"

"Oh my God," said Pinkie. "You sound *exactly* like your mother. Exactly."

"I know," said Cecily, sort of modestly but sort of not, because there were not that many things she could do that Pinkie could not. "*Right?* I've been practicing. I can completely trick my father, if I call to him from another room."

"That's awesome," said Pinkie. "That's absolutely awesome. I wish I could do that."

"You can," said Cecily. "Just record your mom talking, then play it over and over again. You'll get it."

"Here, I'm going to record you," said Pinkie. "It's so awesome, you sound just like her. Okay? Ready? You sure? Ready, set. *Go.*"

CHAPTER 5
NORA

12:13 a.m.

Dear M —
Since you're my fake therapist, I feel I can tell you something I've never told anyone. Ready?

I don't care if Angela gets into Harvard.

I can't say that to Angela, and I certainly can't say it to Gabe, my goodness. I mean, just imagine.

I can't even say it to Cecily or Maya: it is just something, in our house, that is not allowed to be said.

In fact, sometimes I think I would *prefer* that she didn't get in!

I'm sitting back now, and I'm waiting for the lightning to strike me down.

So far, nothing has happened.

Nora was so excited about the potential buyers for the Watkins home — they had requested a second showing — that she stopped at In-N-Out Burger in Mill Valley and picked up dinner for the family. Everyone she knew had recently gone gluten free; she felt like she was sinning just bringing bread into her household. And plain white bread! But: screw it. The potential buyers had loved the Watkins property. They had loved the wine room, the library, the many bathrooms. They had loved the view of the Golden Gate Bridge, the his-and-her walk-in closets in the master bedroom, the glimpse of Alcatraz, of Angel Island, where not so long ago Chinese immigrants waited for their chance to enter America. They had loved the staircase that curled up through the center of the house, and the lush landscaping, and the way you could stand in the master bedroom and feel like you might fall right into the water. She deserved some white bread. They all did.

"Five Double-Doubles," she said. "And five fries. And five chocolate shakes." Cecily was going to freak right out: her favorite food in the whole entire world was a Double-Double from In-N-Out. Maya would probably just drink the shake. (Was Maya eating enough? She had sturdy little legs, but maybe there was some deficit in her nutrition . . . should Nora try to get in with another reading tutor, if the one everyone had recommended wasn't available?) In the olden days, when Frankie was alive, Maya would have fed Frankie the burger under the table, and in the middle of the night Frankie would have thrown up all over the living room — the next day, Maya would have feigned ignorance.

They had eaten at In-N-Out the night two years ago when Arthur Sutton called her out of the blue, six years after she'd left Sutton and Wainwright, the premier real estate agency in Marin. "Arthur says there's an opening. He says he wants *me*. Only me."

Gabe hesitated.

It wasn't just a phone call from Arthur Sutton — it was a phone call that led to lunch at Perbacco in the city, in whose red-boothed extravagance Nora indulged in *salumi misti* and a pan-seared hanger steak and, at Arthur Sutton's urging, one glass, then two, of a gorgeous Valpolicella that was such a dark red it was almost black.

Arthur Sutton was that rare creature in California, a true East Coast West Coaster, born and bred near the stone walls and rolling acreage of Greenwich, Connecticut, but educated on the cheerily sun-splashed Stanford campus. This pedigree, to be sure, was not so unusual; what was different about Arthur was the way he fully inhabited both coasts, rather than constantly documenting and enumerating the differences between the two or the failures of one as compared to the other. (Nora, herself a product of Rhode Island, could not, even after nearly two decades in California, stop herself from using the phrase "back home" to describe her beloved Ocean State.)

Arthur Sutton was fifteen years Nora's senior, and his graying temples, his pressed suits and shined loafers, even the cologne he wore — a subtle and tweedy scent to which Nora could not put a name, for Gabe was not a cologne fan — suggested a gravity and a clarity of purpose that she had always found alluring. In a *fatherly* way, of course. Or at least avuncular. Back when Nora first started with Sutton and Wainwright, she had had offers from six of the seven agencies she'd applied to, but only Arthur had taken her by the hand (figuratively) and shown her how the real estate market worked and how she could make a name for herself in it.

"He wants you back?" said Gabe, two years ago. And he hesitated before saying more, instead taking a giant bite of his Double-Double. Nora, still buzzing from the Valpolicella, had been too wound up to make a real dinner.

"Yes! He wants me back. He says I still hold records in the office. He says they need someone with my . . . how'd he say it?" Here she feigned a brief memory loss, for she knew exactly how Arthur Sutton had said it. "Ah, yes. Someone with my particular combination of *spunk* and *knowledge*."

Maya was five then; Cecily almost eight, Angela fifteen. "We always thought I'd go back," said Nora. "When the kids were older, more self-sufficient." (Were they, though? They were older, anyway. She wasn't sure they would ever become more self-sufficient. When she was Angela's age she was cooking dinner for her entire family twice a week, holding down a part-time job at a now-defunct Newport Creamery, and still finding time to get buzzed on cans of Busch on the weekends down at the beach.)

42

"We did."

"You're hesitating, though," she told Gabe.

"Well. It's just that I remember how hard you had to work, back then. And how much it took out of you. The nights, the Sunday open houses . . ."

Nora decided that the only way to make this conversation go how she wanted it to go was to play midcentury housewife; therefore, like someone straight out of *Mad Men* (the early seasons, before everybody's lives went to hell), she found a rocks glass and poured into it three fingers of Gabe's favorite, the amber-colored Bulleit. Frontier whiskey, said the bottle. Though truly it was California that was the new frontier, right? Years before, Nora had been with Angela's fourth-grade class on a field trip to Columbia, where they'd drunk sarsaparilla straight from the bottle and waded in shin-deep water in search of tiny gold nuggets; she'd experienced a little bit of what it must have been like back then, to be new, in a foreign world, placing one's hopes on a glimmer in the dirt.

Nora considered all of these facts and studied Gabe's Bulleit, which was truly beautiful, like something Cleopatra might have planned an outfit around. "It didn't

43

take that much out of me," said Nora.

That statement was patently untrue. Her job had taken everything out of her, that's why she was so good at it. She was unfailingly on call to soothe the nerves of uneasy buyers and to simultaneously stoke and tamp down sellers' egos.

When Cecily was a baby Nora sold what was then the second-highest-priced property in Marin, a $4.85 million five-bedroom in Tiburon with sweeping views of the bay from every window. The sale had nearly fallen apart at the last minute — buyer's remorse, seller's remorse, every other kind of remorse you could usher into a real estate deal — but Nora had outdone herself. She arranged for the sellers to vacate on the day the P&S was due to be signed, and she brought the buyers — a young couple who had thrived during the dot.com boom and somehow survived its bust — onto the exquisitely tiled patio, where she opened a bottle of Cabernet from her favorite winery, which she coyly called Napa's best-kept secret but which was actually readily available to any tourist with a mid-grade concierge. In the gourmet kitchen she arranged a circle of Cremont, a Rogue River blue, and half a loaf of crusty bread from Boulettes Larder in the Ferry Building on the

J. K. Adams plank that she and Gabe had gotten as a wedding gift, and she brought it out to the couple.

"Take your time," Nora had said, sipping the wine, watching the sun slide into the water. She had slept a total of three hours the night before; this was the most relaxed she'd felt in weeks. "Truly, there's no rush. And if this isn't the right house for you, I promise we will find you the one that is. I want you to be happy." She put the P&S and her favorite Uni-ball Vision pen (fine point, waterproof) alongside the cheese, far enough away that it seemed unobtrusive but close enough to be welcoming, within reach.

"How'd you *do* it?" Arthur Sutton asked her later. "I thought those buyers were gone. I swear I could feel them slip away." Nora shrugged. Cecily was a three-month-old who still woke up at least twice a night to nurse, sometimes four or five times. Cecily's infanthood at that point had left Nora exhausted, sapped, enervated. Cecily was colicky, rheumy-eyed, and dissatisfied, hungry all the time yet never taking a full feeding, giving no indication then of the quirky, bewilderingly lovable kid she'd since become, admired by teachers and students alike, a guest at every birthday party, a magnet, a socialite without the wardrobe.

(Now Cecily was easy. *Easy peasy lemon squeezie,* like the rhyme one of them had picked up at a playground long ago and trotted home, where it had attached itself to their family vocabulary like a leech.)

"No," Nora told Arthur. "They were never gone. They just needed a little extra massaging."

And two years ago Gabe sipped his Bulleit and closed his eyes for a fraction longer than a blink and said, "If you're sure it's the right thing."

"I'm sure," Nora said. "I'm absolutely, positively sure."

Now, while she waited for her order, Nora called Arthur Sutton on his cell. Arthur's home phone number was a closely guarded secret. He'd given it to Nora once, but he'd asked her to use it only in the case of an extreme emergency. "Like a near-death emergency," he's said, as though the word *extreme* weren't descriptive enough. But he was perennially available on his cell. Like, always. She was pretty sure Arthur Sutton didn't sleep. His wife, Linda, had confided as much to Nora during a fit of prosecco-fueled oversharing that took place at the Sutton and Wainwright holiday party years ago.

"Hey," she said now. "It's me, Nora. Listen, these people loved the Watkins house. They *loved* it. I think they may be The Ones." Perhaps it was a bit premature to say that, and if there was one golden rule in the real estate industry it was Don't Count Your Chickens, but Nora felt like she owed Arthur a serving of optimism. The Watkins home had been on the market for a very long time; in real estate parlance, it was *growing stale.* Soon it would move out of the *stale* category and into the *retro* category, whose name Nora had coined herself. (It hadn't caught on yet, but give it time.)

"Wonderful," said Arthur. His voice was as smooth as Dutch gold honey. Though Arthur never slept, he never seemed to be tired, never seemed to be weak. His skin always looked as fresh as that of a young child. Six months ago Arthur had closed escrow on a $4.95 million property in Madrone Canyon that almost fell through at the last minute, and Arthur had never even looked harried. Nora knew he'd worked for it — they all worked for it, they killed themselves (in private, offstage) for every sale they got — but he never broke a sweat. Never second-guessed. Just moved deliberately forward, like a yacht in fine weather.

"I knew you'd find the right buyers," said Arthur now. "I didn't doubt you for a second, Nora. That's why I brought you back!" The Madrone Canyon sale had been a long time ago, and they needed something big, something legit, to take its place.

At home, Nora, lost in thoughts about the Watkins property, was halfway through her Double-Double (was this the same as all the way through a Single?) when she remembered to ask about the appointment with Ms. Vogel.

"Oh!" said Gabe. He had scarfed down his burger and was making serious progress on his shake. Angela was all over the burger and had put her shake into the freezer to drink while she studied. Maya was eating the bun but not the meat. Cecily, still wearing her ghillies and a tank top that read IRISH DANCERS KICK BUTT, looked about as happy as it was possible for a kid to look. *Family dinner,* thought Nora. *Maybe not home-cooked, but we're all here. We're all accounted for.* "It went fine," said Gabe. "Just fine. She knows her stuff, that's for sure. I can see why it's so hard to get an appointment with her."

Nora's phone buzzed, but she ignored it. Family dinner! The time was precious.

"Good," she said approvingly. She

48

watched Gabe and Angela exchange a look. What was behind that look? She swiped one of her last fries through a field of salt. She could feel her blood vessels constricting, but, damn, this was a good dinner. "What'd you come up with?"

"What do you mean?"

"For a list. For the final list of schools."

"We have the list," volunteered Angela. "The list is Harvard."

"That's one school! One word! That's not a list!"

"We don't need a list. Angela's already decided."

Nora glanced at Cecily. She appeared to be listening to the conversation, but when Nora looked more closely she could see Cecily's lips moving in time to an imaginary piece of music playing in her head: *one* two three four *five* six seven eight. Under the table, though she didn't look, Nora knew Cecily's feet were moving too.

"We know she's decided what her *first* choice is. But what about the backup list? What about Williams? What about Amherst, Middlebury? What about *BC*? Plus all the schools out here: Santa Barbara, Santa Cruz. Wasn't that the point of the appointment, to come up with that list?"

"Okay," said Gabe. He drank the last of

his shake and his straw made a sucking sound that, had it been one of her girls making it, Nora would have commented on. Not restaurant manners, she used to tell them. "Here's the thing. She wasn't great. She was like an evil witch in a fairy tale. She scared us."

Angela nodded. "She scared us. She kept talking about all the statistics, about the percentage of admitted students at the Ivies versus the number of applications . . ."

Gabe picked up Angela's sentence and ran with it. "She told us that — Who was it, Angela?"

"Henrietta Faulkner."

"Right. That Henrietta Faulkner was applying to Harvard too."

"I miss Henrietta," said Nora. "Where has she been?"

"She's around," said Angela. "The thing is, I thought she was applying regular admission. Now it turns out she's applying early, just like me. And too many applications from one school can — What'd Ms. Vogel call it?"

"Oversaturate," supplied Gabe.

"Right. Oversaturate the application pool."

Nora was perplexed. Wasn't this the point of the college counselor, to know these things, and to tell them to the ignorant and the blind? She and Gabe were ignorant *and* blind. Angela was too. The three of them were floating on a warm sea of confusion, and they needed people like Ms. Vogel to anchor them. She was sure Ms. Vogel wasn't like an evil witch in a fairy tale. Nora should have been there, she should have been the one to take what Ms. Vogel said and to turn it into something her two crimson-colored family members would understand and listen to. She looked again at Cecily. One two three *four* one two three *four.* She reached over to Maya and pointed sternly at the meat. Nora swallowed the last of her Double-Double and said, "But, Angela. That's exactly why you need to have the rest of your list ready. You can't just apply to one school! I thought we talked about this in the spring. I *know* we talked about this in the spring, the last time you talked to the counselor. You need to cast a wide net!"

"Cliché," murmured Angela, and Nora closed her eyes, scrunched up her face, and tried her hardest to remember how sweet Angela had been in the halcyon days of her toddlerhood, before she knew enough to correct her parents.

"What she needs," said Gabe, "is to focus on Harvard between now and November

51

first. She can't apply anywhere else at the same time anyway. So we'll get through this part, and then we'll reassess as needed."

Nora had lots more to say about all of that, but her cell phone buzzed again. It looked like family dinner was over anyway, so she reached across the counter and picked up her phone. Arthur Sutton? Arthur Sutton's assistant, Grace?

No.

"Nora. Lawrence Watkins here. I thought you'd have feedback on the showing by now. I thought we agreed that you'd call me after each showing, immediately after each showing, and give me feedback."

"Lawrence!" said Nora. She gave to Gabe the universal signal for *I have to take this call* — a vigorous nodding and pointing at the phone — and repaired to Cecily and Maya's room, which had more privacy than the rest of the house, owing to its position near the back.

Lawrence was one half of the formidable Watkins couple — the other was Bee — who had had the Cooper Sudecki built ten years ago and who had insisted on pricing it at $8.8 million, which was approximately one million more than it should have cost. Sellers overestimating the value of their homes was about as common as ninety-five-degree temperatures in East Bay towns like Danville and Walnut Creek, but the prevalence of the practice didn't stop it from being the ultimate challenge for every real estate agent in the business. Nora had tried to talk the Watkinses into pricing their home lower to begin with, when they'd first listed the home with her.

She'd tried to talk them into a price adjustment after the property had been on the market for twenty-eight days, and then after forty, and she'd tried to talk them into it after the usual June rush had yielded a total of zero offers. Zero! She was out a ridiculous amount of money from marketing and advertising at this point, and untold man-hours. Woman hours, too, and mom hours: hours of all kinds, hours she didn't have. July grew slow, as it always did, and August even slower. (As slow, anyway, as the market in Marin ever got.) She'd tried to talk Lawrence and Bee into a price adjustment before September. They'd gone a little lower — $8.5 million — but they ignored Nora's pleas that the number should begin with a seven.

However! A conversation with Lawrence Watkins was something she could feel confident about right now. True, she had neglected to call him, but she could convince him to overlook that. She closed the bedroom door. She tried not to look around the room, but she surveyed anyway. On the floor was a rubber band loom surrounded by zillions of tiny colored rubber bands. Nora took a deep breath and knelt on the floor near the rubber bands. She said, "Lawrence! I'm so glad you called." (She wasn't.) "The showing went long, that's all." (It hadn't.) "Which is a good sign. I was just letting all of the information *gel* in my mind before I reached out."

"And?" said Lawrence.

"It went well," said Nora. She started to gather the rubber bands into a pile but then she realized that Cecily probably had some complicated system for laying them out the way she had and that Nora had better not mess with it. "Very well," she said to Lawrence. "They were already talking about making changes, and you know that's an extremely good sign, when a client can envision —"

"Hang on," said Lawrence. "What changes?"

Backpedal, thought Nora. "Oh, not much. That's not my point, I just mean that they got to that level of conversation very quickly, and typically that's a very good sign —"

"But what changes?" insisted Lawrence.

"It's a *Cooper Sudecki,* Nora. It doesn't need any changes. That house is fucking perfect."

Nora tried not to be offended by Lawrence's language — he swore lustily and often, like a sixty-two-year-old sailor — and she tried not to be distracted by the giant *Riverdance* poster that hung on the back of the girls' door (*The hottest event on 160 legs!*). She tried not to notice that Maya's backpack was zipped up tight, which meant that she hadn't taken out any homework, which meant that Maddie had, once again, not done her job. She tried to channel Arthur Sutton — his smoothness, his fearlessness, his lack of fatigue, though she herself was very, very tired — and she said, "Lawrence, it was just something about the outdoor kitchen. They wanted to add a pizza oven, that's it. No big deal. They don't want to change the essence of the house. They agree that the house is perfect. My only point is that these people could be The Ones. I don't want to get your hopes up, but I got a good feeling. That's all. I'm going to follow up with them tomorrow."

"Tomorrow? Not tonight?"

"Tomorrow," said Nora firmly. She hoped Gabe had picked up the kitchen. She couldn't believe he and Angela hadn't cre-

55

ated a list of colleges with Ms. Vogel! A colossal wait to get on her calendar, and they hadn't created a list. What about all those lovely small East Coast colleges Nora knew Angela would adore if she only gave them a chance? What about Mt. Holyoke, Smith? Or, Heaven forbid, a *different* Ivy?

"Why not tonight?" asked Lawrence. He was starting to sound like one of her children, pecking at her for something she couldn't give them. She had an email to send out to the other parents in Maya's class soliciting last-minute donations for the school auction. Cecily needed a reminder to take a shower; she'd let it go for days if given half a chance. Had anyone unpacked Cecily's and Maya's lunch boxes? And Maya's soccer game had been moved to a different time on Saturday; she'd have to put that in her calendar before she forgot.

"Because," she said soothingly, "they need time to gather their thoughts too. They need to sleep on it. I will touch base with them tomorrow, Lawrence. I promise you. Now you and Bee go have a glass of wine on that gorgeous deck of yours, and I'll be in touch."

"A goddamn pizza oven," said Lawrence Watkins. "How come I never thought of that? That sounds fantastic."

CHAPTER 6
ANGELA

"Oh my God," said Henrietta. "Edmond Lopez? *Angela.* He's not your type at all. He's a total jock."

Angela and Maria Ortiz and Henrietta Faulkner were walking on the bike path on a Sunday morning. It seemed like a funny thing to do, like they were old, like their parents. Going for a walk made more sense if you had a dog, but none of them did. Henrietta had an ancient albino rabbit named Gus, which didn't help because you couldn't walk a rabbit on the bike path. The walk had been Maria's idea and, like most things Maria suggested, people went along with it, because she offered her ideas with style and conviction. Angela's interactions with Maria were sporadic and based entirely on what Angela thought of as TWOM: The Whims of Maria. Take lunch, for example. Sometimes Maria Ortiz ate lunch with Angela and Henrietta and a few other girls from the cross-country team, though Maria was not a runner. Sometimes Maria ate lunch in an empty classroom, working on her poetry. Sometimes she ate outside under a tree, where she spread her papers and her journals out around her and let her long dark hair loose to blow in the breeze. Maria Ortiz was so cool that sometimes Angela couldn't even look at her. Ergo, when Maria beckoned, Angela responded.

"What, are you hanging out with Edmond Lopez now?" asked Maria.

"*No.* Not . . . hanging out with." (Who had the time?) "Just noticing."

Looking at. Admiring. Getting smiled at by, sometimes. Lusting after, if she knew how to lust. Which, by the way, she didn't.

"His sister, Teresa, is a genius," said Henrietta. "That's all I know. She's, like, a legend."

"Yeah," said Angela. "I knew that part. Anyway, he's not a total jock. He's in AP English."

"Fluke," said Henrietta.

"You can't *fluke* AP English," said Angela.

"You can if you got on the track early, and never stepped off when you were supposed to," said Henrietta. "I bet you his sister writes his papers for him."

"I'm sure Teresa Lopez has better things to do than write high school English papers," said Maria wisely.

Angela returned to Henrietta's original point. "I don't think I have a type," said Angela. "Do I?" She didn't have enough experience yet with boys to have a *type.*

Jesus. Silly middle school stuff, then that fumbling with Jacob Boyd at one of the after-prom parties junior year (awkward), and the guy from Phoenix she'd tried to flirt with on the cruise to Alaska in the summer (better, but short-lived). She wished she had a type. But ultimately she'd been too busy with school and cross-country and flute and volunteering et al to figure out her type — let alone to find someone who met that criteria. Maybe she would acquire a type in college. Yes. She would acquire everything she was now lacking once she got to college! "Also, I was only asking what you *knew* about him. You don't have to freak out about it. I didn't say I was going to do anything. I was just curious."

Angela and Maria and Henrietta were all holding Starbucks cups. Whenever Angela took a sip — hers was a latte, though Maria *of course* had ordered four shots of espresso poured over ice, unsweetened, while Henrietta had a hot chocolate with whipped cream and chocolate syrup — she saw her grandmother's disapproving face. Her grandmother was consistently horrified at the amount of caffeine *today's teenagers,* as she called them, drank; when the Hawthorne family visited her in Rhode Island, Angela was served a glass of milk at each meal along with her sisters, as though she were still a little girl. "Coffee will stunt your growth, honey," she told Angela. "You shouldn't have it until you are absolutely fully grown. And even then, in moderation."

(Once she had stage-whispered to Angela's mother, "Do you think that's why she's so petite? Because of the coffee?")

"It's different now, Mom," Angela's mother had said. "You wouldn't believe the hours of homework they have. It's a different world than when we were kids."

Angela adored her grandmother, so she played along, drinking the milk, ignoring the stage whisper. Though sometimes she poured the milk down the kitchen drain when nobody was looking.

"I have a type," said Maria.

"Yeah?" said Henrietta. "What's your type, Maria?" Henrietta was so *eager* that sometimes it just killed Angela to watch her. She was like a puppy — no, more like a little kid dressed up as a puppy for Halloween, overdoing the licking and the jumping for effect. Maya had been a puppy for Halloween when she was five. So Angela knew what was involved.

Maria was six inches taller than Angela, with long dark hair that curled up just at the ends, without even being asked to. She was often mistaken for a college student, or older. She had a long, regal nose and the kind of cheekbones that people pointed out constantly because they were totally notice-able underneath Maria's caramel-colored skin. Maria Ortiz was a walking venti mocha. She didn't play a single sport, never had, didn't care. Even when they were nine, ten, all of them playing soccer, she hadn't played. Her dad owned a fleet of gourmet taco trucks that parked themselves around the city at key times; the lines could go on for a block or more. They were loaded.

Oh, and! Besides the poetry, for which Maria was practically famous, she had the singing voice of an angel. Not just any angel, an angel who had beaten out all of the other angels in Heaven's version of *The Voice*.

Inferiority complex, activate!

Maria was bad at math, though. So there was that. Angela's GPA was higher. Her SAT scores were higher. She had the daughter-of-an-alum card in her pocket. Maria, applying to Yale, did not.

"My type is older," said Maria. "Twenty-two, minimum. High school boys seem *so young*. Don't they?"

Angela tried not to let on how in awe of Maria she was. It was too embarrassing. It sort of seemed like Maria was a different species, living in captivity, and that Angela was some kind of lame tourist wearing khaki shorts and a sun hat and taking photos of her with her iPhone.

Soon enough they happened upon a bench, and huskily, like she was asking them to elope with her, Maria said, "Let's sit."

They sat. The bike path was packed with people of all shapes and sizes. A man rode by and immediately behind him was a little girl on a bike with training wheels. The girl said, "Daddy, *wait!*" in a strident voice that reminded Angela of Maya. Maya had just learned to ride a bike the previous year. Angela hadn't helped her. She'd helped Cecily learn to ride a bike, but by the time it was Maya's turn all of Angela's extra time had disappeared into the great black hole that was homework and extracurricular activities and sports practices.

"Listen," said Henrietta. "I was thinking about it. Do you think there would ever be a tie for GPA? In our class, I mean."

Angela stretched and yawned. Man, she was tired. She was having trouble focusing on Henrietta's words.

"So, do you?" persisted Henrietta. She pulled a pen and a Starbucks napkin from her bag and scribbled some figures. "Let's say, for the sake of argument, that two people started with a weighted GPA of 5.63."

Angela closed her eyes and felt her heart constrict. Did Henrietta have a 5.63? There was no way. If she did, Angela would have known it. Right? There was no way Henrietta had gotten ahead of her without her knowledge. It killed her that Henrietta was applying early to Harvard too, that she was *oversaturating* the pool. Applying early to Harvard had always been Angela's thing, always always. For Henrietta just to come in like it was nothing and apply too . . . well, Angela couldn't help it. She thought that was pretty shitty of Henrietta.

"And the other person has a 5.64. But then person A takes her health requirement, nonweighted, and person B takes an AP/GT class. Both get As. But. Person A simultaneously gets an A minus in a *different* AP class while person B gets an A plus in an AP class. Is it possible for them then to pull exactly even, even if the GPAs were calculated to the thousandths place? Which they're not. But if they were, I mean, what would it take for that to happen?"

"Oh my God," said Maria. "You are giving me such a headache."

"Only an idiot would take their health

63

requirement first semester of senior year," said Angela.

"But for the sake of argument," said Henrietta. "Is all I'm saying. Just humor me for a sec." Henrietta was still writing madly on the napkin. She held the pencil awkwardly, her middle finger hooked over her index finger, and a memory greeted Angela of their kindergarten teacher, Mrs. Doyle, standing over Henrietta and correcting her grip, again and again. All that correcting, all that reminding, and still Henrietta's grip was wrong. Was it bad that that made Angela a little bit happy? Just a tiny bit. It gave her just a *modicum* (SAT word) of happiness.

If Angela squinted at the right angle she could still see *that* Henrietta inside *this* Henrietta. When Henrietta Faulkner turned eleven her parents had taken her and five carefully chosen friends, Angela among them, to Raging Waters, the water park in San Jose, where they'd enjoyed unlimited fountain soda — a true indulgence, since soda was banned from most of their homes — and a Raging Birthday Cookie-Cake. That had been a good day. Angela could still see *that* Henrietta too: sunburned, laughing, the ends of her hair stiff with chlorine.

"I don't know," said Henrietta. "I'm getting a cramp in my brain. Forget it." Then she said, "Do you know? Next summer is the only one we won't have to fill with shit that will look good on our college applications."

"Yeah," said Angela. By next summer, obviously, she would know where she was headed. The thought made her feel sick to her stomach. She could imagine turning in her application to Harvard, but she could not imagine what it would be like to receive a response.

"My summer adviser told me about this one kid's parents who asked a for-profit company to become a nonprofit so he could use it for a congressional award," said Henrietta.

"That's crazy," said Angela, but her heart palpitated at this knowledge — new to her — that Henrietta had a summer adviser. Should she have had a summer adviser? Her father had mostly advised her on what to do with her summers, but maybe she should have had a professional. Shit. A misstep. Could she blame her parents for this one?

Maria tossed back her hair. "I've never done anything just so it will look good on my college application," she said. "Never."

"That's bullshit," said Henrietta. "That is

complete and total bullshit. And I don't believe you. Everyone like us does stuff so it looks good on our college applications. Everyone. That's what we *do*. We're semi-professional college applicants."

"Not me. I don't really care if I get into Yale or not." Maria lowered an enormous pair of sunglasses over her eyes so her expression was now inscrutable. *Inscrutable: not easily understood, mysterious.* SAT word.

"I don't believe you." Henrietta punched Angela on the arm. "Angela, do you believe her?"

"Ow."

"Sorry."

Angela shrugged. Yes. No. She wasn't sure. "I sort of feel the same way about Harvard."

"Right," said Henrietta. "You're so full of shit."

God, it was true: Angela was such a pathetic liar. She wanted to get into Harvard so badly it literally hurt. Ms. Simmons, AP English: "*Literally,* Angela?" Yes, Ms. Simmons. Literally. It hurts so much I can hardly stand it. I want it so much that I feel like there are little pins stuck all over my body, like I am a giant, freaky, hair-made-of-yarn voodoo doll.

"You are so lucky you're Mexican, Maria," said Henrietta. "I would kill to be a minority. I mean, seriously. In this day and age? Applying to the Ivies? You're just so lucky."

Angela said, "*Henrietta!* You can't say that."

Henrietta snorted. "Like you've never thought it."

"Of course I haven't. That's totally racist."

"It's not racist! Racist is when you say another race is *inferior* to yours. Not when you're, like, totally jealous of the other race. Right? I mean, if I said I wish I could have been a slave —"

"You definitely can't say that. You really can't."

"Fuck you both," said Henrietta.

"She can say it," said Maria. "Who cares? *I* don't care."

"So you've *never* wished you could check a different box on your applications? Not once?"

Angela sighed. Okay, maybe once or twice. But she'd certainly never *said* it. There was a limit to how badly you were supposed to want it. Wasn't there?

Just the other day, her mother, visiting her in her room the way she liked to do when Angela was doing homework: "You don't have to work so hard, honey. Give yourself

67

a break. You don't have to make yourself crazy."

How hilarious of her mother. Sweetly misguided. Of *course* Angela had to make herself crazy. She was first in the class! What was she going to do, stop caring all of a sudden? Now, so close to the end? *Now* she was going to let a few things slide? God.

Angela sipped her latte and watched two gray-haired women pass briskly by, pumping their arms. Then came a guy with a golden retriever, who paused to give Maria an approving glance — if Maria noticed, she didn't let on — and a couple of minutes after that Angela rested her Starbucks on the bench beside her, cleared her throat, and presented a question that had lately been plaguing her. She said, "Do you guys ever feel like there's a little voice following you around?"

"You mean a voice in your head? Like a crazy voice?" Maria lifted her sunglasses and cocked her head at Angela. She had gorgeous eyebrows — surprise, surprise — with just the right amount of arch to them. Angela's eyebrows were so pale they were mostly invisible.

"Sort of." Angela closed her eyes and lifted her face to the sky. "But not like a crazy voice that's telling me to *do* something, like jump off a bridge or sacrifice a family member so this unknown god can pull out their heart and eat it. It's more like a recording of all the things that have ever been said to me, running in an endless loop in my mind." As soon as she said it, she wished she could *un*say it. She felt just as naked as she would if she stripped off her clothes and ran three two-hundred-meter repeats down the bike path.

Gabe! Look, honey, look what Angela did at school today. Best in the class, her teacher said.

Angela, did you study?

Angela, did you pick up your room?

Angela, sing louder!

"No," said Maria serenely. "No, I don't think so." She tipped her head back and lifted her face to the sun.

"Um, *no*," said Henrietta. She crossed her arms over her chest like whatever form of craziness Angela had just confessed to might be contagious.

"Okay," said Angela. "Never mind, it's stupid. Forget I said anything."

Who's the one in the blue shirt? What's your name, young lady? Angela? Last name, sweetheart? That was a fabulous race you ran, very tough, ever thought of going out for cross-country?

Did you, Angela, did you? Have you, Angela? Will you? Angela! Angela!

CHAPTER 7
NORA

3:12 a.m.

Dear Marianne,
Do you know I still haven't told Gabe about what happened all those years ago?

Some people say it's normal for spouses to have at least one secret from each other. Do you think that's true?

This is why I worry so much, why I always have. One mistake, Marianne! And a lifetime of worry.

"How long until I don't need a car seat?" asked Maya.

"You have to be eight," said Cecily. "California state law."

"Not true. Hannah doesn't sit in a car seat and *she's* not eight."

"Then she's going to get arrested."

"Girls!" said Nora. She would have rubbed at her temples like a harried mother in a movie but she had both hands on the steering wheel, ten and two, just the way she'd

70

taught Angela.

"But she has to be eight," said Cecily. "I'm not making it up, I'm just telling her."

"Mommy?" said Maya. "Is Hannah going to get arrested?"

"Actually," said Cecily, "Hannah won't get arrested. Her mother will."

"Mommy!"

"Cecily," said Nora sternly. "Don't tease your sister. That isn't like you at all."

"I'm sorry," said Cecily. "Maya, I'm only kidding. Really, I'm sorry. Nobody's getting arrested, promise. Come on, let's do your math facts. Do you have your flash cards?"

Nora was only one-eighth involved in the conversation. They were on their way to Cecily's orthodontist appointment. The other seven-eighths of Nora was trying to (surreptitiously and illegally) check her email to see if an offer was going to come in on the Watkins home, concentrate on the late-afternoon traffic, make a mental to-do list for the auction project for Cecily's class, and work her way through a troubling dream.

At a stoplight in the rearview mirror Nora looked at her two daughters, one dark, the other light. One sturdy, one light as a cloud. Cecily was holding up the flash cards for Maya. Maya's concentration was utter; she

71

looked the way Gabe did when he was trying to tame a thorny situation at Elpis. She even chewed on her thumbnail in the same way. Funny, wasn't it, how two parents combined the same stuff and it came out in completely different ways in different children.

"That's it," said Cecily. "Done, you got them all."

For a moment there was blissful silence from the backseat.

Then Cecily said, "Albert Einstein couldn't read until he was ten. Does that make you feel better about Maya?"

Maya said, "Hey!"

Nora glanced in the rearview mirror. "I don't feel badly about Maya." *Bad,* or *badly*? She could never remember. She'd have to ask Angela.

"Einstein was dyslexic. Maybe Maya's dyslexic."

"She's not dyslexic. Remember? We had her evaluated, that man with the square glasses came over to the house. She'll get there, eventually. Everybody's different. You'll get there, honey." It never helped Nora to hear about Albert Einstein, and yet people were constantly trotting him out as a reason not to worry about Maya. Albert Einstein also never combed his hair and had

72

trouble tying his shoes and evidently couldn't keep track of any of his personal items — he was forever losing things. Umbrellas, apparently, presented a special problem. He lost a lot of umbrellas. This was supposed to make her feel better? Nora didn't want Maya to be Albert Einstein. She just wanted her to be a second grader who could make her way through a *Ramona* book on her own.

"A kid in my class has braces." Maya said.

"Well. That's crazy," said Nora. The sun was hitting her eyes at a very inconvenient angle. Where did it end? Was everything going to continue to come toward these kids earlier and earlier so that they emerged from the womb with their teeth wired, wearing glasses and helmets, scheduling math tutors?

"Mom? What do you think will happen if Angela doesn't get into Harvard?" That was Cecily.

Nora shifted and signaled into the right lane, preparing to exit the freeway. No more three-thirty appointments; it was too tight after school. She'd try for four o'clock next time.

"Nothing will *happen.* Life will go on, as it does. She'll be fine."

"But what will she do?"

The car in front of Nora, a silver Tahoe, slowed, then came to a dead stop. All around her, cars came to a dead stop. Traffic, at three thirty in the afternoon. This couldn't be rush hour. But it was. Rush hour, like orthodontic treatment, was coming earlier and earlier.

"I don't know, Cecily."

She exited. Not far now.

"I think she'll do something really bad."

"Really *bad*?" The Tahoe lurched ahead a couple of feet and stopped again. A ball of dread sprouted in Nora's chest. "Cecily, that's ridiculous. Don't talk like that. What do you even mean?"

"Sorry," said Cecily. "Nothing."

Then Maya said, "Why does Angela cry in the afternoons?" Clear out of nowhere.

Nora almost sideswiped a car pulling out of the orthodontist's parking lot. She took a deep breath, pulled into a parking space, and said, *"What?"*

"She does," said Maya. "When Maddie's there, she cries in her room."

"No she doesn't," said Cecily. "I've never heard her."

"You're not there," said Maya. "You're at Irish."

There was a little man with a hammer tapping away on Nora's skull. Now she could take her hands off the steering wheel and rub her temples properly. Only for a second, though, because they were ten minutes late to the appointment.

"I think she's crying about college," said Maya. "I think she doesn't want to leave us and go live somewhere else where she has to share a room."

"That's probably it," said Nora, and the man with the hammer tapped harder. Why *was* Angela crying in her room? She thought of Angela as a little girl with the fat legs squatting down to look at a sand crab on a Rhode Island beach and her heart tore a little bit.

"Okay," said Nora. "Here we are. Unbuckle, Maya, come on, we're late."

"Is Cecily going to have to get braces?" asked Maya. Languidly she reached for the buckle of her seat belt.

"Faster," said Nora. "Come on, Maya."

"You're always *rushing* me," said Maya tranquilly, and Nora, who wanted to say, "Everybody else is always rushing *me*!" said calmly, "I'm sorry, sweetie, you're right, I'll try not to rush you. Take your time."

"I hope so," said Cecily. Pinkie got her braces at the end of third grade and ever since then Cecily had been trying to construct her own version from paper clips and

75

earring backs, both of which she insisted were *totally clean* and *completely safe.* "I want blue ones. They would match my solo dress. That would be *awesome.*"

Nora stole a glance at her email.

"Can I get blue ones? Mom? Mom?"

"Just a sec—"

"You always tell *us* to put down our technology and pay attention to the person who's talking."

Damn it. Fair point. Anyway, there was nothing on the Watkins home.

"So can I? Get blue?"

"Yes. No. I don't know, Cecily, we have to wait and see what he says." Did blue braces even exist? Could an email have come in just now, while she was locking the doors? Could she check again? Was she letting work take over her life again; had she learned *nothing,* that time? For just a second, Nora allowed her mind to wander. Back to that moment when her entire world could have changed in an instant, in the dash of a head against the floor.

That's why she held on to it so tightly now.

She took Maya's (sticky) hand and led her across the parking lot. Was it terrible that she had never told Gabe about that day? No. One secret, they were each allowed one secret. That was okay. Everybody said so.

CHAPTER 8
GABE

At the table in the conference room, Gabe waited for the prospective clients.

He was early to the meeting — the first Elpis guy in the room, he was there even before the snacks — so he stared for some moments at the giant circular graph that was the centerpiece of the Elpis philosophy. It was divided into thirds, and each third was labeled with one of the three magic words. Align. Prepare. Execute.

Kelsey, the firm's super-young, super-hip office assistant, who wore clothes that looked like cupcake decorations and who lived in up-and-coming NOPA and regularly went to places in the city that Gabe had never even heard of, much less visited, stuck her head inside the conference room. "They're running late," she said. "You don't have to wait in here. Go back to your office — I'll call you in when they get here."

"I'm good here," he said. "But thanks."

The word *Elpis* itself was, in Greek mythology, the personification and spirit of hope. When Gabe first joined the company, when he was a young man with a single pair of Dr. Martens wing tips and a serious Nirvana habit, Elpis was a gutsy, scrappy little firm that had no business competing with the likes of McKinsey and Bain, and yet chose to anyway. They'd had a tiny office back then, in Outer Sunset. This was patently ridiculous. Nobody did business in Outer Sunset. They made their name in the dot.com boom, advising the heck out of the companies that sprung up in the Bay Area like slugs after a rainstorm. Now they had the twentieth floor of a building on Sansome Street, right near the Transamerica building. From the conference room where Gabe now sat he could see the Oakland Bay Bridge.

When he first came to San Francisco he'd lived in a shithole in the Mission with two idiotic, half-baked roommates, and his rat-trap Subaru was broken into three times before he finally abandoned it. Now he lived on a quarter acre in Marin in a town with some of the best schools in the country. Three beautiful daughters, a wife. Everything had changed.

Gabe's strength now was exactly what it was back then. He'd barely gotten that first interview (the economy was struggling and it seemed like no one was looking to hire; thank God for Nora's friend). But once he was sitting across from the founding partners, he knew exactly what they were looking for in a candidate, he handed it to them on a silver platter — and he'd been delivering on it ever since. That counted for something. Didn't it?

Companies came into Elpis and sat at this very table and ate Danishes and drank gourmet coffee and claimed to want all sorts of things. They wanted to bring a new product to market, or they wanted to undergo a dramatic reorg, or they wanted to engender a culture change or become proactive in e-commerce or develop a cross-functional initiative.

And typically they did want at least one of those things, sometimes more. But really what it all came down to was that they wanted someone to listen. It was that simple; that was, at heart, what every single person walking across this green earth wanted. That's what the ranch hands wanted back in Wyoming, when they bitched and moaned to Gabe about how hard it was to hand-feed the cattle in the winter. They didn't want to stop doing their jobs; they just wanted someone to nod and furrow his eyebrows and offer a Bill Clinton–like expression of sympathy and understanding so they could go back to doing what they did best.

The door opened again. This time Kelsey

had a woman with her, even younger than Kelsey herself. The woman had chin-length, swinging dark hair with blunt bangs. She wore a silk blouse and a pencil skirt. She was tall, nearly as tall as Gabe, and yet somehow she looked like a child who had dressed up in her mother's work clothes. Not that the clothes were too big, it was just that — well, they sat oddly on her, as though somebody else had picked them out. The client? Impossible. She didn't look so much older than Angela.

"I forgot," said Kelsey. "They wanted the intern to sit in on the meeting. Gabe Hawthorne, Abby Freeman. Abby Freeman, Gabe Hawthorne, one of the partners."

Abby Freeman said hello and shook the hand Gabe offered, and Kelsey left. Abby Freeman's handshake said, *I wrestle alligators in my spare time.*

"We have something in common," said Abby Freeman. She had a face that was not conventionally attractive — her eyes were small and far apart, and her lips weren't generous. But she was *unconventionally* attractive, in that intense, feline way that some women were. Gabe had never gone for that sort of look. (Most women with it scared him.) Abby stood there with plenty of confidence, like she didn't know her clothes looked wrong on her. In fact — you could argue — she stood there in a way that did not say, *I bow down to you, partner in the firm.*

Gabe said, "Oh, yes? What's that?"

"Same alma mater."

He said, "Is that right?" He tried to smile but his lips seemed to be stuck weirdly to his teeth. He hated it when people brought up Harvard when he wasn't expecting it. Made his eyelids itch.

The door opened again. The clients, the members of his team, all coming in together, led by the indomitable Kelsey. A rush of blood to the head. Gabe lived for this part. He was Don Draper when it came to meetings like this. He cleared his throat. Abby Freeman stood next to him, as though they were man and wife, greeting guests at a dinner party.

"Ah," said the leader of the client team, holding out a hand, grasping Gabe's firmly. "The man we've all been waiting to meet."

CHAPTER 9
NORA

12:15 a.m.

Dear Marianne,
I had seventy-eight different things to

do today. I was supposed to buy supplies for Cecily's around-the-world project, and make an appointment with Maya for the reading tutor, and check in with Lawrence Watkins. But instead I went into Cecily's bookcase and I found an old copy of *Betsy-Tacy,* the third book in the series. It had both of our names in it. Remember when we used to put our names in our books? After my name it said, the Great. Nora the Great, I used to call myself. How narcissistic is that?

Deep Valley, Minnesota, the early nineteen hundreds. Snow fell in November (no global warming), baked goods were plentiful and not frowned upon (no gluten sensitivity), and friendships were thorough and everlasting (maybe there were class ranks, but it didn't seem like people battled for them in quite the same way).

I turned to my favorite chapter in book three: A December snowfall, the kids sledding down the hill by the light of the moon (no streetlights. Okay, maybe there were streetlights. I'm not sure. Probably gaslights). Betsy fell off a sled and sprained her ankle. And she was out of school for weeks. Weeks! Just healing her ankle, limping around her house, writing her little stories on the old trunk. Nobody said, "Betsy, you're going to miss so much." Nobody said, "Betsy, you'll never get into college now." Nobody said, "Betsy! Your after-school activities! Your reading tutor! Your dance class!" They left her alone, and she rested her ankle, and she got better, and life went on. And they all ate more cake.

The offer came in lower than asking, but truthfully Nora thought it was reasonable, even generous. Lawrence and Bee begged to differ. Well, they didn't really beg. Mostly they just differed; more specifically, they refused at first to entertain what they considered an abysmally low number. *Marianne,* wrote Nora in an email in her mind. *Can you imagine a world where a number that begins with a seven, as in seven* million *dollars, is considered abysmally low?*

"Counter, then," said Nora, as gently as she could when she presented the offer to them — *in person,* as Lawrence had requested. Lawrence and Bee did not like to have important conversations over the phone. They were like a couple of shady Russian diplomats who preferred to meet in smoky bars or corner cafés where nobody went. Or, in this case, on the leather stools in front of their massive kitchen island. Nora sat between Lawrence and Bee, like an only child out to dinner with her parents. "These are solid buyers," she continued. "You don't want them to walk away. You *really* don't want them to walk away. If they walk away, they're not coming back." The buyers had made that very clear to their agent, who in turn had made it very clear to Nora.

She brought the offer to Lawrence and Bee at six thirty in the evening, which was a terrible time both traffic-wise and family-dinner-wise. Nora had just released Maddie from her duties, and Gabe wasn't home. Angela was ensconced in her room with post-practice homework. (Was she crying?) Who was supposed to make dinner? Cecily? Unlikely. Nora had never found time to teach her to cook anything. She hadn't taught Angela to cook either. She cut up a bunch of raw vegetables, on which Cecily and Maya began to nibble while they watched the Disney Channel in the living room and Cecily did her heel raises.

"Homework?" Nora asked, laying the plate on the coffee table like Communion gifts at Mass.

Maya said, "Don't have any."

"None?"

"Nope."

Well, that didn't seem right. She'd tackle that one when she got home.

Cecily waved a thin arm toward Nora and said, "Later." They were watching the show with the talking dog who wrote a blog. Nora didn't think Angela had ever expressed even a teaspoon of interest in the Disney Channel. Nora stood for half a second and found herself laughing at the dog, who was observant and sardonic, just the right balance for the busy, wacky, blended family. To boot, he looked like some kind of border collie mix, Nora's favorite breed after Newfoundlands. A little-known fact about Nora Hawthorne was that she had always been a sucker for talking animals. In this show, only the kids in the family knew the dog could talk. Brilliant.

They had a no-TV-before-homework rule, like any respectable modern family, but Nora was in no position to play cop.

When Nora brought the offer over she focused at first on Lawrence, because she thought he was the holdout, had always been the holdout. He was the one who had refused to lower the price back in the summer, when Nora had sat on this very same stool, sipping at a white sangria that Bee had pressed into her hands, and explained to them that the market was seasonal and finicky and that the time for a change was now. But when she looked directly at Lawrence she saw that she'd been wrong; his gaze was open and guileless, while Bee's was shrouded. *Bee* was the holdout. Bee, with her copper-colored hair, her matching copper-colored lipstick, was the Oz who moved the machinery of this marriage. *A-ha.* Nora should have known it.

Forty-six minutes later, Bee bent. An hour in, she broke. The Watkins submitted a counteroffer. The buyers countered the counter.

"We're getting somewhere!" said Nora. She patted Bee on the hand, tapped Lawrence lightly on the shoulder as she passed him on her way to one of the six and a half bathrooms. Nora called home — Gabe had arrived in the interim and opened a box of Annie's Mac and Cheese — and stayed put. She knew Gabe could do better than Annie's; he'd been raised on ranch food, good beef and venison, hearty chili and stews, and his mother had made sure that all of her sons knew their way around a kitchen. But now was not the time to quibble.

Nora left the room to call the buyer's agent and to verbally present the counter-counter. She walked around the living room and peered at some of the artwork on Lawrence and Bee's walls, which Nora was sure meant something to people who knew more about art than she did. She opened the door to the ridiculously stocked wine room and wondered how on earth Lawrence and Bee were going to get all of those bottles out when it was time to move, and where they were going to put them. It wasn't her problem, but she couldn't help thinking about it.

While she inspected the Watkins home, she talked. She used the ultra-reasonable voice she had trotted out time and time again during Angela's transition through puberty and into young adulthood, when every conversation was a minefield waiting to explode. She explained about the merits of the home and how they justified the price tag. She reminded the buyer's agent that Cooper Sudecki was no longer designing homes in the Bay Area, nor anywhere else for that matter, and that of the dozen homes that bore his name very few were likely to hit the market in the next five years.

She knew the other agent well enough to tell it to him straight — the sellers were not bending any further. Their counter-counter was firm, this was it, take it or leave it. Etc.

The buyers took it. Hooray! Nora called

Gabe to check in. All three girls had eaten. Maya was plugged into her Hooked on Phonics CDs. Angela was doing homework and Cecily was practicing her Irish dance solo. Gabe had the fuzzy voice that signaled to Nora that he was into the Bulleit.

Champagne all around. Lawrence, in an unguarded moment, hugged Nora. Even Bee hugged Nora. They had reached an agreement! The long local nightmare was over.

Chapter 10
Angela

Angela was at her desk. She was having trouble concentrating. There was still a month to go until Halloween. Even so, Cecily and Pinkie had spent much of the afternoon — Cecily's sole afternoon free from Irish dance practice — working on their costume, which was some sort of Siamese two-headed zombie situation: *Guinness World Records* meets *The Walking Dead,* while Angela went to French club and cross-country practice and showered and snuck into her room past Cecily, Pinkie, Maya, and the babysitter Maddie. Maddie and Maya had been looking together through a picture book — *The Day the*

Crayons Quit — and Maddie had been scrolling through her texts at the same time. It was a *prodigious* (SAT word) display of multitasking.

Sometimes Angela felt really weird in front of Maddie the babysitter. She was only, what, three years older than Angela? But she had a boyfriend and her own cherry-red CR-V and she was practically done with college. Angela was never sure if she should treat her like a peer or a grown-up. ("Oh my *God* you're going to *totally love* college," Maddie had said to her recently. "Just be careful with the beer, you can't believe how many carbs are in there, I blew up like a *balloon* first semester freshman year.")

Now it was after dinner. Angela was making her way slowly through *Angela's Ashes.* "Not a prescient choice, I hope," her father had joked when he saw it on her desk. *Prescient.* Having or showing knowledge of events before they take place.

Angela was wearing an old pair of flannel pajamas and a Harvard sweatshirt her father had given her two years ago. It was too big then but now it almost fit. With the exception of the absolutely gigantic bulletin board, the centerpiece of which was still the calendar with November first circled, Angela's walls were bare. Over the summer, before her senior year kicked into full swing, she had stripped them of all the childhood memorabilia that she deemed juvenile or distracting. The family photo from a trip to Disneyland five years ago, when Angela and her father rode Space Mountain six times in a row: gone. The poster of Mumford & Sons sitting on an old-fashioned sofa in front of a backdrop of fake trees: also gone. The ribbons from elementary school swim meets. Gone gone gone.

Crappy day, all things considered. Earlier, at practice, Henrietta Faulkner beat Angela on the last two of six hill repeats. Even Angela's usual mantra — *the only way to win on this hill is to train on this hill* — repeated to herself over and over had failed to produce. She had thought about it while she took a shower and had decided that she'd taken the first three hills harder than she needed to. Way harder. Showing off, for no reason. Probably trying to show Henrietta which one of them deserved to get into Harvard. She'd hung on for the fourth hill but she had nothing left for five and six. She had been absolutely *depleted.* So after much *deliberation* Angela had determined that perhaps her *hubris* had led to the failure to engage in proper *husbandry* of her resources. To *deleterious* effect. And now she was bathing in her own *ignominy.*

Henrietta never beat Angela on hills. Nobody ever beat Angela on hills. Hills were her thing. Because she was light, and because she was agile, and because she could scamper over the rocks like a mountain goat, she'd won many a race on the uphills alone. *The only way to win on this hill is to train on this hill.* Truer words were never whispered to oneself.

But today, Henrietta Faulkner had beaten Angela so soundly on the last two repeats that when she'd said "Good workout" and held her hand up for Angela to tap at the end, Angela, panting angrily, hadn't even had the good grace to tap it back. She'd pretended she hadn't seen it, and then she'd concentrated on stretching her calf. What a jerk she could be when she didn't win. Major character flaw. Usually she was able to hide it. But not always!

Could it be the pills?

No. Perish the thought. Angela didn't need the pills. Angela didn't even have any more pills, she'd had only a handful, and she'd used them all.

Except there was one problem. She could really use a pill, just to get through tonight's homework. *Angela's Ashes,* a statistics quiz, flute practice . . .

She couldn't ask Henrietta for any more *now,* not after that workout. First of all, who knew if Henrietta even had any pills. If she did, Angela didn't want to show any cracks in her armor by asking for them. Now that Henrietta was applying early too.

The senior class had entered a new level of intensity; they eyed one another warily, like animals circling before the kill. Angela's class rank was *precarious* as opposed to *immutable* and Angela didn't want to do anything *impetuous* that would *substantiate* any rumors of her weakness.

Her mother knocked and opened the door simultaneously. Angela tried to be annoyed but in fact she was grateful for the interruption. She liked when her mother visited her: it made her feel warm and cozy and taken care of, like a bear in a children's book. Bears in children's books usually had very caring mothers. They baked a lot and wore aprons. Angela's mother did not wear aprons, and she didn't have much time for baking. But still.

Seriously, Angela really was lame. Maria Ortiz probably never hung out voluntarily with her mother. (Maria Ortiz's mother had been a famous model in Mexico, BTW. Which explained a lot.)

"Hey there, sweetie."

92

"Hey. Hi."

When Cecily was really small, maybe two, she used to stand outside Angela's room calling, "I come in? I come in?" Angela always let her in — Cecily was too freaking cute not to. Almost eight years was a big difference; when Cecily was born Angela had been old enough to help out for real, baths, spooning baby food into Cecily's toothless little mouth. Even diapers! Angela and Cecily were too far apart in age to be competitive with each other, the way Henrietta and her younger sister were and the way that sometimes even Cecily and Maya were. Angela and Cecily simply coexisted. Cecily's first word had been "Anla," because she couldn't pronounce the *g*. (Angela's first word had been *libro,* owing to frequent viewings of a Spanish Baby Einstein video; her father had run with it as *substantiated* evidence of her bilingual capabilities, which were then nurtured in a series of early-childhood foreign language programs.)

"I didn't see you much today."

"Yeah," said Angela. She twisted a piece of hair around her finger. "I know."

A crappy day, the crappiest of the crappy. Angela was having trouble concentrating on *Angela's Ashes.* It all seemed very far away and irrelevant and *Irish*. She was on chapter four, the First Communion chapter.

They dried me. They dressed me in my black velvet First Communion suit with the white frilly shirt, the short pants, the white stockings, the black patent leather shoes. Around my arm they tied a white satin bow and on my lapel they pinned the Sacred Heart of Jesus, a picture with blood dripping from it, flames erupting all around it and on top a nasty-looking crown of thorns.

What a scene. Man oh man. First of all, white stockings on a boy? Poor thing. The Hawthorne family as a whole had zero religion. Well, that wasn't exactly true. Angela's mother had grown up attending St. Thomas More parish in Narragansett, a brown-shingled, high-steepled New England church with a low dark wood altar to which Nora dragged the entire Hawthorne family anytime they visited what Angela's father always (ironically?) referred to as "the homestead." Angela was *perennially* surprised to learn that her mother knew all the responses and spoke them along with the rest of the congregation, and that she even sang along with some of the hymns in a lilting, mostly in-tune voice. Except for those times Angela never heard her mother sing.

In California: no church. Which was fine with Angela. Angela's father had grown up "with the ranch as my chapel." And Sundays, of course, belonged to open houses: real estate as religion.

"Just wanted to check in, see how your day was."

"Checking in" was Angela's mom's *euphemism* for being extremely worried about her state of mind. Angela's mother thought Angela worked too hard. She thought Angela pushed herself to extremes. She thought Angela didn't laugh enough, didn't hang out with her friends enough, didn't eat enough or drink enough water or get enough sleep. Didn't plan to apply to enough colleges . . .

When Angela's mother was young she had so much free time that she and Angela's aunt Marianne were *bored* half the time. Blah blah blah, and etc. Angela loved her mother to the ends of the earth, but sometimes her mother just didn't get it.

"Fine," she said. "Not bad."

Angela's mother sat carefully on the edge of the bed. She folded a T-shirt that Angela had left crumpled on the floor and said, "Yeah? Good day?"

Sometimes Angela wished she were still small enough to curl up on her mother's lap, like Maya was.

Did she have to say it again? "Fine," she repeated, trying not to sound testy. But feeling it. Her mother was no longer acting like a bear in a children's book.

What a smart girl. Look, Gabe, it's a chapter book, she read it all by herself!

"Everything okay at school?"

Unbelievable. "Sure. Same as ever."

"Lots of homework?"

Angela yawned. "Always."

"Everything *really* okay?"

Angela eyed her mother. "Yes, Mom, sure. Why?"

Angela, did you do your homework? Did you did you did you.

"Oh, it's nothing. Just that Maya said something about she heard you crying sometimes in the afternoons —" Her mother stole a *surreptitious* glance at the calendar.

"*Crying?* Me? Why would I be crying in the afternoons?"

"I don't know. That's what I'm asking you."

Angela put on her best exasperated face. In fact she had been crying in the afternoons. She couldn't explain it to her mother any better than she could explain it to herself. She was not, in general, a crying sort of person. She tried to make her expres-

96

sion *impassive.*

"So you haven't been crying? Angela?"

"No, Mom, I haven't been crying." Angela bit down on her lower lip, hard. God.

Angela, did you practice?

Angela, kick the ball! Angela, reach for the wall!

Her mother exhaled audibly and rubbed her hands together like that was that and said, "Good." Then she said, "Mrs. Fletcher called earlier."

Instinctively, Angela checked her phone, which she kept on the desk but which she turned facedown and muted while she was doing homework. "I didn't get any calls."

"The home phone." Angela's mother looked around the room, seeking, no doubt, another pile of clutter to which she could bring order. But with the exception of the recently folded shirt Angela did not allow clutter; her room was as neat as a pin (seriously, what did that mean?). All the clutter in this room was smack-dab in the middle of Angela's mind. Which was a crowded and bewildering place.

"She did? She called the home phone? Nobody calls the home phone." Angela chewed at a fingernail. She thought painting them black might have helped her kick the habit, but so far it hadn't.

"Just telemarketers," agreed her mother. Then gently moving Angela's hand away from her mouth, "No nibbles, honey." (That's what she used to say to Angela when she was young, Cecily's age, and had first begun biting the nails.) Angela thought about protesting the choice of phrase, but she was too tired. She let her hand fall to her lap. "But anyway. She wanted to know if you could babysit, on Friday night."

"Babysit?" Angela had stopped babysitting regularly for the Fletchers. Too busy, for one thing. And for another, Joshua Fletcher was a sweet kid (sort of, sweet*ish,* anyway), but he had so much untamed energy that Angela spent half the time running around just making sure he didn't hurt himself. When the younger Fletcher, Colton, was eleven months old — Angela was thirteen — Angela had been there when he'd taken his first steps; she'd thought to capture it with a video taken with her newly acquired phone, and Mrs. Fletcher had been forever grateful. Recently Joshua had been diagnosed with ADHD and the Fletchers had gotten divorced.

"Do you think you might do it, Angela? She's really in a bind, she sounded desperate. Things have been tough for them, and she never even asks anymore, she knows

98

you're so busy. It's the night before the auction and I realize I asked you to stay here with the girls and I hate to take up your whole weekend. But." Angela's mother put the heels of her palms to her forehead and massaged the skin outward. Angela had asked her once why she did that and Nora had said, regretfully, "Trying to smooth away the wrinkles."

Angela said, "I don't know . . . there's a meet on Saturday." She flipped through *Angela's Ashes.* So many more pages to go. Her flute, still in its case, seemed to be reprimanding her.

"Oh!" said her mother. "You're reading *Angela's Ashes*! I loved that book." Then, channeling Cecily's dance teacher, the eminent Seamus O'Malley, Nora said, "Bit of a downer though, yeah?"

Angela allowed herself a small smile: her mother was trying. *Assiduously.* "That sounded British," she said. "Or South African."

"Listen, honey, you know I don't try to dictate your schedule to you but this time I would really, really appreciate it. If you would help out Anna. She's had a hard time since the divorce and I have a feeling" — here she lowered her voice, as though the walls were listening — "I have a feeling that

99

she might be going on *a date.*"

Henrietta Faulkner had beaten her on two out of six hills. There was so much more to go in *Angela's Ashes.* Five fifteen a.m. practice every Friday. Volunteer tutoring for National Honor Society: twenty-five hours required over the course of the year. She hadn't even started thinking about that. The term paper for AP English. (Virginia Woolf?) The Harvard application . . .

But she was so close. A little over a month, she was almost there. She just had to get through a little more. The first-quarter grades would be sent on to Harvard just as soon as they were ready. She didn't want to work so hard and come in second, *geez.* Angela just had to *marshal* her forces and show some *tenacity.* Valedictorians were made, not born.

When she'd turned seventeen Aunt Marianne had sent her, *wow,* a gift certificate for JetBlue for $500. Angela didn't even know airlines did gift certificates.

I don't know where you'll land after your senior year, *the card said.* But I want you to be able to get home anytime.

Sometimes Angela felt like taking that gift certificate and flying far, far away.

(What did Aunt Marianne mean, though, that she didn't know where Angela would land? Didn't she think she could get into Harvard?)

"Okay," Angela said, sighing mightily, tearing at a cuticle with her teeth. "Friday night? I can't stay out late, because of the meet Saturday. I want to be asleep by eleven. But I'll do it."

Chapter 11
Cecily

Cecily could tell by the look on her mother's face that this wasn't the best idea in the world.

Actually she thought Maddie was picking them up, and that would have made things easier. But now she remembered that Maddie was going away for the weekend so her mother was taking the afternoon off work. Maddie probably wouldn't have noticed what Cecily had with her, literally. Maddie never noticed anything.

Still, Cecily was in it now, so she kept on going. *Keep on keeping on* was what her father always said. Maya was already in her booster seat, looking out the window, wiping at her eyes.

Her mother's mouth was a straight line in

her face. She definitely wasn't smiling. She lowered the passenger window and stretched across the seat to lean out of it.

"What's wrong with Maya?"

Maya swiped at her nose. "Stupid boys," she said.

"Nothing," said her mother. "Some idiotic kids made fun of her for her reading. For her *not* reading."

"They called me dumb," confirmed Maya. "I don't care though." But her eyes were wet and bright and she was blinking rapidly.

"I am outraged," said Cecily's mom. "I might talk to their parents."

"No!" said Maya, horrified. "Don't do that!"

Cecily's mom took a better look at Cecily and said, "Cecily. What is in that cage?"

Cecily looked at the cage as though surprised to find it in her hands. She shifted and tried to open the door but she couldn't do both so she set the cage down on the ground.

Maya unbuckled and spilled herself out of the car and crouched on the ground and crowed, "It's *Roland*! From the science lab! Hey, Roland, come here, you little cutie. Is he coming to *our house*, Cecily?"

Now Cecily's mom was out of the car too. Someone in the car behind her was starting to honk. You were supposed to keep moving in the turnaround line. Cecily's mom shot that car a look and the honking stopped.

"Cecily. Is that a *rat*?"

"No! It's Roland. He's a *hamster*. I signed up to take him home for the weekend. He can't stay alone. I mean, he can, but he'd rather be with people. He's really social, he gets lonely on his own."

Her mother sighed and definitely did not crouch down to look at Roland. "Don't you need permission from your parents for that? Isn't there a form?"

"I forgot it. But Mr. G. let me take him anyway."

"What do you mean, you forgot it? I never signed a form."

"That's what I mean. I forgot to have you sign the form."

Her mother was frowning at the cage. Roland hopped on his wheel and showed off a little bit.

"He's nocturnal," said Cecily. "But I guess he's up now because of all the excitement."

"Wonderful," said her mom. "Nocturnal, perfect. Get in the car, girls, I think this car behind us is going to run us over if we don't get out of the way."

"With Roland?"

Her mother frowned again. "Well, I guess

so. We can't leave him at the turnaround, can we?"

"No. And I think Mr. G. already left."

"Perfect." Her mother put two fingers in the center of her forehead and pressed.

They loaded themselves into the car, and Cecily put Roland's cage on the seat between her and Maya. She held on to it with one hand and twisted her body to look at him.

"He looks a little bit like Frankie, if you look closely."

"He does," said Maya. "He does look like Frankie. Aw, his little nose. I love him. Roland, I love you."

Her mother, from the front seat: "How can he look like Frankie? He's a *hamster* and Frankie was a *dog.*"

"Best dog in the world," said Maya softly.

"They have the same expression," said Cecily. "They really do, if you look closely."

Roland hiked himself up on the wires of his cage and studied Cecily, twitching his nose. His whiskers.

"If that thing gets out," said her mother. "We'll never find him."

"That's because he's a dwarf hamster," said Cecily. "He's tiny. That's what Pinkie has too. I won't let him get out, I promise."

Her mother looked in the rearview mirror. Cecily couldn't see her face but when she spoke next it sounded like there might be a little bit of a smile creeping into her voice. "He doesn't look like Frankie," she said. "I do not accept that comparison. But he is a little bit cute. For a hamster."

Cecily missed Frankie so much that sometimes when she thought about him she felt like her stomach was crawling into her throat and choking her. Cecily had never known the world without him, and then suddenly he was gone. And she had to get used to a whole new world.

She was never bothered by his gas attacks the way everyone else was, and she didn't even mind when he drooled on her hand. Which — by the way — he did a lot. Cecily could tell by his eyes that he trusted her and that he believed that Cecily would do whatever he needed for him. Which she would, because she understood him.

Empathy, her mother called it. Her mother always said Cecily had empathy spilling right out of her.

CHAPTER 12
NORA

4:37 a.m.

Dear M:
Auction night. You would hate the auction, dear sister, champion of the underdogs. And if you came to the auction you would be an active participant in the
  odd
  unsettling
  fascinating
  exhilarating
  disturbing
world of privately funded California public schools.
  Don't ever go to the auction, Marianne.
P.S. Did I tell you about the hamster?

There was a cocktail hour with an open bar, purposely held at the same time as the silent auction bidding. There was a four-course sit-down dinner served by the country club staff in bow ties and cummerbunds. There was a professional auctioneer with a bald shiny head and a vest. (Nora read in the auction program that he'd started his career doing cattle auctions, and she squinted at him, imagining him in Gabe's old Wyoming stomping ground, wearing flannel and pointing out the merits of a Texas Longhorn. What did this guy think, transported from a *cattle auction,* of all places, where he literally had to *step over shit* to get his job done, to a country club ballroom filled with some of Marin's finest?) There was lots of cheek kissing on the part of the women, as though they hadn't just seen one another the day before in the pickup line, and hearty handshakes on the part of the men. Nora looked around, accepted a cheek kiss from Melanie Schubert and doled out one to Jules Morris, the room parent in Cecily's class. They sat with Skip and Cathy Moynihan, Pinkie's parents. Angela and Cecily and Maya were home together — this was rare, but the fact that Angela was home was saving Nora approximately eighty dollars in babysitting costs. They were eating pizza and watching a movie that Nora was sure was inappropriate for Maya, but she hadn't thought to ask about it until it was too late. Was that why Maya couldn't read, too many inappropriate movies at a young age?

No, Angela could be trusted. Couldn't she? Of course she could. She had just sat for the Fletcher boys the night before. But she'd be exhausted from being up early for the meet, and Nora knew Angela was kicking herself over a very respectable second-place finish — a bit of a surprise, but everybody has off days. Angela might not even be sitting with the girls, she might be in her room, working on the Harvard application. Should Nora call to check in? Was that what a respectable parent would do, or was that what a helicopter parent would do? Oh, God, was Nora a helicopter parent?

Nora inhaled deeply. School auction night.

The live auction began. In her head, Nora started an email to Marianne.

First, she wrote, *there was the farm-to-table dinner.*

The farm-to-table dinner for twelve people went for $8,000. A week in Tahoe, summer or winter, winner's choice: ten grand. A weekend in the Mulholland Suite at the Huntington: $5,000. A ride on a Rose Bowl parade float. Scuba diving lessons. A getaway in Carmel with two days of spa treatments. A shopping trip to Dubai! The big-ticket item. Twenty-five grand for three couples.

Under the glare of the lights over the stage ballroom, the auctioneer was beginning to sweat. Perhaps, after all, the cattle were easier.

Nora sipped from her wineglass and

looked at Gabe. Had Gabe been distant lately? She knew he was involved in a big project at work, a company called Bizzvara. *Ridiculous* name.

Gabe was dressed to kill, in a Brioni jacket Nora had given him for Christmas the previous year. It looked just a bit looser than it had at Christmas. Had Gabe been working out more than usual? Was he trying to impress someone besides Nora? She remembered when Melanie Schubert's husband had left her the previous year; Melanie had cried on Nora's shoulder at a PTO meeting and said, "How'd he have *time* for an affair? I would never be able to fit infidelity into my day."

Gabe reached for her hand and squeezed it. No, she was being crazy. He wasn't distant; he was merely entranced. He held his paddle at the ready. Every year he bid on a variety of items, and most of the time he lost out to someone else. But he kept up the volley, valiantly, energetically, cheerfully, like a tennis pro from a middling club transported suddenly to the courts at Wimbledon. It was sort of adorable.

Principal for a day for one lucky child went for a cool $2,500. *That's two thousand, five hundred,* Nora mentally typed to Marianne. Reserved parking in front of the

109

school for a year nearly incited a riot; it was decided, eventually, that it would be shared between the two highest bidders. The shining parental faces, the strapless dresses, the perfume, the alcoholic buzz that pervaded the room like campfire smoke at Yosemite.

There was a break. The room itself seemed to sigh, releasing palpable quantities of tension. Nora saw the auctioneer gulping water off to the side of the stage. Someone handed him a napkin, and he mopped at the top of his head.

"Do you think he's okay?" she whispered to Gabe. He was absorbed in the program, but then he looked at her and smiled and he was the same man she'd fallen in love with in that bar in Noe Valley: the bright-eyed sexy optimist with the old sneakers and the beat-up Subaru. "I think he's fine," he said. "Look, he's ready to rock and roll."

"I'd bid on the Adirondack chairs myself," said Cathy Moynihan, leaning so close to Nora that Nora could see the remnants of a pomegranate seed (salad course) wedged between two of her molars.

Dear Marianne, thought Nora. *Hold on to your hat while I tell you about the shopping trip to Dubai . . .*

Marianne might read Nora's email in the wee hours, before she went off to her job as a public defender in Pawtucket, Rhode Island, making the drive up 95 from Narragansett, where the scenery got grimmer and grimmer after you passed the crown jewel of the state, the Providence Place mall (fantastic mall, by the way; if that mall had existed when Nora was a teenager she would have happily become a mall rat). Marianne was currently defending a man accused of stabbing his girlfriend sixteen times and then leaving her for dead. Sixteen times! Try as she might, Nora could not wrap her mind around the specifics of this crime. The girl had lived to tell about it, but only barely. And there was Marianne, pulling on her Talbots suits each day, hopping in her battered Toyota and going off to defend him, innocent until proven guilty and all that. (If Marianne were telling this story she would say carefully that the man had *allegedly* stabbed his girlfriend.) If Marianne were at this auction she would grab the microphone from the auctioneer and ask everybody why it was okay that each child in the fifth grade at their school had an iPad for their own personal use while kids in Concord and Vallejo sometimes struggled to find a pencil or a notebook. People would look around uncomfortably, not knowing what to say, so Marianne

111

would answer for them. Marianne's answer would be: It's not okay! So let's do something about it! She had always been a rallier, an organizer, the Energizer Bunny of social justice. Marianne was good and pure, the champion of the little people, while here Nora sat, transfixed (literally) by the lights of the chandelier.

"But it wouldn't be right," continued Cathy Moynihan, and for a second Nora thought she was talking about social justice. "Since you and I practically made the Adirondacks, right, Nora? Give someone else a chance!" Cathy laughed merrily and inspected her manicure.

Nora wasn't sure if she would be friends with Cathy if Pinkie and Cecily weren't so close. They were like blood sisters, those two, with a friendship so effortlessly deep that Nora sometimes felt an unwelcome twinge of envy watching them. Nora felt that way only about Marianne, her actual blood sister, who lived nowhere near her.

Nora felt then a tug of nostalgia for Rhode Island that was so strong it caused her eyes to fly open. On the other side of the cavernous room, from a faraway table, her old friend Amanda Hill, whom Nora hadn't seen for ages, not since Amanda and her family moved out of their neighborhood and into a gorgeous four-bedroom, three-bath a few miles away. Beautiful pool, with the Tahoe-blue tile that turned the water the color that made you feel like you were always on vacation in Mexico. (Nora hadn't been back at work yet when they sold the house in the old neighborhood; they had chosen someone in Sally Bentley's office, and secretly Nora thought they had taken less than they needed to — if they had been her clients she would have told them to hold firm, patience should trump volume and speed.)

At one time, when the kids were young, and before Nora had gone back to work, Amanda and Nora had been very close. Amanda had a daughter Cecily's age, and a son who was Maya's age, and after Nora shipped Angela off to school for the day Amanda and Nora would do those things that nonworking mothers did, like push their strollers up and down the bike path for hours and sit outside Starbucks while their toddlers babbled to one another and spilled overpriced crunchy organic snacks all over themselves. Talking about nothing, everything, sex, their younger selves, working versus not working, whose husbands left wet towels where. How nice it was to see Amanda.

"Were you sleeping?" Gabe whispered to her.

"Of course not," Nora said. "Don't be daft." She didn't normally say things like that but she'd been binge-watching *Downton Abbey* when she couldn't sleep and the phrase slipped out of her, unchecked. She rubbed her eyes. The auctioneer was nowhere to be seen — changing his shirt, maybe, in the men's room — and that's what accounted for the low buzz of conversation that had taken over the room, broken by the occasional female shriek of delight or surprise.

Amanda drew closer. She wore a look of barely contained glee, like someone who has just discovered that her child has won a prize but is waiting for somebody else to make the announcement.

"Hey!" said Nora, sitting up straighter, holding her arms half open for the requisite half hug, which she'd never seemed to master. Cathy had vacated her seat to go, like an intrepid explorer, in search of more wine, so Nora pulled out the empty seat next to her for Amanda. She couldn't believe how happy she was to see Amanda, who, though she was dressed in an off-the-shoulder number that included a gold belt buckle, was easy to remember in black exercise pants and a tank, marching deter-minedly along the bike path, pale hair swinging. They'd gotten along really well, they'd shared the same sense of humor, and they were annoyed by the same things. The latter, to Nora, was one of the building blocks of true friendship.

"Nora." Amanda smiled. Her smile looked different somehow than it used to back in the fast-walking-stroller days. Tighter. Had Amanda had something done? Botox? But Botox didn't tighten up your mouth, did it? That seemed like it would certainly defeat the purpose. Nora knew very little about Botox or any of Botox's brethren. She had once brought the topic up to Marianne, and Marianne had laughed so long and so hard (and really, in an uncharacteristically un-charitable way) that Nora had let it drop. Now she just avoided looking full-on in the mirror when the lights were very bright; it seemed an altogether less expensive long-term solution. "It's good to see you," Amanda continued. It *almost* seemed like she said that perfunctorily, a little mechani-cally, but maybe Nora was imagining that because the buzz in the room had become louder.

"How're the new digs?" Nora leaned forward eagerly. "I haven't seen you in for-

ever."

Amanda seemed to be looking not quite at Nora but at something just behind her and to the left, which, when Nora turned briefly, she could not identify. "Well. Not so new anymore, you know. It's been three years. But good. We love it over there. It's a great neighborhood."

"Don't I know it," said Nora. She could have gotten them thirty grand more for their old house, easy.

"A much better fit for us, all things considered," said Amanda.

"I can see that," said Nora. Though she couldn't. She had loved having Amanda in their neighborhood. She had hoped Amanda would stay forever, until they were too old to walk quickly on the bike path — until they were old enough to instead just sit quietly on the front porch. In rockers. Although, truthfully, people in their neighborhood never sat on the front porch, in rockers or otherwise. All of the action, all of the living, happened in the privacy of gated backyards.

Just after returning to Sutton and Wainwright, Nora had sold a home near Amanda's new house to the Miller family. Nora had pulled the ultimate coup on that one, being the seller's agent but finding the buyers as well: that was the hat trick, the grand slam, the hole-in-one of real estate. She split the commission with herself! And then handed a good chunk of it over to Arthur Sutton, of course, who was so grateful that he and his wife, Linda, took Gabe and Nora to Saison for one of the most extravagant meals of Nora's life. It was a win-win. Proof that she'd done the right thing, going back to work!

"How *are* the Millers?" Nora asked now. Gabe was deep in conversation with another fourth-grade dad who was only vaguely familiar to Nora. Golf, probably. Or tennis. Men at the auction loved to talk about golf and tennis. These were the stepping-stones of their friendships, since they didn't have the school pickup line or yoga over which to bond. Nora didn't really have the pickup line (Maddie often did that) or yoga either. Nora wished she were the yoga type, but she was too high-strung for it. Far too impatient. Linda Sutton had dragged her along to a class in Cow Hollow once (she called it *girl time*), and as much as she adored Linda, Nora had spent the whole class wondering if everybody else could hear her heart hammering away inside her rib cage because she was so anxious about an open house she was holding the next day at a four-point-eight-million in Tiburon. After, they had gone for green juices at a juice bar near the yoga studio, where Linda had cheerfully forked over twenty-one dollars and fifty cents for two glasses of liquefied spinach and lemon. Nora was so hungry after that she'd stopped at In-N-Out on the way home for a shake.

"Do you ever see them?" Nora asked. "The Millers?" Loretta and Barry Miller had been mildly difficult to deal with. Loretta was one of those red-haired, freckled, slightly pointy women who had about them a semipermanent air of dissatisfaction that seemed neither to grow stronger nor to abate, whatever circumstances they found themselves in. ("A bit of a sourpuss," Nora's mother would have called her.) There were some issues over the inspection, if Nora remembered correctly, a potential leak in the hot tub for which a very expensive leak specialist had been called in, on Nora's dime. But it was nothing that wasn't smoothed over with the right combination of charm and solicitude on Nora's part. People panicked right before they bought an expensive property, she understood that. And there had been no leak in the hot tub after all, though the specialist had to empty the whole thing and refill it to verify that.

(This, again, had occurred at Nora's expense: people outside the industry simply did not understand how large the monetary outlay was for real estate agents prior to a sale, when life became one gigantic, expensive gamble.)

Nora looked eagerly into Amanda's face. She felt like hugging her (a whole hug, none of this half nonsense), or dragging her into a private corner of the ballroom to have a genuine chat. Seeing Amanda again served as a reminder of the fleeting days of Cecily's toddlerhood, of those endless mornings when they were looking to fill the time instead of acquire more of it. Everybody had been so young then! Cecily still had luscious rolls of fat along the backs of her thighs. Life was simpler. It might have seemed hard then, but in retrospect, it was easy.

"Funny you should ask," said Amanda. She smiled her odd, tight, unfamiliar smile again. Was it funny? Nora couldn't stop staring at Amanda's altered mouth. (Had she had those collagen shots that made your lips look fuller?)

"Because in fact," continued Amanda, "they're having some issues."

"Doesn't surprise me *at all,*" said Nora. She took a big sip of wine. "I always found her a little trying. Right? I figured he'd snap one day." This was the sort of thing she and Amanda would have talked endlessly about in the old days. Juicy marital gossip about virtual strangers over a latte.

But then she noticed something: Amanda wasn't gossiping back. She was looking quizzically at Nora. "Not those kinds of problems," she said finally. "Actually I'm pretty friendly with Loretta."

"Oh," said Nora quietly. She looked around for Gabe but he was still engrossed in conversation. She heard the words *St. Andrews* and *royal and ancient.* She looked around for Cathy too — any port in a storm — but she had been waylaid on her way back to the table with the wine. It might be years before she returned.

"Problems with the house," said Amanda. "With their expansion plans."

Nora said, "*Expansion* plans?" She had never heard about any expansion plans. The Millers' house was gigantic, already renovated, and the Millers had no children. What was there to expand? She looked one more time into Amanda's eyes, searching for something, but her expression was sphinxlike, unreadable, and at last Nora understood why her smile looked odd. Not because it had been surgically altered or puffed up or trimmed down, but because it simply wasn't the same smile Nora remembered. It wasn't sincere.

The auctioneer returned not too long after that, but when Nora looked back on the conversation it seemed like it had been hours, because Amanda spoke slowly and deliberately, and (Nora thought) a touch condescendingly, explaining the situation. It was simple, yet potentially devastating. The Millers wanted to build a guesthouse. (In the old days, Nora would have said, "What do they need a *guesthouse* for?" and Amanda would have said, *"Riiiiiight?"* and one of the toddlers would have tripped on something or spilled a juice box and she and Amanda would have collapsed in caffeine-fueled giggles.) But Amanda now seemed to think it was perfectly reasonable for the Millers to want a guesthouse, an additional two bedrooms and a bath, a kitchenette. The problem, she explained, was that a landscaper they had called in had let them know that a couple of properties in the neighborhood had a rare species of a plant called the Marin dwarf flax. And theirs was one.

"Not just rare," whispered Amanda. *"Endangered."*

"Oh, God," said Nora. She was beginning

to remember something. She was beginning to feel sick to her stomach.

"And they seem to think," said Amanda, "that this should have been disclosed. Before they bought."

"But —" said Nora.

"I know," said Amanda. She patted Nora's knee companionably, the way you might pat an elderly dog who could no longer make it up the stairs. "I'm sure you didn't know."

The room whipped around Nora. The problem, of course, was that she did know. She *had* known. She just hadn't taken it seriously. She remembered now that one of the sellers, Mrs. Cantrell (she remembered the name because she always mixed it up with the word *chanterelle,* and funnily enough there was something mushroomy about Mrs. Cantrell's face), had mentioned something about a neighbor finding an endangered plant on the property that abutted theirs, and how it had become a whole thing when they went to get approval from the town for some upgrade. And how the neighbor had seen what *looked like* the same plant in the Cantrells' yard. And Nora had said — what? Probably something hurried and idiotic, like, *We should look into that.* Before she had promptly forgotten all about it, before the mention had floated away on a wave of laundry and lunch boxes and homework and Frankie's visits to the veterinarian. They had never disclosed it because they'd never really looked into it. For the love of God, it was a *plant.* Maya was starting kindergarten that year, Gabe was working overtime at Elpis, Angela was worrying over the SATs, and Nora needed that sale to close on time. A plant.

"I just didn't want you to get blindsided," said Amanda softly. "My understanding is that if their plans get shot down, ultimately this could be your responsibility . . ."

Indeed it could. If Nora had known about and failed to disclose the existence of an endangered species on the property to the buyers, the buyers could sue her. If Nora's errors and omissions insurance didn't cover the sale price of the home, Nora could be forced to cover the entire cost herself. That meant the Hawthornes would have to sell *their* home, the home her children had been babies in, had toddled around in, barechested, wearing only diapers. The home where they'd lost their first teeth, said their first words, written their name for the first time in those stilted, crooked, adorable mostly backward letters that all kids started with.

Her fault.

Nora closed her eyes and tipped her head back.

When she opened them she could see Amanda making her way back across the room, and in her place at Nora's table were two new bottles of wine. She could see Cathy Moynihan, who was once again leaning in toward Nora and studying her with a look of consternation and concern.

"Nora?" said Cathy. "You're white as a sheet. Whiter. Here, let me get you some water." Cathy reached for the pitcher, which was sweating almost as profusely as the auctioneer had been. A little of the water sloshed over the lip of the pitcher and onto the rose-colored tablecloth and Cathy said, *"Whoopsie,"* and giggled. "*Some*body's had a lot to drink."

"Wine," whispered Nora, sitting up. "Not water."

"You sure?" said Cathy. "You don't look —"

"Definitely wine," said Nora, pushing her glass toward Cathy. Her instinct was to reach for Gabe — her rock, her anchor, her Wyoming cowboy — but she wasn't ready yet to tell him this potentially ruinous bit of news. She needed to find out, first, how bad this could get. So she steadied herself by pressing her hands flat on the seat of the chair and sitting up as straight as she could, concentrating on the auctioneer, who had definitely changed his shirt and looked rejuvenated, like an athlete recently emerged from a locker room shower after the big game.

"Oh, *good*!" said Cathy, clapping her hands together girlishly. "Next after this one is the Adirondack chairs. I simply cannot *wait* to see what these go for." She reached out a manicured hand and grasped at Nora's forearm — a gesture that, on any other day, would have irritated Nora to no end, but that currently she hardly noticed.

"Neeeeext up," cried the auctioneer with renewed vim and vigor. Perhaps he had showered in the men's locker room, all dark wood and gleaming gold. He looked like a new man. "The foooooourth-grade class projects!" Cathy Moynihan squeezed Nora's forearm ever more tightly. Nora was too weak to protest, too undone to remind Cathy how sensitive her Irish skin was, how easily she bruised. Cathy's fingerprints might be imprinted on Nora's arm for days to come. With her free hand Nora lifted her wineglass to her mouth and took a long and extravagant swallow. Better. More. A photograph of twelve Adirondack chairs flashed on the screen. Cathy inhaled sharply. "They look *gorgeous,*" she said. "Right, Nora? Gorgeous."

Marin dwarf flax, thought Nora. *I cannot believe I'm going to be undone by something with that idiotic name.*

"We have twelve hundred. Do I hear *fourteen* hundred?" cried the auctioneer. "Fourteen hundred, do I hear *sixteen?*"

Dear Marianne, thought Nora. *You are not going to believe what I found out at the auction.*

Roland the hamster began his cardio workout around midnight.

Great, thought Nora. *Perfect.* Cecily had begged to have Roland's cage in her room, on top of her dresser. Cecily and Maya's room was just down the hall from Nora and Gabe's, but Roland seemed to have woken nobody else in the house but Nora. Go figure.

Nora tiptoed to the younger girls' room and looked at her middle daughter, who slept on, oblivious. She had thrown the covers into a tangle at the bottom of the bed; beneath her T-shirt Nora could see her ribs moving. Nora stood for some time in the doorway until Roland hopped off his wheel and nosed his way to the side of the cage. Nora could see his outline because of the nightlight in the hall. She put her face close to the bars of the cage and whispered, "Okay, guy. We get it. You're super-fit. Now go to sleep." Roland twitched his nose at her. Had Cecily fed and watered him? What else was required of the Hawthornes during Roland's sojourn? What if he got sick? Or escaped. What if he — horror of horrors — *died* while in their care? It could happen. Goldfish seemed to drop dead for no reason whatsoever, why not a hamster? Nora breathed in deeply and tried hard not to feel the weight of another living creature who required something from her. "Just don't need too much, okay?" she told Roland. "I'm sort of at my limit . . ."

Maybe Roland didn't nod, not exactly, but something about his face signaled a gentle acquiescence, and Nora appreciated that. He did look a little bit like Frankie.

Back in her own bed she poked softly at Gabe's back, which was turned away from her. Nothing. The drinks at the auction, of course. Though any happy alcohol effects had dissipated for her. She wanted to tell Gabe about the Marin dwarf flax. She wanted to and she didn't want to. She didn't want to stress *him* out — Lord knew he already seemed stressed out enough. Freaking Bizzvara. But she'd want *him* to tell *her*

127

if he were in a bad way. She didn't want to keep secrets from Gabe. She never kept secrets from Gabe.

Except the one. But that was such a long time ago.

Nora's heart was beating to wake the dead. She didn't even know what Marin dwarf flax looked like. But she had to be prepared. *By failing to prepare, you are preparing to fail.* Who had said that? Mussolini? Ben Franklin? Well, either way. She got out of bed again and made her way to the kitchen, where she kept her laptop on the built-in desk. She sat down, opened the laptop. She felt like a dirty porn addict, feeding her habit in the middle of the night, while her husband and children and the school hamster slept.

And then, into Google, where we type our deepest desires and our most wretched fears and everything in between, went three words: Marin. Dwarf. Flax.

Deep breath. Scientific name: *Hesperolinon congestum.* Rank: Species. (Whatever that meant.) Higher classification: *Hesperolinon. An annual herb, which is known to occur only in San Mateo, San Francisco, and Marin County, California.*

"Aww," said Nora, despite herself, in the voice you might use to respond to a baby bunny on display at an agricultural fair. The Marin dwarf flax was quite pretty. The picture showed a small white flower surrounded by a couple of light pink buds. It was really *very* innocuous looking. Nobody could sue anybody over this.

Nora felt suddenly lighthearted; she imagined herself telling the story one evening at a dinner party. *Oh, and then I couldn't sleep, but that was partly because the school hamster was keeping me awake — you know they work out like little fiends, those things, wish I had the energy! So I looked it up, and you wouldn't believe it, there was nothing to it, it was just a little flowering weed. Can you imagine that I let myself get so worked up about it? That I thought I could lose my job over a weed?*

She read on, and ever so slowly the lighthearted feeling began to dissipate.

Unfortunately, its traditional range from Marin to San Mateo has seen enormous population growth over the last century, and many of the serpentine habitats, never very abundant, have been destroyed or degraded.

Shit. Well, that was quite the conundrum. Nobody liked population growth more than realtors. And yet that very same population growth had destroyed a species that Nora had failed to disclose to the buyers.

In for a penny, in for a pound, as her mother liked to say. Her fingers typed the next search term while her brain somehow detached itself and floated somewhere close to the ceiling. How many times had she wanted to Google this sordid little topic in the past year? Too many to count, and yet somehow she'd stopped herself each time. Because she hadn't really wanted to know.

There went her fingers, typing away, spitting out the letters. *Early head trauma,* her fingers typed. And: *Reading difficulties in childhood.*

Deep breath, the deepest of all breaths. Ready, set, enter.

Nora felt Gabe before she saw him. Or maybe she saw his reflection in the window but didn't quite register it. She slammed down the lid of her laptop. Gabe looked perplexed and rumpled, like a child just roused from a nap. "I woke up and you were gone," he said. "I got worried."

"Hey," Nora said, swallowing the shaking in her voice. "No need to worry. I was just — I couldn't sleep. Just doing a little bit of work, while I was thinking about it."

He rubbed his face and said, "Goddamn Skip Moynihan and that bourbon. I feel like I died and went straight to hell."

"You don't look so good," she said agreeably. "Did you take some Advil?"

"Several." Gabe extended his hand to her and, like a parent to a child, said, "Come to bed, Nora-Bora. Come to bed with me."

She took his hand and followed him, intertwining her fingers with his. He would forgive her, if she ever told him. Right? The only reason she'd never told him was because he'd been so adamant that she not go back to work so soon after Maya, and if she'd listened to him then maybe she would have been more care—

"I had the craziest dream," said Gabe, climbing into bed and pulling the cover up to his chin. "Really crazy, and now I can't remember anything about it, not one detail."

"Then how do you know it was crazy?" Gabe didn't answer — in the three seconds it had taken Nora to ask the question he'd fallen asleep. She switched off the light and lay in the darkness, eyes wide open.

Even Roland had given up the chase: no sounds from Cecily and Maya's room. He must have curled up in his wood shavings and gone off to sleep. That sounded nice, sleeping in wood shavings, hiding from the world in your slumber.

But not Nora, no, no. Nora was wide awake; Nora might never sleep again.

CHAPTER 13
GABE

October

"So," Gabe said to Abby Freeman, "what is it you wanted to talk to me about?"

They were sitting at Barrique on a Thursday just past six o'clock. Abby had suggested five thirty, but to Gabe six seemed much more appropriate because by then many of his coworkers would be on their way home for the evening, if not already gone. He didn't need any raised eyebrows.

More appropriate for what? For having a casual, one hundred percent innocent drink with the new intern? Yes. For that.

Not that any of it was appropriate. Mostly what was inappropriate was how extra-confident Abby Freeman was.

"Ah," said Gabe, when Abby asked him, earlier that day, if she could pick his brain, somewhere outside of the office, without all the distractions. Gabe had never liked that expression. *Pick your brain.* Made him think of Hannibal Lecter. Also he found many more distractions outside the Elpis office than he did inside. So he said, "I'm not sure if . . ." He studied Abby Freeman's smallish and close-together eyes, over which she wore a pair of reading glasses with flowered frames. She wore pumps and a dark skirt that fell just above her knees. He thought she would have tamed her wardrobe just a bit by now (other Elpis interns that Gabe could remember had all worn jeans), but if anything her attire had gotten fussier, more like what a middle-aged attorney might wear. Abby Freeman was like the anti-Kelsey; Kelsey, that day, had shown up with just the tips of her hair dyed a neon pink. It was possible, of course, that Abby's fussy clothing was some sort of ironic statement on business attire that he was missing. It was all so exhausting, getting older, not knowing which statements were ironic and which were not. He let his sentence trail off and tapped at some papers on his desk: the printout from the new client meeting, which had gone fantastically well. They were almost there.

"Oh, it's perfectly innocent," said Abby Freeman, perhaps telepathically picking up on his concerns. "I just have some professional questions. I'm trying to figure out what direction to go in. My treat, of course. Just so you know there's no funny business going on."

She smiled. Abby had a nice, expensive-looking smile. It softened up the sharp features of her face quite a bit. She was actually pretty when she smiled.

But. *Funny business?* Gabe was forty-six years old and had been married for eighteen of them. He had never cheated on his wife. Never planned to. And *funny business* was such an old-fashioned phrase. Was that ironic too?

"How about Barrique?" she said. "It's not far from here. They have a fabulous wine selection." Who *was* this girl? Kids these days, in addition to being ironic, were so intimidating, and so sure of themselves. Probably that came from the generally accepted parenting tactic of allowing each kid to believe he or she was spectacularly brilliant and talented, even in cases where the opposite was true. Gabe was as guilty of that as anyone. (Angela, though, it should be noted, *was* very, very smart. No way would Gabe be pushing this Harvard thing if he didn't think she stood an excellent chance. And not that he was pushing it. Not really. Right? She was pushing *herself,* she'd always had gallons of drive and ambition.)

"I know where Barrique is," Gabe said, to show that he still had the upper hand. Truth be told, he hadn't been to Barrique. It was newish, but that was no excuse. Actually it wasn't that new anymore. When he and Nora were younger and lived in the city they made it a point to try a new restaurant or bar within two weeks of its opening. They were proper hipsters then.

Abby Freeman scarcely looked old enough to drink legally, though Gabe supposed that, if she had already graduated from Harvard, she was. When Gabe graduated from college he had never tasted wine in his life — he certainly wasn't equipped to invite someone two decades his senior to a private-label wine bar.

He squinted at Abby Freeman and imagined Angela as an intern. He imagined her dressed up in work clothes and asking for advice. He imagined Angela knowing which place had a fabulous wine selection and which did not.

It scared him, to think that in just five years Angela would be the same age this girl was now, with a job and maybe even a professional-looking blouse. He'd want someone like him to be nice to Angela, right? Of course he would.

"That sounds great," he told Abby. "I'm

happy to help. That's what internships are for, right?" He tapped again at his pile of papers and glanced at the screen of his computer to see if any vital emails had come in while he was setting up a platonic date with the intern.

"Right," she said.

At Barrique they claimed a table for two. The seats were tall and futuristic orange, and Abby, perched atop one of them, studied the wine menu intently, running her finger up and down the list; she made Gabe think of his daughter Maya, still struggling to read in the second grade. Poor Maya. When she was one, she used to sleep on her stomach with her little butt raised in the air and her cheek pressed into the crib mattress. It killed Gabe every time, that she could sleep like that. It was so goddamn adorable. She'd wake up flushed and warm, like she'd just come from the gym. He hated to think about her struggling with her reading. He hated to think about her struggling with *anything*. Apparently somebody at school had made fun of her. He wanted to punch that kid. Could a forty-six-year-old punch a second grader?

Probably not.

Abby shook herself out of her coat and laid it carefully across her lap. She pushed her glasses up on her nose and said, "The barrel cellar is the way to go. If you haven't been here before. I'm going to have the Sangiovese. You should have that too. It's really good. My dad is part owner of a winery in Sonoma. I've known about good wine since I was ten."

Abby Freeman had put down her menu and was looking at Gabe in a manner that he couldn't exactly read. Was she looking at him in a *sexual* way? Lord, he hoped not. He wasn't exactly sure what constituted a sexual look from someone of that generation, but he hoped it wasn't this: Abby's lips were parted slightly and she wasn't so much meeting his eyes as she was looking just past him and nodding slightly, as though Gabe had said something worth considering.

Occasionally, at home, Nora roped Gabe into watching a few episodes of *Girls,* which, if he were to be honest with himself, he'd have to say that he quite enjoyed, except for two things. *Girls* served the dual purpose of terrifying him at the thought of unleashing his three innocent daughters into the world, and also of letting him know that the sexual mores of females in America had changed rather dramatically since he was in his twenties. Girls now seemed to be so forthright about sex, about how little it meant or could mean, about their desires and how to meet them and how *not* to meet them and what body hair to remove and what body hair to keep as it was.

To prove that he was the adult in the conversation, Gabe said, "How do you like Elpis?" See? Nothing sexual here. Just business talk.

"I love it, so far. It's so *exciting.*"

"Yes," he said platonically. "It's a great firm."

When the wine arrived Abby tipped her glass toward his and said *Cheers!* in a way that — he wished he would stop thinking like this — again reminded him of his daughters, dressed up for a tea party, or clinking glasses of nonalcoholic cider at Christmastime. Of course, it had been some time since Angela had participated in a tea party. But Cecily and Maya sometimes partook still; they used a tea set that Gabe had brought back years ago from a work trip to China. Occasionally they roped him into sitting cross-legged on the living room floor with them while they placed goldfish crackers on the tiny saucers and passed them around. Maya was very strict about how many goldfish each person got.

"Do you like the Sangiovese?"

Gabe whipped himself back to the present. "I do," he said. "Great choice." He should, as the adult, have asked *her* how *she* liked the wine. But she had beaten him to it.

Outside, the traffic on Pacific Avenue zipped along. There was lots of horn honking and the intermittent squeal of brakes or tires. "Now," he said (paternally), "what sorts of questions do you have? I'm happy to help anyone just starting out. I was in your shoes once."

Abby folded her hands on the table in a formal way. Her posture was perfect; her nails, like Angela's, were bitten down to the quick. Interesting. She looked at him in a way that he might, if asked, describe as appraising. "I want to go for my MBA in two years, so I need to make the most of the time between now and then. I was hoping you could help me figure out the best path. At Elpis. To get me there. I'm thinking Sloan, or HBS. Business school is *so* competitive."

Gabe nodded affably. Business conversations he could do. He took a big sip (a gulp, really) of his wine and said, "Smart to start at a place like Elpis. We're small enough that you can see a lot of different facets of the business. If you went to, say, a McKinsey or a Bain as an intern, they'd stick you

139

in a corner somewhere and put you on data entry. Or they'd put you on *research,* but it wouldn't be necessary research, not like you'll be doing for us. It would be busy work."

"That's what I figured," said Abby. She was so eager; she was like that hamster Cecily had brought home from school recently. How lucky Gabe felt not to be in Abby Freeman's position. The world had become altogether more competitive since he was young and hungry. He didn't truly envy any of the young, not the interns, not his daughters. By the time Maya was old enough to apply to college she'd need a 6.0 GPA and a sizable bank account to attend a state school.

"Everybody at Elpis has been so nice," said Abby. "But you seem like — the most approachable of the partners. The kindest."

Gabe was flattered. He didn't always feel kind. He often felt tired and short-tempered, especially this year, especially with Angela applying to college, especially with Angela applying to *Harvard.* He didn't want it to rattle him as much as it did. And yet! It was, just at the moment, the single most important thing in the world to him, that she get accepted. Was he proud of this fact? No. Would he ever admit this to anyone, ever? No. But there it was, as certain and undeniable as the red wine stain on Abby Freeman's white teeth.

He turned his attention back to Abby and said, "Ask away."

"Joe Stone in HR told me that you're from Wyoming. That sounds so exotic."

"It does?" He took a few seconds to wonder why Abby Freeman and Joe Stone from HR had been talking about him at all.

"Yeah. I've never met anyone from Wyoming."

"Exotic," he said, "is not usually how people describe my background. Although my wife does sometimes call me the Rhinestone Cowboy."

Abby looked at him blankly.

He tapped his fingers on the table and sang, *"Riding out on a horse in a star-spangled rodeo . . ."*

She smiled and giggled. Was he making her nervous? Maybe he was acting like the weird uncle at the family Christmas party, the one who shows up in sideburns and a vintage suit coat, drunk.

"Never mind," he said. "You're too young for that song. *I'm* practically too young for that song. Anyway."

Abby took another sip from her wineglass. She closed her eyes and tipped her head

141

back at a certain angle when she swallowed, like a real connoisseur, and she took her time before speaking again. "Believe me, it sounds exotic to someone from here. Everyone in the world is from the Bay Area. I mean, not everyone. Obviously. But it's so totally *not* exotic. Lots of people at Harvard were from around here. I bet that wasn't the case with Wyoming."

Gabe tightened his hold on the stem of his glass, looked into Abby Freeman's small eyes, and released a carefully calibrated chuckle. "No. No, it wasn't. I don't think too many people in my class knew how to vaccinate a calf."

"How do you?"

"How do you vaccinate a calf?"

Abby nodded.

"Not much to it, really, you just get the needle in them right away, soon as you get your hands on them. Trick is to make sure they're tied down nice and tight to the table. And you don't look into their eyes." Gabe felt his ranch voice returning to him — a slight twang, a careless lengthening of the multisyllable words — and he tried his best to tamp it down. Usually the ranch voice came out only when he was around his brothers.

"Huh," said Abby. "I'll keep that in mind."

He tried to imagine her seated at the head of a table in a conference room someday, barking out orders. It was uncomfortably easy to imagine.

"You never know when it might come in handy," he added. Had they moved from business talk to witty banter? Seemed too soon for that. He hadn't given her any advice yet.

"My dad wants me to go to med school," said Abby. "Like my sister. She's an anesthesiologist in Manhattan."

"Do you want to go to med school?"

"No."

Gabe took another long drink of the Sangiovese. "Then you shouldn't. If you want to go to business school, you should go to business school." It was so easy to dispense advice to other people's children, when you had no vested interest in the outcome.

"My sister is miserable half the time," said Abby. "Actually it used to be half the time. Now's she's pregnant and working seventy hours a week, so she's miserable all the time."

"Well," said Gabe, "it's a difficult time, pregnancy." When Nora was pregnant with Angela she cried for twenty minutes every afternoon. For several weeks in the middle of the pregnancy she'd been unable to host her own open houses; Arthur Sutton had to step in for her.

Gabe let his eyes roam around the bar, which was beginning to fill with a sophisticated after-work financial-district crowd, plus a considerable smattering of hipsters. Gabe remembered (sort of) what it was like to live in the city, to go out for a drink after work without having to worry about traffic on the way home, family dinner.

"What house were you?"

"Excuse me?" Gabe thought he might have missed the beginning of the conversation.

"What house were you. At Harvard."

"Oh." Gabe's heart jumped a little bit and he rushed to explain. "My wife is a realtor, so when I hear something about a house . . ." He wondered if maybe he could persuade Abby to travel down a different conversational path.

A group of young women, maybe six or seven years older than Abby, sat themselves at two of the shorter, light-colored tables. There was a lot of hugging and some localized shrieking. One of the young women had a little mewling baby in one of those front-sling things, which didn't seem to dampen her enthusiasm for hugging or being hugged. Nora had used one of those; he remembered Angela in it, peering out like a possum with her moon eyes. Funny, he couldn't recall either of the other two girls in it.

"So . . . ," said Abby, peering at him from around the rim of her wineglass when she lifted it for her final sip. Gabe still had half of his left. He was not, all things considered, as much of a wine guy as he sometimes pretended to be. He preferred bourbon or beer. Again Abby said, "What house?"

Gabe cleared his throat. Abby's expression was inscrutable. That was a good SAT word: *inscrutable.* Of course, Angela's SAT scores were already signed, sealed, delivered.

Carefully, as though he had been charged with pronouncing each letter of the word individually, he said, "Adams."

Abby said, "I was Eliot."

Gabe looked around the bar. The shrieking pentagon of women had ordered three half liters. The traffic was still going strong. The light was fading.

"Eliot's a good one. I had some friends in Eliot."

"How'd you like Adams?"

"I liked it. I loved it." He paused, searching for a way to elaborate. Finally he said, "It was a long time ago."

Abby signaled to the waitress. "I'll have

another," she said. "Something different this time . . . let's see, wasn't there a Pinot?"

"We have two Pinots: a Sonoma, and a Russian River Valley."

"I'll have the Sonoma." She smiled and turned back to Gabe. "Make my dad proud, you know." She paused to glance at her phone, then said, "Sorry," and smiled again. "What was your favorite thing about Harvard? Not the weather, of course."

Gabe chuckled again; the chuckle was starting to come sort of naturally now. That was good. He could do this. "Actually I liked the weather. Reminded me of home. My wife would move back there if the rest of us would. She's a New Englander. But I think it's better here. Everything's better here."

Abby's second glass of wine was a third of the way gone. For a slender person, she could really throw it back. "So then what was your favorite thing? Did you ever pee on the John Harvard statue?"

Gabe shifted. "Once."

"You're lying."

How right she was. "Okay, fine. I didn't. But I always felt like I should have." When he took Angela for her Harvard tour last year he had allowed her to rub the toe of the statue's left foot for good luck.

146

"It's not even John Harvard, you know. On the statue."

"I know. They didn't have a picture of him so the sculptor used his friend's face." Was it getting a little warm in Barrique? Gabe rolled up his sleeves.

"Did you do the Primal Scream?"

The undergraduate streaking, midnight on the last night of reading period. "That," said Gabe, "I did do."

Maybe Gabe was paranoid or actually crazy, but it *almost* seemed like Abby Freeman was *quizzing* him. He was starting to sweat. "Didn't you have some more questions about Elpis?"

The baby in the sling began to cry — it was the sort of cry that rose above the general hubbub of bar noise. A primal scream of its own.

"I did," said Abby Freeman. "But can you believe it? I've forgotten what they were. I guess I should have written them down." She tipped back her glass and swallowed the rest of the wine. "And I just remembered, I have to meet a friend. But this conversation was really helpful, all the same."

All of Gabe's organs seemed to suddenly cave in on him. The thudding of his heart was loud enough that he thought Abby

147

might hear it. He put his hand against the table to steady himself. Abby was squinting at him. He cast about for his poker face and wired it on, secured it as tightly as it would go, and said brightly, "No worries! We can pick this up another time."

She knows, he thought. *She knows.*

CHAPTER 14
ANGELA

Seven and a half milligrams, the night before.

Butterflies in Angela's stomach. Edmond Lopez was in the back of the room, tapping his pencil.

Or were they heart palpitations? She wasn't sure. Could be the pills.

On the way to class Henrietta had grabbed Angela's arm and said, "Have you finished your Harvard essay?"

"No." Angela had started it several times, but had yet to get past the fourth paragraph.

"Me either." Pause. "Ever wish you had a dead parent to write about?"

"No!" said Angela, genuinely horrified. "Of course not. Have *you*?"

"Of course not, me either," said Henrietta, a little too quickly. "I've just heard kids talking like that, that's all."

"What kids?"

"I don't know. Just kids." Because Henrietta's hair was pulled back into a ponytail Angela could see that the tips of her ears were turning red. This was Henrietta's tell, a sign that she was embarrassed.

Ms. Simmons was wearing clothes that looked like they came straight out of the laundry hamper. And not the clean laundry hamper. Rumpled tan pants and an off-white sweater with a gray smudge on one sleeve. Angela felt embarrassed for her, but she liked Ms. Simmons (liked her a *lot,* actually, she was smart and super-engaging) so she tried her hardest not to notice.

Ms. Simmons had young children — she talked about them all the time. A boy named Orvis (seriously) and a girl named Charlotte. ("After Charlotte Brontë, *natch,*" said Henrietta.) Orvis went to a progressive preschool in the city and Charlotte was too young for school. Apparently Mr. Simmons was a stay-at-home dad. She had mentioned that to her mom once and her mom said they must have a trust fund: so close to the city on a teacher's salary!

One of their first assignments, an in-class exposition of two poems, had earned Angela the word *Marvelous!* in Ms. Simmons's red felt-tip pen. (Henrietta had gotten *Good work*. With no exclamation point. Angela had never asked Maria.)

They used a book called *Joy of Vocabulary* to study for biweekly quizzes. Angela was such a nerd that she really did get joy out of the vocabulary. She *loved* vocabulary. Correction. She *apotheosized* vocabulary. *Dichotomy. Tithe. Inchoate.* Beautiful, specific words with beautiful, exact meanings. *Antepenultimate:* coming immediately before the next to last. I mean, come on. What a perfect word.

Ms. Simmons cleared her throat and rustled some papers on her desk. Then she said, "So far this quarter we've been reading deeply for meaning *and* pleasure. And in particular the pleasure that comes from understanding meaning. I want you to think about that, when you're choosing your topics for your extended essay. Really *think* about that."

The extended essay was due the Friday before Thanksgiving.

"Just my luck," Henrietta whispered. "Right after my birthday."

Angela didn't approve of the phrase *just my luck.* In her view, luck was negligible. You made your own luck.

Angela wouldn't turn eighteen until February. It sort of drove her crazy that Henrietta was older. In the row behind her she heard Edmond Lopez tap-tap-tapping on his desk with a pencil. She tried not to notice. She definitely tried not to think about his beautiful full lips and the way he looked in a baseball cap. Which he was not allowed to wear in class, but usually he did it anyway until a teacher asked him to remove it. Ms. Simmons hadn't asked yet; maybe she hadn't noticed.

Angela turned around once. Edmond grinned at her. She thought for a second about how nice it might feel to lay her head on Edmond's muscled chest (it would be smooth and caramel colored) and stay there for a long time. And then . . . well, who knew. She grinned back and tried to maintain her *tenuous* hold on her equilibrium. Her equilibrium had been questionable all day, maybe all week. All month, really. Maybe it had been tenuous forever and she was just starting to notice. Or more likely it was the pills.

("What's the *matter* with you, Angela?" her mother had said to her just the day before, when Angela dropped a water glass on the kitchen floor, then burst into uncharacteristic tears and stomped off to her bedroom. It was bad behavior, uncharacter-istic, but she couldn't help it. The glass shat-tered, but she didn't even clean up the mess. She'd been a total jerk. But it wasn't her, not the real her. It was some other being that took over sometimes, since she began taking the pills. A jittery, unfriendly alien.)

"Angela?" said Ms. Simmons. "Did you have a question about the essay?"

"Nope," said Angela. "Sounds great."

"Good," said Ms. Simmons. "My expecta-tions are high for all of you." Was it Angela's imagination, or did she fix Angela with a look that was especially meaningful? Angela swallowed hard. What was it like to be Edmond, with way fewer expectations on him?

What was it like to be anyone else, anyone at all?

She'd have the Harvard application off in less than a month. She was almost done. She had her test scores (enviable), her two letters of recommendation (stellar). Tran-scripts (to die for, obvi). She had to finish the Harvard questions and the essay. The essay was rattling her. (What would it feel like to press *Submit* on that application, to have it out of her hands? Then she could settle down, relax. Nail the extended essay for Ms. Simmons. Run her heart out. Graduate. Move on with her life, away from high school. And etc. She tried to quiet her heartbeat. She was almost there.)

Angela glanced over at Maria Ortiz, who was smiling in a way that seemed private, like Angela was trespassing just by looking at her. *God.* There it was, that little burst of jealousy that popped out around Maria. Not that her poetry even *rhymed* or anything, not that people necessarily *understood* it, at least Angela didn't. But still, she'd been published. She was an actual published poet. Angela felt weird and inferior whenever she thought about that. Thank God for her GPA, and for her math talent. She was going to hold on to that valedictorian position if she had to grow claws to do it.

CHAPTER 15
NORA

11:16 p.m.

M —

Remember that time I went out to see you and Mom and Dad with Maya when she was tiny? Well, of course you remember! It's not "that time," it's "THAT TIME," in caps and bold. I was so stressed out back then. (Not like now,

153

when I am the picture of calm and serenity, right?) People said so many things to me in those days. Sometimes I got the honest: "You look exhausted." Sometimes it was the misguided rallying cry: "I don't know how you do it!" Or even the downright bitchy (just that one lady in Safeway, really, she was awful): "If you can't get off your cell phone long enough to control your children, miss, maybe you shouldn't have so many." (It was a work call! I was submitting an offer!)

But nobody ever said, "I'm afraid you're going to hurt the baby."

How come nobody ever said that, Marianne? I would have listened. I would have paid attention. I would have.

Nora was in the middle of the inspection for the Watkins home. She was so happy about these buyers that she felt like singing. This would make the Marin dwarf flax situation infinitely better; when (if?) she told Arthur about the Miller house, she would have the Watkins sale in her back pocket. The biggest sale the office had seen in some time.

In California this — the days-long period between when an offer was accepted by a seller and when the buyer signed off on the inspections — was called the *investigation* period, which Nora always found a little over the top, as though they were all members of a secret government organization charged with uncovering foreign terrorists. But never mind: it was what it was. It was October, and autumn in the Hawthorne house was clicking along on schedule. Well, mostly. There was the reading thing, for Maya. Seamus O'Malley had increased the practices for Cecily's ceili team. Angela was like a seventeen-year-old ghost floating through the house with gray circles underneath her eyes.

The sellers had to vacate the premises, so Lawrence and Bee drove off in Lawrence's midnight-blue Mercedes.

"Take your time!" said Nora, waving them off. "Go have a picnic or something." The old Nora, the better Nora, might have shown up with a basket filled with goodies and a list of three or four wonderful picnic spots within a thirty-minute drive. But she had to stop by Cecily's school before the inspection to drop off her forgotten violin (third time in as many weeks), and then she had to run a check by the Irish dance studio that she knew Maddie would forget to deliver if asked, and they were completely,

155

totally out of food, so she grabbed a few groceries and ran them back to the house, where she noticed a load of laundry that she'd forgotten to start the night before, so she did a quick sort and threw it in, but then she saw that the lint catcher in the dryer had gone dangerously unemptied — there was almost enough lint in there to knit a sweater for an overweight adult — so she paused to clear it, and while doing that she snagged a nail on the lint catcher (did that thing have an official name?) and it broke so close to her finger that it drew blood, so she had to go in search of a Band-Aid in the bathroom that the girls shared. There, appropriately bandaged, she stopped herself from straightening Cecily's hair accessories, strewn over the bathroom like rice at a wedding, the lovely little boxes she'd purchased from the Container Store unused. She was almost late for the inspection (an offense of the highest order), and there was certainly no time to organize a picnic for anyone. Though it would have been nice.

Lawrence and Bee waved back; they were jubilant and assured, like grandparents at the height of enjoying their retirement, before it sank in that life was long and there really wasn't, at the end of the day, all that much to do with it.

The buyers were a technology couple (Google stock, Apple stock, Facebook stock: the Triple Threat of the Bay Area) who were now heavily involved in a venture capital firm whose name was not familiar to Nora but that had, when passed by Gabe, elicited a knowing nod and two fingers rubbed against his thumb: the universal signal for bricks of money. It was not a signal Gabe typically employed, but no matter. Money was what they wanted in this case.

The inspector was from New England — Nora picked out his accent at once. Massachusetts, he said, north of Boston, and immediately Nora felt like they were in good hands. He was like the men she had grown up near, friends of her parents, ruddy, good, solid men, salt of the earth, men who had one suit and one set of manners for both weddings and funerals.

"I never go back there," he said, as he whipped out a bunch of forms and offered them to the buyers for signing. Disclosure after disclosure after disclosure. Release from indemnity. God forbid anyone in this industry take responsibility for their own actions, ever. And if a specimen of Marin dwarf flax had been standing there with them, and if plants had heads, surely it would have nodded. "With the weather."

(He said *weathah,* and Nora experienced a small shudder of nostalgia and recognition.) "What's the point? I make everyone come to me. Who doesn't want to visit California, right?"

"Right," said Nora.

The female buyer had just the barest pregnancy bump showing through her fashionably fitted tunic, and though to Nora's eye neither she nor her husband looked much older than Angela — they both had taut, glowing skin and glossy dark hair that suggested a variety of expensive pomades and straighteners — she knew, of course, that they were. They would have to be, to have earned all that money. (She couldn't help it, she put "earned" in air quotes in her mind, though honestly she recognized that her own business would have suffered long ago were it not for the tech dollars around here.) When they entered the home the woman looked at Nora's stockinged feet — she had left her shoes carefully lined up in the entryway — then down at her own knee-high boots, and said, "I'm sorry, I just can't . . . the bending . . . these are impossible to get off."

"No worries," said Nora, though when she pictured Bee's face if she ever found out about the boots she was tempted to kneel

158

down, Prince-to-Cinderella style, and get them off herself, buckle by expensive buckle. The woman put her hand on her belly in the self-protective gesture of early pregnancy, and Nora refrained from asking her how in the world she'd gotten the boots on in the first place.

"Okay, then," Nora said brightly, sociably. "I'll leave you all to it, and I'll be right here if you need me."

One hour, then two hours, then three. Nora was starving. She settled in at the kitchen island with her laptop. She helped herself to Lawrence's wifi — not password protected, very surprising — and tried to look extremely busy, though in fact she was keeping an ear out for all that was going on during the inspection.

The gardens outside the Watkins home were in full bloom, and the sun had emerged from the morning fog and was obligingly outdoing itself, sparkling over the bay, illuminating the Golden Gate. Nora could not have asked for a more perfect inspection day if she'd ordered it out of the Hammacher Schlemmer catalog.

Goodness, she was hungry. Had she eaten breakfast? She'd made scrambled eggs for the girls, which they'd consumed enthusiastically (Cecily) and warily (Angela) and not at all (Maya; she'd asked for cereal, which, as anyone knew, *did nothing for your brain*), but Nora didn't think she'd taken any herself. In her bag she found an elderly Luna bar, which she opened and unstuck from its wrapper. She chewed it very slowly, like a prisoner of war granted her one meal for the day. She opened the refrigerator and pretended to be conducting her own inspection of the appliances, but really she was looking to see if there was anything in there that wouldn't be missed. Blocks of cheese wrapped in wax paper, a corked partial bottle of Chardonnay, a few jars of pâté, unsweetened coconut milk, and a dark jar of flax oil that looked like something you'd buy at an old-fashioned apothecary. Also a couple of eco-friendly take-out containers. Rich people's food, and not much of it. This shouldn't be a shock. Bee was as svelte as a greyhound. That's what she was thinking when her cell rang.

"Lawrence!" She filled a glass with water from the faucet — maybe water would fill her up, wasn't that the oldest dieting trick in the book? — and placed it on the counter. No need for Lawrence to hear her gulping. He might think it was the Chardonnay!

Lawrence wanted, of course, to know how everything was going. When they might be done, when the buyers would see the inspection report. And so forth. When they could do the final signoff on the P&S.

"So far so good," said Nora. "I'm just staying out of the way, you know, letting them do their thing. And it will take a few days for everything to get sorted out. But don't you worry! Nothing should come up, in a house like this."

"It's already perfect," said Lawrence.

"Exactly. More of a formality, in this case, the inspection, you know."

"I know."

From the garage she heard a tap-tap-tapping. Thank goodness Lawrence couldn't hear — he was the type to freak out at any noise at all, at any hint of a noise.

"What's that?" said Lawrence. "That tapping?"

"You *heard* that?" Nora moved the phone away from her mouth and drank a quarter of the water. Somehow it made her hungrier. "Lawrence, it's nothing, they're in the garage. Probably looking at the fuse box." She listened to Lawrence for a moment and then said, "I don't know what he's tapping at. I'm not out there. Do you want me to go out there? No? Okay, exactly right, I think it's better if I stay out of the way." She waited while Lawrence spoke away from the phone, presumably relating this piece of non-information to Bee. "Now, you go off and enjoy your day, Lawrence," said Nora. "You leave the rest of it to me. You have nothing to worry about, not a thing." This was absolutely untrue, but Nora said it like a career liar, like a Vegas poker dealer. A sale like this could get derailed by the most minor of issues; in many ways, the home inspection was the biggest nail-biter of the whole transaction. That's why she felt sick to her stomach: it was a particular kind of torture, waiting here to see what might or might not be uncovered. It was a combination of that and the geriatric Luna bar.

Once Lawrence hung up she checked her email. Arthur Sutton had written back, one word, or really a partial word: *thx.* "That's it?" she said aloud. "Not even a 'keep me posted'?"

She began an actual email to Marianne, who had written to inquire about their holiday plans: Were the Hawthornes making the trip east? Or should Marianne ship gifts? Marianne was one of those super-early holiday shoppers who would have been easy to resent if it weren't for her heart of gold. Marianne never engaged in Black Friday madness, not because the deals weren't good and not because she didn't have her list ready but because by the time Black Friday rolled around and people were lining up at Walmart and Target, preparing for the inevitable fisticuffs over forty-percent-off flatscreens, Marianne was *already done.* No wonder the city of Pawtucket valued her so highly.

Marianne wrote her emails formally, with a salutation and a signature and proper punctuation and spacing. Paragraphs, too. Marianne owned an iPhone but rarely used it for texting, even though, three years Nora's junior, she should have been more tuned in to the power and beauty of electronics. ("Who am I going to text?" asked Marianne. "My dirt-poor clients? Uh, I doubt it." Marianne had just taken on the case of a man who was accused of setting fire to his low-income housing unit. "Did he do it?" Nora wanted to know. "Innocent until," said Marianne. "Innocent until.")

Dear Marianne, typed Nora. *I need to check with Gabe again. Definitely not Thanksgiving. The flights are outrageous and we are swamped. Maybe Christmas? Not sure yet. Crazy fall here, as you know.*

Marianne would understand.

She felt like she should say something more to Marianne, something meaningful and sisterly, but she knew if she didn't send

163

the email now she'd get caught up in the tide of her day and she'd never send it at all.

Just then Nora heard a ticking down the hallway, followed by a sigh of such self-pity and despondency that if Nora hadn't known better she would have thought it had come from a child. But it was no child, it was the female buyer, clicking toward Nora in her expensive boots. She ticked into the kitchen and stood for a minute with a slightly pained expression until Nora, pulling her eyes away from her computer, organized her features in what she hoped was an agreeable manner and said, "Want to sit down?"

"Oh, *could* I?" said the female buyer, whose name, Nora knew, was Courtney. But out of a self-imposed sort of superstition she tried to refrain from getting personal with buyers until all papers were signed. Just in case something fell through. She referred to them, in her head, and with Arthur Sutton and the rest of the staff at Sutton and Wainwright, as Mr. Buyer and Mrs. Buyer. Or Mr. Buyer and Mr. Buyer, as the case may be, this being the Bay Area. It was the same principle that lay behind the idea of not getting too attached to the first puppy you saw in a litter, lest you find out he or she was already spoken for.

"Of course." Nora made a great show of moving the laptop out of the way to make room for Courtney, though truly the island was long enough to comfortably seat a family of ten. "You must be tired."

"You don't even know," said Courtney pleasantly, without blame or judgment, and Nora refrained from saying, *Oh, but I do!* and instead said, "How far along?"

"Five months," said Courtney, with a toss of her sleek, black, tech-savvy hair. She allowed her left hand to linger on her belly in a gesture that was at once self-protective and show-offy. Even Nora, who knew almost nothing about fine jewelry, could see that the engagement ring and wedding band Courtney was wearing were very intricate and very expensive. Courtney went on, "Everybody says I'm so tiny but I don't *feel* tiny —"

Oh, Lord. Marianne would have had a field day with this woman. Heart of gold aside, there was nothing Marianne liked less than a person who wedged a compliment someone else had given her into an unrelated conversation.

"Wow," said Nora sincerely. "I never would have guessed that." It was true. The bump was scarcely visible. This woman was probably the type to put on just the weight of the baby, nothing more, and to walk out of the hospital two days later wearing her favorite pair of pre-pregnancy jeans. When Nora was five months along with Angela she was already indulging so exuberantly in her daily pint of Ben & Jerry's that her obstetrician had given her a stern warning and a handout about *incrementally* increasing caloric intake over the course of a pregnancy. The word *incrementally* was outlined with a neon-yellow highlighter.

Courtney said, "Thanks," and then sighed again. She sighed very prettily, like a high-society lady in an Edith Wharton novel. "Honestly, I'm not that interested in the inspection. I love the house, but I don't care about the behind-the-scenes stuff. The heating, the air-conditioning, blah blah blah. It's all Greek to me."

"It's a great house," said Nora, as neutrally as she could manage. "Really perfect as it is." (*Don't sell it,* sounded a note of caution from Arthur Sutton, coming to Nora as clearly as if Arthur were standing right there in the kitchen with them. *Don't sell the house when it's already sold.*) Courtney looked at Nora and cocked her head and said, "Do you have kids?"

Nora closed her laptop: it seemed it was chatting time. That was fine. She was here to serve. A good real estate agent had to be part therapist, part cocktail party hostess, part badass. Fearless and patient at the same time. She channeled Arthur Sutton, who had taught her never, ever to show anything to a buyer other than the utmost tranquillity, and said, "Three girls. Seven, ten, and seventeen." What was that advertisement from the 1980s? *Never let them see you sweat.* In some ways real estate was just as much theater as theater itself was. More! Because one person was actor and director both. Stagehand too, besides the therapist, the cocktail party hostess, the badass. Very few people understood how many hats this job required.

"Oh, hey, *wow,*" said Courtney. She could have meant anything by that, or nothing. But Nora took it to mean, Man, lady, you are *old.* Courtney had no additional follow-up questions. If you had children yourself you asked things like what grade they were in or what sports they played or if they liked their teachers or where they were applying to college, but if you were newly pregnant you didn't know enough to ask all of those questions. You still, hilariously, thought it was all about you, and your checkups, and what stroller you were going to choose and which of your friends was also pregnant and how much weight you'd gained or hadn't gained, maybe as compared to the aforementioned friends who were also pregnant. Nora had been the same way when she was pregnant with Angela, four hundred years ago. As obvious as it seemed later, you didn't really, truly understand that you were growing a little person in there until that little person emerged, blinking and crying, and looked at you with squinty watery eyes and an expression that very clearly said, *Well. Here I am. What are you going to do with me now?* Although, truth be told, Angela had emerged with a preternatural calm, and her eyes were wide and alert. Cecily had been blinking and crying. Maya had been breech. (Could that somehow explain the reading difficulties?)

Anyway! You didn't know that the complicated lives of children were going to unroll themselves in front of you like a carpet whether you wanted them to or not, and that you would be expected to walk along that carpet for many, many years, always wondering if you were walking the right way.

"Do you know what you're having?" asked Nora politely — she didn't run in many circles with young pregnant women these days, but she remembered that this was a proper question to put forth. That, and

168

Where are you registered? Hilarious! Imagine women in Somalia or Kenya or India talking like this among their friends. No, sir, those women (not to stereotype) just popped them out, strapped them to their bellies or their backs or wherever there was room, and then got pregnant again.

People had asked Nora all the time if she knew what she was having. She hadn't found out, not with any of her children. The prospect made her feel too anxious. She couldn't stop thinking that if she assigned a gender to them then she would have to assign a name, and if a name then they became real people, and if they were real people then they were subject to the whims of nature and biology, where anything could happen, including but not limited to death or birth defects. ("A bit of a downer of a worldview, Nora-Bora," Gabe had said. But Nora, in the throes of pregnancy hormones, weeping once over a mistake in one of her open house listings in the *Chronicle*, couldn't help it.)

"No," said Courtney. "I haven't found out. I want to be surprised!"

Surprise! thought Nora. *Here's a little person who will one day need to get into college! Here's a person who will need three meals a day for the next eighteen years, but*

169

who will eschew more than half of the ones you prepare for reasons of taste or general stubbornness! Here is a person who will have nightly homework, yearly science fair projects; here's a person who will one day go through puberty, and you will have a front-row seat to the show.

"You're going to love parenting," said Nora. "There's nothing better. Except —"

"Except what?"

Nora drummed her fingers on top of the laptop. The inspector and Mr. Buyer were nowhere to be found. The tapping in the garage had ceased. Perhaps they were outside, inspecting the grounds, though most likely the buyers would bring in a separate inspector for that. Most did, at this level. These people, for sure. They had enough money to be crazy with it if they wanted but also enough brains to be smart. She looked Courtney square in her pretty face and said, "Can I give you a piece of advice?"

Courtney said, "Sure?" She smoothed her already-smooth hair with one hand.

Nora took a deep breath. Yes, it was true. She had become *that* woman, the woman dispensing matronly advice. No matter, what she had to say was as true as anything. Courtney was chewing on a cuticle; it was, thus far, the only sign of physical imperfection Nora had noticed, and she'd been looking pretty hard. Nora said, "I know, everybody will say this to you!"

Courtney said, "You're making me nervous."

"Well," said Nora. "I don't mean to. But I wanted to say: enjoy the heck out of that baby."

"Okay," said Courtney automatically, like a child being given instructions for a test.

"Because it will seem so hard, I know it will. But later on, when they're older, my God, when they're applying to college and crying over a test score and they still need you but they don't *need you* need you the way they did before, you're going to wish you had that time back, when they were snuggled up next to you and they needed you, only you. Nobody else, not even their fathers, the way they need you."

"My mother-in-law says stuff like that to me all the time," said Courtney levelly. She shook her head and her hair lifted and settled; it was Disney princess hair, Mulan or Jasmine. (Was she part Asian, Mrs. Buyer? It was hard to say — but there was something exotic about her, something not-quite-U.S.-born-and-bred. Eastern European? Russian? Boarding school, definitely, somewhere far away and astronomically priced. This was going to be one beautiful baby, whatever gender it decided to be, beautiful and rich.) "But I guess I don't really get it. Yet."

Mrs. Buyer stood — gracefully, giving, in her stance, no indication of any physical discomfort. The sun was now shining with a vengeance. Mrs. Buyer walked toward the French doors leading to the deck and Nora imagined her, baby in her arms, striding across the kitchen, a burp cloth over her shoulder, a decaf espresso brewing at the coffee bar. Wearing some sort of luxury robe that Nora could not clearly imagine since she herself did not actually own one; she was a battered terry-cloth girl herself. Perhaps silk? Although that seemed impractical, with the baby. Slippery, and likely dry-clean only. Nora sighed. She knew her business. She knew the perfect buyer when she saw the perfect buyer. Once Nora Hawthorne, Marin realtor extraordinaire, could envision somebody inside a home, making a coffee, holding a baby, it was pretty close to a sure thing.

And then.

"What's this?"

Nora said, "What's what?"

"On the doors, there's . . ." Courtney Buyer was crouching down, inspecting the doors. "There's something in the glass."

"Probably just a smudge," said Nora. That was unlikely, because Bee Watkins was extremely particular about her housekeeping, which she didn't do herself but which she outsourced to a lovely Mexican woman who spoke almost no English but who came in from Vallejo *every single day* to vacuum and dust and Windex the French doors and wash the dinner dishes from the night before. Imagine.

Nora's heartbeat picked up speed. She didn't like the way Courtney was crouching; she didn't like the way she was frowning — it was enough of a frown that it caused a tiny divot to appear in Courtney's Asian/Russian/ European/boarding school brow.

"My goodness, don't crouch like that," said Nora. "That can't be comfortable." In fact Courtney looked perfectly at ease; she straightened her legs with barely a flicker of effort, not even pushing herself with her hands — she looked like a long-legged feline. She must be a yoga aficionado.

Standing now, Courtney was still peering at the glass in the doors. "No, it's not a smudge," she said. "My father owned a glass manufacturer for twenty years in Brooklyn." (Brooklyn! Nora never, absolutely never, would have guessed Brooklyn.) "There are pits all throughout this glass. It's a defect. They'll have to be replaced."

"A defect?" Nora crossed the living room to the French doors. The living room was so big it felt like it took years to cross it. Lawrence and Bee entertained frequently, dozens and dozens of people at a time. Four of Nora's childhood living rooms, maybe five, would have fit inside the living room in the Watkins home. "I can't imagine that. The current owners are very particular." (*Also,* she wanted to add, *I thought you didn't care about inspections.*)

Just then Mr. Buyer and the inspector appeared. The inspector smiled and said, "We're looking good! Just a couple of rooms to go. Great house."

"Not so fast," said Courtney. She crooked a finger at her husband and motioned him closer. "There's something you have to see here."

"What's that?" said the inspector, and Nora, in her brightest, don't-you-worry-about-a-thing voice, said, "Nothing," at the same time that Courtney said, "Something."

Now Mr. Buyer crossed the room too, and he and his wife both leaned in toward the glass. Outside, birds were chirping like crazy, as if they were tuning up for the

Philharmonic. Across the street, a leaf blower roared to life, and a lawn mower started up too. The buzzing and sawing of a contractor's mysterious machinery joined the melody. It was all very elite Northern California, privileged people keeping up their beautiful homes, and the sound was usually music to Nora's ears. But all Nora really heard now was Courtney saying to her husband, in a low, urgent, confident voice used by wives the world over when they knew it was important that they have the upper hand, that they be listened to, that this was A Very Big Deal. All Nora could hear — she'd heard the sound before, in many different guises, though all recognizable to her practiced ear — were the sounds of a deal that was about to fall through.

Chapter 16
Cecily

Cecily knocked on Angela's door. She knew Angela was in there, but at first there was no answer. So Cecily kept up the knocking.

Finally she heard a loud sigh, then footsteps on the hardwood, then the door opened just a smidge, and one of Angela's big blue eyes appeared in the crack.

"Oh," said Angela. "I thought it was Mom or Dad, coming to check on me." She opened the door wider.

Cecily was wearing the black shorts she wore to Irish dance, the white socks, and her ghillies.

"Why are you wearing those in the house?" Angela nodded toward the ghillies.

"They're new," reported Cecily. "I'm stretching them out." She extended a foot toward Angela.

"Why didn't you just get them in a bigger size?"

"Ha!" said Cecily, then realized Angela hadn't been joking. "They're supposed to fit super-tight. So you have to get them really fitted, and then stretch them."

Experimentally, she did a few steps of her hornpipe. The hornpipe was meant to be done in hard shoes, not ghillies, but Cecily wasn't allowed to wear her hard shoes on the wood. They left black marks and scuffs everywhere.

"I'm going to sleep in them all week. So that they're ready for the *feis* in November. It's a big one, the regional." You spelled *feis* one way, but you said it another: *fesh*. Weird, in Angela's opinion. It meant competition.

"Oh," said Angela irritably. "You can sleep

176

like that? That looks really uncomfortable."

"It's not so bad," said Cecily. "Anyway, Seamus says I have an incredibly high pain tolerance. Do you have an incredibly high pain tolerance?"

Angela was looking back at the work on her desk. "I guess so," she said. "Yeah. What I have is an incredible amount of homework. So do you think you could go now, Cecily?" She chewed at her fingernails.

"You're so *grouchy* lately, geez."

Cecily looked around Angela's room. It was smaller than the room that Maya and Cecily shared, but Cecily was still envious that she had it all to herself. Maya talked in her sleep and sometimes even sleepwalked; Cecily had recently woken to find her sitting at her little white desk, completely asleep but with her eyes wide open, trying to open a container of markers. That had freaked Cecily right out.

Her mother said it was stress that made Maya do that. (*How can second grade be stressful?* Cecily asked, and her mother had said, *It can be if you're a struggling reader.*) Her mother got *ridiculously* stressed about Maya's reading, even though she tried not to show it.

"So . . . ," said Cecily. She lay down on Angela's bed and flexed her feet. Angela

177

tapped her foot and looked again at her desk. "When you go away to college can I move into your room?"

"Cecily, I told you —"

"Just answer that one question. One."

Angela smiled her new, weird smile. *Look at me!* the smile seemed to say. *I am all mouth, no eyes!* "I doubt it."

"I'm tired of sharing a room with Maya, though. Don't you think it's stupid that Maya and I have to share just so we keep a guest room free? We don't even have that many guests."

"Sure we do. Aunt Marianne comes at least once a year. And Grandma comes from Rhode Island."

"Not that much."

"No, not that much. But still."

"Pinkie has a room all to herself. And a bathroom."

"Pinkie," said Angela, "has a whole house to herself, and a whole set of parents, because Pinkie is an only child. Pinkie is probably incredibly lonely. Why do you think she wants to come over here all the time?"

"True." Cecily examined Angela's bulletin board. "Who's Timothy Valentine? Why do you have his picture there?"

"That's nothing."

"Is he your *boyfriend*?"

"Come on, Cecily, don't be an idiot."

That one stung. Cecily tried not to let it show. Angela frowned and looked a little embarrassed. "I'm sorry. He's an admissions guy at Harvard, the guy for this region. The *Chronicle* did an interview with him once and Mom saved it for me. So I cut out his picture. So I can bow to him five times a day. Like he's Mecca."

"Really?"

"No. Of course not. It's just so I have a mental image of the guy who might be looking at my application. Personal connection, you know. But seriously Cecily —"

"Do you talk to him?"

Angela looked even more embarrassed. "Sometimes," she said. Then, in a hurry, "Not very much."

"He looks nice," said Cecily. "Friendly. He looks like he'd like you."

"Thanks." Angela opened the door and stood near it.

Cecily looked at Angela's bare walls. "What'd you do with your stuff? Your posters and all that?"

Angela took her chin in her hands and twisted her neck and Cecily heard a popping sound. Then she sighed and said, "I took them down."

"Why?"

"I didn't want them anymore. Cecily, I mean it, I have to do my homework now." She gave Cecily a little push.

Cecily said, *"Ow,"* and stayed where she was. "What are you working on?"

Angela huffed and sighed and sat down at her desk and put her back to Cecily. "Statistics. But after that I have to work on English."

"What do you have to do for English?"

"Do you really want to know? You do? Okay, we have to choose a British author and read two works and some criticism and create an original thesis. It's called an extended essay. Okay? Now get *out.*"

Cecily didn't know what most of that meant, but she was trying to find a way to stay in Angela's room so she said, "Who are you going to choose?"

Angela leaned back in her chair and closed her eyes. When she opened them she turned toward Cecily and said, "Probably Virginia Woolf."

"I don't know who that is."

"That's okay. You don't need to, yet. She went mad."

"Crazy mad or angry mad?"

"Crazy mad. She ended her life by walk-

180

ing into the water with stones in her pockets."

"Huh? I don't get it."

"So she drowned. The stones weighed her down until she drowned."

"But." Cecily was perplexed. "Why didn't she just take the stones out of her pockets?"

Angela sighed. "Because. She didn't want to. She wanted to die. Okay? She wanted to die."

This was horrifying news. Cecily felt a little bit sick to her stomach, and she watched a complicated expression cross Angela's face. "I shouldn't have told you that, Cecily. I don't want you to get nightmares. Forget I said that, okay?"

"I don't get nightmares. I never even remember my dreams." Cecily tried not to think about the stones in the pockets. (Logistically, she wasn't even sure how that was possible, like how many stones you would need and how big your pockets would have to be.)

Cecily lay back down on the bed and covered her face with one of Angela's decorative pillows and mumbled, "Are you coming to my *feis*?"

Angela said, "Cec, I can't hear a word you're saying."

Cecily removed the pillow, sighed theatrically, and said, "Are you coming to my *feis*? My dance competition."

"I know what a *feis* is, Cecily. Geez."

"Well, are you?"

"I don't know. When is it?"

"The ninth. November ninth. My ceili team is trying to qualify for Worlds. We're really good this year. So . . . you should come."

"I have a meet."

Cecily could sense that she was going to get tossed out of the room, so she kept talking. "Do you remember fourth grade?"

"Sort of," said Angela. "Not really."

"The California history year."

"Oh," said Angela. "Oh, sure. The gold rush, et cetera. Yeah, I remember. All those field trips. It was fun. You'll like it." She smiled at Cecily again, the real thing this time, the eyes joining in. But it was still not enough for Cecily. She was drinking up her sister's attention; she wanted more and more and more. She remembered when Angela had helped her learn to ride a bike, running behind her, balancing the bike, letting go and yelling, *You can do it!*

"Did you have to do a paper on a state landmark?"

Angela had taken up her pencil and was writing something on graph paper. She looked up and said, "Probably. I don't remember."

"I'm going to do Coit Tower. Or the Golden Gate. I'm not sure. Hey, Angela?"

"Yes?"

"Are you going to miss us? When you go off to Harvard?"

Angela turned around and studied Cecily. Her mouth twisted in a funny way and she got up without saying anything and opened the door. Finally she said, "Of course I'm going to miss you."

"For real?"

"Yes. For real." Firmly. "I'm sorry I was grouchy. I'm just —" She looked at the ceiling and blinked rapidly. "Never mind. Now get out of here. Go stretch your shoes or whatever. I have to study."

CHAPTER 17
ANGELA

"Hey!" said Kelsey, as Angela pulled open the heavy glass doors with the Elpis logo emblazoned on both sides. "What's *up*?"

Kelsey hugged Angela and Angela absorbed her perfume, a complicated smell that made Angela think of pine trees and rosebushes and maybe the ocean and defi-

183

nitely something metallic. *Odiferous.* SAT word.

"Not much," said Angela. "I had a thing in the city for Student Sharing, so I thought I'd come by and see my dad."

"Sit *down,*" said Kelsey. "Tell me everything, oh my God, I can't believe you're *graduating* next year; when I first started working here you were a *freshman.*" Kelsey's breasts were big and soft and so completely on display that Angela couldn't look away from them. Her smile was wide enough to fall into. In the very back of Kelsey's mouth, sitting atop a molar, were the remains of Kelsey's lunch, or maybe her afternoon snack. Elpis was famous for its snack room. Angela had known approximately five Kelseys since she'd started visiting her father at work: Veronica. Mabel. Juliette. Janie. And now the actual Kelsey. Each one replaced by the next, a revolving door of office assistants who organized activities for Take Your Child to Work Day and kept her father and the other Elpis partners on schedule and in line and then eventually aged out of the position.

Kelsey pointed to a square chair, too modern to be comfortable, and said, "Your dad's in a meeting, but as soon as he's out I'll let him know you're here. Is he expecting you?"

Angela shook her head and got ready to explain her presence when a commotion from down the hall distracted her and Kelsey. Two of the senior partners, Doug Maverick and somebody Angela thought was named Stuart, were arguing over a paper one of them held.

"That's *not* what the data tells us," said Doug. "You know it's not, Stu, you can't keep —"

"Actually," said a young female voice, "I'm with Stu on this one. I think that is *exactly* what the data tells us."

"Oh, God," whispered Kelsey. "Here we go." She rolled her eyes dramatically, impressively.

"Here we go what?" Angela gave in and sat on the modern chair.

"You'll see," said Kelsey. "Just hang on."

Angela hung on long enough for the voice to turn into a person, a young woman, not much older than Angela, though dressed (Angela thought) like a forty-year-old attorney, with a gray stretch wool jacket and matching gray pants. "The intern," whispered Kelsey, "who thinks she's a senior partner."

The gray suit grew closer and closer and finally its owner said, "Angela? I recognize

185

you from the pictures in your dad's office. Oh, I'm so happy to meet you. Finally! I'm Abby." She extended a hand.

"I'm happy to meet you too," said Angela, dutifully shaking, but inside she was bewildered and maybe even a little bit alarmed and also she was thinking, *WTF?*

"Your dad has told me *so much* about you," said Abby. "I feel like I know you." She claimed the chair opposite Angela's, crossed her legs, and leaned in closely. "And I'm sure he's mentioned what he and I have in common."

"Um," said Angela. Angela's father had never mentioned this person to Angela at all (he wasn't in the habit of talking about the *interns* at home), and while she was searching for a way not to say that — she had manners, after all! — Abby said, "Harvard, of course!" with a note of triumph, as though Angela had asked a question and Abby had produced the correct answer. "We both went to Harvard. And you're headed there too."

"I haven't even —" said Angela, but before she could finish Abby fixed her with an odd, almost secretive look. (*Conspiratorial.* SAT.) And then she said, "Let's get a snack."

Angela was starving. They'd had an early practice that morning, a four-mile tempo run. Kelsey was at her desk, answering the phone, "Elpis Consulting!" and rolling her eyes at Angela, like somehow this was all a big joke. "Okay," said Angela. She thought for a second that this Abby person was going to take her hand and lead her to the snack room as though she'd never been there before, but instead she walked in front of Angela and Angela followed along, like a serf.

In the snack room Angela surveyed the offerings. SunChips. Clif Bars. Gluten-free scones baked by somebody named Sunny in Half Moon Bay. A stash of Vitaminwaters and regular bottled water in the fridge with the clear doors. Abby plucked a bag of M&M's out of the candy bowl and said, "My favorite." Angela chose Twizzlers, as she did every time she came to the Elpis snack room, as she'd been doing for a dozen years, because there was nobody here who was going to remind her how badly chewy candy stuck to the teeth. Anyway, Cecily was the one who was getting braces. Angela was all done with the orthodontist.

"So," said Abby, tearing into her M&M's bag with her teeth (with her *teeth*!) and speaking as though she was continuing a conversation they'd begun earlier, "the next thing you need to know about Harvard is that everybody there is terrified. That's your secret weapon, but it took me two years to figure it out." She leaned against the counter and rooted through the M&M's bag. Angela bit into a Twizzler. "Once you know that," Abby said, "you'll be amazed how well you can get along. I wish someone had told me early on, like I'm telling you."

"But I don't even —" Angela had been about to say that she didn't even know if she'd get in, but Abby stomped on her words and said, "In other news, that rule applies everywhere. Now that I'm half a year out, I can see it. *Everywhere.* But especially where there are super-smart people trying to do a good job. People are scared every-where."

Angela was starting to feel a little scared herself. This Abby person was very intense. The way she stared at you when she talked. The way all that fire came out of eyes that were small and close together. There was something desperate there, something striv-ing. Maybe even something *indefatigable.*

"When do the notices go out?" asked Abby.

"Not sure, exactly," said Angela. "Middle of December."

Abby laughed. "Yeah, isn't that madden-ing? You don't know exactly when it's coming, and then — *poof!* — you get an email, and your whole world changes, one way or the other." When she said *poof* she flicked her fingers like a magician. *God,* thought Angela. *What a nut.* But she was also sort of mesmerized.

It could have been the Twizzlers, but Angela felt something knot up and flip in her stomach. She took a Vitaminwater and studied the sensation for a moment. Okay, it was something like this.

Abby was six months out of Harvard.

Which meant that if she was *out* of college and *this* was how she acted, well, then, it didn't end with college. The competing, the posturing. It didn't even end with the end of college. The bullshit that Angela thought she was nearly done with — did it have a finish line? If it did, where the hell was it?

The snack room door swung open and Kelsey popped her head around the corner and said, "You guys cool here?" There was a purple streak in her hair Angela hadn't noticed before. Kelsey was so badass. Angela bet she slept with all kinds of guys, and did it the right way, too (whatever that was, not that Angela would know). Kelsey looked like sex. Whatever sex looked like.

"We're great," said Abby, with a considerable amount of authority. Angela nodded along. "Just getting to know each other."

Angela thought, *We* are?

On the other hand. There was something about this conversation (could she call it a conversation when she hadn't actually gotten a full sentence out? Or was it more like a lecture . . .) that was the opposite of scary, that thrilled Angela for a reason she couldn't quite put her finger on. An *unfathomable* reason.

"Soooooo," said Abby, crumpling the M&M's bag and tossing it toward the garbage. She missed, and got up with a little embarrassed smile to retrieve it. "What else do you want to know about Harvard?"

Then it hit Angela, why she'd felt a little *frisson* of excitement. Pretty simple, really. Her entire life people had been telling her how to get into Harvard: what to do, what not to do, how to think and write and run and be. Now here was someone who took her ability to be admitted for granted, and who was telling her what to do once she got there. The sensation was refreshing, like diving into a cold wave. A cold Atlantic wave, in Rhode Island.

"I heard I have a surprise visitor," said a familiar voice. The door to the snack room swung open for a second time, and Angela said, "Dad!" Her father looked the same as he always did, a little tired, a little stressed, but with an underlying *countenance* that said that if you told a funny enough story about your day he'd give you his full attention and laugh and be sincere about it.

At almost the same time Angela said, "Dad!" Abby said, "Gabe!" and Angela's father's face took on a startled expression. He rarely flushed (that was her mother's department), but now there was a spot of color high on each cheek. Weird.

"Gabe," said Abby again, like nobody had heard her the first time. Angela chewed the inside of her lip. It was odd to hear her father addressed so familiarly by someone so close to Angela's own age. Not just familiarly, but sort of, well . . . for lack of a better word (*There's always a better word,* Ms. Simmons would say), *intimately.*

Intimately! She looked more carefully at Abby, at her father. Her father had a strange look on his face. *Sphinxlike.* He glanced at Abby, then back at Angela, and if Angela didn't know much, much better, she'd think that he looked like a man who'd been caught doing something he shouldn't have done.

Your dad's office.

I recognize you from the pictures.

Your dad has told me so much about you.
What he and I have in common.

"Angela," he said. "What a surprise —"

Her *father* and the *intern*. Oh. My. Freaking. God. Gross. Grosser than gross. Whatever was in her stomach triple-flipped.

"I have to go," she said to both of them. Finally! A complete sentence. She looked at her wrist for a watch that wasn't there. "I forgot, I have — I have a thing. I have to go." She turned out of the snack room, past a bewildered Kelsey, who half stood when Angela passed, and out toward the elevator.

Her *father* and the *intern.* It was such a cliché, they may as well slip on a couple of banana peels while they were at it. It was the plot of every bad movie and a bunch of books, both mediocre and not, and it was happening right now, right here, right in her very own life.

So what? she thought, turning out of the office building and melting away into the early-evening crowds. So *what*? She'd be out of the house by this time next year, so, really, so what.

But that wasn't true; that wasn't how she really felt. She would never let something crappy like that go on behind her mother's back without telling her about it. After the Harvard application was in, she'd find time to investigate.

It wasn't *so what* after all, not with this. It was *so everything.*

CHAPTER 18
ARTHUR

"All right, then," said Arthur Sutton. It was the weekly catch-up meeting. He was sitting at the conference table with Grace, Nora, and the new realtor who had joined the firm the past spring, Seth. Things had been looking altogether better when Arthur hired Seth. If sales didn't pick up soon, Arthur would have to let him go, which would be a shame, because Seth and his young wife had just bought a starter home in San Mateo. A heck of a commute, though, San Mateo to Marin, so maybe it would be for the best.

Arthur cleared his throat and waited until all eyes were on him. In general Arthur loved the weekly check-in meeting; it comforted him to know that things at Sutton and Wainwright were ticking along the way they were supposed to. But today the mood felt somber and gray. It felt like they were at a funeral meal.

"Nora," he said, "you had the second-highest sales in the region the quarter before last, right behind Sally Bentley at Bentley and Associates."

There were few people in the business — really, few people in the world — Arthur truly disliked, but Sally Bentley was one of them. She spent more on advertising than any other agent in the Bay Area. She plastered her photo — coiffed hair, Nancy Reagan lollipop head on a skinny body — all over the city, on buses and billboards, in coffee shops, on grocery carts. She used the slogan "When you think *Sell* think *Sally.*" She bragged about her sales (which, admittedly, were astronomical) to anyone who would listen and to many who wouldn't.

"That's great," said Nora. Her tone was flat.

"But last quarter . . . well, nobody in the office had stellar sales. Madrone Canyon was the last big one." Arthur took a deep breath. "The Watkins home," he said. "Nora? Any nibbles out there?"

Nora shook her head and winced. "Not yet," she said. "I tried to get Lawrence to compromise. I think Bee was open to it, I really do, but Lawrence wouldn't hear of any solutions. I mean, the buyers wanted to knock forty thousand off the price to replace the doors."

Seth said, "That's insane."

Nora said, "Lawrence wants it back on

the market, full price."

Arthur didn't like Nora this way, tense and sad. He wanted to put his arms around her (in an avuncular way) and tell her that everything was going to be okay.

"He held it against me, that *I* didn't point out the flaws in the glass." Her voice was strained; she sounded like she might cry. Arthur really didn't want Nora to cry. He didn't think he could take it.

"You'll find another buyer," he said now, glancing at Seth, glancing at Grace. "No home goes unsold forever."

Actually, that wasn't true. Some of them did.

Nora looked tired. Nora always looked a little bit tired, but now she looked about as tired as Arthur had ever seen her. Was there something else bothering her besides the Watkins sale? Something with one of the girls, or with Gabe?

"Right, I know." Nora rubbed her eyes and twisted her pencil in her hands. "I'm sure I'll find another buyer." It must be difficult to be wife and mother and realtor all rolled in together, with one of her birds preparing to flee the nest. Perhaps that was what was bothering her, the oldest, Angela, almost out of the house. Maybe she needed to talk to someone about that. Nora would

195

never see a therapist. Arthur felt confident in saying that. She was too practical and of-the-moment for therapy. Too busy.

Arthur felt a tug of sympathy for Nora, he did, but still he envied her, too, the unruliness and mess of family life. She was always, during her non-Sutton-and-Wainwright hours, consumed with her volunteer obligations at the girls' schools and field trips and overseeing homework and shuttling them around to the various activities because it seemed that in the modern age you were not allowed to be a child who simply came home from school and *existed:* you had to be well rounded and accomplished and coddled and fed lots of flax and wild salmon and carefully monitored for signs of potential failure.

His non-Sutton-and-Wainwright hours with Linda were lovely, in their home on Marina Boulevard, looking out at the boats. But so very quiet.

"You will," said Arthur. "You're a wonderful realtor. And it's a beautiful home."

"It's overpriced," murmured Nora.

"It's beautiful," said Arthur firmly.

For Arthur and Linda there had been just the one baby. Just the one, a little girl, living only one day, like a mayfly. They had named her Dawn. That's when she entered the world, that's when she left it, that's why Arthur was up before the sun every day of his life since then — he said a little prayer, paid a little homage, as the first threads of sunlight made their way across the sky. Often in the early morning he walked from his and Linda's home down to Crissy Field, where he let the wind whip his thinning hair, and he watched the lucky dogs running along the beach. They had been so young then, Arthur twenty-nine and Linda twenty-six. Still nearly children themselves, it seemed to Arthur now, though at the time, when it happened, he felt older than the hills. A heart defect, not repairable. Dawn had no chance.

Come to think of it, they were *all* very quiet and subdued at the conference table today, not just Nora.

"Grace?" said Arthur. "What's next?"

"I'm sorry," said Grace. "I'm not myself today."

Nora was on that immediately, shifting from tired mode to caretaking mode, stretching her hand toward Grace. "Oh, sweetie. Is it the cat again?"

Grace's cat! How did Nora know what was wrong with Grace's cat? In fact it seemed downright exhausting to be Nora — on top of everything else she was tracking a sick cat.

Grace nodded and took Nora's outstretched hand. Seth looked uncomfortably at Arthur.

If Dawn had lived she'd be thirty-one years old; sometimes Arthur wondered if she'd have been a mother by now, and what kind of mother she would have been. Linda would have made a phenomenal grandmother, with just the right amount of doting, and she'd have been able to counsel Dawn to take it easy, not to worry so much about every little thing. Nora could probably use some of that. Her own mother lived too far away to do much of that for her.

Not all single women over the age of thirty-five lived alone in apartments with felines, Arthur knew that, but Grace did. It was hard to look at her and not think she had come straight from a casting call: the conscientious, slightly grumpy, loyal-to-a-fault secretary. *Office assistant,* Grace corrected him if he slipped. *Don't you dare call me a secretary.* She was Sutton and Wainwright's secret backbone.

"It's just . . . well, she's on a steroid, prednisone, and it's supposed to work immediately but I'm not sure if it's doing anything. I hate to think of her alone, in my apartment. If something happens."

"Do you need to leave, Grace?" said Arthur. There was an impatient note in his voice that he tried to snuff out but that he didn't quite get to in time.

Nora whispered, "I think she should." She rubbed Grace's back.

Arthur and Linda were not cat people — they were not *pet* people, their house was uncluttered and clean as a museum — but even so, Arthur tried his hardest to work up sympathy for Grace. And for the cat, he supposed.

"Okay," said Arthur. "Well, in that case, if we've nothing else to discuss: meeting adjourned."

Grace leapt up.

Oh, for Heaven's sake.

Chapter 19
Nora

"Listen," said Seamus O'Malley, taking Nora's elbow and leading her to a quiet corner of the studio's waiting room, *quiet* being a relative term, since inside the studio a clamorous beginners' hard-shoe class was lurching along under the tutelage of one of Seamus's underlings and on the other side of the waiting room the under-thirteen ceili group — Cecily's — was ostensibly warming up for their practice but was actually engaged in an (illegal) bartering program involving gum and Twizzlers. They were sitting directly beneath a sign that read NO FOOD IN THE STUDIO OR WAITING ROOM. WATER ONLY, PLEASE. But Seamus seemed to be turning a blind eye, so Nora turned a blind eye too.

Usually, out of necessity, Nora just opened the door of the Audi while it was practically still moving and deposited Cecily in the parking lot to make her way into class. Today, though, Nora had a check to drop off and a mother to connect with about a costume piece. She was glancing at her phone, waiting for the mother, when Seamus grabbed her.

"Listen, Nora," said Seamus. Nora took a second, as she always did, to enjoy the way her name sounded when Seamus said it. He was two decades in America but, thank God, the vestiges of his brogue remained. Seamus could say anything to Nora, he could tell her she'd just been diagnosed with a rare blood disease or that a buyer had walked half an hour before closing escrow and still it would sound like he was singing her an Irish lullaby. "Is Cecily okay?"

"Why?" Nora looked at Cecily, who was busy bartering with Fiona.

"She seems a bit shook, is all."

"A bit shook?" It wasn't unusual to be perplexed during a conversation with Seamus. Once he told the ceili team that they couldn't hit a cow's arse with a banjo. Cecily had looked it up on Nora's iPhone on the way home. (*"Oh!"* she said. "It means we're hopeless.")

"A bit unwell. A bit not like herself."

"She looks like herself to me," said Nora. "She looks exactly like herself." She glanced over at Cecily. When were Lawrence and Bee going to drop the hammer on her? How many miles a week was Gabe running, and *why*? Should she take Maya to a neurologist? Had Angela finished the application? And, seriously, what was for dinner?

"I think you know, Nora," said Seamus, "that we need this team to do well. To qualify for Worlds. We've put a lot into this, everybody has."

"I know. Cecily has too." The ceili dresses had run each family $750. "Believe me, Seamus, Cecily has put as much into this as anyone."

"Sure she has," said Seamus. "But the uniformity, that's what's crucial here. Cecily's a gorgeous solo dancer, we all know that. But she's losing her concentration with the ceili and that's where we can't be losing it. Ceili is all concentration, that's all it is."

"I *know,*" said Nora. Seamus's brogue was sounding less adorable.

"See if you can't rein her in a bit, yeah? Normally I would say don't be troubling yourself, you know our Cecily can always pull off whatever we throw at her. But keep an eye, will you, Nora?"

Cecily! Cecily was the light in the darkness, the bird singing in the trees. Worry about Cecily?

"Okay," she said congenially to Seamus O'Malley. It was warm in the studio; Nora wanted to get out of there. She had thirty-eight things to do. Her phone was buzzing. "Okay," she said. She was a wife and a mother and a real estate professional; she could add one more thing to her list. "I will keep an eye, Seamus."

She answered the phone on the way out of the studio. Gabe.

"I think we made a big mistake."

"How's that?" Nora marched toward her car, slid in.

"I think we should have sent Angela to private school."

Nora started the car. *"What?"*

She could practically feel Gabe nodding. "I mean it," he said. "Skip Moynihan told me that the Ivies aren't taking from public high schools anymore. That if you really want to get in you have to come from a boarding school, like that one down in Monterey, what's it called?"

"I don't know what it's called. That's insane. We're not sending our children to school in Monterey."

She backed out of the space.

"I know that. We've missed the boat for that, obviously, with Angela. But if those are the kids who are getting in, maybe we should have — or maybe Cecily, or Maya —"

Nora thought of Angela, worn out, overworked, crescents beneath her eyes: moons beneath the moons. She didn't know how kids stood it these days. She couldn't have. She could barely stand watching it.

"Oh, Gabe. Gabe, Gabe. That is simply a dog you can't walk back. You have done everything you could. *We* have done everything we could. Go back to work."

"Fine," said Gabe sharply, but he stayed on the phone, like he was waiting for her to say something.

CHAPTER 20
GABE

"Or notice the bears asleep at the zoo. It's because they've been dancing all night for you . . ."

Cecily was reading to Maya. Okay, that was sweet. That was very sweet. Gabe, on his way to his bedroom to change out of his work clothes, paused to listen.

Cecily looked up, saw him standing there. She smiled and went back to reading and he felt pinpricks in the backs of his eyes. *Don't cry, you old bastard. It's just two kids reading. No big deal.*

He changed his clothes and returned to the living room.

The scene put him in mind of his own brothers, that was all. Michael and Ryan. Not that they sat around reading books with dancing polar bears on the cover together when they were kids. But they did play with Legos. When they had time. There were always chores on a ranch, endless work. Kids today didn't do many chores. They didn't have time: they were too busy training for adulthood. Also his kids didn't live on a ranch, so there was less to do. In their defense.

From faraway places, the geese flew home,

read Cecily in a clear, firm voice.

The ranch. Gabe remembered a winter sunset, the whole sky a blood orange. The biggest sky in the world. He remembered waves of panic coursing through him when he was a small child, briefly lost in the Dillard's in Cheyenne, his hands grasping a blue silk dress in the ladies' department, waiting for his mother to claim him.

He remembered his brother Michael's high school girlfriend, Lauren Foster, who had eyes like a cat's, light green. He thought Michael would marry her, they all did. They'd all been a little bit in love with Lauren. Okay, Gabe had done more than *be* a little bit in love with Lauren. He'd acted on it. He couldn't help it. Nobody could have helped it — Lauren Foster at seventeen had been an absolute goddess.

A coward move, Gabe.

A decades-old mistake.

The moon stayed up until morning next day, and none of the ladybugs flew away. Cecily moved over on the couch and patted the empty space next to her and Gabe sat down.

Just before his mother's death she told him that she'd seen Lauren at a county fair and that time hadn't been kind to her. This news depressed Gabe. He preferred to think of Lauren Foster as forever seventeen and beautiful, long-legged and tan, sitting at the kitchen table at the ranch house with bare feet and jean shorts and a *bikini* top. Which at the time hadn't seemed nearly as strange as it did in retrospect. In landlocked Wyoming.

So whenever you doubt just how special you are, and you wonder who loves you, how much and how far . . .

His brother had married a woman from Vancouver. He'd never gotten over what Gabe had done. Stupid of Gabe to tell him.

I can't believe you would do something like that, Gabe.

"Now you read," said Cecily. "Just this last page, take your time."

"I can't," said Maya.

"Of course you can. It's just one page, two paragraphs, really. You can do it."

"I don't want to do it. I want you to read."

"Maya . . ."

What an asshole move, Gabe.

"Okay," said Cecily, frowning. *Heaven blew every trumpet and played every horn on the wonderful, marvelous night you were born.*

She closed the book.

"Daddy?" asked Maya. "What was it like on the night *I* was born?"

"Darkest midnight," said Gabe. "Magical. Well, not exactly midnight, more like one

206

thirty or two. But still magical. Angela was born at midnight."

Cecily leaned her head against Gabe's arm. "I remember when Maya was born. Aunt Marianne came to stay with us, and Angela had the stomach bug. I was born in the daytime. Right, Daddy? High noon?"

"That's right," said Gabe. "Lunchtime. That's why you like lunch so much."

"Everybody likes lunch."

"Not everybody."

Gabe took the book from Cecily and studied the cover. Two polar bears doing a waltz, and above the title a full moon, with two eyes and a mouth just visible. The man in the moon.

CHAPTER 21
NORA

1:23 a.m.

Dear Marianne,
There's a three-quarter moon tonight. I don't know the official name for that, but Cecily would. She's doing the phases of the moon at school.

An email went out looking for a parent or two willing to preside over an evening trip somewhere-or-other for proper viewing.

They said "parent" but of course they meant "mother." They always mean mother.

I pretended I didn't get it.

Tuesday morning, eight twenty-three. Nora had seen all three of her girls off to school. Angela had slouched her way out the door to walk with a couple of friends from the neighborhood and Nora had delivered Cecily and Maya to the turnaround circle at the elementary school.

It was all very much the opposite of relaxing, this morning routine, and nothing about it seemed to get easier as time went on. Maybe when Angela was off at college — maybe then it would get easier, for there would be just Cecily and Maya to look after.

Nora did not remember her mother rushing around like this to get Marianne and Nora out the door when they were school-children in Rhode Island. She stood in her robe at the door as they walked themselves to the bus stop under gray New England skies. Surely she provided them with breakfast, but Nora did not recall made-to-order omelets. Cheerios and milk, maybe a raspberry Entenmann's strudel when they were on special at the market. Of course there were only two of them, not three. That made a difference. Suzanne Ramsey, one of the moms at Cecily and Maya's school — mother of four — theorized that no matter how many children you had, everything seemed easier once you subtracted one.

Now, instead of going into the office the way she normally would, Nora was back in her kitchen, scrubbing dried egg from the stove, wiping smoothie residue from the counter, straightening the dish towel hanging on the stove handle, because she had to get to the monthly meeting of the Spring Fling committee for the elementary school.

She was feeling unfairly peevish about the Spring Fling meeting, coming at a very busy time of year: the Harvard application looming, Cecily's ceili team gearing up, the science fair. Maya's class was putting on some sort of play before the Thanksgiving holiday, and Nora needed to go back and read the email to see what was expected of her. Then, of course, there was the dwarf flax, looming over her like a storm cloud. She found herself hoping fervently that something would happen to the Millers' expansion plans — nothing too tragic, not an illness or anything, but maybe a gentle dip in the stock market that would affect their ear-marked funds, or a respectable yet irreparable falling out with the architect —

The dishwasher was chugging along, as it had been since before Nora dropped Cecily and Maya off. The more exclusive the brand, it seemed, the longer the wash cycle. *Ridiculous.* She had time to call her mother, whose phone call from a few days ago she had not yet returned.

"Nora-Bora!" said her mother. "I was just thinking about you."

"You were?"

"Well, sort of. Inasmuch as I'm always thinking about you."

Nora said, "Awww," and was surprised to discover a little catch in her voice. She glanced around the kitchen, refolded the dish towel, and suddenly felt nearly as exhausted as she'd ever felt. She wanted to lean into her mother across the telephone wires, to be enveloped by Aileen's sturdy and freckled arms.

"How are you, Nora?"

Nora sighed. The dishwasher was telling her that forty-nine minutes remained in the cycle. Seriously? She could have hand-washed everything faster. "Oh," she said. "You know, busy. Tired."

"Right," said Aileen. "You're always busy out there, all of you."

"Big fall for Angela," said Nora. She

scarcely remembered submitting her application to the University of Rhode Island. There'd really been no doubt that she'd get in, and she hadn't applied anywhere else. Was she being hypocritical, getting all over Angela for not coming up with another list of schools? Of course she wasn't! It was *a different situation entirely.*

"Well," said her mother. "You *do* rush around quite a bit. I mean, you're like a whirling dervish whenever I see you."

"It's a lot to keep up with!" protested Nora, who wasn't sure about the whirling dervish comparison; she knew from Angela, courtesy of an extra-credit project for eleventh-grade English the previous year, that a whirling dervish was not, as Nora had always believed, a type of bird similar to a roadrunner, but a member of a Muslim order known for its ecstatic dancing rituals.

"You're the busiest person I know," her mother went on cheerfully. "That's what I'm always telling my bird-watching friends." Her mother had, to Nora's knowledge, never watched a single bird until she became a widow. Now she watched them constantly.

"What about Marianne? She defends *murderers*! She works *all the time.* Nights, weekends."

"*Accused* murderers," said Aileen. "Innocent until, you know."

"I know," said Nora.

"But you're busier," persisted her mother. "It's different when you have children, and when they demand so much of you. Now, honey, I have to go — I'm meeting a friend for a morning walk."

"Which friend?"

"Stella. You don't know her. New friend. The leaves are turning. It's gorgeous today."

Childishly, Nora felt pushed aside, and homesick for a New England fall.

"I'll call you soon," promised Aileen. "I want to hear what my beautiful granddaughters are up to. How's Maya's reading coming along?"

"Slowly," said Nora. "She can sound out some words, but . . . well, it's much slower than it should be. I'm trying to get in with this tutor everybody *raves* about but he's got no openings forever. I'm worried Maya will be in tenth grade before this guy has a free slot."

"No big rush," said Aileen. "All in good time, you know. Just because Angela was so early with everything doesn't mean they all will be. You weren't toilet-trained until you were almost four!"

"Mom."

"And Marianne was, what? Two? She practically trained herself, I just pointed her toward the bathroom and off she went."

"Mom. Is this supposed to be helping?"

"I'm just reminding you that everyone develops at her own particular pace. And Nora?"

"What?"

"Take a minute. Take a few minutes. Deep breath. Enjoy every moment. They're young only once, you know."

"I know," said Nora. To herself, after the call had disconnected, she said, "Thank goodness."

By eleven ten, Nora had unloaded the dishwasher, showered, run the dwarf flax problem through her mind for the four hundredth time that week, made her face up minimally, and was on her way over to Suzanne Ramsey's for the meeting.

She let herself in and seven voices said, "Nora!" in unison; the greeting made her feel like Norm from *Cheers*. Suzanne was balancing her youngest, a gorgeous eight-month-old boy with heart-stopping eyelashes, on her lap and trying to eat a croissant without letting the baby grab it out of her hands.

Suzanne nodded toward a plate on the coffee table. "Have one, Nora," she said.

"They're gluten free."

"Oh, no!" said Liza Massey. "Who has an allergy?"

"Nobody, yet," said Suzanne. "But they think Lucas might have a *sensitivity.*"

Lucas said, "Baaaaah!"

Nora bit into a croissant — funny, you didn't think much about gluten until it was gone, and then you realized what an important job it did — and tried to focus on the meeting. She gave a not-very-informative report on the booths, about which she hadn't done much of anything yet ("We've got a long time still," said Suzanne soothingly) and half listened while the head of the entertainment subcommittee and the head of the food and drink subcommittee offered their updates.

Then she allowed her mind to wander. She was thinking about Gabe. She had heard a report on the radio that said that people underwent significant changes in their early twenties — that was why marriages between younger people were more likely to break up than they were if people got married older. That part wasn't really news to her. When she was in her early twenties she'd been a certifiable disaster, living in Rhode Island, dating a man named Brandon who was so unkind to her that he'd

214

once told her she was so pale he felt like he could see right through her. Then one day she'd packed up her rust-colored Corolla and announced to her mother, to Marianne, to all of her childhood friends, that she was moving clear across the country. And she'd done it! Talk about impulsive.

"Another one?" someone said to Nora. Melanie Morris.

"No thanks." She waved a hand. "I'm stuffed."

"No, another *baby*," said Melanie. "You look like you're going to eat Lucas."

"Oh, you've got to be kidding me," Nora said. "I am forty-four years old. Can you *imagine*?" Her hand went involuntarily to her abdomen as if checking for signs of life, a heartbeat, a kick. God help us all. The baby's eyes were following hers. She smiled at him and he considered her really quite seriously before breaking into a mammoth grin.

"Oooooh, Nora," said Suzanne. "He likes you. He doesn't smile that way at everyone."

"Of course he does," said Nora, feeling, despite herself, a little rush of pride. "Babies do."

"No, really, he doesn't. He's *very* strict."

"Oh, Nora," said Lori Schneider. "Did

you get in with that reading tutor for Maya?"

"Bob Huffman?" asked Nora.

"That's the one — he did Craig a world of good. He really turned him around. He is just *flying* through Harry Potter now. I can't keep enough books in the house!"

"No." Nora sighed and looked into her coffee cup and thought about reaching out with one hand to pinch Lori Schneider.

"He's really amazing, is what I heard," said Melanie. "He's the one you want."

"I did not get in with Bob Huffman," said Nora. She tried for a casual, devil-may-care laugh. "Because Bob Huffman is booked until the end of time. And beyond."

"Oh," said Lori. "That's too bad."

"Well," said Melanie, "no surprise, I guess. He's supposed to be almost magical."

A respectful silence fell over the gathering, until Suzanne deemed that it was time to get back to business.

The more interesting part about the news report on the radio was that apparently a similar change came in the midforties; that accounted for the divorces in that age group. Look at the Kelleys from Maya's class; look at George and Rebecca Nguyen, from Cecily's Irish dance studio. All those brains and personalities, morphing into something their partners never expected them to be. Was something like that going on with Gabe lately? Because he'd been distracted and edgy. Going for more runs, working longer. Was he going to come home one day and put down his work satchel and announce that it was all over, that they'd been growing apart for a while now and it was time someone called a spade a spade?

They'd have such a complicated arrangement to work out with the three girls; the thought of it made her feel absolutely exhausted. And who would move out?

Not Nora. She didn't want this divorce — she wasn't moving an inch. Plus she had just organized her closet the way she wanted it.

"Someone's phone is blowing up," said Robin Fox, coming in from the kitchen.

Or probably it was just the Harvard application. Really, it was so (weirdly) important to Gabe that Angela get in. Gabe, who didn't, truth be told, talk all that much about college, who didn't keep in close touch with any of his college friends, who never even went to a *reunion,* was one hundred percent fixated on Angela's application.

That must be what had him on edge. In fact Nora had heard him grilling Angela quite uncharacteristically harshly about her schoolwork and her application the other day: Was *this* thing done? Was *that* part in? What about the AP exams, when were they? Her alumnus interview, was it scheduled?

Nora had to say, "Whoa, easy, cowboy," to get him to stop.

"Blue Coach bag? Nora?"

There were three missed calls from Lawrence. Oh boy. Easy enough to slip out. Everybody was caught up in an animated discussion about the band they were going to hire — last year's had been dismal — and nobody really noticed her. Only the baby, Lucas, watched her, following her with his gigantic eyes that reminded her of Angela's. Moon eyes.

CHAPTER 22
CECILY

"This is called the power selector ring," said Cecily's father. "And this is the eyepiece lock ring. And *this*" — he fiddled with something that Cecily couldn't really see — "is the eyepiece lens. I can't believe I remember all this. It's all coming back to me, it's like riding a bike."

Actually, Cecily couldn't see very much at all of the parts of the telescope. There was only a quarter moon. They were on the roof of their house. "The beauty of a one-story," her father had said.

Cecily's father had held the ladder steady for her to climb up and then he had followed her while Cecily's mother held the ladder for him and said things like *Take it easy, Gabe!* and *Do not let her hurt herself, she has to compete soon* and *Are you sure this is a good idea?*

Cecily hadn't even known that her father owned a telescope; it was tucked inside the closet in the office in a special case with purple velvet lining, like something a wizard would bring along to work. But at dinner, when her mother asked her about how her moon chart was coming along, her father, who hadn't appeared to be listening to the conversation at all, said, "You want to see the moon? *I'll* show you the moon."

"I used to use this all the time on the ranch," he said now. "I guess I was a stargazer." He looked at her expectantly, and obligingly Cecily smiled, although she wasn't sure if this was a joke or not, and if it was she didn't get it.

Sometimes her father looked in the mirror and scrubbed his fingers through his hair and said, *Look what an old man I'm turning into.* He didn't look so old to her — Pinkie's father was bald and he looked older than Cecily's dad — but sometimes when she paused in front of the wedding picture of her parents that sat on one of the built-ins in the living room and saw what he'd looked like then, she could see what he was talking about. There was also a picture of him holding each of the girls when they were infants, his big strong hand palming their little baby heads. She loved those pictures. Now he was wearing a headlamp, which made him look like the pictures of underground gold miners in South Africa that Mrs. Whitney had shown them. Her father definitely had a dorky side.

"Okay, then," he said suddenly. "I think I've got it adjusted. It's not the Hubble," he said now. "But it's better than nothing."

Cecily didn't know what the Hubble was but didn't especially feel like getting into it.

Are you guys okay up there? Cecily?

"Fine, Mom," she called out, though in fact she was terrified of heights and even this distance up made her feel queasy and uncertain. She tried not to look down but instead looked across, over the roof of the Fletchers' house and to the yard beyond.

"Now," said her father. "First rule of looking through a telescope. Before you do it, you look at the object with your naked eye and you observe everything you can. What do you see?"

Cecily trained her eyes on the moon. "A waxing crescent," she reported. They'd learned that at school. "Twenty-nine percent." She'd looked that up online. She closed one eye, then opened it and closed the other eye. "I see the sliver that's lit but I also see the outline of the rest of it. A very light outline. The part that's lit is reflecting the light of the sun, and the part facing away from the sun is in darkness. It takes the moon 29.53 days to move around the earth."

"Very good," said her father approvingly. He cleared his throat in a way that let her know more and better information was coming. "Technically," he said, "it's more like twenty-seven days, but because the earth is continuing to move around the sun during each lunar phase, we observe it as twenty-nine days. If you were a star, for example, observing the phases of the moon, you would see a twenty-seven-day cycle. Okay?"

"Okay," said Cecily. How did parents know so much about so many different things? Her father was looking up at the sky, his hands folded behind him. He sighed deeply and happily and put his hand on top of Cecily's hair and messed it up a little. She didn't mind. Angela really minded when her hair got messed up; she spent a long time on it each morning. "Okay," she said in her mother's voice. "Whatever you say, boss."

Her father shook his head at this. "How can you do that, sound exactly like her?"

Cecily shrugged modestly. "I've been practicing with Pinkie. You should hear *her* do her mom."

"You could take that act on the road," her father said. "Now, when you're ready, put your eye to the telescope. And tell me what you see. I have it set at the right angle, so kneel or bend down or whatever works best for you, but don't touch anything."

The night air was cool and dry. Cecily shivered; she was wearing a thin fleece but had turned down the jacket her mother had offered.

She was prepared to overdo it for her father's benefit. (*Be extra nice,* her mother had whispered when her father was setting everything up. *I think he had a long day.*) Every day seemed like a long day for her father. She was ready to be the cheerful, appreciative kid her father was expecting. She was ready to pretend to be wowed.

She bent until her eye was level with the eyepiece and looked.

She didn't have to pretend at all. She was wowed for real. Up close, the moon was gray and looked like a giant rock. It was covered with pits that looked like you could put your finger right into them. In fact she found she was, embarrassingly, holding out one hand as though she could actually touch the pits. When she realized she was doing that she put her hand down.

She said, "Wow," but that word didn't seem like enough to convey the unnamed emotion she was feeling. It was astonishing, that something that looked so bright and simple from far away, something that sat in the sky night after night after night, looked like *this* up close. That they could just point a telescope (a telescope her father had owned since before she was born and had never mentioned) and see it, just like that, no big deal.

"With the Hubble they can see individual craters. They have specific names, you know. I think the largest is called Bailly."

There was that Hubble again.

"*See you on the dark side of the moon.* That's a line from an old Pink Floyd song. I used to listen to a lot of Pink Floyd."

Cecily sort of wished her father would

stop talking, though she would never hurt his feelings by saying that. She wanted to be alone with the moon.

"Makes you feel sort of insignificant, doesn't it?" he said.

"Yeah," she said. But in fact the opposite was true for Cecily. It made her feel huge and mighty. It made her feel like she wanted something big to happen. More than that: like she wanted to *make* something happen. Like she had a power in her she hadn't known she had. That wasn't it, exactly. But it was hard to explain. Maybe not a power, maybe more like a responsibility. It made her feel like she was the beating heart of the family, or maybe even the heart of something bigger.

Her father let her look for a while and then he cleared his throat again and said, "Had about enough? Your mother's going to send a search party up here."

Reluctantly she moved away from the telescope and allowed her father to use his headlamp to repack it in its velvet-lined case. Every part had its own spot in the case; even the tripod folded up small enough to fit in. It was very satisfying, watching it get packed up like that.

When he'd closed the case Cecily said, "Thanks, Daddy. That was —" she paused, then, for lack of anything better, said, "That was awesome."

"Thank *you,* Cecily. We should do this more often. I can't tell you how —"

His voice splintered off and he lifted his eyes to the sky and Cecily felt slightly embarrassed, the way she did when her aunt Marianne, talking once about one of her cases to Cecily's mother, had started crying. Still talking, but with tears slipping down her face and her makeup all smudged beneath her eyes. (Cecily hadn't known where to look.)

She shifted her gaze down to the ground and this time her stomach didn't drop. Wait until she told Pinkie about this, about looking at the moon through the telescope but also about the way she felt now. She felt like she could fly over the rooftop of the Fletchers' house, and maybe all the way up to the great gray rock itself. She wasn't afraid of heights after all.

She wasn't afraid of anything.

CHAPTER 23
NORA

Nora and Maya sat with a book: *Biscuit Visits the Big City.* Biscuit, the intrepid puppy, was attempting to navigate the

225

streets of Manhattan. Woof, Biscuit. Maya's nose was running slightly and her bangs were in her eyes. Nora smoothed them from her forehead. In twenty minutes, she had to start dinner. She glanced at her watch. Fifteen minutes would be better. Better still would be if she'd already started it.

"Try, sweetie," said Nora. "I just don't feel like you're trying."

She felt an off note in her voice. She tried to tamp it down — Angela could read the *Biscuit* books when she was three but you were *not supposed to compare your children,* every parent knew that. Too late: Maya heard it too and looked at Nora from underneath the hair with a look that said: betrayal.

"I *am* trying," said Maya. "I just can't do it."

Maternal betrayal, the worst kind. It wasn't Maya's fault she couldn't read. It was Nora's fault.

Maybe it would have been easier if they were elephants. Angela had once told Nora that in the elephant world, after a mother gives birth, a bunch of the other female elephants chip in on the work so the actual mother can focus on eating enough to nurse the baby. They were called *allmothers.* What a lovely concept.

"I just — honey, I just don't understand why you can't do it. You know your letters, and you know the sounds the letters make. We've been over the flash cards so many times, sweetie. I know you can do it."

But elephants were also pregnant for nearly two years. So no thank you to that. Nora adored infants but she loathed being pregnant. In fact she was suspicious of any pregnant woman who claimed to love it, because in Nora's mind it simply wasn't possible. She thought of what Maya had looked like as a baby, her face scrunched up like an elderly man's, her delicious legs kicking, and her heart softened. Imagine if someone had told her that one day she'd feel impatient if that little creature was a late reader. She would have said to that someone, "Don't be *ridiculous.* I am *not* going to be that kind of a mother."

"I want to," whispered Maya, swiping at her nose. "I really want to, but I can't."

Before you had kids everyone told you all the wonderful and tragic things your kids would do to you. They'll make googly eyes and you'll fall in love! Wonderful. They'll ruin your figure! Terrible. They'll light up when you walk into the room. Wonderful. When they become teenagers they'll smash up the car and say really rude things to you in public. Terrible.

But nobody talked about the things *you* could do to ruin *them.* That was the dirty little secret of parenting. You didn't find out about that until you became a parent, and by then, of course, there was no going back. All sales final.

When Maya was an infant Nora took her — just her — to visit Nora's parents and Marianne in Rhode Island. Nora's father wasn't up to the trip out to California. Angela was already in school, and they had a good after-school babysitter who could care for her until Gabe got home from work. The same sitter — an elementary school-teacher who hadn't found a job, *perfect* — was willing to work extra hours to care for Cecily too, because a two-year-old and a six-hour plane ride and a three-hour time change were a lethal mix. Maya didn't know her days from her nights anyway. They'd be gone from a Monday night through midday Friday. No big deal — in fact, a bit of a break for Nora, a chance to focus on just the new baby. It was October, Nora's favor-ite month in New England. She'd been working like a maniac, pulling together a sale in Tiburon. Arthur was calling her several times a day.

Nora's mother had said, *I think you're working too hard. Sweetheart, they're only young once.*

(To which Nora had answered, under her breath, *Thank goodness.*)

Gabe had said, *Things at Elpis are going really well, you don't need to do this.*

(To which Nora had answered, firmly, *Yes, I do.*) They didn't need her income then the way they did now with college tuition looming, maybe, but it had taken a while to get back into the market after her last break. She didn't want to lose her client base. She didn't want to disappoint Arthur. She didn't want to be one of those women who slipped out of the workforce when their children were young and then *forgot* how to do it and suddenly found themselves fiftysomething empty nesters turning an old play area into a craft room. Not Nora! No, sir. She didn't even know how to craft.

People said lots of things to her back then, but nobody ever said, *I'm afraid you're going to hurt the baby.*

On Tuesday they drove up to Boston and walked through the Common while Maya napped in the BabyBjörn. Pizza at Regina in the North End for lunch. That night, in the port-a-crib set up in Nora's old bedroom at her parents' house, Maya slept for six hours straight for the first time ever and then woke up and nursed like she'd been on a desert island for two weeks. Absolute heaven.

Marianne took Wednesday and Thursday off from work. On Wednesday they walked at Town Beach, which was deserted but because the day was warm retained a glorious, mournful, end-of-summer feel. The leaves on a few of the trees along Boston Neck Road were beginning to turn.

On Thursday, when her parents were off at a dentist appointment, Nora set Maya, freshly changed, freshly fed, on the bed while she engaged in an argument with her parents' dial-up modem to get an addendum to the contract over to the office in time for the start of the West Coast business day.

She left the room. Number one rule of parenting: Don't leave the baby lying unsupervised on a bed. Okay, maybe not the absolute number one rule, but it was right up there.

And Maya, who had never rolled before, thought that might be a good time to start. She rolled off the edge of the bed and hit the uncarpeted floor in the guest room. The worst noise Nora had ever heard in her life.

The fastest Nora had ever moved, running back into the room from the upstairs office to Marianne's old bedroom where the modem was.

Maya was out for five seconds, maybe ten, seconds that lasted a year each, during which Nora's only two thoughts as she held her were: I've killed the baby. And: Now, of course, I have to kill myself.

Then Maya opened her gummy little mouth and cried. Screamed bloody murder.

"Ambulance?" said Marianne, running up from the kitchen, but Nora said, "*God*, no, just drive us, please. Just drive us, faster that way."

Marianne drove, and Nora sat in the backseat. She'd had to buckle Maya, still screaming, into her infant seat, but she didn't wear a seat belt herself. She didn't deserve a seat belt! She didn't deserve anything. She leaned over Maya the whole time and whispered useless, inane things that nobody could hear over the screaming. There was a divot on the back of Maya's head that seemed big enough to fit an egg into, although in retrospect it probably wasn't. Nora thought a bump might have been easier to take — a divot was such a *subtraction*. Like something had actually been lost, left on the bedroom floor.

First a nurse triaged Maya. Then came a resident, who asked all the same questions that the nurse had asked, and then the attending physician, who did everything all over again. The doctor was older, maybe sixty, with thinning gray hair and deep lines around his mouth. His white coat was slightly rumpled.

Maya scored a 14 on the Pediatric Glasgow Coma Scale! It was almost the highest score you could get. Weirdly, Nora was proud of that, like somehow it boded well for the SATs. She sort of wanted to show the other mothers in the emergency room.

The doctor said, "How long did you say she lost consciousness for?"

Nora said, "Ten seconds, maybe fifteen. No, maybe five. I really don't know. I'm sorry. I'm so so sorry." Like he was going to give her absolution, not medical advice. Like he was a priest.

And Maya blinked at her, as if she were saying, Um, shouldn't you apologize to *me*?

"I don't see any cause for real concern. But we're going to observe her for the next few hours, just to be sure."

Observing sounded nice and gentle. Nora could handle that.

While they were waiting for Maya, Marianne asked, "Should I dial Gabe's number for you?"

And Nora, who had meant to say, "Yes, please," had simply said, "Not right now. I'll call him later."

And didn't. She never told him. Kept it to herself. Something like that, something so terrible, for which *she'd* been to blame, kept it all to herself. That was her secret: that was the one thing.

By the time they flew back to California the divot was no bigger than a walnut. Nothing that couldn't be covered with a hat. Babies always wore hats! Especially on planes, where the temperature was unpredictable. A couple of days later it was an almond, then a sesame seed, and then it was gone.

When Gabe picked them up at the airport he held Maya up in the air and said, "I missed you two!" and tickled Maya under her chin until she smiled. Then he kissed Nora on the forehead and said kindly, "You look exhausted. You didn't work too hard out there, did you? You better not have." Nora sucked in her breath and shook her head and felt like the worst person in the entire world.

Now, so many years later, Maya couldn't read, and it was all Nora's fault. Something had happened in her brain that day, the fall had loosened something that had never been put right, whatever that kindly ER doctor had said. How did they *really* know what went on inside such a tiny brain, when they couldn't see anything? They didn't know, but Nora knew. She had ruined her daughter, and she'd kept it to herself.

If she'd been an elephant, if they'd all been elephants, none of this ever would have happened.

Where were the allmothers when you really needed them?

Chapter 24
Angela

Ten milligrams.

Coach Don had to leave unexpectedly for a family emergency, so practice was canceled. He wanted them to do an easy five on their own if they were so inclined.

Angela was so inclined — she was very inclined, Angela was always inclined, and she wasn't going to do the five easy, either, she was going to hammer it — but she wanted to get some of her homework done first. Besides the regular load (*formidable*) and the Harvard application hanging over her (like a *specter*), she was trying to figure out what to do about the term paper for AP

English. Topics due in a week.

Angela was thinking about all of this as she walked home. If she'd been a high school kid in a movie walking home on a fall day there might have been brilliant foliage framing her and a carpet of fallen leaves she could nonchalantly kick through. That would have to be an East Coast movie, though. They didn't have that kind of *variegated* foliage in California. Much to Angela's mother's *chagrin.* She talked a lot about missing foliage in the fall where she grew up. This fall in particular.

Angela was about to step onto the bike path when a car pulled up alongside her, a midnight-blue BMW. She walked a little faster — it could be a rapist or a kidnapper, even in Marin, and Angela was fast but she wasn't very strong. Then she heard someone say, "Yo, Angela!" so she looked over and the car came to a complete stop. Which, in retrospect, wasn't that smart, because presumably rapists also knew how to say *yo.* Though they probably wouldn't know her name.

But it wasn't a rapist or a kidnapper: it was Edmond Lopez from school, and he was nodding and smiling and reaching over to open the passenger-side door and it looked like he was gesturing to Angela to get in.

Her brain said, *No, thank you,* but her mouth, surprisingly, said, *Sure. Why not?* And she got in the car, feeling more jittery and weird than she did when she thought about Maria's poems being published in those journals. ("Quinceañera," one of them had been called. Geez, how was the white child of two white parents supposed to compete with that? Angela didn't have anything to write a poem about. Her poem would be called something dull and ordinary, like "Making My Bed.")

Once Angela was in the car Edmond turned to her and said, "Want to come over?"

"To your house?" *Duh.* Edmond smiled. His teeth made him look like he'd just stepped out of a Crest Whitestrips ad. He was wearing a baseball cap and a dark blue shirt with the sleeves pushed up past his elbows, and she could see the muscles moving in his forearm when he turned the steering wheel.

"Sure. Yeah. Nobody's home." Edmond smiled lazily. (She could hear Ms. Simmons: *Think of a better way to say it. Can a* smile *really be* lazy? *Really?* Angela might fight that one. She thought a smile could be lazy.

Edmond's was. Lazy and beautiful.)

In the Lopezes' driveway she closed the car door carefully and slung her backpack over her shoulder. Or should she leave her backpack in the car? But that would make it seem like he was driving her home, and maybe he wasn't. If she ran home, she could get a couple of her miles in that way. But what about the backpack?

Oh my God, what was *wrong* with her?

She'd leave it in the car. No, bring it. She brought it even though she felt weird about it, like she was carrying a puppy into a church.

Edmond's house was a converted Craftsman, which Angela knew her mother would call "one in a million" or something else equally corny and *hyperbolic.* Still, it was a really nice house.

Angela left her backpack by the front door and followed Edmond into the kitchen. He offered her a beer from his parents' fridge, which she declined — beer made her feel bloated, never mind the fact that she had at least three hours of homework to do when she got home, plus the run — and then he opened one himself and tipped half of it into his mouth. It was called Super Chili Pepper Madness and on the front of the bottle was a chili pepper dressed in a superhero costume. Soon enough, Edmond tipped the other half into his mouth and said, "You sure you don't want some?"

"I'm sure," said Angela. Even if she liked beer she wouldn't have liked the spicy kind.

Did her father and Abby the Intern ever drink beer together? *Ugh.*

He did the same with the next beer, but he'd turned his head respectfully away from her when he burped. (She was starting to hope he *wasn't* driving her home.) After he was done with that one, he took off his hat and ran his hand through his hair until it looked adorably rumpled.

Edmond's parents were at work, he said; his sister, Teresa, who had gone to Princeton undergrad, was now at Cornell doing graduate work in sociology. Edmond was (his own words) on a different track. Just that one AP English class, which, according to Henrietta, was a fluke. Honors Lab Science, which he was failing. (Even though science was her worst subject, Angela considered it *almost impossible* to fail Honors Lab Science.)

"I don't care," he said. "As long as I can play baseball in the spring." He rumpled his hair again. His hair was very thick and dark and when he ran his hands through it they seemed to imprint themselves there.

"I can help you, if you want," she said. It was just Honors Lab Science; she could ace that class with her eyes closed. Not to be braggy. But. (Was this why he'd picked her up? To help with science? That was fine, she was just wondering.)

"You'd do that?" asked Edmond. One more time with the hands and the hair and Angela's stomach lurched. Sitting this close to Edmond, she was able to take in his scent, which wasn't exactly clean but wasn't dirty either. *Like the soil in a garden before anything has been planted in it.* No, she could do better. *Like the dark side of the moon.* (Ms. Simmons might say, "What does that mean, exactly?" And Angela wouldn't really know. But it felt just right. It was from some old song her dad occasionally sang.)

Seriously, what was wrong with her? She was sitting in an empty house with a baseball player and having an imaginary conversation with her AP English teacher. Lame alert.

She said, "Definitely, I'd do that," and stared at the mosaic backsplash that ran along the length of the kitchen (classy, her mother would say; it was all muted tans with a few hints of gold).

Edmond poured Angela a glass of water

while he drank his third beer and they sat for some minutes in the kitchen, both of them drinking, and Angela felt very briefly like an adult: she was not often in an otherwise unoccupied house with just one person her own age. And by not often she meant never.

"My sister, though," said Edmond, "man, she's smart. She's like you." He fixed his gaze on Angela and she noted that his eyes were darker than dark; the pupils and the irises were pretty much the same color. She hoped her skin was behaving itself, not blushing.

"Oh, I don't know about that," said Angela modestly. Teresa Lopez. Geez. "Your sister's, like, a legend. The teachers still talk about her. She's brilliant."

"Yeah," said Edmond. "I'm sort of lucky that way. My parents don't expect anything from me. But, boy, they did from her. Still do. She doesn't catch a break."

Angela considered this. She had never met Teresa, but in a way she felt like she knew her. She trained her eyes on the built-ins above the kitchen desk and saw a couple of family photos — the Lopezes vacationing in Hawaii, wearing snorkel masks and flippers; the Lopezes at Tahoe, holding ski poles. Edmond looked so much like Teresa that if

not for what she knew to be a five-year difference in their ages they could pass for
fraternal twins.

"So, Harvard, huh?" asked Edmond, as
though continuing a conversation they had
started earlier. He tapped his fingers against
the beer bottle. "How come?"

Angela took a long drink of her water, feeling self-conscious about the sound she
made when she swallowed, and then said,
"My dad went there." She still had to finish
the application. Her heart palpitated, thinking about that. Edmond scrunched up his
face and Angela *intuited* that this was an
unsatisfactory answer. Her breath got
caught in her throat. "I mean, that's not the
main reason. That's *one* reason, I should
say. That's the reason I was first interested.
But when I went there for my campus visit,
I don't know, I just felt really at home there.
You know?" What was hard to get across to
Edmond Lopez was the fact that when her
father had taken her out the previous year,
when they'd driven together along the
Charles River, when they'd followed the
student guide from building to building,
when they'd walked around Harvard Square
and shopped at the Coop and stood outside
the dorm her father had lived in his freshman year, everything about the world felt

right and good, as though Angela were a coin that had been dropped inside the exactly right slot. But she couldn't put that into words. Well, she *could,* but she didn't want to. Too embarrassing. Too pretentious.

Edmond blinked; he had enviable eyelashes, just like Cecily's. Angela's stomach did the weird twisting thing again. Edmond said, "You remind me a lot of my sister. How you're so smart and everything comes easy."

Angela cleared her throat. Okay, she liked Edmond, but a misconception was a misconception. "Oh my God, that's not true. It doesn't come easy, not at all."

Edmond seemed to take that in. Or not. Then he said, "How you're so *serious.*"

Angela felt a whisper of an insult at that. "I'm not always serious." She could be goofy — with her sisters, with her parents, with her friends. She could definitely be goofy. Silly. *Fatuous.*

"I don't mean that in a bad way. I mean it like you know what you want, you're not wasting time on stupid shit like a lot of people do. I like that."

"Oh," she said. Better. She did actually pride herself on not wasting time on stupid shit.

"Plus I think you're really pretty."

Oh!

"Yeah?"

Yeah.

She ducked her head and felt a blush creep to her cheeks. (Corny? Yes.) "Thanks."

"I'm serious about baseball. Come to a game in the spring, you'll see."

She smiled. "Maybe I will." She reached over and lifted Edmond's beer from the counter, took a sip. Just one sip. It was terrible. It burned going down. The actual chili pepper in the actual beer was much less friendly and accommodating than the super-hero chili on the label. She coughed and handed the bottle back.

"What are *you* doing next year?"

"Gap year," he said. "Somewhere in Colorado, to work at a ski resort."

The first time Angela had used the phrase *gap year,* her father, in a deeply uncool way, had thought that people were taking a year off to work at the Gap.

"Wow," she said. "That sounds awesome." Edmond Lopez thought Angela was pretty. That wasn't nothing. That was definitely something.

"Yeah." He stood. "Want to see my room?"

"Sure." She followed Edmond obediently down the hall. Some of the doors (office, bathroom) were open, but others (master

243

bedroom? sister's room? Edmond's room?)
were closed.

Edmond said, "This is where the magic
happens," and opened a door at the end of
the hallway. Angela tried to look like that
was cool with her, even though she was a
little embarrassed for Edmond, for having
said that. Then he said, "I'm totally kidding. I saw that in a movie once and always
wanted to say it." Then she felt better.

Angela said, "Ha," or at least tried to, but
it came out sounding like a noise an asth-
matic troll might make.

Edmond's room had the same turned-
over-earth smell that she'd noticed in the
kitchen. On the wall across from the bed
was a poster of a Giants player that read
JUAN MARICHAL across the bottom in bright
orange. In the corner of the room was a pile
of laundry, presumably dirty, and on the
plain brown wooden desk sat a baseball in a
clear glass case. On the nightstand was a
condom in a white wrapper. No, not one
condom, two.

Geez.

Did he keep those there all the time, like
it was so inconvenient to reach inside a
drawer? *In the heat of the moment.* Was this
his regular after-school activity when baseball wasn't in season, luring nerdy girls into

his room and having his way with them? Didn't his *mother* ever come into his room or a *cleaning lady* who might take a moment to tuck the condoms into a drawer? Should she be *nervous*? She patted the back pocket of her jeans to make sure she had her cell phone with her.

No wonder Edmond Lopez was failing Honors Lab Science. How the heck was he surviving AP English? Well, he probably wasn't surviving it.

Angela tried for a moment to be outraged/insulted/apprehensive but when she looked at Edmond she saw that he was shifting his weight from one foot to the other in a way that reminded her of Maya when she had to go to the bathroom, and she felt a spasm of tenderness for him. Also. He really was hot.

Edmond crabwalked over to the nightstand and performed a maneuver that caused the condoms to disappear into the nightstand drawer. He walked back toward Angela and said, "Sorry about that."

His voice was a little blurry, probably from the beers, and his face was very close to hers. His skin was beautiful, olive and extremely smooth-looking. She wondered what it felt like to touch it. She *wanted* to touch it. She wished she'd had one of those horrendous chili beers after all, for courage.

Edmond must look all kinds of great in a baseball uniform. She'd never been to one of the high school baseball games. She should go. She would go! By baseball season, she'd have gotten into Harvard. Or not. Oh, God, what if the answer was *not*? Not the time or the place for those thoughts, Angela, not at all.

She said, "No problem." *Nonchalantly,* as though it happened to her all the time, having to look discreetly away while a really hot baseball player hid his condoms.

"Want to sit down or something?" he said. "You can sit on the bed." She breathed in the garden smell. It was starting to grow on her. No pun intended. "Or, or. The floor, or wherever you want."

"Sure," said Angela. "But I just have to go to the bathroom first."

"Okay," said Edmond. "I'm going to stretch out for just a sec." He looked adorably sleepy. Angela, by contrast, was as alert as if she'd just popped an Adderall. She crept out of the room and toward the bathroom that she'd noticed before. The bathroom was very feminine, with fluffy pink towels and peach-colored soaps arranged in a semicircle on a square dish. She couldn't picture Edmond using this bathroom. Maybe he used a different one, something with lots of navy blue or dark plaid.

On the way back she paused in front of one of the closed doors, then took a chance and opened it. Teresa's room, obvi. The bed, a double, had a white quilt wrapped tightly around the mattress, and two oversized pillows in bright lavender. The surface of the white desk was empty, and there was a white bookshelf in which all manner of English novels were organized alphabetically. The bottom shelf was heavy on Woolf.

Angela meant only to observe, but next thing she knew she was entering the room, sitting for a moment at the desk, running her hands over its smooth white surface. Then she was opening the bottom drawer, where there were six or seven manila folders labeled in what must be Teresa's neat hand. AP History. AP Calculus. AP English. And so forth.

She opened the AP English folder; inside were five neatly typed term papers, dated, stapled, graded. Two copies of each. Leave it to Teresa to make copies of everything.

One of them: "The Use of Free Indirect Discourse in *Mrs. Dalloway* and *To the Lighthouse*."

Virginia Woolf.

Jackpot. It was too perfect. But *no.* Of

course not. She wouldn't. She wouldn't dare; she would never. She closed the folder and returned it to its place in the drawer.

Geez. *God.* She stood, pushed the chair in, made her way back to Edmond's room.

He was on his back, his arms flung out to either side as though he were trying to embrace something much bigger than he was. Sleeping! *Asleep.*

Good job, Angela. Way to knock him dead with your sexiness. She would never, ever, not in a million years, not even if someone offered her a trillion dollars to do it, tell Maria Ortiz that she had put Edmond Lopez to sleep. She wouldn't even tell Henrietta. She wouldn't tell anyone, not ever.

She walked over to the bed and considered Edmond. He was breathing deeply and evenly; he reminded Angela of the way Maya slept, with great abandon and innocence. She always envied Maya this. Angela tied herself up in the sheets from all of her thrashing around.

She reached out and touched him gently, a feather-light touch, on the cheek. Edmond's cheek felt as soft as it looked. It was like touching silk. Or lambskin. Not that she'd ever touched lambskin. Edmond didn't open his eyes, didn't even move.

She returned to Teresa's room and sat down again at the desk.

Was Angela really doing this?

She wasn't.

She was.

There were two copies of everything; nobody would miss one. "Just in case," she said out loud, although there was nobody there to hear her.

She opened the drawer.

CHAPTER 25
NORA

4:30 a.m.

M —

Today I went to a closing for Arthur. Closings always leave me a little melancholy, which is the opposite of how I should feel. But I can't help it. It's like seeing a fat, jolly baby who doesn't know what life has in store: you're happy for the baby, but you're also a little worried for when it finds out about all the crappy stuff that's coming.

Do you know that's why they use the sound of children laughing so much in horror movies? I learned that on NPR.

This was a good closing, full of positive vibes. A one-bedroom condo on Bush Street. A youngish pregnant couple was selling to a younger unmarried unpregnant couple. Everybody was happy: the buyers, the sellers, the escrow officers.

Once I had a closing where one of the sellers spent the whole time in the corner of the room, weeping into a potted plant.

So why did this one make me sad, when nobody else was crying?

I guess because I know things the other people involved don't know yet.

I know that in this new home they'll make love and fight and sometimes they'll hate each other and other times they'll love each other so completely that the thought of being apart for even an hour will be impossible to bear.

I know that in three years or five years this couple will be back, pregnant themselves, looking for a bigger place, bummed because to get what they want they'll have to move farther and farther out of the city until they're practically in Stockton.

I know that sometimes people buy a new home when what they really need is a new marriage or a new career or some deeper, more radical change that the real estate market can't solve.

What's that famous Confucius quote? Wherever you go, there you are.

Dinner with the Chens, old friends from long ago, when they all lived in the city. A reservation at the Slanted Door in the Ferry Building. In the olden days, they were neighbors in the same building in Noe Valley, at the beginning of gentrification. Now people called it Stroller Valley, but the Chens lived there still, sending their teenagers to private school, walking to their respective jobs.

Angela was eleven months older than the oldest Chen boy. Nora remembered putting Angela in the BabyBjörn and walking up Billy Goat Hill with Silvia on Saturday mornings.

The restaurant was lively, bustling, completely full, with a line. Waiters and waitresses zipped around the light wood tables, carrying bright drinks, gorgeous plates of grapefruit and jicama salad, chicken claypots, the signature cotton candy dessert.

While Nora admired the chicken claypots she engaged in a little bit of recreational worrying. There were so very many things to worry about. But mostly the Marin dwarf flax. She'd been sitting with the information for more than a month now and couldn't figure out what to do. She hadn't told Gabe about it. She hadn't told Arthur Sutton. After the Watkins fiasco, she couldn't afford another misstep.

"How's life on the upper end of the Marin real estate market?" Andrew asked Nora once they were all settled.

"Oh," said Nora. "Not bad. It's a slow time of year."

"You won't believe this one," said Gabe. "Gorgeous home in Belvedere — what was it, Nora? Seven something?"

"Eight point five," she whispered.

"Jesus *Christ,*" said Andrew, whistling softly.

"I mean, that was the asking price," said Nora, suddenly embarrassed, as though she herself had come up with the original number, as though she'd *sanctioned* it. She'd never thought it should be listed that high! "The accepted offer actually came in lower."

"Anyway," said Gabe, taking a generous sip of his rum punch. "So they're having the inspection, and the buyer notices something about the French doors, these little pits that you and I would never in a hundred thousand years notice, and they freaked out."

"Freaked right out," confirmed Nora. "Like nothing I've ever seen, and I've seen a lot of freak-outs."

"Wanted the whole row of doors replaced to the tune of — what was it, Nora? Fifty thousand?"

"Forty," she said. "Forty thousand dollars. And the sellers wouldn't budge an inch. So the deal fell through. Just like that. The buyers walked."

"Man oh man," said Andrew, and agreeably Silvia said, "Can you imagine."

"You should see this place, though," said Gabe. "What's it have, eight bathrooms?"

"Six," said Nora. "And a half."

"Close enough. And a view of the bridge like you wouldn't believe. Really incredible."

Small talk, large talk. Nora had caramelized Gulf shrimp. The Chen boys were on the tennis team at their private school. ("Tennis," said Andrew. "I'm the son of Chinese immigrants who never saw a racket in their lives, and my sons are wearing tennis whites. I don't know whether to be proud or ashamed.")

"So he confuses us all and vacillates," said Silvia fondly.

Some time later, when the Hawthornes

and the Chens were mauling the big swirl of cotton candy the waitress delivered, Nora looked up and noticed a young woman heading toward their table. A *tall* young woman. Strange, but it almost looked as though she was heading for Gabe. No, that couldn't be right. She had a fierce, moving-in-for-the-kill look on her face. She wore glasses and had hair that was cut neatly at her chin. Long ago Angela had had that haircut. Nora adored that haircut on little girls.

She was! She was heading for Gabe. Nora watched Gabe notice the young woman, and she watched a look of panic cross Gabe's face. That was odd, wasn't it? Why did Gabe look so panicked?

The young woman said, *"Gabe?"*

Gabe turned his head toward her and coughed into his napkin. He spent a while on the cough and when he was finished he lifted his head and smiled at the woman and said, "Abby! What a pleasure." He then turned to his dinner companions, gestured toward the young woman, and said, "This is Abby Freeman."

Introductions, smiles, handshakes. Abby Freeman's handshake, Nora noted, was suitably firm. Almost too firm. Andrew rose halfway out of his seat when he was introduced, which Nora thought was very gentlemanly of him.

"I work with Gabe," said Abby. And she smiled. (Perfect teeth. A little mousy in the features, with the smallish eyes. But perfect teeth.) And Nora couldn't help being a little envious of the height. She'd always wanted to be tall.

"She's an intern," said Gabe. There was a dram of color on each of his cheeks that Nora didn't think had been there a few minutes ago. That was definitely odd; her husband wasn't a blusher.

Nora looked at her husband as if he were someone she'd never seen before. Was he having an *affair*?

No.

It was out of the question. It was ludicrous!

Was it? He was still very good-looking. No gray in his hair (unfair) and good skin. Maybe slightly sun-damaged from all of the years on the ranch, but that was perfectly acceptable if you were a man. He ran three times a week (although, admittedly, more lately . . .) and lifted weights in the gym at Elpis on opposite days. He had great triceps, and better-than-average abs.

"Just until December," said Abby.

Aside from the idle wondering in which

every married woman engaged from time to time, Nora had never suspected Gabe of an affair, or anyway not an *actual* affair with an *actual* person. Their sex life was okay, right? Even great, sometimes. Maybe it didn't happen as often as it did when they first met, but really, did it for anyone who had been married for such a long time? Blanca Barnett on the Spring Fling committee claimed five times a week with *her* husband but honestly nobody believed her.

"Abby's father owns a winery in Sonoma," said Gabe. Was he sweating?

It wasn't a real possibility, an affair. Until now. Abby wore perfectly fitted jeans and a chunky bracelet. No earrings, no makeup. Much easier to pull off that look in your twenties than in your forties. Also, when you were tall.

"Oh, he's just a part owner," said Abby, waving one thin arm as if to indicate that anyone with half a brain could partially own a winery. The chunky bracelet slid up and back down again.

Nora found that she was nearly bursting with horror but that an exactly equal part of her was filled with a definite exhilaration — the kind that's brought on by the possibility of something truly dramatic happening. Right here at the Slanted Door, in front of half of San Francisco. She shivered. A scene!

"December?" Nora said. "Then your internship ends?"

What would Nora do, once this affair was confirmed? Would they get a divorce? Would she get the house? What about the kids? She definitely wanted the kids. Especially Cecily. No, you weren't allowed to think things like that. You weren't allowed to pick just one. She wanted all the kids, of course.

"I'm hoping to get a full-time job at El-pis," said Abby Freeman.

Gabe was definitely sweating. Nora passed her napkin to him under the table, but he ignored it.

"Good for you!" said Nora brightly. If this young thing thought she was going to climb the Elpis ladder by sleeping with her husband she had another think coming. Under the table, she grasped Gabe's hand.

"Well," said Gabe. "It was nice to see you, Abby. See you at work on Monday."

"That's right," said Abby. "See you Monday."

Nora kept her eyes on Abby's face as she departed. There was no long, lingering look that passed between her and Gabe. No secret code. No tiny folded note that said *Meet me for sex in the ladies' room at the end*

257

of the Ferry Building.

"She was . . . a little bit odd," said Nora. "Right?" She looked to Silvia for confirmation. "Gabe? What was that all about? You're turning pink. You never turn pink."

"Nothing," he said. "Just that I hate mixing work with social occasions."

"Ohhhhh. Bizzvara," said Nora. "Is that it?"

Silvia looked confused. "What kind of a name is Bizzvara?"

"High-tech," said Nora. "They've run out of real words to use, so now they just make them up."

"Well," said Gabe. "Not exactly."

"Isn't that right, though? That's what you told me."

"I guess so. Sure, sort of. Anyway, this is a company that used to be in the e-commerce space but is now moving sort of radically into managed services and they're looking for a consulting company to —"

"That's okay," said Nora. "You lost us at managed services. We don't need to go into the whole thing." She smiled at Silvia, smiled at Andrew, and said, "Bizzvara is a nutcase client."

That's all that was going on here; the intern reminded Gabe of Bizzvara, and the last thing he wanted to do at the Slanted

Door, where the line for a table was now well out the door, was think about Bizzvara.

She and Gabe had had sex two nights ago, and it had been lovely. Well, sort of lovely. Maybe Nora had been a little rushed and distracted. Maybe the dwarf flax had appeared in her mind during an *inconvenient* moment. Maybe she had sneaked a glance at the clock on her nightstand to calculate how much sleep she could get if they finished up on the sooner side. But still! If he was having an affair with a twentysomething, surely he wouldn't have bothered with her forty-four-year-old body.

Right?

And the Catalan Farm spicy broccoli at the Slanted Door *did* live up to its name. And Gabe had eaten a lot of it. Surely that accounted for the sweating.

Right?

Divorce, splitting up the kids. Ugh.

Nora would get custody, of course, but they would go to Gabe once a month. One complication with that would be that she would move back to Rhode Island in a heartbeat, to be closer to her mother and to her sister, and then they'd have to fly the kids back and forth. Very expensive.

But it was unthinkable, the whole thing. That young woman wasn't Gabe's type at

259

all, not at all. He would never go for someone with such small, scary eyes.

Would he?

"Shall we get another cotton candy?"
asked Silvia.

"And more drinks!" said Nora. She felt
light-headed.

"Gabe?" she said later, when they were in
bed. "Is there something you're not telling
me?"

A deep and abiding silence. Maybe he was
asleep . . .

"Gabe?"

The sheets shifted. Awake.

"Did you hear me?"

"I heard you."

"Well, is there?" She steeled herself.

"I *hate* Abby Freeman."

"You what?" They had always taught the
girls not to use the word *hate* when they
were young. They were supposed to say, *I
don't care for asparagus* or *Spelling is not my
favorite subject.*

"I'm sorry. I just — I sort of do."

Quickly Nora cataloged five things she
loved about her husband. Just in case this
was the end. (Could this be the end?) He
made a fabulous apple pie. He looked good
in a gray T-shirt. He was an honest-to-God

cowboy. When his mother was alive he never forgot to call her on her birthday. He gave a good foot massage. He was funny!

That was more than five — and she could keep going. See? They were fine. She could name fifty.

In a tiny voice, the tiniest of all voices, she asked the Question. "Do you hate her because you tried to have an affair with her and she rejected you?"

"*What?* Nora, no. Of course not."

(Did she believe him? There were times when Gabe hadn't been one hundred percent honest. He and his brother Michael no longer spoke, all because of what had happened with Michael's high school girlfriend. That was pretty dishonest.

But that was a long time ago. And the girlfriend had seduced Gabe. Was Gabe really to be blamed for that? She bet he was extremely seducible, back in the day. Ranch boys were, Nora guessed. All that fresh air and manual labor resulted in voracious appetites, sexual and otherwise.)

When Cecily's goldfish had died two years ago Gabe had taken the morning off from work and brought the *carcass* to the pet store to pick out an *exact match* before Cecily got home from school.

Nora wouldn't have done that. It wouldn't

261

even have occurred to her.

She waited a beat. "Vice versa?"

"No. Trust me, that's the furthest thing from her mind. And my mind."

Nora stared at the moon glancing in through the skylight. You *always* recouped your investment when you added skylights to a home.

"Then why do you hate her?"

"It's like I said at the restaurant. She's very intense, work-wise. She always wants to talk about Bizzvara. Constantly asking for career advice. You know how that generation is, *me me me.* Makes me crazy. It really, truly, makes me crazy. Like they want to rule the world, but they don't want to put the necessary work in to learn *how* to rule it. They just want things handed to them. She just — she represents something that I really despise."

Nora settled her head against her pillow. "That's it?" she asked. "Really and truly, that's why you hate her?"

"That's it. I swear. Scout's honor."

She thought of Gabe in a scouting uniform. "Were you really a scout? I can never remember."

"I was."

"There are still so many things I don't know about you. Or that I forgot. How is

262

that possible? We've been married for ten lifetimes."

"Right. I know. At least ten, maybe more."

"More."

CHAPTER 26
NORA

2:15 a.m.

Dear M —

I keep dreaming about Rhode Island. I dream about the beach, of course. That's an obvious one. But I also dream about other things, like the lady who used to work at the drive-through at the bank. Remember her? Her two front teeth crossed over each other, you and I were fascinated by that. If she lived in Marin she would have gotten braces in kindergarten. She always gave us lollipops. I remember it like it was yesterday, sitting in the backseat of the station wagon. Summer, humid, no air-conditioning, the backs of our thighs sticking to the black vinyl car seat.

Such an ordinary memory, I wonder why I'm dreaming about it.

Isn't it funny? All these years out here, and suddenly all I can think about is going home. Simpler times, I guess that's what I'm longing for.

I peeled back the layers to reveal the truth that I haven't been admitting to anyone. Do you care to hear it, Marianne, honorary therapist?

I want to go home. Not for a visit, but for good.

When Nora and Marianne were young they used to play a game called One Genie, Three Wishes. They played lots of games! How was it that they had so much time for games? They were smart girls, they were productive members of the childhood community in Narragansett. Nora had been an avid Girl Scout, from Daisies all the way to whatever they called it when you were so old there was something faintly humiliating about it. (There was an "adult" category at many of Cecily's *feises,* and Nora felt a definite twang of embarrassment when she passed by the rooms where these women were competing. They looked like a bunch of librarians who had gotten drunk at the holiday party and had taken to the dance floor. No offense to librarians! But. Some things were better left to the young.)

For six years running Nora had sold more cookies than anyone in her troop, and one year she sold more than any scout in her region.

Marianne, for her part, had been a phenomenal soccer player, and this was back in the days before all girls played soccer as a rite of passage.

So. Three wishes, the genie says to you. Because despite the soccer, despite the scouting and the tooling around the neighborhood on their three-speeds, and the catching of lightning bugs during endless summer evenings, and the Monopoly that went on for hours or days during blizzards, and Boggle and Scrabble and Clue when they tired of Monopoly, Nora and Marianne still had time for this game.

Just one wish, Genie, thought Nora now. Just one. You can keep the other two, I don't even need them. And my wish is this! I would like to take each of my children at a particular age (of my choosing, Genie) and I would like to put them in a glass jar, like a mason jar. (The logistics I'll leave up to you.) And I would like to be able to take them out and play with them and listen to them and *enjoy* them the way they were before the world got its teeth into them. If their older selves, their current selves, could spend a minute talking to the smaller versions that would be really cool but it's not totally mandatory.

What's that, Genie? What ages? That's easy. I hardly have to think about that. Angela, age three, because she had this adorable lisp and she called strawberries *strawbabies* and because she went through a phase where she said, "Goodbye! I love you!" to anyone, *anyone,* like the clerk at the gas station or patients waiting to be called in to see the dentist. For Cecily I would pick five, kindergarten, because she wore her hair in two braids with ribbons at the ends and she had this great big belly laugh that a lot of kids have outgrown by that age but that she hadn't. People have turned around in the grocery store when they've heard that laugh, and I am not kidding, Genie, when I tell you that every single person who hears that laugh laughs too. You can't *not* laugh back at it. It is quite literally not possible.

Maya: age four. She took gymnastics and she thought the balance beam was called a balance *bean.* I never corrected her because I didn't want her to stop saying it. It killed me every time.

Is that a strange wish, Genie? Keeping my kids in mason jars? You would know, I guess, you live in a bottle. But don't judge me for it. Don't judge me for wanting to take the very best of them and keep it locked up where nobody else can get to it. You're not a mother, are you, Genie? Your sexuality seems kind of amorphous to me, so I'm guessing not. And if you're not a mother, you don't know. So don't judge.

Nora had many productive, useful things she could be doing with her morning — she wasn't due into the office until noon, because she had to work into the evening. She had one showing for the Watkins house (she could tell already that the buyers weren't solid, but at this point she had to chase every possible lead) plus a pile of paperwork that wouldn't be ready until later that afternoon. She'd planned to take the morning to catch up on a bunch of things around the house and maybe even exercise; optimistically, she'd put on yoga pants and an embarrassingly underused lululemon top the girls had given her for Christmas the previous year. There was a pile of Maya's clothes she wanted to go through for donation pickup, and three calls she was supposed to make about Spring Fling donations. Dry cleaning to drop off for Gabe. And for once in her life she wanted to get the family Christmas card made up in November so she could put it in the mail in early December. So far she had accomplished none of these things.

One problem: her laptop was at work, and that's where she stored her pictures. Then she remembered that they'd taken some gorgeous photos on their summer vacation in Alaska with Angela's iPhone; those might be on Angela's computer right now, having been uploaded through the mysterious "cloud," whose workings Nora still did not quite understand. ("It's in the cloud!" people said so happily, so casually, like that just explained everything. It put Nora's teeth on edge.) Anyway, it was worth a shot. She tiptoed into Angela's room, as if she were trespassing. But she wasn't *trespassing,* she was very innocently looking for family vacation photographs for the family Christmas card. In a house on which she paid a good part of the mortgage. (Depending on the real estate market in a given year.) She was allowed. And besides being allowed, she was, parentally speaking, entitled. They had a rule that Nora and Gabe were allowed to look at any messages or social media posts that Angela put out or received. Truly, Nora forgot to do that most of the time, and anytime she did remember she discovered such inane chatter that she didn't have the stomach for it, all the silly abbreviations and emoticons, all the non-sense.

Of course, everybody was silly as a teen-ager, everybody did things that would make their parents blush if they knew about them. Nora certainly had! The difference was that now it was so terrifyingly *public* — anybody could witness your shame or humiliation or insecurities. It was there for anyone with a data plan to see.

Nora had mostly instituted the rule be-cause she'd learned about it a few years before at a "parents and technology" semi-nar when Angela was in middle school. Because, really, it was *Angela*! She didn't even have time to be up to no good. She barely had time to be up to good.

Nora tapped a button on the keyboard to bring the screen to life and thought about how nice it would be to cross the Christmas card off her to-do list. Wouldn't that be a coup! She'd shock everyone who'd ever known her. She imagined Marianne's face when she reached into her mailbox.

Angela had her iMessages open on her computer. Could Nora have closed the iMessage screen? Sure, she could have. But she didn't. As she watched, a group mes-sage popped up, four unfamiliar numbers with local area codes.

Anyone know where Addy is?

And then a reply from another number, *nope.*

Nora stared at the screen and wondered who Addy was. Maybe it was a nickname, short for Adeline or Addison or Adelaide, a nice, solid, old-fashioned name for a nice, solid, old-fashioned girl, someone who might wear a maxi skirt to school. But Nora had never heard of Addy.

Well, of course she hadn't heard of everyone! There were scores of students at the high school, and really Nora knew only a fraction of them, whereas she knew all the kids in Maya's and Cecily's classes.

So that was that.

She was moving the cursor toward Angela's iPhoto library when another message popped up, this one from Angela herself, texting from her phone: *no I wish,* and then the original questioner texted, *2 bad* and then Angela texted, *IKR*?

Nora wanted to reach through the computer and tell Angela, *Stop texting at school.* She wanted to tell her, *You're too smart to say* "yeah" *and* "I know, right?" She wanted to hit reply and ask who Addy was. She wanted to scroll through every other message on Angela's account and see what she was missing out on. She had the right, of course. It was part of the agreement as long as Gabe and Nora paid the cell phone bills. But she didn't *really* want to. Because she was getting a funny sensation in her belly, a Viper-roller-coaster-at-Six-Flags feeling. (The last time Cecily had coaxed her on the Viper Nora had thrown up semi-discreetly in a garbage can just past the exit.) She felt sort of like a voyeur, sure, but, a thousand times worse, she also felt like a stranger. Someone who didn't know her own child.

Of course, she *knew* her daughter.

She knew lots about Angela. She knew that when she was a child she liked applesauce with cinnamon in it and toast with a great deal of butter on it. She knew that the only subject at which she did not naturally excel was science. She knew that she liked light blue but not navy, red jelly beans but not black, spinach but not kale, Katy Perry but not Pink. She knew that until she was seven she liked to sleep with her door open and her closet light on. She knew that she was a cautious driver and a prolific texter and better at the butterfly than the backstroke. She knew that she sometimes forgot to put her running clothes in the hamper but never forgot a friend's birthday.

See?

There was a time when Nora knew *every-*

thing about her daughter. Everything. But now she knew so little.

And here it was, nearly eleven, her exercise clothes were still pristine, she hadn't done a damn thing about the Christmas card.

CHAPTER 27
GABE

It was called the Common Application, but to Gabe there was nothing common about it. Of course he'd known forever that this day was coming, but he couldn't quite believe that it had actually arrived.

His progeny. His eyes felt moist and he had to blink and look away before another family member noticed and perhaps made fun.

It was all just very, very remarkable, that was all. That they had arrived at this point.

Angela's laptop was open on the kitchen desk and Angela sat in front of it, squinting at the screen. Her posture was perfect. Deadly, even. Her posture said, *Let's do this thing.* Gabe couldn't believe nobody else in the family was similarly in awe of the moment. Cecily and Maya were already in their pajamas and in fact Maya's bedtime had come and gone, unnoticed. They were all hyped up because Halloween was only two days away.

Gabe thought about pouring himself a bourbon, to celebrate this moment, this night, the submitting of Angela's Harvard application.

Also, there was one other thing. He was nervous.

Well, why not? He poured two fingers, then three. Why the hell not. Big day.

Abby Freeman's face appeared briefly in his mind's eye and he made every effort to ablate it. *Pop.* There it went, into oblivion.

"I can't believe this is happening," he said, to nobody in particular. Cecily and Maya had repaired to the living room to sneak in a show on the Disney Channel, and Nora was loading the dishwasher with the dinner dishes.

Angela took a deep breath and let it out slowly, the way she did before the start of a cross-country race. Her hands, poised over the keyboard, were shaking. (Maybe *she* needed the bourbon?)

"Can you just check it all over for me one time?" asked Angela.

"Absolutely!" said Nora, but Angela twisted her shoulders and whispered, "Sorry, Mom, I meant Dad."

"Right," said Nora. "Of course you did. I knew that." She clattered some dishes in the sink to indicate that she wasn't of-fended.

"Dad?" said Angela. She turned her face toward him and all he could think about was the way she'd first looked at him from the confines of the hospital blanket on the night she was born, after her first feeding, when the world was calm and her belly was full and she was just getting used to this thing called life.

"I thought you'd never ask," he said. (In fact, he had been terrified that she wouldn't.) "I'm just going to — Do you mind if I take it into my office, so I can concentrate?"

"Nope," said Angela, and she handed over the computer carefully, the way you'd pass off an infant.

Gabe had cruised the College Confidential message boards, and he knew how very, very many people were out there, about to press *Submit* on this same application. He hoped Angela never cruised the College Confidential message boards; they were a minefield of ultracompetitive students, with a bunch of low-grade procrastinators mixed in. These poor kids wondered if they should disclose their mental illnesses in their essays (definitely not, was the consensus); they wondered how to get by on four hours of sleep while playing high school football; they wondered how competitive the White House internship program was and what would happen if they decided to drop an AP class senior year. They gave Gabe a serious case of agita.

When Gabe returned from the office he handed the computer back to Angela. He half expected that things would be different, that the universe would have somehow reordered itself in his absence. But all was just as he'd left it: the canned laughter from the television, Angela sitting at the kitchen desk. The only change was that the dishwasher was now beginning its cycle, issuing semicontented noises.

"Go ahead," he said. "Submit it. Knock 'em dead."

Angela took another deep breath and pressed some things on the computer. Then she said, "Okay. That's it. It's done. It's in."

"It's in!" cried Nora. "What should we do, to celebrate? Champagne?"

"We can't drink champagne," said Cecily, from the living room. "We're kids."

"A sip isn't going to kill anyone," said Nora. "And I meant Angela, actually, not you and Maya."

"No — no," said Angela. "I don't want champagne. I just want —"

"What?" said Gabe, way, way too eagerly. "Anything you say."

"I just want to go to bed," said Angela. Her shoulders slumped forward, and Gabe drank the rest of the bourbon down straight.

CHAPTER 28
NORA

November

Nora carried Cecily's dress bag, and Cecily carried the bag with her shoes (light and heavy), her socks, her makeup, snacks (carbs and fats), water (bubbly and still), a variety of bobby pins (long, short, medium), and her iPod Touch, on which she had loaded her solo music for last-minute practices, as well as some Taylor Swift for inspiration and Shakira for energy and good vibes.

In the car Cecily put in her earbuds and stared out the window. It was a long drive, all the way to Sacramento. Gabe and Maya had gone to Angela's meet instead and then they had to hustle over to Maya's soccer game. At one point Nora turned around and said, "What's up, sweetie? You don't seem like your usual peppy self."

Cecily shrugged. "Just nervous, I guess."

"You're never nervous," said Nora.

"I know. But this time I am." Cecily could

usually dance her heart out no matter if she was in the studio practicing or in front of the harshest judges in the world. That's what made her so good.

By now Nora had been to enough *feises* ("Pronounced *fesh*," a helpful, more experienced mother from the Seamus O'Malley School of Irish Dance had explained to Nora five years ago when Nora, seeking to har ness some of Cecily's astonishing energy, and to make contact with her own latent Celtic roots, had first stepped foot inside the studio) that they no longer overwhelmed her in the same way that they once had. Still, there was something unsettling about the scene: the girls with the ringlets of their wigs bouncing, the sparkles on their solo dresses catching the light (Cecily's, handmade by someone always referred to reverently just as "Gareth," no last name, too famous for that, like Madonna or Cher or Prince, had cost $2,300, *significantly* more than Nora's wedding dress). The youngest girls in plain navy or black jumpers, like Catholic school girls set free for recess.

And so much makeup everywhere: on the girls themselves, on the mothers, and also on the younger set of female adjudicators, who were themselves recently retired from such competitions and who dressed, for reasons Nora had never been able to fathom, like they were going out to a secret Manhattan nightclub. They wore dresses or skirts that went no more than halfway down their thighs, and heels higher than Nora had ever dared to wear in any circumstance. They had a proliferation of long hair, as though their tresses, so recently liberated from the confines of the competition wigs, were celebrating their hard-earned freedom by showing the world what they could do.

And the mothers! If you looked closely at each one you might see some variation among them but they were, as a whole, a downtrodden lot, following behind their daughters like handmaidens behind a queen, scooping up items that had dropped, dispensing tissues and sock glue (this, a whole separate phenomenon, actually *gluing* your clothing to your *body*), and holding hand mirrors, their vices clearly on display, whether they be diet soda or nail biting or constant smartphone checking. Nora's was a Starbucks concoction, a venti salted caramel moccachino with an extra shot, which rang in at more than five dollars. (Worth it.)

There were dozens of teams in Cecily's age group, and Cecily's was third to last, but Nora didn't mind a bit. She loved watching ceili dancing. She found herself a good seat with Molly Flanagan, the only Seamus O'Malley mother who did not entirely stress her out.

Nora loved the ceili dancing even more than the solo dancing. She loved watching the girls synchronize their steps. She loved the way the dances were the same no matter where you saw them, step for step, beat for beat. She loved that the dances were, at heart, social numbers, their roots firmly set in the Old Country.

Cecily's team was performing the High Cauled Cap. Nora had seen this dance so many times she thought she could perform it herself. Eight girls, four dancing the ladies' part and four dancing the gentlemen's part. The steps themselves were not difficult, compared to some of the things these girls did in their solo dancing, but it was the precision that counted: Were the arms all raised at the same level? Were the stationary dancers pointing their toes at the same angle? When all eight dancers stamped and clapped, were they stamping and clapping at the exact same time? To earn a spot at Worlds (in London, next year! Nora already had two restaurants picked out, and she had secretly booked a hotel room.

Totally refundable, of course), not only did Cecily's team have to get recalled into the second round, they had to place in the top ten once they did.

Which shouldn't be a problem. This particular team had been dancing this particular dance for two full years. They were like sets of identical twins who knew each other so well they could complete the other's sentences. They had it *down.*

Finally: Cecily's turn. Nora took a big sip of her salted caramel moccachino. She forgot about how many calories and grams of fat and sugar were lurking in each sip. She forgot about Angela's Harvard application, wending its way through the admissions process. She forgot about the French doors in the Watkins home and the fact that Maya couldn't read. None of that mattered. *This* was what mattered. This was what it was all about, all the lessons, all the driving, the washing of the practice clothes, the doing of the hair (those wigs didn't put themselves on; nobody but an Irish dancer and her mother knew what really went on under there, the tributaries of small ponytails, the stacks and crisscrosses of bobby pins). It all led to this. The pleasure in the action itself, the joy in the doing.

But something wasn't right.

Cecily's team was off.

Their timing was scattered. A toe pointing a fraction of a second too soon, one girl's arm lifted too high. Not by much, but still. Not perfect. Not top-ten perfect.

And then. On the most basic of steps, a simple side step, one leg became tangled in another. The dancer stumbled, tried to recover, though truly there was no recovery from a stumble. And then she was down.

Nora gasped. Molly Flanagan grabbed Nora's hand and squeezed. The audience inhaled collectively and loudly.

Cecily.

CHAPTER 29
ANGELA

A knock on the door. Cecily. Her mother had said they must all be extra-nice to Cecily, after what had happened at the *feis*. In fact, said her mother, if Cecily doesn't bring it up we shouldn't bring it up either. Pretend you don't even know about it. Talk to her about something different, like . . . oh, I don't know. Movies.

Movies? Cecily never went to the movies. She was always at dance practice, or hanging out with Pinkie, looking at the screen on Pinkie's iPhone.

282

Earlier that day her father had taken Pinkie and Cecily and Maya and Maya's friend Penelope out for ice cream, to Lappert's in Sausalito, *ostensibly* to cheer Cecily up. She had gotten her favorite, guava cheesecake. Pinkie had probably gotten *her* usual: rum raisin. Maya got vanilla bean no matter where she was, or just plain vanilla if there was no bean available. So boring. Angela didn't know Penelope well enough to predict. And Angela's dad would have gotten one of the coffee flavors, probably the Kauai. Angela's mother had an open house and Angela herself had declined the invitation. She had masses of homework. Now she was upset with herself: she loved Lappert's.

But the rough draft for the AP English term paper was due the following day, and Angela had. Not. Even. Begun. Even after nearly an entire day spent in her bedroom, contemplating Virginia Woolf, she had. Not. Begun. What was going *on* with her? She never struggled with papers like this; she was *never* behind. She never just plain didn't start.

The knock repeated.

"Come in!"

"Hey," said Cecily. She was wearing flannel pajamas, not dance clothes. Seeing

Cecily out of her dance clothes was like seeing a dog without its fur. She simply didn't look right. The pajamas made her look young and Christmas-morning innocent. They had pictures of smiling snowmen marching across the top. Cecily loved Christmas. I mean, duh, most kids loved Christmas. But Cecily really, *really* loved Christmas.

Angela said, "Hey." The cheating would be easy, she'd determined that much. Like taking candy from a baby. Which, when you thought about it, was an odd expression, because babies were not supposed to have candy. She knew that from all of her babysitting at the Fletchers' house, back when the children were young. Also just from general common sense, of which she had plenty. Babies and candy equals no.

She used to have plenty of common sense, but then again she used to be someone who would begin a term paper with enough time to complete the assignment properly. She used to be someone who would not steal a paper from a girl's bedroom while an extra-hot baseball player snoozed in the room next door.

"We're not going to Worlds, Angela. The ceili team." Cecily slumped against the wall. Angela motioned toward the bed but Cecily shook her head and remained standing. "I know Mom already told you and you're pretending not to know."

"I'm not pretending not to know," said Angela. "I'm just . . ."

"Just what?"

"Just not bringing it up."

"Well, it's up," said Cecily. "It's all kinds of up."

"I'm sorry, Cecily. I really am." Angela *was* sorry. While she had never quite understood the appeal of Irish dance (it freaked her out that they didn't move their arms, and that they didn't smile), she knew how important it was to Cecily. And she didn't like seeing Cecily in this state, *downtrodden* and *forlorn.* Cecily was uniformly happy and easygoing. That was her role in the family unit. The way Angela understood it from the psychology class she'd taken junior year, the middle child, especially the middle child of siblings of the same gender, could be either the dissenter, sowing drama and conflict wherever she went, or the stabilizing force. The peacemaker. Cecily was definitely the peacemaker.

Setting Cecily aside for a moment, Angela's mind clicked on along its own invisible, inevitable track.

There were two kinds of cheating. There

was the unsophisticated sort of cheating, the kind engaged in by students in standard or maybe even Honors classes. Internet cheating, the classic Google-and-copy. You found something somebody else had written on the topic. Maybe you massaged the sentences a little bit, maybe you altered the paragraphs. But mostly you just copied. Simple to perform, simple to catch. Not that everybody who did it got caught, but. Most teachers, when handed a paper of surprising quality or sophistication, plugged a few sentences into a search engine and summoned the guilty party for a confession.

Junior varsity cheating, cheating for beginners. It happened all the time.

"Because I fell. That's why we're not going. We didn't even recall." Cecily looked into the mirror and rearranged her hair. Cecily typically wore her hair in a ponytail but now it was down; that, too, accounted for her not looking quite like herself.

"You look pretty with your hair down, Cec," said Angela. "You should wear it that way more often." Virginia Woolf famously thought herself ugly but when Angela looked at the best-known picture of her she saw a great beauty. The solemn, hooded eyes, the long straight nose.

"Thanks," said Cecily dully.

And then there was Angela-Hawthorne-style cheating, an altogether more sophisticated method, a multistep process requiring forethought and planning.

She had never done it before; like the Adderall, she'd never needed to.

But she simply could not bring herself to write this paper. She'd spent so much of October on her Harvard application that she just didn't have time to do it the right way; she didn't have time to read two works, to read the criticism, to create an original thesis, to write the thesis. The application had been electronic, but she felt like she'd boxed up her heart in a Priority package and shipped it along to Cambridge at the same time. She didn't know if or when she'd get the heart back.

The paper Angela had taken from Teresa's room was sophisticated, sure, but once she'd read it through it seemed perfectly reasonable that Angela might have come up with it. She was valedictorian, after all. She could recognize indirect discourse when she saw it.

"Seamus O'Malley's teams *always* recall," said Cecily mournfully. "This is the first time in, like, forever that they haven't."

When Angela was Cecily's age, in fourth grade, she'd written a paper on imagery in

The Ballad of Lucy Whipple (a gold rush tale) that was so good that (Cecily told her) the teacher used it as an example to this day.

Angela said, "Ceci—" and realized she didn't know what to say next. She said, "I'm really sorry. I'm sorry that happened. But it was just a mistake! You can't beat yourself up for a mistake."

Teresa had referenced a critic named Gérard Genette, who'd written something called *Narrative Discourse: An Essay in Method.* She'd chosen two examples from each book. There was Mrs. Ramsey in *To the Lighthouse,* thinking, about the character named Lily, *With her little Chinese eyes and her puckered-up face she would never marry; one could not take her painting very seriously; but she was an independent little creature, Mrs. Ramsay liked her for it, and so remembering her promise, she bent her head.* And there was Clarissa Dalloway, running into Hugh Whitbread: *They had just come up — unfortunately — to see doctors. Other people came to see pictures; go to the opera; take their daughters out; the Whitbreads came "to see doctors." Times without number Clarissa had visited Evelyn Whitbread in a nursing home. Was Evelyn sick again?* "Woolf's use of free indirect discourse here serves a dual purpose . . ."

Perfect, perfect, perfect. Two exquisite examples of free indirect discourse.

Angela had still been wavering a couple of weeks ago when it was time to have Ms. Simmons approve her thesis. She wasn't ready to commit herself; she might still come up with her own. So it had been simple enough — too simple — to fix Ms. Simmons with a look of mild bewilderment and to say, "Oh, but you *did* approve it, don't you remember? I'll bring it in tomorrow to show you again."

Teachers, like parents, were too busy to keep track of everything. Ms. Simmons forgot to ask again the following day.

"I know Mom told you already, but I'm just telling you again. Just to make sure you understand. We didn't qualify, we're not going to London. And it's all my fault. Even if it was a mistake it was still all my fault."

Angela said, "Oh, *Cecily.* I'm sorry. Really I am." Virginia Woolf had lived in London when she used free indirect discourse.

Teresa's paper was in the bottom of Angela's desk drawer, in the very bedroom in which she and Cecily now stood. She had not yet copied it, had not yet handed it in as her own. She was a thief and a liar, but she was not yet a cheat. If she changed her mind she could still reverse course; she could still come up with something mildly original to say about Virginia Woolf.

Of course everything original had already been said about everyone.

But now that she had Teresa's paper, now that she'd gone through the trouble of *procuring* it and hiding it and admiring it and practically memorizing it, now that she knew it as well as she might know a paper she'd written herself, it seemed inappropriate not to use it. Even uneconomical.

Cecily was still talking about London, bless her skinny little self. "Some people will still go for solos, but not me. I did bad in those too, I was all messed up after the fall. Seamus wouldn't talk to me."

"Really?" said Angela. "What a jerk."

"Maybe," said Cecily dolefully. "But I see his point. He worked hard for us."

"You know, I never trusted the guy," said Angela. "I know Mom's halfway in love with him, but."

Cecily said, "Gross."

"I think she just likes his accent," added Angela. It *was* sort of gross to think about, her mother and Seamus O'Malley. They were both so old.

After they handed in the rough drafts they'd begin the peer-guided edits.

Cecily leaned over and placed her hands flat on the floor with her legs straight. Angela would never have that kind of flexibility, not after all the running. Cecily was like an extra-stretchy rubber band, no bones, just skin and muscle.

Cecily said, "I think I'm going to stop for a while. Stop dancing. Do you think I should?"

Perhaps a convenient absence on the rough-draft date — she *was* feeling a tickle in her throat, wasn't she? But at that point Ms. Simmons *might* reach out to her parents to inquire why a usually on-the-ball student had faltered. Or her mother might take a peek at the school portal, where all the grades were posted.

Better not to think about it, not right now. There were a few hours left in the evening.

Cecily said, "Angela? Do you?"

Angela considered her little sister. When Cecily returned to an upright position her face was its normal olive color. Angela's would have been scarlet. If she hadn't witnessed, if she didn't remember so clearly, when her mother was pregnant with Cecily, if she hadn't seen Cecily in the hospital when she was a mere ten minutes old, reclining against her exhausted mother's chest, she would seriously wonder if Cecily was adopted.

This was no different from when Angela had helped Cecily learn to ride a bike, steadying her, running alongside her, letting her go until her balance caught. She was helping her, pure and simple. "Well," said Angela. "It's not the kind of thing colleges look at. Right? Unless you're, like, the very best in the whole world. Maybe this is a good time to pick up something new. What about fencing? You'd be good at that, I bet, from all your dancing." She chewed on a fingernail. What a terrible habit. Ick. She wished she could break it. "Quick feet and everything. I wish I'd done fencing." How come nobody had ever put Cecily in a Harvard sweatshirt? Or Maya? It was always Angela, every time, it was her, her, her. Sometimes it seemed so . . . well, just unfair. So unfair.

She was definitely feeling a tickle in her throat. If she stayed home from school tomorrow and if both her parents were at work she could get tons done on her statistics homework and figure out what she could do for her National Honor Society volunteer hours. She could sleep a little, too. God, she'd love to get some extra sleep.

Cecily said, "*Fencing?* I don't even know what that is really. Is that where they wear those masks?" Cecily's face looked like a crumpled version of itself and Angela understood that she had misread what Cecily wanted from her.

"Sure," said Angela, beginning to falter. "That's fencing. The masks, and the swords. They dress in white, usually. They wear knickers."

"Why would I want to do that?"

"Why not? It's really cool. Maybe not the knickers. And they're, like, *giving* away scholarships for it, is what I heard. They need girls who are good at it."

"Who's 'they'?" said Cecily suspiciously.

"Colleges."

"Well, I'm not doing it," said Cecily, with uncharacteristic grumpiness. "I don't care about college. Fencing isn't what I love."

How many things in her life had Angela done when she didn't want to, and how many other things had she stopped doing because they led nowhere? She had enjoyed swimming, for example. But to be a competitive swimmer you had to commit to it one hundred and twelve percent: early mornings, afternoons, everything. And she knew she couldn't to that. So she stopped. And ran. The next week's meet was a big one, regional — Angela tried not to think about that. "I mean, *no,*" Angela said. "You should not quit. You work so hard at this, Cecily. You're so talented."

Angela placed her hands on Cecily's shoulders and pulled her toward her. She looked deep into Cecily's brown eyes. She could feel Cecily's shoulder blades through her skin. Cecily had grown taller this fall; she was meeting Angela's gaze almost evenly. Soon she would surpass her. "Listen to me, Cecily. Then you keep doing it. If it's what you love, you keep doing it."

Cecily said, "I don't know if I love it . . ."

"Are you happy when you're dancing, Cecily?"

Angela had already dropped the ball; she'd dropped it weeks ago, when she hadn't chosen a topic, hadn't written an outline, hadn't read any literary criticism. She couldn't just pick it up now like it was no big deal.

How would she get caught, anyway? Ms. Simmons hadn't been the AP English teacher when Teresa wrote that essay; Mr. Strickland, now the department head, had been. Ms. Simmons wouldn't *recognize* it. Teresa didn't even go to the school anymore.

Geez.

"Yes," said Cecily. "I'm happy when I'm

dancing. Happier than I am doing anything else."

To ace this paper, to secure her GPA, her class rank, once and for all. This was the last time as a high school student that she'd ever have to worry like this. This was the final shitty hurdle in an extremely long race.

"Then keep dancing, Cecily. I mean it." She was still holding Cecily by the shoulders. She squeezed them in a gentle, sisterly way, and Cecily smiled. "Keep dancing!" said Angela.

In a way, Angela was not doing this for herself. Look at her parents, who had given her so much, who had worked so hard for her, given her every advantage. She couldn't fail them now.

In this way, in Angela's mind, the action became noble.

Fifteen milligrams. Maybe twenty.

CHAPTER 30
GABE

Gabe was in his office, looking over the Bizz-vara presentation on his computer, when Abby Freeman knocked on the door and let herself in. If he were Don Draper he would have had a secretary to stop her. Why wasn't he Don Draper? Gabe raised his eyes and

then lowered them back down, being careful to make himself look busy. Since the
drink at the wine bar he'd felt exceedingly
uncomfortable around Abby Freeman. She
looked young (she was) and harmless (she
wasn't). She was a wolf in sheep's clothing,
if he could permit himself an idiom.

"Hello!" said Abby. "I just came by with a
couple of questions. I hope that's okay."

"Shoot," said Gabe. *Shit,* he thought.

"I was talking to someone, I forget who it
was, and they mentioned that you don't
have an MBA." She stood in front of his
desk and swayed a tiny bit in the heels she
was wearing.

So they were doing this. Here. Now. This
was it. He met her gaze. "I don't."

"That's unusual, in this industry. Highly
unusual. Wouldn't you say?"

"That's right." *Highly unusual* seemed like
a strange phrase for a girl Abby's age to be
using. A young lady.

Abby picked up a family photograph Gabe
kept on his desk in a plain silver frame. The
photograph showed the Hawthorne females
on the beach in Rhode Island during a family trip two summers ago. No, it must have
been longer ago than that; Cecily's front
teeth were missing. Three years ago? Nora
had sunglasses pushed up on top of her

296

head. She was holding Maya, who looked a little too big to be held and slightly embarrassed about it. Cecily was wearing a bright green bikini and her collarbones and ribs were sticking out. Everyone was suntanned and happy. Gabe had taken the photo. He remembered how hard it had been to get everyone to look at the camera at the same time; finally he'd given up. Angela was looking off to the side just a little bit, hair caught by a summer breeze. As if (this occurred to him only now) she were looking toward the future. His heart constricted a little bit at that thought. "Beautiful family," said Abby.

"Thank you." *Put down my family.*

"I really enjoyed meeting Angela, that time she came by. I see a lot of myself in her."

No you don't, you witchy woman. Bite your tongue. Abby put the photo back incorrectly, and Gabe angled it toward himself, the way it had been. "I mean, really almost unheard of, not to have the MBA. Am I right?"

Gabe sighed. "These days, certainly. But keep in mind, when I started Elpis was *tiny.* Three people in a run-down office in Outer Sunset. We were scrappy. They weren't as worried about degrees then as they were about gumption. People skills. Excellent communication. Experience. All of which I

297

had." Gabe took a second to remember those days, the tech boom new, the city bright and promising. The bars full of paper millionaires. Everybody was smiling, all the time. They all thought it would last forever. "There were the founders, and then they hired me. Four of us, then that doubled, then that doubled, and so on." He paused and turned from Abby to look out the window, over at the little bit of the Transamerica that he could see, though he was too close, of course, to see the top. He'd lived here so long that he remembered when the twenty-seventh floor was still an observation deck. They'd taken Angela up there when she was little.

"And you never went back for your MBA?"

Jesus H. Christ. Maybe you should be interning at a law firm. She could give Nora's sister, Marianne, a run for her money.

"I thought about it. I wanted to. But then my oldest daughter was born, and I couldn't go full-time. I needed the job."

"Nights, though? Weekends?"

Keep it cool, Gabe. He sort of felt like he was in an episode of *The Good Wife,* being questioned like this. He lifted his hands in a what-do-you-want-me-to-do gesture. "Didn't work out. Wasn't really necessary,

298

at the time. Now, of course, you'd never make partner without it. You'd never get hired without it. But it was different then. I learned on the job."

"Mint?"

"What?"

"I mean, can I have a mint?" Abby nodded toward the bowl of Wint O Green Life Savers on Gabe's desk, next to the picture.

No. Please leave my office and let me look at the Bizzvara presentation on my own, and please take your uncomfortable line of questioning with you.

"Of course. Absolutely. Help yourself." If she had been his daughter, he would have instructed her to say, "*May* I have a mint."

Abby took a mint and unwrapped it quickly, then stuck it in her mouth. The mint made a cracking sound when she bit down on it. *Man oh man,* thought Gabe, *if this is how you always eat hard candy, Abby Freeman, you are going to have some real problems with your molars by the time you're my age.* He felt a spasm of satisfaction at that thought. Of course, Elpis had a good dental plan. They were about to pay for Cecily's braces. Nora had pristine teeth; she was a nut about flossing, never needed anything but her regular six-month check-ups. Maya was still losing teeth. Gabe loved the lisp that little kids got when they were missing a front tooth. He looked at his laptop and tapped a few keys, although the document was locked. He was just reviewing it, giving it the final once-over. Actually the team had done an *outstanding* job on this presentation. Bizzvara was going to eat it up.

"Is that the Bizzvara presentation?"

Gabe nodded.

"How'd it come out?"

"Great," he said, "really great. You all did a fantastic job on it. The analysts told me you had some good insights."

Abby looked pleased. She took another mint and sat down in the chair across from Gabe's desk.

"I'd like to be one of the key presenters."

Gabe laughed out loud at that, and Abby blinked at him. "With all due respect, Abby, you're an intern. We don't let interns present to new clients. Sometimes — *sometimes* — we let them sit in the room. But that's it. And even that, not very often."

"I'd like you to make an exception."

"I don't think I can make an exception."

"Here's the thing," she said. "I think you can. Because there's something I know about you that I'm guessing you don't want getting out around the office."

Was it Gabe's imagination, or were the walls closing in on him?

He cleared his throat. "Excuse me?"

"I know your secret."

The rush of blood to Gabe's head was so sudden and so loud that it almost made him dizzy. A mortified little voice in his head whispered, *Here we go.* Dully, he said, "Secret?"

"You see, there's a little habit I have, a little Google habit. I Google everything."

Gabe wanted to wipe the floor with Abbie's smug expression, but the best he could manage was to say, "Everybody Googles everything."

"I guess I should say I Google *everyone,* when I land in a new place. Like here, at Elpis. I Googled all of the partners, just to make sure I had all the information." She smiled. "Did you know Doug Maverick has done *three* Ironman triathlons?"

Gabe did know that; he'd known Doug Maverick forever.

"And did you know that Stu's son plays Division I lacrosse at Dartmouth?"

Yes, Gabe knew that too.

"And it was weird, because I didn't find what I was looking for about you —"

"Abby," he said firmly. "I'm afraid I don't understand what you're talking about. And if you don't mind, I really need to get back —" *Admit nothing.*

Joe Stone from HR walked by the office and waved enthusiastically, like a child riding on a carousal might wave to his parents standing outside the gate and snapping pictures. Gabe noticed that his own hand lifted and waved back at Joe; he could feel that his own lips smiled. He was pantomiming the movements of a man whose world was not about to come crashing down. He cleared his throat again. *Think of her as cattle, Gabe. Make her do what you want, even if she wants to do the opposite. Prod her, Gabe. But he was mute.*

"Want to know how I know? After my Googling proved to be, well, *disappointing,* in your case, I did something nobody in this company ever bothered to do. I called the registrar's office. At Harvard."

A voice that sounded a little bit like Gabe's spoke. "I'm offended, Abby, that you would insinuate something like this. Offended and, well, frankly, disappointed. Also, I don't believe that any person can just call up and check someone's résumé. And even if you could —"

Abby took three mints this time. "You'd be surprised, what you can find out, if you have a relative who works in the registrar's office. Like my aunt does. I think you'd be really surprised." She smiled again. "The records at Harvard go back, gosh, decades and decades and decades. Electronic, now, of course, but before that, microfilm." She folded her hands like a little girl at church. "And would you believe that there *was* a Gabriel Hawthorne. But he graduated in 1938."

Thank goodness Gabe wasn't blushing; he'd be able to feel it if he were. Blushing was such a dead giveaway. No, he knew that if he looked in the mirror he'd be drained of color, white as a sheet, a ghost, a freshly painted wall. One of Gabe's knees was knocking against the other. *Admit nothing.*

"So you never peed on the John Harvard statue. You never lived in Adams. You never did the Primal Scream, except maybe when you were born. Not only did you never graduate, you were never enrolled. You never matriculated. My guess is that you never even *applied,* but of course I don't know that for sure. They don't keep records of every applicant. Can you imagine if they did?" She looked him straight in the eyes and said, "So many people want to go to Harvard. So many people."

"Listen," said Gabe. Abby looked at him expectantly. "It's not what you think." He stopped there because the truth was that it was exactly what she thought.

"Someday, when we have a little more time, I'd love to hear the story, about how you got away with it. No hurry, of course."

"Abby —"

"I'm not going to do anything about it *today,* or anything. But there are a couple of things I'd like."

Somehow, he got his voice to work. He sounded almost normal, casually nonchalant. "Okay, Abby. Out of sheer curiosity, what would you want? If what you're saying has any basis in fact. Which I'm not saying it does."

"I want to sit in on the Bizzvara presentation, for one."

Deep breath. "Fine, okay, done. But you can't present."

He thought of Nora, of his daughters. He thought of his brother Michael, the only person who'd called him on it. Who'd been disgusted by it. *A coward move, Gabe.*

"I want to present Bizzvara."

What an asshole move, Michael had said. He didn't care about Lauren anymore at that point. He'd forgiven that, but not this.

"You know you can't do that."

"But I want to." She folded her hands and tapped her index fingers together. It was the gesture of a much older person; he wondered where she'd picked it up. "I want it on my résumé, that I presented to a major client. And I would never, ah, *lie* on my résumé."

Deeper breath. Deeper, now. Steady. "You can present a little bit. Just the beginning. I'll let Dustin know. You can do the intro. But then you have to hand it over to the manager. You have to. Anything more than that would look — well, it would look unprofessional."

"Got it," she said. "And I want" — she paused to unwrap yet another mint — "I want a job."

"Pardon me?"

"When the internship ends. Full-time, with benefits. Analyst position, associate track. I want to be working here when I apply to business school."

Gabe thought of a bar in Noe Valley, a beautiful girl with skin that glowed from the inside out. *Hey, I'm Nora. Nice to meet you. I just moved here. Wyoming? What's it like living on a ranch?*

"Abby. You know I can't promise that."

"If you can, your secret is safe with me."

"I can't."

"You're a partner."

"Not a senior partner. They make deci-

305

sions like this, the founders. I don't have the power to . . ."

"You're a smart guy. I mean, not *Ivy League* smart or anything." Abby plucked five mints from the bowl and held them in her hand, considering them. Then she closed her fist over them. "But smart enough. You have some time. My internship goes through December. You'll figure it out."

CHAPTER 31
NORA

3:03 a.m.

Dear Marianne,
After Cecily's debacle at the *feis* she went back to the Seamus O'Malley School of Irish Dance. I thought that was very brave of her. I told her she didn't have to go — I wouldn't have gone, myself. But she's braver than I am. She's like you, Marianne, afraid of nothing. So she went, and when I picked her up — I did not entrust this delicate task to Maddie — she got in the car and promptly burst into one thousand tears. She said it was terrible. They didn't talk to her, her Irish dance friends; they

pretended she wasn't there. Those little bitches. I swear to God, I could pummel their pale little faces.

Nora wanted to wait until the moon was nearly full. Earlier that day she had asked Cecily, and Cecily checked her notes, fiddled around on a couple of websites, and pronounced the full moon just a couple of days away. She didn't want to wait a couple of days. A couple of days might be too late. Almost full was close enough.

A Steller sea lion, a humpback whale, for Christ's sake: these she could get on board with preserving. Even the California red-legged frog — she could see the value in that. Red legs were unusual, Nora granted the world that. Particularly on a frog. She'd looked it up: the frog looked like it had been dipped in Kool-Aid. But the Marin dwarf flax? Seriously? A *plant* was going to undo everything she'd toiled for, her entire career? All those Sundays spent in open houses, the evenings away from her husband and her children, cajoling buyers, convincing sellers. No, sir. No, it wasn't. Nora had worked too hard for this. She'd sacrificed too much.

It was easy to get out of bed without waking Gabe. He slept like he was getting paid to sleep. His concentration was utter, and his breathing was deep and even. Had Nora's beloved Frankie still been alive, this would have been more difficult; Frankie slept like a menopausal woman, nodding off easily but after an hour or two waking at the slightest noise and remaining restless after that.

Quiet, now, slipping out of the house on little cat feet. Quiet!

Nora couldn't remember the last time she'd been outside after midnight. As she drove, she thought once again of the gold rush settlers, driving their wagons west and west and west or taking ships around the tip of South America. She was under the impression from overseeing Cecily's fourth-grade homework that the South American route was the preferred one, although that seemed crazy: the trip took something like five to eight months. Not that dragging a wagon full of complaining kids across the entire country would have been any picnic either. If Nora had been a gold rush settler she would have been so impatient with the slow pace of the wagons that she would have called the whole thing off, turned back home. Gabe would have had to call upon some of his endless supply of patience to try to calm her down. "Come on, Nora-Bora," he'd say. "Just a little longer. We can make it." And she would have sighed heartily, looking around the plains, and said, "Seriously? Is *that* what they're getting for a log cabin these days?"

Cecily told her that San Francisco had a population of only two hundred before the first gold was discovered. Imagine! There were more parents than that in the volunteer database at Cecily's school. It was not even a town; it was an outpost, the raw beginnings of something, that's it. At the start of the gold rush, Cecily had said, the nuggets were so big and so blatant that gold seekers could pick them up right off the ground. Nora took a moment to imagine what that must have been like, gold more common, more easily located, than the insidious Marin dwarf flax. The promise and exhilaration of that!

Driving, driving, on her way to the Miller property, no big deal, just driving, a drive she'd made dozens of times when the home was on the market. The house had been a snap to sell. It had practically sold itself. The market had been on an uptick then. There was almost no inventory in Marin. She could have sold that home to at least a dozen families, it was simply her bad luck that it had gone to Loretta and Barry Miller, who, instead of being happy with what they got, wanted to *expand.* Go figure.

The moonlight dancing in San Rafael Bay was truly lovely. Nora should make a point to get out late at night more often. She should look at the water more often. She didn't take the water here as seriously as she took the ocean in Rhode Island. She saw the water almost every day, either the bay or the majestic Pacific, but these weren't real *beaches;* these weren't places you could go with your friends and stick your toes in the sand and get a good old-fashioned sunburn while you drank soda (or beer poured into soda cans) and gossiped. If you were only halfway sane and a tremendously talented surfer you could go to Mavericks near Half Moon Bay, and certainly the view of the ocean lashing the cliffs was breathtaking. But if you were just a regular person, just a person who wanted to hang out at the beach, you were mostly out of luck. *Water water everywhere and not a place to swim.*

These thoughts occupied Nora for much of the short drive, but then her anxiety returned with renewed strength and vigor. She should turn back, she should forget this whole expedition, let fate run its course. *Turn this wagon around, Gabe. Girls! We're going back. No gold for us.* If the Millers sued her, the Millers sued her. If they lost

310

their home, they lost their home.

Okay. What if? So they'd sell their home, and live — *where?* And pay for Angela's college tuition — *how?* They wouldn't be able to. The Hawthornes would become one of those families you heard about who made one mistake and, *kaput,* there went their lives. People would say things about them like, *They were doing so well! Why'd they go and risk it?*

Or, worse, *I always knew there was something about them. Don't you think, in the end, they got what they deserved?* They would become a cautionary tale, like the baseball manager with the doomed land investments or the brilliant businessman who bet it all on one horse.

Nora didn't want to become a cautionary tale. She wanted to keep her regular life. She wanted to continue working for Arthur Sutton. She wanted to take care of her children and love her husband. (If he wasn't having an affair with the intern and planning to divorce her. Although if he were having an affair and not planning to divorce her she'd have to divorce *him* once she found out, in the name of feminism and also because she couldn't imagine ever sleeping with him again after he slept with someone else. Nora was monogamous to the core.)

She wanted Angela to get into Harvard because it would make Angela and Gabe happy and would give them more reason to go east. She wanted to visit her mother and Marianne in the summer and take a day trip to Newport and eat a lobster roll at Monahan's. Cecily loved the lobster rolls at Monahan's, and Maya loved the mozzarella sticks.

And to keep all that, she needed to do this.

She took a deep breath, exhaled audibly. She found a classical station on the radio and was momentarily calmed by the music; her mother used to listen to classical music in the afternoons, and the sound brought to mind coming in the door after school, the hiss of an iron across white dress shirts, the sound of the oven door creaking open. Nora was too type A for listening to classical music at home. Or, for that matter, for ironing. They sent Gabe's shirts out to the dry cleaner's for pressing, and Nora herself favored clothes that tended not to wrinkle, or that wrinkled in such a way that the wrinkling seemed purposeful.

When Nora reached the Millers' street she did something she hadn't done since she was in high school, cruising toward the beach at Narragansett in Stuart Mobley's old Buick: she turned off the headlights and coasted quietly to a stop.

She was dressed like a cat burglar, in all black: black yoga pants, never used for their expressed purpose, and a black turtleneck that called to mind either Steve Jobs or an East Village poet from the 1970s. Nora detested turtlenecks and had had to reach deep into the archives of her closet to recover this one.

She had with her a backpack with a flashlight and a small trowel she'd found in a mislabeled bin in the garage. She got out of the car on her little cat feet and headed around to the back — the Millers had no front fence, just the one along the back. No dog, which was a plus. Also, they weren't home. They were in Hawaii, drinking cucumber and pineapple mojitos and eating farm-to-table vegetarian dip at the Ritz-Carlton on Maui. (Nora, in a fit of envy and curiosity, had looked the menu up online.)

I'm not doing this, she told herself. *I am not. Doing. This.*

And yet she was! She was doing it. Here she was, closing the car door softly, softly, so softly that she didn't hear so much as the whisper of metal on metal. Here she was, sneaking around to the backyard. Here she was turning on her flashlight, shining it along the back fence. Here she was, looking, looking. Looking for the plant that was keeping the Millers from expanding their already-large home.

Except. Here she was, and here was the flashlight. But where was the plant?

Here she was, looking harder, looking more. She had thought it would be easy. But she'd neglected to consider something obvious. The Marin dwarf flax was a *flowering* plant. Flowering plants didn't flower all year long, at least that's how it worked in the botanical world that Nora imagined, though she knew little about it herself.

She had thought that under the light of the (nearly) full moon, with the pinky-white flowers glowing against the fence, it would be easy to pick them out. Loretta Miller had said there were only a few plants, three or four; she had told Amanda that it was astonishing and irritating that such a small number of plants — a smattering of weeds, really — should keep them from expanding. This job should be easy. *Easy peasy lemon squeezie!*

But the goddamn plants weren't flowering. It was November, not the middle of summer. Nora shined her flashlight along the edge of the fence. What did the dwarf flax look like when it wasn't flowering? She should have brought her iPhone in her backpack so she could take a quick look, but she'd left it in the car. Not worth going back for: too risky, even though the Millers were on vacation.

An anomaly, Loretta Miller had told Amanda. *Just our house, and the house next door.* So maybe the plants were right on the border with the neighbor's yard. But which neighbor? There was a house on either side. Nora crept to one side of the yard and shined the flashlight at the corner of the fence. She was too warm in her turtleneck. How did Steve Jobs stand it? Of course, he had a total of zero body fat. Lot of good that did him, in the end. Don't be uncharitable, Nora. Just focus on the task at hand.

Well, she'd just have to pull up anything that looked like a possibility.

The back door opened. The outdoor lights came on, illuminating the pool, illuminating the chaise lounge chairs that (Nora knew) the Millers had purchased from the sellers for a very good price, illuminating the palm trees that stood sentry around the pool, and illuminating (Nora was certain) Nora herself, standing in her cat-burglar suit, holding a trowel and her ten-year-old's backpack.

And then a voice spoke: a strident, possibly frightened female voice, a voice that did not belong to Loretta Miller.

"Hey!" said the voice. "Hey! Is someone out there?"

What was Nora supposed to do? Answer, not answer? She was, of course, out there.

"I'm calling the police," said the voice. "Don't you dare come any closer. I'm calling the police."

Housesitter, thought Nora. Of course. Typical. Loretta Miller wasn't going to leave her house unattended during a vacation. At the same time she thought, *Police!* How formal. In Rhode Island people would say *cops.* And at the same time she was thinking all of that she thought, *Don't just stand there, Nora-Bora, you idiot. Run!*

But she couldn't run. Her feet were frozen; her legs were paralyzed. And from a great distance a mind that didn't seem to belong entirely to her wondered, *Is this what it feels like to die of shame?*

CHAPTER 32
ANGELA

After the team warm-up, a slow jog out on the course for a little more than a mile and then back again, checking out some of the more *ominous* hills, the team split up, each to his or her own particular pre-race routine, gum chewing or water sipping or a final anxiety-laden trip to the trio of porta potties along the edge of the woods. Angela liked to stay near the school banner, which was held up by two rusting metal poles that the coach screwed into the ground.

Twenty minutes until race time.

Angela started with a little Mumford & Sons for relaxation, while she was working on her hamstrings, laying her jacket on the cold ground and stretching herself out on top of it. She rolled out her tweaky left calf with her massage stick. At that point she switched over to a little Lumineers, then some Avett Brothers, music that she did not always listen to at home, due to the fact that her parents also listened to it, and that made it faintly embarrassing, but which she liked anyway. She pulled up her socks, exchanged her regular running shoes for cross-country spikes, tied them. She checked to make sure the laces were even with each other, and that each loop was the same size as each other loop. An acceptable quirk, or a sign of a touch of OCD? She wasn't sure. She wasn't sure it mattered. At this point. She double-knotted them, then triple. Many a cross-country runner had been undone by an untied shoelace, and she didn't want to be that guy. (*Remember Angela Hawthorne? Class of 2014? She was a star cross-country runner, and then there was that one time she didn't tie her shoelace tightly right before that big regional meet and she face-planted into a tree root, had to have three different surgeries on her front teeth? Didn't get into college? Yeah, that girl. You don't want to be that girl.*)

She put her hair into a ponytail that was not too high (swung too much), nor too low (made her neck sweat), and she wrapped the elastic three times. Not two, not four. Three.

Ten minutes to race time.

She flipped through her iTunes library and upped the ante: Katy Perry. *Roar.*

A shadow crossed in front of her. Angela tried to ignore it, but then the shadow sat down next to her and resolved itself into Henrietta Faulkner. Angela glanced at her watch. Eight minutes to go. Runners were gathering near the line. Two incredibly tall, incredibly skinny girls in green uniforms were doing strides across the grass. They looked as fresh as a couple of daisies. Cliché.

You held me down but I got up . . .

"Hey," said Henrietta. Angela pulled the earbuds from her ears. Seven minutes.

"Hey," said Angela. She didn't like to talk

318

before races. Everybody knew that. *Everybody.*

"Senior year, huh, I can't believe it. Can you believe it? Last meet of the season. Last meet ever, for high school." Henrietta Faulkner was nervous; she was terrified. And when Henrietta was terrified she wanted to talk. Angela, who was also terrified, wanted to curl up into a little ball.

"We still have track in the spring," said Angela.

The music was coming through the earbuds even though they weren't in Angela's ears anymore. Henrietta's face lit up. "I *love* that song," she said.

"Yeah," said Angela. Everybody loved that song. Angela was so unoriginal.

I am a champion and you're gonna hear me roaaaaaar . . .

"But track," Henrietta said. "That's not the same as this. Not for us. We're cross-country girls, you and me."

Angela thought, *You and I.* But she nodded, looking over the line of trees, looking at the path that led to the first hill.

Five minutes. She stood up, stretched her calf. She didn't want to agree too heartily with Henrietta Faulkner, although of course she was right. They were so much alike, the two of them. Good students. Fast runners.

319

Cross-country girls. Even their ponytails hung from the same part of their heads. That's why they had been friends, way back when. If she squinted she could still see the old Henrietta, the eleven-year-old with the striped bathing suit whose strap tied in a thick knot around her neck, hair tangled from the water slide, face smeared with blue frosting from the Raging Birthday Cookie-Cake.

"Yeah," Angela said finally. "I guess you're right."

Henrietta stood along with Angela, and mimicked her quad stretch. After she released her foot she leaned toward Angela and said, "I heard something."

"Yeah?"

"I heard that the Harvard coach is here today."

"You *did*?"

"I did. I don't know who he's watching, there's a girl from Novato who's applying too and also I think one from Redwood, then of course there's *us*" — here she delivered a friendly-ish punch to Angela's upper arm — "but I'm so nervous I could just throw up, aren't you?"

"Well, now I am," said Angela. She'd had her usual pre-race breakfast, a slice of whole-wheat toast spread with almond butter, but she could feel it churning around. Why hadn't Henrietta kept that to herself? God.

But once said, the words could not be unsaid. They were out there, and now Angela was scanning the crowd of spectators, wondering which one he could be.

"I'm sorry," said Henrietta. "Maybe I shouldn't have told you. Should I not have told you?" Henrietta was looking at Angela uncertainly. She looked almost like she was going to cry. When had Henrietta become such a bundle of nerves? She used to be tougher than nails, able to hold her own in any situation; she used to ooze confidence. At the infamous eleventh birthday party she'd been the only one out of all of them to go down the Triple Slammer Flume, and she hadn't blinked. Some adults went up there and freaked out and had to go backward down the ladder to get out of it. Not Henrietta. She'd just hopped on her rubber mat and she'd *gone.*

"Well," said Angela. "Yeah, I guess I wish I didn't know. But I know now. So . . . whatever."

They both scrutinized the crowd standing past the starting line. They were looking for — what? A man in a crimson jacket that said COACH on the back? A man with a clipboard and a fountain pen? A man with his palm out, holding their fates? All of the spectators simply looked like parents: a little excited, a little nervous, a little grumpy, a little chilly. Most of them held take-out coffee cups and they stamped their feet on the ground like horses at the Kentucky Derby.

"I'm sure he's not here for me," said Henrietta. She was talking really fast now, like her words were racing one another. "If either of us is getting in it's you. I'm mostly applying to get my parents off my back. It's a super-big deal to them."

Instead of saying "Mine too," Angela said, "Don't be ridiculous," too sharply. More gently she said, "You have as much of a chance as I have." Though, of course, obviously, she didn't believe that. They wouldn't *both* get in early, would they? And if only one of them was to get in, well, it would have to be Angela. *Right?* She was valedictorian. She was the better runner. She was team co-captain. She was smarter.

Four minutes. Angela turned off the iPod, put it in her bag, stripped off her final layer of warm-ups. She was wearing the bun huggers, which looked and felt like underwear. Henrietta was wearing shorts. Personally Angela thought everyone should wear the bun huggers in a big race like this. They

322

were more legit. They made Angela feel invincible, like she was Katy Perry herself, flying through the jungle, painting the elephant's toenails, palling around with the monkey.

Time to line up. They all moved toward the starting line: girls from Tamalpais, Redwood High, Novato. Girls with fishtail braids or ponytails or hair cut super-short to show off their fierce expressions and their hard bright eyes. Some of them bounced on their toes but others remained very still, poised at the starting line. If Angela looked too closely at any of the runners' faces she saw her own emotions reflected too well in their faces. They were all pale, slender, nervously intense, not blinking. Breathing audibly already.

You had to get out hard. That was key on this course — any course, really, but especially this one, because half of it was single track. Once they got into the single track it was hard to pass. Impossible. Plus Angela's specialty was going out hard, freaking out everybody else in the race, and then surprising them by not dying. It was part nature and part art.

Two minutes.

"Two minutes!" called the official. The tension increased by a notch, two notches, three. Angela's coach stood on the sidelines with the rest of the coaches, blowing into his hands and rubbing them together, exchanging a word or two with the men or women beside him. He knew better than to give instruction at this point, especially to Angela. He knew she had a good chance of winning the whole thing if she kept her head in the game, though neither of them had said that out loud, not since the beginning of the season. He knew that Angela, like all good runners, was fifty percent steel and fifty percent crazy and that on any given day one could overtake the other. Did he know about the Harvard coach?

Angela thought she might throw up for real now. It sometimes happened, right before races, though more commonly after. Angela wouldn't mind if she threw up after the race, that would just prove she'd run as hard as she possibly could. But she didn't have time now.

One minute. The longest and the shortest sixty seconds of Angela's life.

The gun.

Go.

They were off.

The thing about cross-country, well, about running fast in general, was that it hurt. Hurt like hell. Hurt like hell the whole time you were doing it, and it only felt better when you stopped. Why had Angela picked such a *painful* sport? Cecily wasn't in pain when she was dancing; Cecily was in *ecstasy* when she was dancing. Angela's friend Brynne Jacobson wasn't in pain the *entire* time she was playing soccer. She had to run fast a lot, but not continuously, and she had teammates. She got taken out of a game, and she was able to sit on the sidelines and cheer while she drank Gatorade and waited to be brought back in. Where was the passing in cross-country races, where was the resting? Angela thought it would be nice if you could pass off a little bit of the pain to someone else, just for a minute. Even thirty seconds would do it. But it wasn't a team sport. Except for the scoring, it was the most individual of all the individual sports.

These thoughts kept Angela busy for the first quarter mile. She had gotten out well. The people standing near the start were just a blur of light and color. Harvard coach or no Harvard coach, they blended in with the trees and the clouds and the other girls breathing around her. Time to fly.

("Is that normal?" said Angela's sweet, naive mother, after Angela's first meet, freshman year. "That you all sound like you're hyperventilating the whole time? I

325

mean, is that okay?" "Perfectly normal," Angela told her. "If you're running as fast as you can.")

She had gotten out well enough, okay, but not first. Not as well as she usually did. She preferred to break free of the pack before the pack even formed, and to pretend that she was running alone. There were two girls ahead of her, one from Tamalpais, one from Novato. Angela had raced against both of them before. The girl from Novato — Casey something — was within Angela's reach, first figuratively and then literally. She had gone out harder than she usually did. She had channeled Angela! She had a long blond fishtail braid, very pretty. Angela gained on her, gained enough that she could see the little wisps of hair coming out of the braid, could see the red elastic at the end of it, could watch it bouncing against Casey's school tank.

Three point one miles, a standard 5K. This was Angela's best distance, not just on the trails but on the road and even on the track, where many runners would rather stick pins in their eyes and then blink than run a 5K. You had to have nerves of steel for a 5K on the track; you had to be able to beat back the boredom and keep your head in the game while you went around and around the same damn circle. Angela could do that.

Angela did some math; math was another good way to keep her mind occupied. If she ran eighteen minutes, which — by the way — would not be fast enough to win the thing, then she was already one-ninth done. Good. Only eight-ninths to go! Piece of cake. And hopefully she'd run faster than eighteen minutes, so the whole thing would be over sooner. The faster you run, the more it hurts, and the sooner you're done: the paradox of distance running.

If only she could pass this Casey what's-her-name.

Casey from Novato, sensing Angela behind her, picked it up a notch, just a hair, barely perceptible. That was fine. That was okay. As long as Angela also picked it up a notch, stayed on her shoulder, didn't let her pull farther ahead. Angela didn't hold back on her breathing: sometimes that could disrupt another runner, throw them off guard a little bit, to hear someone's lungs exploding. She let it rip, stayed on Casey's shoulder. Casey was playing a good mental game, not acknowledging Angela. She didn't turn her head, didn't nod or say anything. She was acting like a girl all on her own, just running through the woods on a November morning for the heck of it. That was smart. That was how Angela liked to play it too.

They were four minutes into it now. Still on Casey's shoulder. Lots of time for strategy. Where was the girl from Tamalpais? She had made the second turn into the woods already, ahead of Angela and Casey. Not a great sign, that she was that far ahead. Not the way Angela preferred to race. But not unfixable. The girl from Tamalpais had probably gone out too hard, and she'd pay for it later. Pretty common, especially in a big meet like this. Angela watched Casey's fishtail braid swing back and forth, back and forth. Was Casey the Harvard applicant the coach had really come to see? Possible. Angela knew nothing about Casey from Novato academically, or at all, really, except what she looked like running a 5K. Did she have siblings, were her parents here? How had she gotten her braid so perfect? Angela had never mastered the fishtail, though Cecily was pretty good at it; she'd refined her skills on her American Girl dolls, Kaya and Josefina in particular. They had the longest hair. In addition, Cecily and Pinkie spent a lot of time doing each other's hair. When they weren't doing weird things with Pinkie's iPhone.

She was letting her mind wander now. Too much? It was a delicate balance, to let your mind wander just enough to keep it off the pain but not so much that you lost focus. Exquisitely difficult.

God, it hurt. Her lungs, her legs. Even her eyes stung. How much longer?

It would be better, of course, if Angela were in front of these two, but it was early. Only — she checked her watch — only five minutes in. Five minutes into a race that would last (hopefully!) fewer than eighteen minutes. Seventeen-thirty, if she had a good day. But what if the Harvard coach *was* here to see Casey? And what if Casey beat Angela in front of him?

Okay, Casey from Novato, thought Angela. *You're history.*

Deep breath, suck in all the air you can.

Quick feet, big blast.

And Angela had passed Casey from Novato. She kept the speed up for five extra steps to make sure Casey didn't pass her right back, then she settled in. Casey might have cursed; Angela wasn't sure. Maybe she was just wheezing.

Eight minutes down. Almost halfway. Ten minutes, then eleven. Lungs bursting, maybe broken. Casey hadn't gained on Angela, but Angela hadn't gained on the girl from Tamalpais. The course turned again, into a single track, up a hill: where was she?

Then! The course turned back on itself just ahead. A flash of green through the woods, a glimpse of black hair. There she was. She was maybe thirty seconds ahead of Angela.

Ten minutes down. Seven to go. *You can do anything for seven minutes, Angela Hawthorne. Anything. So pick up the fucking pace.*

She picked it up. She was gaining on the girl in green . . . gaining . . . gaining. She was invincible. She was the champion, louder than the lion.

And then the unthinkable happened. She slowed down.

Angela Hawthorne — Harvard applicant, a runner of such talent that in middle school the *high school* coach had seen her at the Fourth of July road race and *recruited* her while she chomped a banana and gulped from a bottle of Powerade handed to her by a race volunteer. . . . Angela, who had once (embarrassingly, in a moment of extreme weakness that had now become, to Angela's great chagrin, part of family lore) pushed a fellow preschooler from the top of the slide because she wanted so badly to be first — had slowed down. She was bonking. Everything around her started to blur, and she felt so light-headed she thought she was going to pass out. She blinked hard, shook her head, tried to make her legs go. But her feet were two bricks now, and lifting her legs felt like lifting two logs out of a swamp. She couldn't go faster. She was moving backward! She looked up, but all she saw were the redwoods, stretching their way to the sky.

More footsteps behind her, like a herd of antelope running through the plains. More heavy breathing. One of the girls sounded like she was on the edge of cardiac arrest. But she wasn't, because the next thing Angela knew she was passing her, and then more girls, not just Casey from Novato but other girls too. More than Angela could count, or wanted to: they were antelope no longer, now they were wolves, running in a pack, urging one another on.

And the final humiliation was that the last one to pass her was Henrietta Faulkner, who had the nerve to tap Angela on the shoulder and wheeze, "Good race!" as she went by.

No! It wasn't too late. Was it? Fourteen minutes in, fifteen. There were girls behind her and girls ahead of her but Angela Hawthorne might as well have been on an island.

Marooned.

She didn't have it. She had no gas. No-body heard her roar.

She crossed the line looking straight ahead and went immediately for her bag. She pulled on her warm-ups. Her legs were lead. She didn't look for her parents, didn't look for her coach, certainly (God no!) didn't look for the Harvard coach. The girl in green from Tamalpais was throwing up in the grass while her mother (Angela sup-posed it was her mother) stood next to her, rubbing her back and holding a water bottle. Casey from Novato was joking around with a teammate. Henrietta Faulk-ner was checking her phone, studiously not seeking out Angela. She knew better.

"Eighth," her mom said cheerfully later, on the way home, Angela stony-faced in the backseat, but also surprisingly hungry, as though she, not the girl from Tamalpais (Meghan Green, it turned out), had been the one to throw up. But she hadn't run fast enough to throw up! She wanted pan-cakes, and she knew her parents would take her anywhere she wanted, do anything to make her feel better. She could ask for the most expensive pancakes in all of San Francisco, she could request solid gold pancakes, and her parents would get them for her.

But she didn't deserve pancakes, so she didn't ask for them.

"I mean, *eighth,*" said her mom. "Sure, I know you would have preferred first, but eighth out of how many? Like sixty, right?" Her mother was rubbing at her temples and inspecting her eyebrows in the rearview mirror.

"Ugh," said Angela. She didn't want to look at it that way. Her mother twisted around in the front seat to look at her. Her father remained silent. He had said almost nothing after the race, just clapped her on the back in a manly way that made her feel like they were office coworkers and said, "Hey, nice job." They both knew he was lying.

She didn't say anything about the Harvard coach — she couldn't stand to tell her father that. That would crush him like a candy cane caught underfoot.

"That's okay," said her mother now. "Not every day can be your day. That's just how the world works."

"That's a stupid course," said Angela. "I *hate* that course, you can't see where you're going. It's such an advantage to the home team." Angela wanted to claw at something.

She settled for kicking the back of the seat the way Maya did when she got mad. Her mother managed to ignore this so she kicked harder and felt a little bit better. But not much.

Her mother was looking out the window and gnawing at her thumbnail. Odd: her mother was not a nail biter.

To her father her mother said, "Can you get Cecily from Pinkie's and Maya from Penelope's after you drop me at home? I need to jump in my car and be in the city in — let's see" — she scrunched her nose and tapped her fingers on her wrist, though she wasn't wearing a watch — "let's see, in forty-five minutes. Geez, I hope the traffic isn't too bad. Do you think it will be bad?" Her mother's voice sounded odd, more frantic than usual.

"Shouldn't be," said her father.

Angela looked out the window, pressing her forehead to the glass. The sun had come out after the race. Its brightness was a slap in the face. Where was the mist, the fog, the cloud cover?

She wanted to take a long, hot shower and crawl into her bed and sleep for the rest of the day and into the night. But she had a massive psychology project due on Monday, and she didn't have time to sleep.

"The pedestrian traffic on the bridge is going to be crazy. But the car traffic shouldn't be bad." To Angela's ear her mom sounded a little panicked. Angela's mom was made of velvet wrapped around steel, but, man, she could sometimes be undone by the weirdest things.

"Right," agreed her father. He glanced in the rearview mirror but didn't address Angela. What if he knew about the Harvard coach? Should she tell him, just to get it over with? Then again, maybe Henrietta was wrong. Maybe the coach had never shown. "When the weather's like this, everybody and their brother wants to walk across the bridge."

"We haven't done that in a long time. I mean, as a family." Now her mom was inspecting her teeth in the mirror. Once she had gone to a showing with a minuscule piece of an almond between two teeth and she still wasn't over it. "Remember that time when we tried to go when Maya was too young and she started crying that she couldn't make it? And we were smack-dab in the middle?"

Angela looked at her cell phone. A text from Mrs. Fletcher, who knew it was last minute but wondered if Angela might possibly be available to babysit that night. She texted back: *So sorry my parents need me at home 2nite.* Thinking about the Fletchers gave Angela a stomachache.

Her father said, "Hmmm . . . ," and her mother fiddled with the car radio. Comforting, Saturday-morning National Public Radio voices.

Angela tried not to notice that her parents' lives were continuing. They didn't seem to notice that hers was over. Her mother was heading to a showing. Her father was going to pick up Maya and Cecily, and probably Pinkie too, and bring them back to the house, which would be annoying on the one hand but also okay because Angela didn't want to be alone with her father. Maybe Cecily and Pinkie would watch a movie or go outside and tool around on their scooters. Maya would play with her American Girl dolls. Maybe someone from school would text Angela, see if she wanted to go out, maybe felt like going to that party at Jacob Boyd's house (his parents were in Napa for the weekend). But the thought of the party at Jacob Boyd's just made Angela feel more tired. She didn't want to see Edmond Lopez. She did, but she didn't. Mostly she didn't.

Also, there was one time just after the *debacle* at his house when he'd jostled

336

against her leaving AP English and she'd looked up at him (more hopefully, more expectantly, more *girlishly* than she meant to) and she was pretty sure he'd sneered at her. He had definitely sneered at her. And what had Angela done? She hadn't sneered back, no. She hadn't even avoided his gaze altogether. She'd smiled! The stupidest, most vulnerable, most needy and ridiculous smile, a smile that said, *Give me one more chance. Oh master.*

Just to make sure her humiliation was complete.

Besides all of that, Angela was hopeless at parties. She was self-conscious in the truest sense of the phrase: so freakishly conscious of everything she said or did that she couldn't enjoy herself.

Her mother twisted around in her seat again. Angela saw now that she was wearing her real estate makeup: eyeliner, a hint of shadow. Mascara. Of course. She probably had a pair of heels stashed in her car, along with a lipstick. She probably wouldn't even need to go inside the house; she'd just get in her car and go.

"Sweetie?" she said. "It's just one race, you know." Her voice really did sound odd, almost the way a voice sounded when its owner had been crying. But what would

Angela's mother be crying about? "It's not the end of the world."

Angela snorted.

Then, because she felt bad about snorting, she said, "I know it's not." She meant to speak nicely, but the words came out like they had knives attached to them. Also, she didn't believe her mother. It did feel like the end of the world. The end of something, anyway.

She texted back to Mrs. Fletcher. *Nvr mind, sorry I can do it*

CHAPTER 33
GABE

Gabe was in front of the house, inspecting the variegated sweet flag for signs of rust. It was a golden fall day, Indian summer, though in California Indian summer was a different beast altogether — not brief, as the term implied in other parts of the country, it could last most of the fall here, up until the rainy season, which passed for winter out here. Earlier that day, just for kicks, he'd checked the weather in Laramie: a high of 38, a low of 15. Snow possible in the late afternoon. He allowed himself to picture, for a moment, the ranch in winter. The cold! Biting at his fingers, at his toes, at any exposed patch of skin. Feeding the cattle from hay hauled in on a flatbed, when they couldn't get to the grass because of the snow. A hard, brittle life. No country for old men, that was for sure. And here he was, standing barefoot on his emerald-green lawn, wearing a short-sleeved gray T-shirt and jeans. He could have had shorts on if he'd wanted to. Angela, headed out for a long run with her team on one of the rare Saturdays without a meet, was in a tank.

In California, people did not put *weather permitting* on their invitations to outdoor events. In California, the weather always permitted.

Gabe knew that Nora, even after so many years out here, still missed the (ridiculous) weather patterns of the East Coast, the unforgiving humidity, the extreme cold. The snow. But not Gabe. He woke up most days and thanked God (in whom he did not believe) that he'd done what it took to land himself out here, build a family, keep them there. In paradise. Some might say against all odds.

He heard his name and turned around to see Anna Fletcher marching toward him. He raised a hand in greeting. They never saw the Fletchers anymore, not since the divorce. Which was a shame: they lived right across the street! In happier times they'd gone back and forth to dinner at each other's houses. Sometimes it was just impromptu drinks and apps. Angela used to babysit all the time for them; they had quite a social life, from what Gabe remembered, until Alan Fletcher woke up one day, walked into the kitchen, announced that he wasn't cut out for family life, and took off for a bungalow in Oceanside.

Gabe gave Anna Fletcher a big welcoming smile — looking at her, he felt a tug of wistfulness for those early days, tortilla chips and sangria on the Fletchers' patio. He almost hugged her.

"Anna! Long time no see."

When they first knew Anna she had been voluptuous and sensual, with a short and daring haircut. ("I never say no to dessert," she'd said once, and Gabe couldn't help it, he thought that was one of the sexiest things a woman could say. Though not sexy enough, apparently, for Alan Fletcher.) Now she was three shades paler and twenty pounds lighter ("Divorce diet," Nora said). She'd grown out her hair, too, into a disappointingly ordinary style. And she was most definitely not smiling.

"Gabe, hello. I was wondering. Is Angela here?"

"Out for a run. But I can pass on a message!" He was still trying to be jovial, still attempting to coax a smile out of her. She had had a gorgeous smile, back in the day. It really stood out against the shorter haircut. "Are you looking for a sitter? I don't know her sched—"

"No." Anna shook her head. "I am *not* looking for a sitter." He saw now that she was holding a small green bottle. "I am looking, in fact, for my son's medication."

"Excuse me?" Gabe dropped the joviality; he was genuinely confused.

"For my son's medication. For Joshua's Adderall, which he takes for his ADHD. And which Angela has stolen from him."

"Which Angela has *what*?" Gabe's hackles were raised now: somebody was accusing his little girl! "Uh, I'm afraid you must be mistaken."

Anna sighed and looked heavenward, then leveled her gaze at Gabe. "There used to be thirty pills in this bottle. Now there are twenty-two. Angela is the only person outside of my kids and me who's been in my house lately. And I don't keep medicine where my kids can reach it, believe me."

Gabe backed away from Anna; he backed right into the variegated sweet flag, which was really, come to think of it, quite delicate.

341

Even if he was barefoot. "I don't understand," he said. "Why would Angela take Joshua's medicine?"

"Are you kidding?"

Gabe wasn't; he was thoroughly perplexed. Anna sighed in an exasperated way.

"It's all over the Internet, Gabe. Adderall is a stimulant. The drug of choice among high school students. *High-achieving* high school students, in particular. They use it for mental clarity. They use it to stay awake, sometimes all night. They use it as a *study drug.* Don't tell me you don't know anything about it."

The variegated sweet flag crunched under his feet. The soil was still damp from the morning's watering by the in-ground sprinkler system. "I don't know anything about it," Gabe said. "Really, truly, I don't."

Anna sighed again. "Talk to her. Look it up. Stealing prescription medication is a felony, Gabe. A *felony.* I could press charges."

Gabe's heartbeat picked up ferociously. He could feel the tips of his ears growing red, the way they did when he was embarrassed or scared or really drunk. A felony! "What about — what about, well, don't you have a cleaning person?" Everybody on their street had cleaning people.

"It wasn't my cleaning person, Gabe."

"But —"

Anna was becoming fed up with Gabe; he felt like a chastised schoolboy. He was at a loss for words; he was at a loss for actions too. Then Anna's expression softened; her features relaxed to create the face that Gabe remembered from the long-ago cocktail parties. "If you talk to her, if she apologizes, to me, in person, I won't go any further than this." This was probably the face that Alan had fallen in love with initially. "She's a great kid. She's always been so wonderful to my boys, Gabe. I mean, my God, she captured Colton's first steps on video for me! You know I love her. But this is unacceptable. This needs to be addressed."

Gabe said, perhaps too eagerly, "She loves your boys too, Anna. She always has. She always came home and told me all the cute things they said . . ." (Angela, in fact, had never done this. She was a responsible, solid babysitter, but it was not her great passion. She was not the person who couldn't resist smiling at a baby in a shopping cart. Now that Gabe thought about it, actually, it *was* surprising that she'd made time for babysitting during this very busy fall . . . or, in light of this conversation, not so surprising.) "She's just . . . I can't imagine why she would do something like this. She's just under such pressure this fall. Incredible pressure."

"I'm sure she is." Anna nodded crisply, and her features tightened up again. She shook the bottle one more time. "I mean, jeez. Harvard! That's a big deal. What we expect of our kids these days is ridiculous, right?"

"Right."

"But still. These drugs are not meant for people who aren't prescribed them. It's a real epidemic among these teenagers. The side effects are worse if you aren't treating the underlying condition."

Gabe said, "Side effects?"

"Stomachache. Difficulty sleeping. Headache. Appetite suppression. Bouts of teariness, when the drug wears off. That's usually in the late afternoon with Joshua, because he needs it for school. But with these other kids, teenagers taking it to stay awake at night, who the hell knows when the drug wears off. It's no joke."

Gabe thought about Angela picking at her dinner, Angela with dark circles under her pretty blue eyes. Angela coming in eighth in a race she was qualified to win. He thought about Angela in prison, in an orange jump-suit, like that pretty blonde on that series

344

Nora had just started watching on Netflix. He felt like punching something.

Anna laid a hand on his arm. She'd always been like that, touchy-feely, which Gabe attributed to her South American roots — she was from Colombia. He didn't mind. It was oddly comforting to have a moment where only he and someone who was now mostly a stranger knew something about Angela. "It's okay, Gabe," she said. "It's really not the end of the world, I promise. But you'll talk to her?"

"I'll talk to her." This was all his fault, there was no escaping it now. The pressure he put on her, to do something he'd never done himself. All his fault.

Best to get it out of the way immediately. Gabe didn't wait until Angela had gotten herself a glass of water, until she'd stretched her hamstrings or her calves. He certainly didn't wait until she'd taken a shower. He got to her as soon as she entered the house. Nora and Cecily had dropped Maya at a reading tutor (Nora had managed to track down an available one — not the one everybody raved about, but better, they all hoped, than nothing) and gone shopping for supplies for Cecily's science fair project, and he didn't know when they'd be back.

Angela was sweating, still breathing hard. She was wearing a black Nike running cap pulled down low enough that her eyes were almost obscured. Her cheeks were pink. She looked happy, content; she looked the way Gabe remembered feeling after a day out with the cattle, the satisfaction of a job well done, the eagerness for a well-deserved rest. Some of the best sleep of his life he'd had in his boyhood bedroom, aching down to the very bones, the memory of the cold still gliding out of his muscles. All the beds in the ranch house, even his parents', had plaid flannel sheets and thick wool blankets that scratched at your chin when you pulled them up.

"Sit down."

She was confused. "What? Dad, I just got back. I'm sweating. We did eight."

"I don't care if you did eighteen. Sit down." He motioned to a stool at the island. Then he filled a glass of water for her from the refrigerator.

She said, "Dad?" Uncertainly.

"Anna Fletcher came over." He watched her face carefully.

"Dad —"

"She wasn't happy."

Several emotions crisscrossed Angela's face at once: hesitation, recognition, embarrassment, defensiveness. He watched as she settled on defensiveness. Inwardly, he approved (it was the mark of a smart negotiator, never to admit wrongdoing right away). Outwardly, he was livid.

"*Dad,* it isn't what you think . . ."

"Oh yeah?" Gabe surprised himself with the force with which his fist hit the island (goddamn granite, on the ranch they'd had Formica, which had suited everyone just fine, though the fashionable East Coasters, hobbyists, really just weekenders, who had bought the ranch from his mother had changed that — they'd made the kitchen white. White!). "If it isn't what I think, what, then, is it? Did you or did you not take pills from Joshua Fletcher? From an eight-year-old child?"

Angela stood, refusing the water. (Another mark of a good negotiator: don't act like you need anything, even when you do.) Her chest was still heaving. "It's more complicated than that."

"It's not. It's pretty simple. You did or you didn't. Which is it?"

Angela studied her feet. Then she took off the hat, placed it on the island. Bits of her hair were sticking to her forehead in a way, nearly comic, that almost detracted from her air of utter certainty and control. But

347

not quite. She looked at Gabe squarely and said, "I did."

"Oh, Angela. Angela! *Why?*"

"Because I needed them."

"Why?"

"To stay awake. To study. To do the fourteen hours of homework I have every night." (It was, in fact, just as Anna Fletcher had said. How was it that Gabe knew nothing of this phenomenon? He must be a terrible father, isolated from his children's worlds like this. When he'd woken up that morning he had been completely unfamiliar with a drug called Adderall.) Angela took a deep, quivering breath and continued. "Everybody uses stuff like that, Dad. Everybody in the top third of the class, anyway. If not specifically Adderall, then something. Massive energy drinks, other stuff, who knows. All kinds of things."

Gabe made his voice as level as he could manage. It was a struggle: he wanted to scream like a toddler. "Am I to believe, Angela, that the top echelon of your class has all stolen prescription drugs? That they have all committed a felony?"

Angela shuddered at the word *felony,* and briefly he felt sorry for her. She was the little girl who used to push a fake lawn mower around the yard behind him. She used to leave Post-it notes for him on the bathroom mirror every morning with messages like SMILE ALL DAY LONG and YOU ARE THE BEST DADDY OUT THERE. She was the girl who had tried to stay awake all night waiting for Santa when she was seven, and who had eventually fallen asleep in the dog's bed, her arm held firmly under one of Frankie's gigantic paws. Both of them drooling.

"No, but. They take them from their younger brothers or sisters. Or they lie to their doctors, fake symptoms for ADHD to get a prescription. Some kids' parents take them to the doctor for just that reason. Some of the kids who get prescriptions, they sell them. I didn't do that. I'm not *selling* drugs, Dad. Or buying them at school. I just . . . I just borrowed. Just a little bit, a couple of times, when I really needed them, just these last couple of months. Just to get through the last stretch."

"Let's be very clear here. You didn't borrow, you stole."

She sighed, started to roll her eyes. Must have thought better of it because she stopped. "Because that was the only way to do it. I never even took any before this fall. I just did it to keep up, not for any other reason. I'm not, like, some crazy drug addict, Dad. You know I'm not."

Gabe paced the length of the kitchen. Outside, the day sparkled on, oblivious. He could see the Fletchers' house, the English daisies in the front garden blooming ferociously. "That's not a good argument, Angela. That makes you sound like Lance Armstrong, and look how that turned out for him. Next thing you know you'll be acting awkward and unapologetic on *Oprah*."

"That's not funny."

"Actually, I don't think any part of this is funny."

"I don't either." She folded her arms.

"Well, then." He stopped moving, folded his arms in the exact same way as she had: a parody of a game they used to play, where Angela would try to replicate Gabe's expressions. Happy. Sad. Confused. Scared. Silly. (*How about irate, my darling daughter. Can we try irate?*) "At least we agree on something."

She snorted. "Yeah. That's about all we agree on."

He was momentarily thrown off balance by the venom in her voice. His little girl, sneering at him! "What's that supposed to mean?"

It didn't take long — three seconds, four. She turned the full force of her fury on him.

"You expect me to do all of this!"

"All of what?" He was genuinely confused. He felt exposed, nearly naked.

"You expect me to be *perfect* at *everything*. To win every race, be first in everything. You always have. And you expect me to do it without any help. And you're shocked when I can't. Well, I can't. Nobody can. So there." Childishly, she stamped her foot. He almost laughed, except this wasn't funny. None of this was funny.

"I do not —"

"Don't think I couldn't tell that you were disappointed about that race, the one that the Harvard coach was at."

Gabe swallowed.

"Ha!" she said. "That's why I didn't tell you. If you could see your face now, how disappointed you look, how worried. You're frantic."

Carefully, Gabe rearranged his features, made them as neutral as possible. He said, "I'm not —"

"You are! Of course you are! I don't know if the coach was there or if he wasn't, and I don't know if he was watching me or the girl from Novato or Henrietta Faulkner. Who knows. But I ran like crap, I think we can all agree on that. So that's one more disappointment for you."

351

"For me?"

"Yes, for you. You want me to go there so badly, Dad, it's so obvious. That's why I'm working so hard, that's why I took the pills. That's why."

"But." His voice came out smaller and altogether less manly than he wanted it to. "But *you* love Harvard. *You* want to go there."

"How do I know if I want to go there? I never had a chance to decide. It's *your* school that *you* went to that *you* picked for me that I never had any say in." Her voice broke, and then recovered. "You don't do that to Cecily, decide things for her like that. You don't do it to Maya."

Gabe couldn't stop pacing, back and forth, back and forth, a lion in its den. Pacing was a way not to have to look directly at Angela — maybe not to have to absorb what she was saying. He said, "Cecily is only ten. She's a long way from the SATs. Maya is seven!"

"You bought me a Harvard sweatshirt when I was two."

Gabe nodded. This was true. Point to Angela. He tried another angle. "Cecily," he said, "is a different person altogether. Our expectations for her are different. As they should be. And Maya is different from both of you. But let's get back to the case in point, which is the fact that you stole prescription drugs. Something like this, it could *ruin* you. All this work you've done, all these years. Gone. Just like that." He snapped his fingers. He had a very effective snap, louder and assertive. He'd honed that skill on the ranch, where it had come in handy in myriad ways.

Angela bent and peeled off her running socks. They were old and battered, gray from too much washing. Gabe felt exactly the same way as the socks looked. She tucked them into a neat little roll and put them on one of the kitchen stools. Her toenails were as short, as ravaged, as her fingernails. (Did she chew those too?) "Well, this is what it takes to get there, Dad, into your precious Harvard."

Gabe winced. Then he thought about Abby, and about his job, and he winced harder.

"Maybe not when you went there, but now. *This is what it takes.*"

Even so. He was the father here. "You think so? You actually think you can convince me that that makes it okay to do something illegal? You think every person who is going to get admitted to Harvard this year is a felon?"

She evaded that question handily. He could see her working the angles in her mind. This kid was going to be a phenomenal businesswoman one day. Then she set her lips together, the pretty little lips with which she used to proffer a goodnight kiss from the safety of her princess comforter, and said, "You try it."

Gabe said, "Huh?"

"I challenge you. Try for a month. Trying living in my shoes and see if you can do it. Do my homework for a week and see how that goes. Go to these practices, listen to the kids at school talk about their GPAs and their class ranks. All. Day. Long. Do it."

"Don't be ridiculous. I'm not going to —"

"One week! Kill yourself for one week, working for something you don't even want."

"We're back to that again? This is now, officially, something you don't want?"

"I don't know if I want it. I don't know! I never had a chance to figure it out! Like I said, it was all decided for me."

Where was Nora? Gabe was foundering in this conversation. He cast a hopeful look at the driveway, wondering when she might turn up. Nada. Empty. Across the street Anna Fletcher was climbing into her Infiniti, sunglasses on. No kids with her;

maybe the kids were with Alan.

"Let me ask you this, Dad. Why do you want me to go there so badly?"

Here was a question Angela had never asked him; he'd assumed, he supposed, that they all already knew the answer. But what was the answer? Did *he* know it? He wound his way through the bewildering maze his brain had become.

"Because," he said finally. "It's the best."

Angela smiled: a knowing smile, not very sincere. The problem with having a smart child, he thought, as he had many times in the past seventeen years, is that they were more than able to outsmart you. "Technically," said Angela, "by the way, according to *U.S. News and World Report,* Princeton is better."

"Touché," said Gabe. "It's one of the best, then. And I want the best, or one of the best, for you. I always have, and I always will."

"But," said Angela, "why?"

"Because you deserve the best. You're so smart, Angela. You work so hard. Your potential is limitless. So shouldn't you be among other people like that? Shouldn't you have the chance to spread your wings as far as they'll go?"

"Why?"

355

This line of question was becoming borderline annoying; hadn't Angela given up the *why why why* game at age three? It was highly unoriginal. She was better than this.

"So you can get a good job," he said finally.

"Like yours?"

"I have a good job, yes. That I worked really hard to get, and that I work every single day to do well at. Every single day. So I don't need you to teach me about hard work."

"So you want me to go to Harvard *like you did* and get a job *like you have* so I can, what? Stress about living in an expensive city and struggle to buy a house and raise a kid who I can then put pressure on to do the exact same thing?"

Gabe stared at her. Put that way, it seemed an unappetizing choice. He didn't answer; his energy was flagging. But it seemed that Angela had plenty for the both of them. She regained her seat at the island and considered Gabe. "Would you say that you, with your Harvard degree, are, say, happier than the guy who pumps gas at the Fuel and Save down the street?"

Gabe cleared his throat. "I don't know that guy."

"The one with the snake tattoos up his

arms. Always wears a white T-shirt."

"I don't know," said Gabe. "I don't know him. But if you held a gun to my head, yes, I would say I probably am."

"What about the rangers at Muir Woods? The nurses at Pacific Medical Center? The guy who blows our leaves?"

Gabe didn't know what to say to any of this. Finally he said, "I don't know." Really, truly, what did any of them really know of other people's happiness?

"When I look at you," Angela said, "I don't always see happy."

Gabe shifted uncomfortably. "What do you see?"

"I see worry," she went on. "I see stress."

"It's a stressful year," he said. "Lots of pressure on everyone."

"I know," said Angela. SMILE ALL DAY LONG, the little Post-it notes had said. He had saved that one; he should pull it out, stick it back on his mirror. Might be helpful. Then he thought, *Damn it. She's turning the tables on me.*

He was struggling to find a way to turn them back when they heard the Audi pulling up outside. And gone, suddenly, was the confident negotiator, the CEO in training. Angela's voice became tiny, childlike. She looked like a little broken bird. "Who are you going to tell? Are you going to tell Mom?"

"I don't know. Yes. No. I don't know." He was genuinely perplexed. What good would it do to tell Nora at this point?

"What is Mrs. Fletcher going to do?"

"She said as long as you apologize, she won't do anything. Won't press charges. But you need to do it. You need to go over there as soon as she's home and apologize. In person. Sincerely."

"I will. I definitely will." She put the hat back on, scooped the socks from the stool.

"And," he said. "It wouldn't hurt if you apologized to me too."

"Oh! No, you're right. I'm sorry, Daddy. I'm really sorry."

She was halfway down the hall on the way back to her room when he heard her turn back. He was watching Cecily and Nora disembark from the Audi. Cecily held a giant paper bag from the hardware store with some official-looking metal tubing poking out of the top. Geez. What kind of science fair project were they in for this year? Last year they'd had to put up with a thorough swabbing of the kitchen counters and the toilet seats and even the inside of Gabe's cheek so that Cecily could then grow batches of bacteria in little petri dishes.

"Dad?" said Angela. "Daddy? I didn't mean it, what I said."

"Which part?"

"I do want it. I do want to go there. I just — I just lost it back there." She came all the way over to him, stood on her tiptoes, kissed his cheek. He didn't even mind the sweat.

"You do?"

"I do."

He felt his heart swell and then constrict as he watched her disappear back down the hallway.

He'd started this train, and now he couldn't get off.

He watched from the window as Nora and Cecily carried their packages toward the side door.

It was all going to be all right.

Wasn't it?

"Hey," said Nora, handing him a bag, kicking off her shoes. "What'd we miss here?"

5:20 a.m.

Dear Marianne,
You didn't tell Mom about what I told you about the Millers' yard, did you? I didn't think so. I knew you wouldn't. You've always been such a good keeper of secrets.

You know, sometimes when I'm awake in the middle of the night it seems *almost* funny, what happened there. I mean, can you picture it? I was dressed like a burglar! I had a child's backpack! I was ready to steal an endangered plant! Which is absolutely a crime.

And then I couldn't even find the plant. I am not worth my salt, as a criminal. Marianne, your clients would be ashamed of me.

Thank goodness that housesitter was as nice as she was. I'm not sure I would have been, in her place. I promised her that when the Millers come back from Maui I'll take Loretta Miller out for coffee and tell her everything. And by everything I mean a tale I will concoct that will not involve the fact that I was going to dig up the plant. I will paint it more like an exploratory mission, totally inappropriate, but not as illegal as it was going to be.

I think, if I play my cards right, I can keep from telling Arthur about it. If I do a really super good job with Loretta Miller. If I turn on the charm full-force. And I will be the best realtor he ever saw from here on in. I will find new buyers for the Watkins house if I have to scrape the pavement for them. I will make myself indispensable. I will prevail.

Do you think I can prevail, Marianne? I really, really want to prevail.

Cecily and Pinkie were bent over the iPad, their heads so close that if Cecily's hair hadn't been darker than Pinkie's it would have been impossible to distinguish one from the other. They reminded Nora of sisters, of what she and Marianne must have looked like thousands of years ago, bent over the Monopoly board or a vigorous game of Clue. Marianne was aces at Clue — it was no wonder, really, that she'd gone into criminal justice. Nora constantly guessed Miss Scarlet, even when all evidence pointed to the contrary. She just didn't trust the look of her.

"What are you girls doing?" asked Nora, flying through the living room on her way to the kitchen. Maddie had called in sick today, very inconvenient, so Nora had come home early from Sutton and Wainwright to collect Maya and the fourth graders at school — she had promised Cathy ages ago that Pinkie could have a playdate at their house.

"Nothing," came Pinkie's answer, and "Research," came Cecily's, or perhaps it was the other way around. They were basically the same person, so it was hard to tell.

Cecily was "taking a break" from Irish dance. She might go back after the holidays; she might not. She didn't want to talk about it.

"Think of all the time you'll have," Nora had told her, even though it seemed to her like the wrong decision. "You'll have your afternoons back." Though, in truth, as the number of things to do had decreased, time itself had, unfairly, done the same. The Hawthorne family seemed to be exactly where they had always been, without enough hours in the day. It was the perplexing equation of the modern age.

Nora passed through again — she was trying to get ahead so that when Thanksgiving came she'd be able to take a couple of days and relax after the big day itself. Maybe with a book! Nora couldn't remember the last time she'd read a full book, cover to cover. Maybe she'd finally get around to finding out what all the fuss was over *Gone Girl*. Grace from the office had lent it to Nora ages ago and Nora hadn't even cracked it.

This time the girls had moved slightly apart from each other, the iPad on the table between them. Nora paused. "Is that the Golden Gate?"

"Yes." Cecily placed her body slightly in front of the screen. "We're supposed to do a report on a state landmark. Three pages."

"What have you learned?"

"Opened on May 28, 1937," reported Pinkie. "Six hundred thousand rivets in each tower."

"We found a documentary. We're renting it from iTunes, on your account. Is that okay? It's just a rental, two ninety-nine."

"Okay," said Nora. "Sure. I'm glad you're getting ahead of it."

CHAPTER 35
ANGELA

Angela's hands were shaking so much she had trouble pushing the Fletchers' doorbell.

From inside she could hear multiple chimes, a piece of music that was vaguely familiar to her but that she couldn't place. Didn't matter, but it gave her something to think about instead of what was coming. (She should know the music, though, after all those flute lessons. *Did you practice, Angela?*)

Footsteps, then the door opened to reveal Mrs. Fletcher, who smiled a half smile and said, "Angela."

"I came to apologize," said Angela. (I came to *expiate* my selfishness. My felony. For which, of course, the evidence is *incontrovertible.*) She coughed to cover the fact that her sentence accidentally went up on the word *apologize* like a question. She knew better. Ms. Simmons was all over them for that, in class. Especially the girls. (*Never sound uncertain, ladies! It diminishes how hard you've worked to get where you are. Never ever ever.*)

Mrs. Fletcher didn't say anything. She appeared to be waiting. Probably to hear Angela say the exact words, like how if you went to Alcoholics Anonymous you had to come right out and say, *My name is so-and-so, and I'm an alcoholic.* At least on television. Angela had never been to a real

Alcoholics Anonymous meeting. She thought of Edmond gulping down his chili beers. Maybe he should go.

Mrs. Fletcher was still waiting. Ugh. *Fine.* Fair enough.

So she said, "I apologize for taking Joshua's pills. I don't know what got into me."

Mrs. Fletcher's smile stretched out: it was now approximately three-quarters of a smile.

"I'm really sorry. I've brought them back, what I took." Angela had put the rest of the pills in a Baggie like the kind her mom used to pack Cecily's and Maya's lunches in. (Though Angela, as part of the Green Team, had tried to get her to switch to something reusable.)

Angela presented the Baggie to Mrs. Fletcher, who accepted it and nodded quickly. God. They were practically doing a drug deal. They may as well be standing on the street corner in West Oakland. She wondered what would happen if she tried to make a joke about that. Nothing good, she imagined. Drug jokes probably didn't go over well with someone from whom you'd actually *stolen drugs.*

Angela was hoping that was that, but. That was not that. Mrs. Fletcher motioned to Angela to come inside. She led her through the kitchen, where she stopped to place the bag on top of the refrigerator. Out of Angela's reach. As though Angela might feel compelled to steal the pills a second time! Please.

Angela followed Mrs. Fletcher out to the patio (into the *maelstrom,* she thought), where Mrs. Fletcher poured two glasses of lemonade from a pitcher in the outdoor refrigerator and handed one to Angela. Angela's mother, by the way, would kill for the Fletchers' outdoor refrigerator. Or so she always said. Angela looked around for Colton and Joshua. All things considered, as far as little boys went, they were pretty cute. Colton always smelled like cinnamon.

"The boys are with their dad," said Mrs. Fletcher, before Angela had a chance to ask. "A little getaway down at the beach."

"That sounds nice," said Angela. Mrs. Fletcher pointed to a chair and Angela sat down in it. She wasn't going to disobey, at this point. Geez. Imagine. She was here seeking *clemency.*

Mrs. Fletcher didn't sit. She leaned against the bar — the outdoor refrigerator was built into a granite bar with a sink and cabinets and a shelf fully stocked with all kinds of liquor — and shook her head. "It isn't nice. It's horrible."

"Oh," said Angela. *Whoops.* "Why is it horrible?"

"He loads them up on sugar and forgets to put sunscreen on them. And then they come back all hopped up on crap and it takes them *days* to get back to their normal routine. Just *days.*" She scratched vigorously at the nape of her neck and said, "It's awful, I hate it."

"I'm sorry," said Angela. She took a sip of the lemonade. Mrs. Fletcher turned to face a collection of bottles on top of the bar and tipped a little bit of vodka into her lemonade, then considered Angela for a long moment. It seemed that Angela was expected to say something. (What, though?) Eventually she said, "I'm not using pills anymore. I'm not, like, addicted to them or anything. I just needed them to get through a really tough time this fall. And I'm really, really sorry." She folded her hands contritely next to her lemonade glass. She *was* really sorry. She felt terrible.

Mrs. Fletcher nodded, as though that was just a casual comment, not the reason Angela was here. In fact she sort of brushed over it. Then she said, "You know what's funny, Angela?"

Angela shook her head: she did not know what was funny. She drank more lemonade.

"I used to be so envious of your family. Your parents with their perfect marriage, and you three perfect little girls."

Angela tried not to be offended at the word *little.*

Mrs. Fletcher tasted her lemonade, shook her head and frowned, and tipped a little bit more vodka in.

"This was a few years ago. When I felt like I was spending all my time just trying to get Joshua to sit still, pay attention. *Focus,* I used to tell him. You're just not *focusing.* I didn't know there was something *official* that could be done, in the beginning. To help him. God, it was so hard! Every single day was exhausting. The fights Alan and I had, you can't imagine. And I would look across the street and see the five of you piling in your car, or playing soccer on the front lawn — and I was just so envious. Those pills saved Joshua, you know."

Angela shifted her weight in the chair and tried to nod and smile bravely. How much easier this conversation would be if she hadn't actually *stolen* the pills that had *saved* Joshua. Mrs. Fletcher's face was open and honest and under any other circumstances Angela might really have enjoyed talking to her. But. She wanted to bolt like it was the last two hundred meters of a 5K.

Finally she said, "I understand."

"I don't think you do," said Mrs. Fletcher. "But why would you? I don't expect you to, not really. You're, what? How old are you now? Seventeen? Eighteen?" She looked over her yard, which was small, but meticulously maintained, with not one stray leaf or weed. There was a lemon tree in the corner.

"Almost eighteen."

"Okay. And I'm sure people tell you these are the best years of your life."

Angela nodded. Actually nobody had told her that in a while. (If this was the best, she wondered, what was the worst? Man oh man.)

"In some ways they are. Your metabolism, for example, will never again be as good as it is now."

Angela never thought about her metabolism. Was she supposed to?

"But the truth is, Angela, I remember being your age. And it's not that easy."

"Thank you," whispered Angela. More lemonade, down the hatch. "Thank you!" It really wasn't easy. It was really, really hard.

Mrs. Fletcher drank lustily, put her glass down, and said, "It's confusing. It's really fucking confusing. Life, all of it, whether you're eighteen or eighty. I know that. I'm not as jealous of you all now as I used to be. It's hard for everybody in some way, right?"

Angela wasn't sure how she was supposed to react. In general, in her day-to-day life, adults did not say *fucking* anything to her. There was a *paucity* of cursing adults in her life.

"But you know what else?"

Angela's lemonade was gone. The ice cubes hit her teeth as she took her last sip. Carefully she asked, "What?"

"It's no prize being my age either. Divorced. Single mother. Shuttling the boys back and forth. Do you know Colton left his gym sneakers at Alan's house two weeks ago and you cannot imagine the drama we went through trying to get him to school without them. It was gym day, and we didn't notice until the morning, and all hell broke loose. Seriously, all hell. Not a tragedy, right, in the big scheme of things?"

Angela wasn't sure if this question was rhetorical or not but after some time she whispered, "Right."

"But it almost undid us, I swear." Mrs. Fletcher was now looking off into the middle distance, as though she were an actress in a play talking to an unseen audience. Monologue time. "Just those sneakers." Now she looked directly at Angela.

370

Angela held her gaze. Mrs. Fletcher must have gotten those eyelash extensions that many of Angela's mother's friends were getting. "I never thought this would be me. I thought Alan and I were going to be together forever and then he just . . . Oh, never mind, I shouldn't have brought any of this up." She put her face in her hands and let out a noise that sounded like *ppppuft.*

"I'm sorry," whispered Angela. "I'm sorry about everything." And she wasn't being *specious.* She meant it.

"I know," said Mrs. Fletcher, her face still packed away inside her hands.

Angela said, "I'm really sorry I took the pills. I will never, ever do anything like that again." She stood. "Thank you for the lemonade. Thank you for not —" She paused. *Pressing charges* seemed too crime-drama-ish. (Seriously, though, thank God she hadn't . . .)

Finally she said, "Thank you for understanding."

Mrs. Fletcher opened her arms, and there was nothing for Angela to do but step into them. Mrs. Fletcher's hug was surprisingly strong — almost violent — but Angela didn't let herself squirm or pull away. She had sinned, and this was her penance. She even hugged back, just a little bit at first, and then, when she found she was still entrapped, a little bit more. Mrs. Fletcher's back was firm and muscled; hugging her was like hugging a bunch of tennis balls. It wasn't bad, the hugging, though admittedly it was a little strange. Angela hadn't hugged anyone not related to her in a long time. All in all, though, the hugging made Angela feel a little better about everything. Not just about what she'd done — but maybe like she was helping Mrs. Fletcher out too. Maybe Mrs. Fletcher didn't get hugged enough, now that Mr. Fletcher — *Alan* — had left her and was busy getting the children sunburned and feeding them bad food. So: a net gain.

Eventually Mrs. Fletcher released her and held her by the shoulders and looked deep into her eyes. Definitely, on the eyelash extensions. Nobody had eyelashes like that naturally, except maybe babies. "Be careful out there, honey. It's a wild world. You take care of yourself. You have no idea what you're in for."

"Okay," said Angela.

When she was outside the front door, and sure Mrs. Fletcher couldn't see her, she ran.

CHAPTER 36
NORA

10:14 p.m.

Dear Marianne,

I'm not even attempting to go to bed yet (tonight, at all? not sure yet) because I know I won't sleep. Everybody else is in bed (even Gabe! he's snoring a little bit in that way that gives me a hint of what it might be like one day to be married to an old man). Maya is sleeping with no fewer than fourteen stuffed animals (I counted) but her favorite is still that pink unicorn you gave her two Christmases ago. Angela is never, ever in bed this early, and maybe she's not asleep, but when I crouched down to look for the strip of light under her door I saw nothing. So I didn't even knock; I just slunk off.

I remember when she would never go to sleep without a goodnight kiss. Even when she was eleven, twelve! Then all of a sudden it stopped. All of a sudden, I didn't know when her day ended.

A couple of hours ago I got off the phone with Pinkie's mom (Cathy, not that you need to remember that). She was livid! Absolutely livid. I don't remember a time when Cathy Moynihan has actually been angry with me. She's one of those extra-sweet, super-cheerful, always-on-top-of-things people who never seem stressed and volunteer for everything and then take on work the other volunteers (me, often) sign up for and never get to. She does it all with a smile, etc., while at the same time baking healthy muffins with ingredients like hemp and chia seeds. And pinning things on Pinterest. She's like a movie version of a mom.

Of course she has only one child and she doesn't have a job. I can't help thinking that makes it easier on her.

Anyway. She was livid because earlier today when Pinkie and Cecily were watching what I thought was an innocent documentary about the building of the Golden Gate Bridge for a school project they were actually watching — on *my* iPad, using *my* iTunes account — a documentary about all the people who have committed suicide by jumping off the bridge. It's called *The Bridge,* and I guess Pinkie was so upset by it that she couldn't go to sleep tonight.

Don't you dare watch it, Marianne. I sat down with it after I got off the phone with Cathy. (Luckily the rental was still good; you know how much I hate renting something twice, Marianne. It rankles my frugal nature.) It's beyond upsetting. Seriously, don't watch it. Whoever made the documentary interviewed the parents of these poor souls, so you get a lot of regular people sitting on plaid couches and petting their lap dogs and wondering where they went wrong in their parenting.

One guy took out the recycling for his parents before he went and jumped. Like it was any other day.

Can you imagine? And Cecily and Pinkie watched the whole thing.

I see that bridge every day. It's the backdrop to so many of the homes I sell. The sun rising near it, setting over it: it's a symbol of all that people love about this city.

After I watched it I marched into Cecily and Maya's room and I said, "This is the information you need, Cecily. The main span is 4,200 feet. The total wire used is 80,000 miles. That's what your teacher wants to know. Not this other stuff."

And you know what she said, Marianne? She said, "If I was there, Mom, I would have saved him."

I said, "Who? The guy who took out the recycling?"

She said, "Any of them."

I see that comment as proof of Cecily's essential, irrevocable goodness. She has a solid gold heart, this child of mine.

She must have inherited it from you, Marianne.

CHAPTER 37
GABE

"Ah," Gabe said to Abby. They were standing on the Golden Gate Bridge. "*This* is what it's all about, isn't it? This is what makes living here worth it, what makes up for the traffic, the expense. Look at that view." Mount Tam to the north, the city to the south. Alcatraz in view. A sailboat with pristine white sails passing underneath. Beautiful.

A gaggle of Japanese tourists passed them, chattering and pointing. Then came a woman in a sari. On the west sidewalk (they were on the east) he could see a couple riding bicycles. It was warm for late November, must be mid-sixties. Abby peered at him with those odd, close-together eyes. It was strange, standing here with a woman almost his same height. She moved in closer. She parted her lips just a little bit, like she was going to kiss him.

"Oh, no, Abby," he said. "You're facing the wrong way. You've got to look out, to appreciate it." He put his hands on her slender shoulders and turned her. Gently! So gently, so she could see the twilight purpling of the sky. He could feel the vibrations from the traffic underneath his feet.

She turned.

"Look at that," he said, in his most tender and accommodating voice. "It's like nothing else in the world, this bridge. It means so much to so many people."

It would be so easy, from there. A push, a fall, a tragic accident, a young and promising life snuffed out.

So easy.

"Gabe? Gabe? Earth to Gabe . . ."

Gabe jerked back to reality. He and Nora were making homemade spaghetti sauce. This was a highly unusual occurrence, the two of them cooking together on a Friday night. They used to do it quite often, before kids. In his dismal little apartment in the Mission they'd once attempted Lobster

377

Thermidor. It had been a certified failure, and they'd paid through the nose for the lobsters. But there was lots of wine involved, so it was fun. Like most things with Nora were fun.

He pulled himself back into the present.

"You have to skin the tomatoes before you chop them, you nitwit. That's why I have the water boiling. Remember? You make the little X at one end and drop them into the water for exactly sixty seconds, no more, no less."

"You're talking to me like I'm someone who never watches *Chopped,*" Gabe said, channeling his normal voice.

If he pushed Abby off a bridge, Nora would never lovingly call him a nitwit again. He'd never make homemade spaghetti sauce again; he might never eat it again. Plus, wouldn't it be difficult to push someone tall off a bridge? Much easier to push a petite person, you'd have physics on your side. Though the rails on the Golden Gate were pretty high, no matter the size of your victim.

You're a sick bastard, he told himself. You know that? A sick, sick bastard.

Tomorrow, he would tell them at Elpis. Tomorrow, he would make it right.

Or if not tomorrow, then definitely the next day.

CHAPTER 38
MELVIN

Melvin Strickland sat in the teachers' lounge with a Starbucks coffee and a croissant. He was supposed to be watching his cholesterol and his blood pressure and everything else a man of his age (fifty-six next week) should be watching; his wife, who worked as a hospital administrator at Kaiser San Francisco, had sent him off for the day with a container of fruit salad and another container of hummus. To go with the hummus was a snack bag filled with baby carrots. He felt like a preschooler, unpacking this food from his satchel. So he supplemented.

Melvin Strickland had been teaching at the same school for two and a half decades. He'd seen his own children, three of them, two boys (easy) and a girl (more difficult than the two boys put together), through their own high school years. There had been some bad moments, and many good.

Melvin Strickland had seen thirty-one of his students accepted at Ivy League colleges. He remembered the best students he'd ever had — he could, when called upon, also remember the best work of the best students: his mental filing cabinet was extremely well organized. He figured in two and a half decades he'd graded north of 28,000 essays. He'd written hundreds of recommendation letters. He was, to put it gently, exhausted.

So when Leslie Simmons approached and sat down across from him the day before Thanksgiving (without asking), Melvin found himself decidedly this side of happy. Leslie unpacked, in short order, a Greek yogurt, a whole-wheat wrap with (she told him) almond butter, and some sort of salad, heavy (naturally) on the kale. Leslie was in her late thirties. Smart but scattered. Still had young children at home, preschool and younger, which explained the scattered. Degrees from Johns Hopkins and Stanford, which explained the smart.

"It's such a treat," Leslie said now. "To come in here every day and worry only about my own food, not what anyone else is eating, not cleaning up anyone else's messes."

"Ah," said Melvin charitably. He remembered those days, but only barely. Mostly he remembered them fondly, but his wife was always reminding him that the sheen of nostalgia did a lot to conceal the reality. She was pragmatic nearly to a fault, which was why she was so highly valued at Kaiser.

Leslie was going at the salad with what could only be called gusto. "I think these five lunches are the best part of my week." She smiled at him. She had a pretty smile. "I love Mondays. Sometimes the end of the weekend can't come fast enough for me."

This was a depressing confession, but Melvin didn't let on. Instead he inquired politely after the AP English Lit class — the crown jewel in the school's English department, and one that had been bequeathed to Leslie this year. By all accounts she was doing well.

"Oh, it's wonderful," said Leslie. She had come to them via a school in Antioch, where parental oversight was zero and student fervor a negative five. They were lucky they had nabbed her when they did, before she burned out. "Sometimes I can't believe how smart these kids are," Leslie said, "and how hard they work. How much they *care*. My word. I mean, some of this work — they really blow me away, these kids. I didn't learn that kind of critical thinking until college."

Melvin had been born with critical thinking skills. He thought of his years-old novel, rewritten so many times that it no longer bore much resemblance to what it had originally started out to be, which was a satire of a high school writing workshop.

"For example," said Leslie, "you should see some of these extended essays . . ."

Melvin felt his mind beginning to drift. His children would be home for Thanksgiving, and he couldn't wait.

Leslie was saying, ". . . far and away the best in the class. Might be the best I've seen, for high school."

Melvin was listening, but not really. In fact he was thinking about his novel, and whether or not he was ready to pull it out again, tackle some revisions. Maybe over the Christmas break. *Winter* break! They weren't allowed to say Christmas, not in this day and age. Since when was he old enough to use a term like "this day and age"? He felt like he was nineteen a lot of the time, until he looked in the mirror and saw an old man staring back at him. But the novel. He could strip it down to its barest bones, set right everything that had gone wrong. And if the details seemed dated (the setting was the late nineties), well, he could fix that. He could move it up a decade, add a few iPhones, a Twitter reference.

"Are you okay, Melvin?"

"What? Yes, of course." In fact, he had felt short of breath for a moment, but the sensation passed. Must have been the thought of unearthing his novel.

"Good. You looked a bit off there for a sec." Leslie was still talking, enthusiastically spooning yogurt into her mouth at the same time. "Virginia Woolf," she said.

Melvin perked up a little. He loved Virginia Woolf. Then his mind trotted off again. He wondered if the satire in his novel still held up. Perhaps he should change the setting from a high school to a college — a fictional version of a small liberal arts college, maybe in the East, or the Midwest. The Midwest could be funny, though Melvin wasn't that familiar with it. Maybe a road trip was in order, over the summer. His wife got two weeks off from Kaiser. They could rent a Winnebago, stop at the Grand Canyon on the way out. He'd never seen the Grand Canyon. A change in setting might solve some of the novel's more cantankerous problems. California as a setting for fiction was sort of overdone, in his opinion. Apologies to Steinbeck.

"The use of indirect discourse in, let's see, it was in *Mrs. Dalloway* and *To the Lighthouse*. Just spot-on. I mean, I did *graduate* work on Virginia Woolf, and I don't remember writing anything like this. Melvin? Melvin? You okay?"

Somewhere deep inside Melvin Strickland's formidable memory, a bell rang. "Hold on," he said. "Do you have that paper?"

"Not on me," said Leslie, holding up her hands to show that they were empty, save a fork on which reclined a forgotten piece of kale. "But I'll remember to show it to you, at some point. Plans for Thanksgiving, Melvin?"

Chapter 39
Nora

"Please, Linda," said Nora. "Come fill your plate." The Hawthornes had the Suttons over for Thanksgiving dinner any year they didn't go back east. Nora set up the dishes on the sideboard. She had thought about canceling the dinner this year, because she had trouble looking Arthur in the eye after what had happened in the Millers' yard. It would have been terrible if he'd known about it, of course, but it was nearly as awful that he didn't. Nora didn't like keeping secrets, even if they were of the self-preservation variety.

But instead of canceling she'd gone full

steam ahead: a new set of holiday place mats from Crate and Barrel, three complicated side dishes she'd never made before, a piecrust she'd had to wrestle into the pie plate because the timing of it had to be perfect. Two lovely red wines she'd researched carefully, plus a bottle of champagne to serve with the appetizers.

"Don't bother with Linda, Nora," said Arthur. "She's on day thirteen of a twenty-one-day cleanse. I said to her, 'Who starts a cleanse during the holidays?' but she just smiled and handed me a hemp seed smoothie." He raised a hand to the side of his mouth like he was telling a secret and stage-whispered, "I dumped it." He was extra-jovial because he and Gabe had started in on the cocktails early.

"Oh, you did *not*," said Linda, punching him playfully on the shoulder. "You loved it." Inwardly, Nora rolled her eyes. Normally she thought of Linda and Arthur as the world's greatest love story, but just at the moment her nerves were slightly on edge and she didn't quite have the stomach for anything that might make her feel inferior.

"Anyway, the cleanse is not so restrictive. I can eat most of what's here." Linda repaired to the sideboard and returned to the table with a tiny helping of squash.

"Besides, this way I'll be done before Christmas." She smiled and Nora released an internal sigh. She loved Linda Sutton to death, but she did not approve of cleanses. Through gritted teeth she said, "Why don't the rest of you go up."

"I might skip the turkey. I'm thinking of becoming a vegetarian," announced Cecily.

Nora sighed, outwardly this time. She had about as much patience for vegetarians as she had for cleanses. "No, you're not a vegetarian, Cecily. We had a pepperoni pizza last night!"

"Pepperoni isn't real meat."

"Where do you think it comes from?" asked Angela. "The garden?"

"No, but," said Cecily. "It doesn't *seem* real."

"Why vegetarianism?" asked Linda, with genuine interest. She leaned toward Cecily.

"My teacher says that cow flatulence is causing global warming."

"That's *ridiculous,*" said Nora. She looked helplessly at Gabe. He'd grown up on a ranch, he'd know! But Gabe was busy pouring wine for all the adults save Linda, who covered her glass with the flat of her hand and shook her head regretfully.

"Actually it's true," interjected Angela. "The methane the cows release is *way* more damaging to the climate than carbon dioxide. One cow can release, like, two hundred pounds of methane per year."

"Aren't you fortunate not to have a brilliant child?" Nora said to Linda and Arthur. She thought she saw Linda flinch, but that was probably because she'd noticed the melted butter in the squash.

"What's flatulence?" asked Maya.

"Farts," said Cecily. "Cow farts."

Maya said, "Gross."

Gabe said, *"Cecily!"*

Cecily said, "Sorry."

"Well, it's just completely uncalled for," said Gabe. "We have guests here, and I don't know how the conversation got so —"

"You're right, Daddy," said Angela. "I'm sorry I started it." She shot Gabe a look that Nora — if she had to put a name to it — would probably call guilty. That was odd. Nora made a mental note to look into that later.

"Please don't start being a vegetarian until tomorrow," Nora said. "Any of you. I was up at six with this turkey."

"I'm not a vegetarian," said Angela. "But I'm not that hungry." Gabe was looking sharply at Angela. What on earth was going on around here? Nora said, "Gabe? Not you too, right? Please, not you too."

"I'll eat enough turkey for all of you put together," said Gabe loyally. "I'm not scared of a little meat."

"Thank you," whispered Nora. She could always count on Gabe.

Gabe, bless his heart, piled his plate to the sky. So did Arthur. So did Nora, out of spite, and Maya, because Nora served her and she didn't have a choice. She'd never eat it all, but Nora felt better that at least one of her children had a groaning plate.

"Well!" said Nora, once they were all seated. "Should we have a blessing?" Her children and husband looked surprised, the way they always did when Nora's childhood religion snuck its way into the household. *Interloper!* they seemed to say to the prayer. *You don't belong here, now get on back to where you came from.* But obediently, they all bowed their heads and folded their hands in their laps.

Now that she had the floor, Nora realized she couldn't say any of the things she wanted to say. Which were, in no particular order: God, would you help Maya's reading. God, would you help Angela's Harvard application. God, would you help that snarky little intern have some misfortune befall her. God, would you help Cecily find something else she loves to replace the Irish dance hole. God, would you make sure people eat this turkey because it's organic and grass-fed and free-range and all of the other good things a turkey can be and it cost eighty-three dollars before tax and besides that I have no idea what I'm going to do with the leftovers.

This was not what prayer was supposed to be, of course. You were supposed to pray for the poor and the hungry and the sick and the dying and all of the other unfortunate people roaming the earth. You were supposed to pray for people trapped in hospices or South American mines or prison camps in the Middle East. You were not supposed to use up all of your prayers trying to keep your little healthy and fortunate family in the cocoon of health and fortune into which they'd happily been born. *Bad girl, Nora,* she thought. *Selfish and bad. You deserve nothing.*

So she went instead for brevity. *Lord, thank you for the lovely meal you have given us and the opportunity to be together with family and friends on this holiday, and Lord, help those less fortunate, amen.*

"Amen," said everyone together, and Nora was so happy about that that she said it again, louder, evangelist-style: *Amen.*

CHAPTER 40
ARTHUR

It was five o'clock on the Friday after Thanksgiving. A quiet day, of course, but Arthur went in anyway. You never knew when something might happen. Grace came in for two hours and then slunk out.

Arthur was starving. After Grace's departure, the office was empty. Only Arthur remained — Arthur, and the ghost of Jimmy Wainwright, Arthur's business partner for so many years. The Jacob Marley to Arthur's Scrooge, though Arthur and Jimmy were nice men, charitable men, men who contributed to the community and would never say an unkind or judgmental word about the poor. Linda dragged Arthur to the American Conservatory Theater's production of *A Christmas Carol* at the Geary each December, and Arthur always felt a tear or two develop in his eyes during the first act, when poor old Ebenezer worked alone in his office. You weren't supposed to feel sympathy for Scrooge in the first act, Arthur knew this, but he allowed himself the exquisitely painful luxury of it anyway. It had been ten years since Jimmy died and Arthur missed him like crazy. He couldn't bear to remove his name from the business, and so he kept it there, as homage, faithfully, the way a hunter might display in his lodge a photo of a beloved and expired coonhound.

Tonight it would fall to Arthur to turn off the lights and lock the door. Two years ago, right before bringing Nora Hawthorne back on, Sutton and Wainwright had combined its original office space with the vacant office next door — a failed cupcake bakery — and renovated the office, adding exposed brick where there was none, and brushed metal signs with the firm's name printed in a sophisticated-but-not-overly-trendy font, and a table with a top-of-the-line cappuccino machine.

Wow, he was really, really hungry. He felt a sudden and intense pang of nostalgia for the way Linda had cooked when they first met, six hundred and fifty-two years ago: spaghetti carbonara, rich with bacon fat and cream. Beef Wellington. Bourbon shrimp flambé. Linda had been an energetic and bold cook, not afraid of sauces or cream or butter. Especially butter. She'd try anything. She'd eat anything, drink anything, go anywhere. She was up for whatever.

Linda and Arthur Sutton spoke of baby Dawn only once a year, on her birthday, the fourth of December, and the rest of the year they said nothing. People who hadn't known them then didn't know about it. No need; Arthur Sutton didn't want anybody's pity. Life was hard on everybody, in one way or another. Who didn't carry a little heartbreak around with them, tucked away somewhere? All things considered, he was fortunate. He had his marriage, which he treasured above and beyond everything else in the world. He still worshipped his wife's body, all these years later, and making love to her, as he did often, and gratefully, still felt like the elegant magic it had been the very first time. He had his work, which he also treasured. He was a lucky, lucky man, living in the Bay Area, in a gorgeous home purchased three decades ago and renovated into urban perfection. He felt only occasional yearnings for Connecticut, where he had grown up, for his parents, long since passed away, for his old faithful golden retriever, for the playing fields at Brunswick School, where he'd come of age as a day student.

But sometimes, looking at Nora Hawthorne's daughters, and at Nora herself (though of course Arthur wasn't quite old enough to be Nora's father), he imagined what could have been, and the sense of melancholy he felt for Dawn was nearly enough to undo him. Cecily in particular:

there was a joy about her, a vivacity, that he knew Dawn would have had. Linda sensed this too, he was sure of this, though again they never spoke of it. Every Christmas, approximately one week after *A Christmas Carol,* Linda took Nora and her three girls to see *The Nutcracker* at the Opera House. After, they had hot chocolate at Tosca Cafe. It was one of the highlights of Linda's year, and they had carried on with the tradition even during Nora's hiatus from the job.

Arthur looked through the snack basket next to the cappuccino machine. Grace faithfully filled the basket each day before leaving, which was good, but she purchased the snacks on the advice of Linda, which was bad. Everything was all-natural, gluten free, sugar free, soy free. Taste free!

Because of Linda's latest cleanse, Arthur had no hope of a good meal at home. Linda had expunged from the house all grains and dairy, and she had relegated to the locked wine room anything remotely alcoholic. Thank goodness for Nora's Thanksgiving meal the day before. Though Nora had been acting a little mercurial, had she not? It wasn't just Nora, actually — the whole Hawthorne family had seemed a little off, not quite their usual sunny selves.

A complicated business, family life.

Not that he would know.

Arthur wanted a thick steak, a baked potato with butter, and a good Scotch followed by a glass of Cabernet. He wondered if he could get a seat at the bar at Alexander's without a reservation. Worth a shot? Maybe. He was putting on his coat — the fall evenings were downright chilly now — when the office phone rang. He hesitated. He could taste the steak already, the Scotch, the Cab. But: five o'clock on the Friday after Thanksgiving. That wasn't a typical time for the office phone to ring. It could be important.

"Sutton and Wainwright," he said. *Scrooge and Marley.*

"Arthur! Sally Bentley. I was hoping to reach Nora."

Arthur said, "Sally!" with more enthusiasm than he felt. "Hello there. Nora's off for the day from the office. Did you try her cell?"

"No, I didn't try her cell." Sally sounded as though she'd rushed to answer the phone, even though she was the one who had called. "But I wanted to catch up with her, about the Watkins listing. I know she must be feeling . . . ah, how shall I say it? Frustrated? Disappointed? Maybe a teensy bit envious?"

"Envious?" said Arthur. Why would Nora be feeling envious about the Watkins listing? Arthur waited, thought about the baked potato. Butter. *And* sour cream. It wouldn't kill him to have both, this —

"Oh, *Arthur,*" said Sally regretfully. "I thought for sure you knew, about the listing. That Lawrence canceled with you all, and is listing with me. I'm so sorry, Arthur. I just *hate* to be the bearer of unwelcome tidings."

Arthur experienced several undesirable sensations all at once: cold and hot, fury and indignation, a curious suctioning feeling in his gut that he recalled feeling only once before, when he and Linda did a wine tasting in Napa followed by a balloon ride (you were supposed to do it the other way around).

It was ruined now: the seat at the bar at Alexander's, the Scotch. Even the goddamn sour cream was ruined. He had never lost a listing to Sally Bentley. She might have represented volume, but Sutton and Wainwright represented *class.* Look at the exposed brick in the office, look at the cappuccino machine!

"And I hate to kick a person when they're down, Arthur."

"Who's down?" said Arthur. "I'm not

down. I couldn't be more up." In fact he was starting to feel a little bit down.

"Why, about what happened at the Millers' house, of course. Over on Sycamore. Last week."

Millers, Millers. Rang a bell, yes, Nora's listing, some time ago. Sycamore. Yes. Slightly difficult buyers, but nothing Nora couldn't handle. She'd handled them beautifully, in fact. With grace and aplomb, typical of Nora. It was coming back to him now. The Millers on Sycamore. Beautiful home.

"Loretta didn't call you? I thought for *sure* she'd call you. You know I've known Loretta forever, it's just that I never got along with her husband — long story, Arthur, pretty hilarious, remind me and I'll tell you sometime. Really just a big misunderstanding. In fact, that's why they approached your office and not mine when they were looking to buy. Which was a blow to me, of course. I've always been in favor of letting bygones be bygones —"

"What on earth," said Arthur testily, "are you talking about, Sally?" Forget the potato. Now he just wanted the Scotch, and the Cabernet. Maybe an order of the shichimi fries. His stomach muttered.

"I'm talking about Nora. At the Millers' house. You know about this, right? Oh my goodness, Arthur, wait a minute, do you really not *know* about this? *Nora* didn't tell you? *Loretta* didn't call you? Well, they haven't been back from Maui for more than three or four days but I thought for sure she'd call you immediately."

Arthur listened. His stomach dropped down, then down again, into a place he hadn't known it could go. He was no longer hungry and he wasn't thirsty; he didn't want the Scotch nor the Cabernet nor the shichimi fries.

Well, maybe the Scotch.

Definitely the Scotch.

CHAPTER 41

State Landmark Report
By Cecily Hawthorne
Mrs. Whitney's 4th Grade Class

The Golden Gate Bridge is one of California's most famous landmarks. It is also one of the most famous bridges in the world. It opened to cars on May 28, 1937. The day before people were allowed to walk across it. There was a line of people waiting to cross by 6 a.m. that day. There were 18,000 people in the line. One man walked across the Bridge and back again on stilts the first day it was open! His name was Florentine Calegeri, and he was really good on stilts.

The Golden Gate is not golden. Many visitors to San Francisco think it is going to be and are surprised. The Bridge got its name because it goes over the Golden Gate Strait. The strait was named by a person in the United States Army in 1846.

Eleven men died building the Golden Gate Bridge. 96 men died building the Hoover Dam, which opened one year earlier, in 1936. So that is an interesting number. You would think a lot more people might die building such a big bridge. Ten of the men died in one single accident on the bridge when it was almost done. Everybody who worked on the bridge had to wear a safety belt and a hard hat. There was a safety net put under the bridge during the building and that saved 19 men. The net allowed the men to work faster than they would have because they were not afraid of falling and dying, which I would be if I worked on that bridge. The ten men who died were all on a piece that fell through the net. That must have been really scary.

The Golden Gate Bridge is a Suspension Bridge. The Golden Gate is not the longest suspension bridge in the world. But it used to be. Now it is ninth. The longest one is in Japan and other long ones are in China, Hong Kong, Denmark, and New York.

You can still walk or drive across the bridge. I have done it and it is fun. It is 1.7 miles long. It can be tiring if you have to walk back across. A good idea is to have someone pick you up at the other end. Some of the things that are not allowed on the bridge are electric scooters, roller blades, roller skates, and dogs unless they are service dogs. Also you can't bring a wheelbarrow, not that you really would want to! You also cannot scatter ashes from the Bridge. You aren't allowed to drop or throw anything at all. If you do you will get in big trouble.

The Golden Gate Bridge is one of the most popular suicide destinations in the world! But lots of people are saved every year by Bridge Patrol or by regular people who happen to be on the bridge. So that's good. Sometimes people jump from the bridge and survive, but not very often. Usually if you jump you die. Bridge Patrol officers use patrol cars, bicycles, and motorized scooters to go back and forth across the bridge and to try to stop people from jumping.

The chief engineer of the bridge was Joseph Strauss. He died in Los Angeles almost exactly one year after the bridge was done. There was also another man that had a lot to do with the design of the bridge but he had a big fight with Joseph Strauss so Joseph Strauss got all of the credit. The other man finally got credit in 2007.

There are 600,000 rivets in each tower. A rivet is a pin or bolt that holds together two pieces of metal. The Golden Gate Bridge did not get damaged in the famous earthquake in 1989. The Bay Bridge did. That's a different bridge that goes to Oakland.

The color of the bridge is called international orange. The bridge is always being painted a little bit at a time. The U.S. Navy wanted the bridge to be painted with black and yellow stripes to make it easy to see. But they didn't get their way.

The Golden Gate Bridge is one of California's most famous landmarks. To many people it is what they think of when they think of San Francisco.

CHAPTER 42
ANGELA

December

It was five o'clock in the evening and Angela was parking (badly) on Fillmore Street. Her mother had wanted to accompany her — embarrassing, but kind of sweet — and now that she was trying to parallel park she sort of wished she'd taken her up on the offer. Angela had many fortes, but parallel parking was not one of them.

This was Angela's interview with a Harvard alumnus.

"I can do this alone!" she insisted.

See me, the note from Ms. Simmons had said on her extended essay, and she burned with shame, thinking about it. She couldn't even meet Ms. Simmons's eyes in class anymore.

"I won't come *in* with you," her mother said. "I'll just make sure you make it there safely, and then I'll leave you to it. I'll go get a cup of coffee."

"I thought you didn't drink coffee after one in the afternoon."

"I'll get a decaf."

Maya, piping up from the living room: "You could have wine."

"I don't drink wine at five o'clock on a Wednesday."

"Yes, you do. Sometimes you drink it earlier."

"Okay, Maya, that's enough out of you."

Angela wanted to go it alone. She wanted it to be perfect. She dressed carefully, in an outfit she'd chosen from J.Crew earlier in the fall for exactly this purpose — gray toothpick pants, an embroidered tank, and a matching cardigan, all of which she would probably never wear again. Wasn't her style. She could hand it down to Cecily, except it *definitely* wasn't Cecily's style. Also Cecily was almost as tall as Angela. Maybe one day it would be Maya's style. Did Maya have a style? Not yet, but she'd get one. Everybody did, eventually.

Nope, she couldn't do it, she couldn't parallel park in the city this close to rush hour. She pulled out of the space — only the nose of the car was in there anyway — and found a garage, forking over thirty-three (?!) of the forty dollars her mother had given her for this very reason.

Susan Holloway, class of '76, was a partner at an environmental law firm: Bennett, Collins, Holloway. All of the names seemed very lawyerly. Angela understood only in a general sense what environmental lawyers did; she hoped it didn't come up. She was ushered from the main lobby, which was decorated with tastefully framed photographs of waterfalls and breaching humpback whales, into Susan Holloway's office by an assistant with a perfect blond bun and a tasteful suntan. She must, Angela decided, following her down a long bright hallway, use one of those doughnut things to get the bun so perfect. Angela had tried to use one before but could never get it right. Cecily was really good at using doughnuts; she used them with her Irish dance wig. Back when she used to wear an Irish dance wig.

"Okay," said the assistant, letting air out through a space between her front teeth. "She'll be with you in just a moment." Angela sat in the chair the assistant pointed to and braced herself. She pictured Susan Holloway, class of '76, as tall and sternly Scandinavian, maybe like an Old Norse princess. Watching through the fog while the ships rolled in.

Deep breath. She dug her fingernails into her palms. She felt like she was waiting for

403

a doctor to examine her.

"*Hello.* You must be Angela. Who else would you be!"

Angela turned, rose. Susan Holloway, class of '76, turned out to be one of the few adult females over whom Angela towered. It was refreshing. She had tight little dark curls (*a crown of curls?*) and thin lips that disappeared when she smiled. She looked like a friendly hamster. She looked like the one Cecily had brought home that one weekend.

Angela cleared her throat, channeled her mother, and said, "It's so, so nice to meet you, Ms. Holloway. Thank you for taking the time to talk with me."

If it was possible, Susan Holloway smiled harder; the smiling looked almost like physical exertion. A little vein popped out in the center of her forehead.

"That's a nice firm handshake you have there, Angela. Who taught you that?"

"My father." Angela thought of her father's giant rancher's hands, brown and strong. He used to birth calves with those hands. Disgusting, of course, but also fascinating.

"Well. Good for him. Thank you for coming out to my office. Any trouble finding the place?" Angela shook her head, trying not to think about the botched parallel parking job. "No? Just shot right over the bridge from Marin, did you? I love Marin. I always said if I ever leave the city that's where I'd land. But I never left, so I never needed to land!" She paused, and into the space she left Angela inserted a noise that was supposed to be a laugh but that sounded like *humpgh.* "Anyway, I really do appreciate it. I used to conduct these interviews from my home, in the evening, but I think the office just makes so much more sense. People tend to be a bit more at ease in a formal setting, ironically enough. And now I don't have to make sure the kitchen is cleaned up!"

Susan Holloway sat down and Angela regained her seat in front of the desk. "I'm so sorry," said Susan Holloway, "that I have to sit behind this giant desk. I used to have two chairs in front of the desk but it seems as if someone has absconded with one of them."

Angela laughed agreeably. Susan Holloway sort of scared Angela. She was like a hummingbird on Red Bull — even when she was sitting still she gave the impression of darting about.

"Can I offer you anything? Water? Tea? Or did Alva already offer you something?"

Alva. So she was the Scandinavian one,

the assistant. "No, thank you, Ms. Holloway. I'm goo— I'm fine, thank you." Ms.
Simmons: *You are good, in general. At least I
hope you are. But in this situation you are fine.*

"Oh, let's dispense with the formalities,
shall we? Although I do appreciate it. Just
Susan, please."

"Okay. *Susan.* "

"What a sweet smile you have, Angela, and
beautiful blue eyes. I couldn't say that if I
were a man interviewing you, could I? But
here I am, a woman, so I am free to comment. Doesn't seem quite fair, does it? I
came of age — *professionally speaking* — in
the late seventies. Where nothing seemed
quite right. These interviews are often as
much of a learning experience for me as
they are for Harvard, you know! Though I
do tend to babble on. You must let me know
if I'm babbling, will you do that? Yes? No? I
hope you will. I'm just looking through your
file here, Angela. I reviewed it before you
came in. The academics are stellar, of
course. No surprise there. We don't get
many early-action applicants who are not.
In some sense you're all starting from the
same place in that respect, are you not?"

Ooof. True enough, but Angela didn't
need to hear it. She leaned forward in her
chair and tried to appear alert but not overly

eager, the way she'd rehearsed in the mirror at home. This in itself was difficult; she almost tipped right out of her chair.

There was that voice again, sniping at her. *Higher, Angela. Faster. More more more.* There were the voodoo-doll pinpricks. There she was, wanting it so much it literally hurt.

"So why don't you tell me about your extracurricular activities. That's always the first question they like us to ask. They're stricter about the format here than you might guess. We have meetings and so forth where they tell us how to do this, check in with us. Give us tips. Make sure we're still *worthy.* So far I've passed the test, I guess. Which is good for me. I like to keep tabs on what the younger people are up to. Anyway, I have it all here on my sheet, of course. But I like to hear you tell it to me yourself. So I get a real sense of things, of what's important to you. So anytime you're ready. Why don't you start with your varsity sports."

Deep breath. Deeper. She'd practiced this one. "Well. My sport is mostly . . . I mean, these days, it's running. I used to swim and play lacrosse and soccer. But it got to the point where I had to pick one. So I picked running."

Susan smiled again, the lips pulled tight across her front teeth. "A runner! I was a runner, back when I still had my own knees. The artificial ones just don't *bend* as much, you know?"

Angela didn't know, but she nodded and smiled as though she did.

"But they are supposed to be astonishingly enduring. This last one should take me almost to the end."

Another smile: her politest, smartest, Ivy Leaguest smile.

"Wonderful sport," said Susan. "Best distance?"

"Cross-country. Five kilometers on the track." What a nerd she was. Nobody liked a 5K on the track; it was simply the ugly truth that she didn't have the speed for anything shorter.

"A distance runner! I was a sprinter, myself." Angela was surprised that Susan Holloway's hummingbird legs had enough muscle to get her through a sprint. "Never quite had the endurance for the distance. Seemed like a lot of pain for not much reward. Although I'm sure you feel differently."

Actually, Angela didn't. "I'd be a sprinter if I could. But I don't have the speed."

"Grass is always greener," said Susan.

"Am I right?"

Damn straight, thought Angela.

"What else? Music?"

Practice, Angela, practice.

"Well. I've been in the all-county band for three years now."

Did you practice?

"Instrument?"

"Flute."

"Wonderful. A beautiful instrument."

Angela, don't forget your music book. Don't forget your cleats. Your bathing suit. Your book report, your science fair project, Angela. Your lunch.

"I'm an officer in my school's chapter of the National Honor Society." (*See me,* in Ms. Simmons's felt tip.)

"Position?"

"Secretary."

"Okay. Well, still counts as a position, right?"

She should have gone for vice president. There was a sensation in her stomach she couldn't put a name to. Not exactly nausea, but maybe nausea's younger cousin.

"And, let's see, French Club. Any officer position?"

"Vice president."

So there.

"That's fine. Next?"

"Senior-class president, this year," said Angela, wondering what, exactly, Susan Holloway meant when she said, "Fine." Also, she should have led with senior-class president. What was wrong with her. What was *wrong* with her? Was she flubbing up the interview? Her heart was starting to race. Also, there seemed to be a small creature (a woodland fairy?) inside her skull, banging on it with a mallet.

"Wonderful. That's the big kahuna, as they say. Maybe not as big as student government president."

That was Henrietta. Damn it.

"But still, big. If I were you, I would have led with that. But never mind. It all comes out in the wash, doesn't it?"

Does it? And a woodland fairy wouldn't be mean enough to bang with a mallet, would it? She'd have to ask Maya. Maya knew everything about fairies.

"What else?"

Angela, did you find a charity organization yet? Harvard's going to want to see that, you know. Start thinking about it. Two charities, if you can.

"Student Sharing — that's where we do volunteer outings. For example, ah, last month we attended a Justice Education Day at the Saint Anthony Foundation in the

Tenderloin. In the spring we're planning a fund-raiser for the new dining room they're building."

"Very rewarding, I'm sure."

"It was. And . . . let's see. Speech and Debate."

"How did you find that?"

Angela scratched her palm. If her mother had been here she would have said, *How did I find it? I looked it up on Google. Ha ha ha.* Her mother loved a corny joke. And her dad liked her mom's sense of humor. But maybe the intern was funnier.

Duh. Even Angela knew that people did not generally begin affairs because the new person was *funnier* than the person they were married to.

Angela hated Speech and Debate. "Well. I liked it. I get nervous, sometimes, talking in front of people. But my aunt in Rhode Island is a lawyer, she works with some really tough cases, and so I guess I try to imagine sometimes that I'm her when I'm up there. That someone's life depends on how I do, you know? That helps. She's a really good lawyer."

When was she going to say something to her mother about the intern? She'd told herself it would be after she submitted the Harvard application, but now she realized

411

she was waiting to find out if she got in before she stepped up her investigation.

"I like that. I like that answer very much. Very honest. Just hang on a second while I note that down . . . Okay, noted. Please go on."

Angela felt extremely pleased by that, the noting down. Excellent sign.

"The last three years I did Best Buddies, but not this year."

"Is that some sort of a dog charity thing? You'd think I would know every activity out there, having done these interviews for so long. But every school does things differently."

Angela smiled. "Um, no, it's not a dog charity. It's working with disabled students. Sometimes, um, before or after school, but sometimes having lunch with them, that sort of thing." *Stop saying um.*

"I see. Did you like it?"

"I loved it." This was one hundred percent true. There was a girl in their school, Mary Lou Wilkerson, with cerebral palsy. Angela ate lunch with her twice a month junior year. She had terrible depth perception, the worst. It killed Angela every time she helped her with her lunch tray, it just about did her in to watch what a mess Mary Lou was, and how she just kept trying anyway, just kept

412

keeping on, smiling her lopsided smile, eating her French fries. *God.* Poor Mary Lou. Angela had to blink rapidly a few times to get herself back into interview mode.

"What did you like about it?"

"I, ah, well." *Don't say ah, either.* "I liked helping. I liked trying to see my world through their eyes, and their world through mine. It's so competitive at my school. It was really nice to step away from that for a little while, and just *be,* you know? Just try to make someone laugh." She thought, *Nailed it,* and then instantly felt like the worst person in the universe. Using Mary Lou Wilkerson for her own gain like that. She was definitely a monster.

"Why only three years?"

Shit.

"This year I didn't have time anymore. With applying to college and everything. I had to give some things up."

Angela, is the application done? It's October, you know. Not much time now.

"You sound wistful about that."

Wistful was such a pretty word; it made Angela think of ladies playing tennis on grass courts wearing long skirts. "I guess I am. I miss it." She never saw Mary Lou anymore.

"Let's see here. This says Green Club?"

413

"Recycling. We do can drives, water aware-ness week. We do a thing on Earth Day where we go to an underprivileged school and help build something, like a playground slide." Angela had cut her post-workout showers down to three minutes because of Green Club.

"How do you spend your summers?"

"This past summer I worked for three weeks as a volunteer docent at the Explor-atorium."

"It's lovely, isn't it? The new building by the Pier. I'm so glad they moved from that rusty old building they were in. Although I've heard that financially it hasn't been the boon for memberships they were hoping for."

Angela scratched at her other palm. How much longer? "I — um, I don't know about that. But it is beautiful, yes."

"And the other weeks?"

"Let's see. I did four weeks as a counselor in the Rec and Park for my town, for a multi-sport camp. One week I went on vaca-tion with my family, to Alaska." Maya had almost fallen off the boat during a whale-watching cruise, but other than that it had been a spectacular trip. Henrietta's summer adviser had probably told her not to go on any family vacations this past year. Shit, why

414

didn't Angela have a summer adviser?

"Wonderful! Any summer job that carried throughout the whole summer or into the school year?"

Angela almost laughed, then caught herself. It was actually legitimately funny, that Susan Holloway thought that anyone with the schedule Angela had just detailed would have time for a job. She didn't know anyone in the top of the class who held down a job along with everything else. Her mother, as she reminded them *often,* had scooped ice cream at Newport Creamery throughout her high school and college years. She talked a lot about the famous Awful Awful, and she brought the whole family there every time they went east so they could all experience it. (Awful Awfuls were actually to die for.)

"Um. No, not really. After Alaska we started summer training for cross-country, and the AP course work . . . and I guess that was it." The summer had gone by in a blink. Half a blink. One careful reading of *Jane Eyre,* some statistics work, the beginning of the Harvard application, and whoosh, it was over.

"I see. Now, Angela, why don't you tell me what the last book was that you read that wasn't a school assignment. You look

415

surprised."

Angela *was* surprised. Reading for pleasure! It was almost funny. "Well, it's just that . . . well. Let me think. No, that wasn't. . . . It's just that, with all the reading for school — I have five AP classes this semester — I actually don't have time to read anything else. I wish I did."

See me, from Ms. Simmons, written right across the top of the extended essay. Horrifying. She felt herself starting to blush and so she tried to think of very cold things: icicles, skiing in Tahoe, cold showers at summer camp.

"Anything at all?"

Angela's mind was a wasteland; she couldn't think of the title of a single book. Not one. She felt like she'd just taken all of her clothes off and was sitting in front of Susan Holloway completely naked while Susan Holloway checked for flaws.

"Well. Isn't that a pity. I finally had a chance to read *Gone Girl.* I felt like I was the only person on earth who hadn't read that. Made me uncomfortable, in the end. I suppose that was the author's intention. But thank you for your honesty. It's refreshing. I'm looking at my watch here and it seems like our time is almost up, if you can believe it. I have so many more questions I could ask. I didn't even ask you where you see yourself in ten years! Which is a standard. And believe me, I get a wide variety of answers. The smart alecks always tell me they see themselves five years out of Harvard." Susan Holloway chortled.

"I have more time if you do, Ms. Holloway." She really didn't want to answer the ten-year question, though. That sounded awful awful.

"Susan."

"Susan."

"I'm afraid I'm off to an engagement. I have to meet someone to go to the symphony, and I have the tickets. I don't know why, but I seem to be the one with the tickets always. The most organized of my group, I guess." She smiled again, and the vein came back out to say hello. "I wish I did have more time! It's been a delight. Do you have any questions for me, Angela? You look like you might."

Her father had said it would be good to have one question in her pocket, just in case. She scraped her mind, she scraped her pocket, but nothing came up.

Well, something came up, but it was not Dad approved. Definitely not.

Don't ask it, Angela. Do not ask that question. You idiot, you complete idiot. Don't.

"I do, actually. I do have one. It's sort of . . ."

Don't do it! Stop it. STOP *it.* The words were gearing up, ready to launch out of her mouth.

"Yes?"

Quick, think of something else.

"I've been wondering . . . well, I've been wondering if you think that Harvard . . ."

"Out with it, Angela. He who hesitates in this world is lost, as I'm sure you know. Especially at the Ivies." Another chortle. Angela had been under the impression that mostly chubby, jolly people chortled, but apparently that wasn't the case: you could be elfin and chortle anyway.

"I guess what I'm wondering is. This is something I'd like to ask my father. But I think the question would upset him." Deep breath. Go ahead, what do you have to lose? Only everything . . .

"Is it all that it's cracked up to be?"

A long pause. Angela thought she might just go ahead and check her bag for poison, in case she had any to take.

Then Susan Holloway unleashed a peal of laughter that was so long Angela thought it might have been built in parts and strung together in a warehouse.

"Ha! How *refreshing.* I love that question.

Nobody has ever asked me that before. I'm just going to take a sip of water here. Let me think about this a moment so I can answer properly. In my experience, Angela, nothing is really and truly all that it's cracked up to be."

I knew it!

"But Harvard comes pretty close. For me, it was paradise, it positively opened my eyes in every way, shape, and form. Made me what I am today, absolutely."

If I don't get into Harvard, it might be because of that question. Or it might not. And I'll never know.

"Best of luck to you, Angela, it's been a real pleasure. There's that firm handshake again. You must tell your father he did well to teach you that. Are you going to have any trouble getting out of the city? No? Well, you seem like a capable young lady to me. I will say, though. And I'm sure I'm not supposed to say this. But when I look at what you kids have to do today, just to stay even, never mind to get ahead — well, it makes me glad that I'm through it all, and well on the other side. I'd be happy to have the *knees* of a seventeen-year-old, make no mistake about it. But the rest of it? You can *have* it. Oh, don't look so crestfallen. You're going to do fine. With these grades and these scores. You sure you know your way back? I think this city can be so confusing for young drivers. Okay, then, so nice to have met you, Angela."

Once she was back on the sidewalk Angela's entire body sagged with relief. She was so happy to be done, she could have kissed the homeless man who was collecting money on the sidewalk. Instead she gave him the remaining seven dollars from her mother's parking money. It wouldn't hurt, she thought, if Susan Holloway happened to be looking out the window at the exact same time. Extra points for charity.

Susan Holloway, class of '76 and part-time hummingbird, seemed to have taken a shine to Angela. Right? Or did she act head over heels in love with every early-action applicant who sauntered through her door? What did Susan mean, telling Angela she was going to do fine? Fine getting into Harvard, or fine when she was rejected from Harvard and had to rebuild her life? Who knew. Angela had either aced it, or she had flubbed it completely. She just had no idea which —

Higher, Angela. Faster. Better better better.

Practice makes perfect, Angela. It wouldn't be a saying if it weren't true.

More.

CHAPTER 43
GABE

It became easier for Gabe to be away from the office than it was for him to be there. He'd checked with HR about the possibility of hiring Abby Freeman full-time when her internship ended in December; he'd even gently floated the idea by two of the senior partners, and he'd gotten the same answer from all of them: Elpis wasn't hiring recent grads, no matter how good they were, no matter what a phenomenal job they'd done (as Abby had) of handling the beginning of the Bizzvara presentation. The internship program at Elpis was meant to be finite — a stepping-stone to business school, perhaps — and they might welcome the return of those interns once they had their MBAs, particularly if they had MBAs from the top schools. But not before.

The world had changed dramatically since that grubby little office in Outer Sunset.

And they wouldn't consider making an exception? For an extremely bright intern?

No, Joe Stone told Gabe, no, they wouldn't. And why, might Joe Stone ask, was Gabe taking such an interest in the career of Abby Freeman?

No reason, said Gabe, except he thought

she was very talented.

He did *not* like the look Joe Stone gave him.

If he had a client meeting, obviously, Gabe's presence was expected, and he showed. But when he didn't, it was simple enough to disengage. Disappear. Hide out. A matinee, once. *Captain Phillips,* a nice long movie, though riveting all the same: he bought Junior Mints and Twizzlers both and chased them with a large Dr Pepper. Another time he met Skip Moynihan at his club in Novato for a leisurely nine holes, followed by drinks and lunch in the grill room. Three hours gone, just like that. It was easy, in the digital age, to disappear for long periods of time and yet be instantly accessible. It was so easy, in fact, that Gabe wondered why he'd never thought of it before. Look at all he'd been missing.

One day in early December he crossed the Bay Bridge and headed out to the East Bay. He rarely had reason to cross the Bay Bridge, but a guy from the Bizzvara team had mentioned some good hiking out that way.

In the olden days, when he and Nora were new to each other, and new to the Bay Area, they'd been inexhaustible: Stinson Beach to Mount Tam, Bonita Park, Pedro Point

Headlands, an overnight camping trip once to Point Reyes, where they'd made it to the northernmost tip of Tomales Point and had seen two red-beaked, red-eyed oyster catchers. Since the kids, the hiking had slowed considerably, and now they hardly ever went.

Gabe had researched a few possible hikes carefully on his laptop at work. Yelpers, it turned out, were quite prolific with their reviews of hiking trails; it was surprising to Gabe that so many people had so much time not only to hike but also to post comprehensive reviews and even photographs of their hikes.

Eventually he chose Las Trampas because the Yelpers (Chloe C. from San Ramon, Larry B. from Walnut Creek, Stephanie H. from Alamo) talked a lot about the trails being quiet, sometimes nearly deserted. Gabe was about as anxious as he remembered being anytime in his life, so quiet and deserted seemed like just the ticket. He was anxious about Angela. Had they done everything, every single thing, they possibly could have? Should she have stayed on the swim team longer, learned more languages? What had happened to her in that last cross-country race, which she should have won handily? Was it the Adderall? He was anxious about that, too, and about the fact that he hadn't told Nora yet — he should have, but he was worried that Nora would blame *him* for pushing Angela to a point where she became a felon. A felon! Geez. Then, of course, he was anxious about the situation at work, so anxious that he hardly wanted to think about it. He was anxious about Maya; should they get her tested for a learning disability again?

No shade, and very hot in the summer (everybody on Yelp talked about the heat), but in December he should be fine hiking Las Trampas. The rains hadn't come yet; it wouldn't be slippery. (The Yelpers had warned about the slipperiness after the rains. The Yelpers had thought of everything.) In fact he had heard in a piece on NPR that the rains might not be coming at all this year. The snowpack in the Sierra Nevada was lower than it had been in decades. California had a severe drought coming. It was gold rush dry.

Gabe was no stranger to drought; Wyoming was the fifth-driest state in the Union.

He parked in a residential neighborhood on a street named Camille. Pretty houses, lots of renovation going on. Nora would have something to say about that. She'd be able to look at the houses and pinpoint which renovations would increase the curb appeal and which would not.

Gabe had found a reasonable hike, four miles, steep, but (so said the Yelpers) worth it for the view from the ridge.

He didn't bring his phone, didn't bring his wallet, locked his car. Didn't even bring a bottle of water, because he didn't have one with him. Bad hiking form. He started up the trail, which didn't, in fact, seem so steep after all. Had the Yelpers exaggerated? He paused at the trailhead to read the sign about what to do if you saw a mountain lion. These were things he already knew, having grown up in a mountain lion state. But he read it anyway, as a refresher. Make yourself appear as large as possible. Make noise. Act like a predator. Throw stones or branches. Don't turn your back, don't run. Back away slowly. If attacked, protect yourself. (Not bad advice for dealing with Abby Freeman either, was it?) He had seen signs like that all over California, but he had never seen an actual mountain lion here. In Wyoming you could hunt them. In California, of course, land of the liberals, you could not.

He paused and squinted — it was midday, and, despite the season, the sun was strong. He began the ascent.

Okay. Now he saw what the Yelpers were yelping about. The trail went from flat to incredibly steep in three seconds. He had read about people trail running, even mountain biking, up here, but for the life of him he couldn't imagine that. He could hardly walk.

It felt good, though, working his quads like this, up and up and up. His calves were straining. He was starting to sweat. He was overdressed, to be sure, in his work clothes, but he'd found a pair of sneakers in the trunk of his car. So that was something.

He seemed to have the place to himself. The rocky trail was bordered by trees in the beginning, live oak, bay laurel. Farther on, the trail opened up and the trees gave way to more varied vegetation — he recognized black sage and buck brush but there were others that he did not know.

He was breathing hard, working hard. He felt the knot of anxiety begin to loosen. He let his thoughts wander. He thought of the first time he'd seen Nora, at that bar in Noe Valley. She'd been so beautiful — she still was! Love of his life. He thought of the births of each of his children, he thought of the day he'd gotten the job at Elpis. Happy moments, all of them, joy, joy. He was a lucky man. (*But what if you lose it?* asked

426

the bothersome voice inside his head. *What then?*)

In some parts the ascent was so steep that Gabe had to grasp for tree roots and make his way up on his hands and knees. He passed a woman walking two golden retrievers. The woman and the dogs all eyed him warily, and he supposed that in his untraditional hiking clothes (khakis and a dress shirt, the sleeves rolled up to his elbows, the sneakers) he probably looked like some sort of pervert trolling the trails, the Pee-wee Herman of the East Bay. No matter. His lungs were filling and expanding, the December sunshine was now joyously unrelenting. The bothersome voice was receding. This was the California dream, right here, a piece of unpopulated land, his for the taking.

Halfway through the ascent he passed a cluster of cows. If the Yelpers hadn't mentioned the cows he would have been wholly taken aback, but he knew from his Internet research that the parks service leased out part of the land for cattle grazing. It didn't look like much to graze on to Gabe's eye, all this scrub, but he supposed the cows knew what they were doing. California cows, like California people, were probably more adventurous, more accustomed to

427

adapting to changing circumstances, than those from Wyoming. One of the cows looked at Gabe and made a halfhearted lunge toward him, then seemed to change her mind and turn away.

"Easy does it," said Gabe, which was what he used to say on the ranch. He'd learned that from his father. He could practically hear his father talking to the cattle in that gentle and encouraging way he had — as though he understood what they were going through, what they were up against.

More sweating, more breathing, in and out, in and out. Gabe's father had died from kidney failure, one year after Gabe and Nora started dating. Gabe tried not to think about the fact that he was only a decade away from the age his father was when he died — his father had seemed downright ancient to Gabe in the last year of his life — and concentrated instead on the trail in front of him. It was easier to ascend if you didn't look more than three steps ahead. He tripped once on a tree root and went down on one knee, but no harm done, he recovered, though now there was a hole in his khakis.

Angela could have flown up this mountain; she was in the shape of her life. Cecily could have slip-jigged up it. Maya would have walked for about six minutes and wanted to turn back. What about Nora? She would probably have a showing, wouldn't be able to make it.

At last — at last — he reached the ridge. And it was worth it, every drop of sweat, every uncertain breath, the cows, the judgmental dogs, all of it. To the east, he could see the majestic Mt. Diablo, bright green at the base, brown at the top. To the west, the darker green Oakland hills. Breathtaking, in every possible way.

Under his feet the dirt was dusty and dry. He sat for a moment on a little patch of scrubby grass — the khakis were now mostly a loss. He was definitely regretting not bringing water. But it was beautiful here, and in almost every way more similar to Wyoming than any place he was likely to find in Marin. Why had he never hiked in the East Bay before? He felt, after so many years away, like he was home.

Maybe it was the familiarity of the landscape, and maybe it was the cow sighting, but there on the ridge Gabe experienced a sensation he hadn't had since his boyhood, when sometimes he would look around the ranch, at the cattle grazing in the distance, at the long low ranch house where his mother cooked stews and chili, the two bedrooms he and his brothers shared, and revel in and marvel at the smallness of his place in the world. One person, one person's troubles or decisions, took up such an insignificant amount of space.

By the same token (the hills in the distance seemed to say), you got only one chance on this big green earth. You had to make the most of it. You had to do it right.

Have you done it right? the voice asked him. Not exactly, he told the voice. Not entirely. But I'll make amends. When he got home, that very day, he would tell Nora everything. Open a bottle of wine, pour them each a glass, spill the tale of his shame and woe while she fixed him with that empathetic look that made her so good at her job. He'd ask for her forgiveness, maybe even her sympathy. Definitely her advice. He'd take whatever it was he had coming. Would she still love him? He wasn't sure. He didn't know what he'd do if she didn't.

That felt better. That felt really good. The decision made, he stood, stretched his arms above his head, bent down, and rubbed at his tight calf, ready to begin his descent.

And then he saw the mountain lion.

Midnight

M —
Do not go crazy on Christmas gifts this year. I still think it's ridiculous what you spent on Angela's birthday last year. I feel like I should pay you back . . .
    Remember that genie we used to talk about when we were kids?
I really could use him right now.
Where the hell is he?
Xo.

Typically Nora loved going to Arthur and Linda's house. She loved Arthur and Linda separately, and she loved them as a couple. She loved the food Linda served when she wasn't on one of her restrictive diets and she loved the way they talked to her children, with interest and respect and the assumption that they could carry on an adult conversation without being talked down to. She loved the way Arthur and Linda still linked fingers when they were walking down the street, and the way Arthur stood if Linda entered a room he was in, and gave an odd little formal bow, like Carson on *Downton*

Abbey. She loved the house itself: prime real estate right on Marina Boulevard, meticulously decorated and perfectly kept up and absolutely free from clutter in a way that a home with children could never be, not in its wildest dreams. No matter how much Nora tried to keep her home looking like that she simply couldn't do it. Her children were too prodigious with the bobby pins and hair elastics, the glasses of lukewarm water left around, the Rorschach-test globs of toothpaste abandoned to dry in the sink. It was hopeless, it would be hopeless until they all went off on their own, and by then Nora would be too old and too sad and too lonely to care about tidiness.

Nora was hoping Linda would be there too, to break up the tension a little bit. But no, Arthur said, Linda was out at a yoga class. Hot yoga three times a week, and some other type of yoga whose name he could never remember three other days. Sundays off sometimes, but not always. Over the past few years Linda had become very serious about her yoga. You could practically see the tendons in Linda's neck present themselves, a new tendon every time Nora saw her. It made Nora feel positively fleshy.

At the moment, though, rather than fleshy,

432

Nora was feeling extremely tense. Her own neck muscles were tied up in such a knot that she could feel them bunched under her skin, like an actual knot in an actual rope. A bowline, or maybe a clove hitch. She had learned all sorts of knots in the Girl Scouts back in Rhode Island. Not that she'd ever had to use any of them in any real-life situation. *(The paperwork is due to the mortgage counselor! Quick, somebody tie a cow hitch!)*

She'd been really good at the knots, which was sort of ironic, since these days she couldn't *un*tie a knot to save her life: not a knot in a shoelace or a necklace or even the string that held up the ancient, hopelessly unfashionable pair of gray sweatpants that she'd donned regularly as maternity wear when she was pregnant with Cecily and which Gabe had politely asked her to burn after the fact. (She hadn't. They were ridiculously comfortable.)

On the other hand, she was feeling oddly *un*-tense, sort of the way she imagined a prisoner on death row might feel when, after years and years of imagining the event, he was finally asked to choose his last meal. (Spaghetti carbonara, Nora would choose, with a green salad and a large glass of Chianti. Espresso crème brûlée for dessert. Because it wouldn't really matter if it kept you up. Ba-da-dum. This question came up in their family a surprising amount. Gabe would have ribs and a bourbon — ever the ranch boy — and Cecily would have a Double-Double from In-N-Out, with fries and a chocolate shake. Pizza for Maya. Come to think of it, Nora couldn't remember what Angela would have. She'd have to ask her later. It seemed suddenly like a very bad sign, that she couldn't remember this important fact about Angela.)

After Arthur greeted Nora at the door he left her for a moment without apology or explanation (she hadn't heard a phone ring, no summons from the hallowed offices of Sutton and Wainwright), so she stood at the front window and looked out onto Marina Boulevard. Maybe he just needed the bathroom. Although Arthur never seemed to need the bathroom — he seemed somehow above and separate from the basic operations of the human body. She'd seen him eat, of course, many times, but he never expressed hunger before the fact nor satiety after it.

Arthur and Linda's home was detached, though the neighboring houses were so close that if you were upstairs and your neighbor was too and you cared to pass a cup of coffee from one house to the other you could both lean out of the window and accomplish this with little to no incident. Theirs was Spanish-style stucco, tan in color, though farther down the street some of the attached homes bore bright pinks and yellows.

It was a beautiful neighborhood, unpretentious (yet still expensive), neither edgy nor progressive, but simply beautiful, with the gulls crying overhead and the boats rocking in the water and the Palace of Fine Arts rising in the distance. Standing here, Nora could allow herself to imagine the area thousands and thousands of years ago, when American Indians lived on the dunes where the homes now stood, and then, more recently, after the big quake in 1906, when real development first began in preparation for the Panama-Pacific International Exposition in 1915. If Nora could travel back in time she'd like to see that. The Liberty Bell, all the way from Pennsylvania for a visit. The Tower of Jewels, covered with cut glass, but underneath, of course, just plaster and burlap, easily demolished after the fair. Then came the Loma Prieta quake in 1989 — Nora was twenty then, happily partying at the University of Rhode Island, the quake didn't register with her — and a lot of the neighborhood crumbled. Whole buildings, flattened. The marina even had its own personal firestorm. Now everything was rebuilt, earthquake-sturdy, reinforced and then doubly reinforced, with the price tags to prove it.

It was a glorious day, the sun was high in a sky that looked like gossamer, the light clear and almost springlike, although in less than a month it would be Christmas. The marina was plump with sailboats, and the bridge watched over the entire scene, like a benevolent parent, a good and wholesome nanny. Maybe even a god, if you believed in such things.

The genie grants you three wishes. First wish: Let me keep my job. Second wish: Let me keep my house. Third wish: Let me keep my sanity.

"Drink?" said Arthur. He appeared out of nowhere, like a ghost. The ghost, thought Nora, of employment past.

Nora said, "Um." It was just before noon. While she was equivocating Arthur moved toward the bar. Ever graceful, he didn't walk there so much as he floated, and Nora thought of the old dance studio in a shopping center not far from her childhood home, surrounded by an insurance company, a nail salon, a FedEx office. Some-times her mother had to go there for various errands — though certainly not the nail salon; Nora's mother had had exactly one manicure in her life, the day before Nora's wedding — and Marianne and Nora would sit in the car and watch the ballroom dancers sail by the windows. Older couples, mostly, though sometimes they would see a bride and groom in training, or, once, hilariously, a pair of blushing teenage girls. Nora would bet real money that Arthur Sutton had grown up taking ballroom dancing lessons, and not in a grim little suburban shopping center, either.

Arthur turned his back to Nora while he was at the bar — not out of any lack of manners; his position was dictated by the setup of the living room — so Nora had no idea what he was pouring. It certainly wasn't wine, which Nora might have preferred. When Arthur handed her the drink — something goldish brown, on the rocks — she felt like an executive from *Mad Men,* sipping away on a Wednesday morning in the office. ("No, Don, I really don't think we should go for that account, and let me tell you exactly why . . .")

Arthur Sutton, ever the gentleman, raised his own glass, gave a small chivalrous nod in Nora's direction, and said, "How's the family?"

"Oh," said Nora. She shouldn't have been surprised by this question — the little niceties were part of Arthur's character, as much as ambition and drive were part of Angela's and an ear for slip-jig music was part of Cecily's — but nevertheless she was unprepared to enter the arena of small talk. Not now, not today. She could still call up the sensation of the dirt from the Millers' lawn on her knees (her burglar suit had been inadequately thin; if she planned to take endangered-plant killing up as a career she would certainly have to budget for more appropriate clothing). She could feel, again, the sense of semi-detached excitement she'd experienced on the way there, the memory that had been called up of riding in Stuart Mobley's old Buick toward the beach. Then the panic rising in her throat as she heard the Millers' back door open, saw the silhouette of the career-destroying housesitter peering out into the lawn. She remembered thinking, *Well, that's that, then. It's all over now.* The new frontier, broken and burned. The California dream, gone.

No, she didn't feel much like small talk. She just wanted to present herself for the chopping block and get on with her day, head in hand. (First wish, Genie. Get this conversation over with quickly.) But she took a deep breath and said, "They're well, Arthur. Very well. Thank you."

Arthur nodded, and Nora took (or mistook) his pleasantly blank expression as a signal to keep talking. She helped herself to a giant sip of her drink. It scorched its way down her throat, but she made a point of not reacting, and soon enough her innards were filled with an overwhelming and not entirely unpleasant sensation of warmth, even well-being. So that was why people drank the stuff. She thought of Gabe's amber-colored Bulleit, which made her think again of the gold rush settlers, wearing their hats and their suspenders, drying their socks over an open fire, sweeping out their tents with their cornhusk brooms. The card games, the whiskey, the eternal optimism of the new frontier, coming by land, coming by sea, whatever it took. She remembered, on Angela's field trip to Columbia, learning about how fire had destroyed the newly built town in 1854. All but one building, gone. Did those miners give up and go home, tails between their proverbial legs, returning to the East Coast or the middle of the country or wherever it was they had come from? No, sir. They regrouped, they rebuilt, they used brick instead of wood. Then, three years later, another fire. The capacity this state had for rising from the flames was truly mind-boggling. Without the gold rush there'd be no California as they knew it today, no pricey Marin real estate, no rigorous public high schools. No blue jeans.

"And we're just waiting to hear about Angela," Nora said into the gap. "About, you know, Harvard. Early action."

Arthur nodded and smiled. "Well, Harvard would be crazy not to want Angela."

"That's what I think. But of course I'm a bit biased." Nora's smile felt loose on her face. This stuff hit you faster than wine. No wonder the characters on *Mad Men* were always doing heedless things. Nothing seemed of much consequence when your ribs were on fire.

Arthur took a seat opposite Nora — the two couches in the room formed an L, with a small square table in between. He leaned in close enough that Nora could see a stray hair popping out from one of his eyebrows, which were usually well tamed. She looked deep into his eyes and saw there a bewilderment and a disappointment for which she knew she was responsible. She steeled herself: she was lying on the guillotine, waiting for the blade to fall.

"I think of you like a daughter, you know, Nora."

Nora could no longer meet Arthur's gaze — it was too dangerous, like looking directly at the sun. Instead she looked at her hands. She was still holding her glass. Arthur hadn't offered her a coaster and this was not the sort of house where you put your glass down without a coaster. (The coffee table in Nora's childhood home still proudly wore the rings from many a beverage set down in haste or ignorance. Can after can of Diet Pepsi consumed by Marianne and Nora, before the wars against artificial sweeteners commenced.)

She took a large sip and tried for a bit of levity. "For me to be your daughter you'd have to have been fifteen when you had me, Arthur."

"True." A false smile, only the mouth moving, nothing in the eyes. He tapped two fingers together, a gesture Nora knew from years of experience to indicate not that he was thinking about something but that he'd already decided.

While she was busy avoiding Arthur's eyes she looked at the side table between the two couches. She saw there a photograph she had never noticed. It didn't fit the décor at all, and Arthur and Linda were not people

441

who left things out when they didn't fit the décor. (This, of course, was a luxury afforded only the eternally childless.) It was as though somebody had just been looking at it and had forgotten to put it away.

Nora resisted the urge to pick it up, but, emboldened by the drink, she allowed her gaze to linger on it, and confirmed that it was what she thought: an ultrasound picture in a little gold frame.

Nora had one of those from when she was pregnant with Angela, and another one from when she was pregnant with Cecily. Her pregnancy with Maya had also necessitated (because of her *advanced maternal age*) an amniocentesis, with a terrifying large needle and lots of waiting to find out that everything was okay. She had never framed her ultrasound photos. Hers were in her nightstand drawer, along with a collection of Chapsticks that seemed to multiply like rabbits. She'd always intended to take them out and put them in the girls' baby books. The photos, not the Chapsticks. Man, this drink was strong. It was difficult to put anything in her daughters' baby books, since she'd never actually created the baby books in the first place. Someday she would.

Arthur followed her gaze and said, "Oh." Carefully he reached for the photo and placed it facedown on the table. "Linda was looking at that earlier. She must have left it out."

"Is that —"

"Nothing we need to talk about now," said Arthur. "Just something from a very long time ago."

But Nora persisted. She couldn't help it. She loved Arthur so dearly, and respected him so formidably, that she had to know. She thought, she supposed later, that by asking she could possibly take on some of his pain as her own. Just in case he couldn't carry it all by himself. Her voice seemed dwarfed by the large room, and dwarfed, too, by the information it was seeking. Out on the boulevard a siren screeched by. "Was that . . . was that your baby? Yours and Linda's?"

"It was," said Arthur.

"Oh, *Arthur,*" said Nora. "Arthur. I never knew."

"*She* was," said Arthur. "But she didn't live. She didn't live past the first day." His voice caught and he gave a meaningful nod that signified to Nora that she was not to take the conversation any further. Then gave a quick shake of his head, as if to banish all memories, and repeated, "It was a very long time ago." Nora understood in that instant that everything she thought she'd known about Arthur and Linda Sutton had been based on incomplete information. The uncluttered house, the tickets to *The Nutcracker* with the Hawthorne girls: these things now took on a different, darker patina. Even the yoga obsession. She understood that what she'd always believed to be a conscious choice of Arthur and Linda's had been no choice whatsoever. You never quite knew another's story, did you, if you hadn't walked by that person's side their whole long lives.

"This is difficult for me, Nora. Maybe as difficult for me as it is for you, I'm not sure."

Nora nodded — they were finished with the first conversation, then, and on to the next — and bit her lip. She felt suddenly like crying. She couldn't speak. Her bag lay by her feet and she pulled it into her lap and searched for a tissue, which she didn't find. Arthur, again channeling an English butler, slid a box toward her. Where the box had come from Nora couldn't say — she hadn't noticed it anywhere in the room before. It seemed to have appeared from the very air.

Arthur downed the rest of his drink, and Nora saw that his hand shook in a way that suggested that this was possibly not his first drink of the day. *Goodness,* thought Nora. *This is almost as hard on him as it is on me.* (Please, Genie, let Angela get some sort of scholarship. Let the Millers decide not to sue me.) Arthur went on. "You are one of the best I've ever seen in this industry." He paused and nodded, confirming the truth of his own words, before continuing. "Probably the very best. You're better than I am. You're years better than Sally Bentley. The things you understand about people, about what makes them tick, what they want and don't want from their lives, what their homes represent to them — well, it's rare."

Nora whispered, "Thank you." She clutched her tissue and kept her gaze on the facedown picture frame. From another room, a clock struck the hour. Twelve chimes, high noon. Leave it to Arthur to own a clock that still struck the hour. If Nora had a clock like that, which she didn't, she would never remember to keep it properly maintained. You had to take care of things like that, you had to respect the craftsmanship that went into them. She thought of the Tower of Jewels: cut glass on the surface, burlap and plaster underneath. That was more her style. "You could have excelled at so many things, Nora. And I've thanked my lucky stars more times than you know that you chose to be good at this, and that you chose to do it with me."

Nora nodded again. Big compliment. There was a boulder stuck in her throat. It was too big to swallow around.

"But you made a big mistake, at the Millers'. A very, very big mistake. As you know, of course. And you put the reputation of the firm at risk."

This time Nora didn't even have it in her to nod. Nora had read somewhere that when they trained doctors to let a family member know a patient had passed away they had to use the exact words, "and he died." Because otherwise people willfully misunderstood the message; they allowed themselves to believe there was still hope. Had Arthur Sutton read the same article? Because so far he'd said only that she'd made a big mistake. There was room for hope.

"I'm sure you know you can't continue working for me. Nora, I have to let you go."

And: he died. Arthur had read the article.

Three wishes, Genie? Oh, screw it. What's the point.

Nora might have been okay had she not spoken, but the very act of opening her mouth to utter the pitifully inadequate trio of words ("I'm sorry, Arthur") released a

446

torrent of tears over which she had zero control. She took a great, gulping breath; she was like a toddler having a tantrum in the cereal aisle, trying to regain control of herself so her mother would let her out of the cart.

As inadequate as the words was the tissue, and the next one she selected, and the one after that: she was soaking through all of them. She didn't know where to put them so she collected them in her lap. Arthur said, "Oh, Nora," and he moved closer to her and placed a comforting, paternal hand on her back. She could smell that tweedy cologne and the sharp scent of the liquor on his breath. "I'm so sorry, Nora."

"*You* don't have anything to be sorry about," sobbed Nora. "You didn't do anything wrong."

"I hate to see you this upset," said Arthur. "I hate that this has happened. I hate that you felt — well, for lack of a better word — *desperate* enough to do this. After the Watkins incident."

"Yeah," said Nora from around what was now her fifth tissue. "Me too." Desperate was the perfect word for it. She hadn't put it that way, even to herself. Desperate. That's exactly what she'd been: desperate to pull those little plants out of the ground, desperate to save the sale, desperate not to get sued, not to get in trouble. Desperate enough that she hadn't even told her own husband about it. Now she'd have to tell Gabe about this, and her children. The other mothers at school — soon they'd know, if not the specifics of her job loss then at least the fact of it. ("I'm so *glad*!" Cathy Moynihan might say. "We'll get more of your time now, Nora!") They'd want her in the classroom; they'd want her painting Adirondack chairs and going into the science lab or helping out on some art project that she'd be hopeless at. They'd all assume it would be good for Cecily and Maya and Angela but it *wouldn't* be good for any of them, to have a dreadfully depressed, hopelessly unemployed mother around more. It wouldn't be good for anyone.

There wasn't enough air in the room for Nora. There wasn't enough air in the entire city of San Francisco to fill her empty lungs, her empty heart. Because Nora wasn't crying just for her job; she was also crying for Cecily falling on the stage, and for Angela coming in eighth in a race she wanted to win, and for Maya trying to hold her tears in after school, and for the tiny unborn baby in the ultrasound picture, and even for this glorious city that rebuilt itself again and again, the phoenix rising from the ashes. She was crying because it was so hard to be a parent, but it was also hard — look at Arthur, look at Linda! — *not* to be a parent. It was all just so, so hard.

"I'm so sorry," she said again. She knew she should pull herself together, get up from the couch, gather her things, exit as gracefully as she could manage. "I'm trying to — I mean, I can't —"

"Take your time, Nora," said Arthur. "I'm going to go back into my office for a minute, I'll be right here if you need me. Please, take all the time you need."

CHAPTER 45
GABE

At first Gabe thought it was one of the golden retrievers, back for a visit. A flash of tawny brown, silent in the already silent hills, one in the afternoon, nobody around.

"Jesus *fucking* Christ," said Gabe softly, and he knew Nora would disapprove of his language but he hoped this one time she might forgive him. Under the circumstances.

The mountain lion was on the skinnier side — bad sign, Gabe knew, that meant it wasn't hunting effectively on its own. It was below Gabe, looking up at him, not yet advancing. But Gabe couldn't descend without passing it. He was close enough — just — to see the yellow eyes. The animal held Gabe steady in its gaze. Neither man nor beast moved.

And then Gabe realized it: the drought. Not enough food or water sent the animals out of their usual locations, into residential areas, sometimes. Or maybe just a well-traveled hiking trail they would typically avoid.

The mountain lion, standing now, somberly beautiful, almost innocent (though not), whiskers, snub nose, softly rounded ears, like a house cat (though not), mouth closed over what (Gabe knew) was a formidable set of teeth. And the paws! Oversized, compared to the size of the lean body, like a Labrador puppy that hadn't yet grown into its own. Though of course it had. Those paws could kill with a swipe. The teeth, of course, presented the greater danger.

A plaid quilt, pulled tight around his bed at the ranch house. *Will you marry me, Nora?* His father's funeral, his mother crying into an old-fashioned handkerchief Gabe hadn't known she owned. A Lego set spread out in front of a fire, construction vehicles in primary colors, working with one of his brothers, his concentration utter. *No,* his brother said. *The wheel goes over here. Let me do it.* An infant Cecily grasping at his finger. *Will you marry me, Nora?* His father lifting him into a saddle for the first time. *There, you'll be all right, easy does it.* A grilled cheese sandwich dipped into a bowl of tomato soup. A bull elk. A rifle hiked over his shoulder. A yellow school bus rounding the corner. The steering wheel of a pickup, Gabe's hands steady. Maya toddling toward his open arms: her first uncertain steps. October snow in Wyoming, a bison calf trekking through the drifts. *Nora, will you make me the happiest man alive?* Angela on his shoulders at the Harvard–Yale game. A crisp New England fall day, colors so bright it almost hurt to look. His hand on Nora's thigh, on her beautiful pale neck. *I'm sorry, Mr. Hawthorne, but I couldn't reach anyone else in your family. I'm afraid I have some bad news about your father.* Center field on a day as hot as blazes, running, running, a pop fly to the middle of the glove. A beautiful catch, everybody said so.

It was true, then, about your life playing before your eyes. Wait. Did that mean he was going to . . .

And one thought ridiculous enough to push its way to the surface, glinting in the sunlight so quickly — like the flat edge of a knife — and then disappearing before he really had time to grasp it, was how embarrassing it was going to be to die here, in the early afternoon, in the East Bay (of all places!) on a Monday, a workday, when he was supposed to be at Elpis. To add to that, his bladder had given way and the front of his khakis was soaked.

No.

Remember, he told himself, you're an animal too. He tried to recall exactly what the sign at the trailhead had said. Make yourself big. Don't back away, don't run. Make lots of noise. Throw rocks, throw sticks, throw anything. If attacked, fight back.

Carefully, carefully, his eyes on the mountain lion, he bent and felt for a rock. When he bent, the animal took a step forward. Considering. Gabe straightened.

Lots of noise, the sign said. Don't retreat. Don't turn your back.

Later, a couple of hikers pretty far away, on the Hemme trail, reported an unearthly noise. They thought it might be coyotes — mating, maybe, or fighting. God-awful, they said. One of them tried to capture the sound with her iPhone but by the time she got the video on (she had the new iPhone, and, annoyingly, the camera often froze) it was over and done with.

But it wasn't a coyote. It was Gabe Hawthorne, father, husband, partner at San Francisco–based Elpis Consulting, opening his mouth and letting loose what he would think of later as a primal scream. *The* primal scream. It was a sound he never would have guessed he had inside of him, and it echoed over the mountains and bounced back again. Arms above his head, waving. The rock, thrown at the animal, who, when struck, had such an expression of bewilderment that had the circumstances been different Gabe might have felt sorry for it.

And the mountain lion fled.

The khakis were now a complete loss. The torn knee, the urine. A little extra digging in the trunk eventually revealed a pair of crumpled track pants, not clean, necessarily, but serviceable enough, and Gabe climbed into the passenger seat to make the switch, praying that no dog walkers or — worse — young mothers with strollers wandered by at this most inconvenient of times. The residential street was mostly quiet, though down the way from where he was parked Gabe could hear a leaf blower and the distant drone of saws or drills:

453

instruments of the upper class's inevitable, insatiable quest for more and better.

He stopped at a gas station in Alamo on the way to the freeway and bought a bottle of water. And if the man at the cash register noticed the incongruity of his dress shirt and his track pants; if he noticed Gabe's hands shaking, and his knees too; if he looked deep into Gabe's eyes and understood that here was a man who had fought death and won, well, he said nothing about it.

And there was no point in keeping the secret anymore. He'd go home, and he'd take a shower, and when Nora got home he'd tell her everything. *Everything.*

Something about the house didn't look right. Gabe squinted at it. What was it? It was the driveway. It was Nora's car, in the driveway, at three o'clock in the afternoon, on a weekday. Something must be wrong. Nora had said she had a packed day at the office. She had said she'd never get it all done.

Nora was sitting on the couch in the living room watching television. This was odd in and of itself: Nora never watched television. In fact she rarely sat down. Also: she was crying. Nora seldom cried. The last time he remembered seeing her cry was when Frankie died.

"Hey," he said. He slipped off his shoes. "Hey, Nora. What is it? What's wrong? Where are the kids?" His first thought, of course, was, *Angela! Harvard!* But it was the first week in December and she'd only just had her alumni interview. No, it was too early for that. He was ashamed, maybe, at the relief he felt when he realized Nora must be crying over something else.

Then he thought, *She knows!* He imagined Abby Freeman showing up at the door, inviting herself in, releasing Gabe's lie into the atmosphere.

But it was neither of these things. "Nelson Mandela died," she said. "Didn't you hear?"

Gabe sat down next to her. She held a Kleenex box in her lap and on the floor was a giant pile of used tissues: a veritable mountain. She must have been at this for quite a while. He glanced at the television: cable news. He said, "Of course I heard. Lead story on NPR." He had been only half listening. He had almost been mauled by a mountain lion! South Africa seemed very far away.

She took a deep and shuddering breath, and blew her nose loudly, and said, "What are you *wearing*?"

"Oh. I, ah, worked out at the gym before I came home." Another lie. "I thought you'd be at work," he said.

She waved a wet tissue toward him and said, "Came home early." She paused and looked at him. Her eyes were rimmed with pink, like an albino rabbit's, and there was a small bright circle of red, Rudolph-like, on the tip of her nose. He thought Nora was beautiful, but she did not have the skin tone that lent itself to handsome crying. She pointed the universal remote at the television like a weapon. On the screen, hundreds of South Africans were dancing, swaying, singing, crying. "Some of these people aren't going to sleep for days, they said. To honor him. Can you imagine? For *days*." Her crying began anew.

Gabe hadn't known that Nora cared so deeply about Nelson Mandela. He wasn't sure he'd ever heard her talk about apartheid, or South Africa. Or, really, any part of Africa. South *America* she'd expressed interest in. Chile, Brazil. But Pretoria? Soweto? He moved closer to her and rubbed her back.

"Even the children are crying, Gabe. Crying and dancing. Even these little kids, what are they, five, six? They get this. They grasp the significance of it. Look at that little boy swaying."

Gabe looked at the little boy swaying.

"Maybe," he said carefully, "maybe they're crying because they see all the grown-ups around them crying. You know how kids are. Suggestible." He hadn't meant any harm by the statement but Nora fixed on him such a look of venom that he wished he could take his words back.

"Why aren't we more like that?"

Gabe definitely couldn't tell her now. Definitely not. On the screen he saw flashing images of the great man from various stages in his life, interspersed with footage of the mourners. "Well," he said. "You're Catholic. And a New Englander. And Irish! Those aren't groups that are known for dancing in the streets, whatever the reason."

She wiped savagely at her nose. "Not as a *family*. Besides, you're not exactly Johnny Emotion. I mean as a *country*. Why aren't we more like that as a country? Who do we mourn like that? Who has this country ever mourned like that?"

"I don't know. Kennedy?"

She sighed. "It wasn't the same."

"We weren't born then."

"I know. But I've seen footage of the funeral procession. It wasn't the same. Everybody just stood there somberly. No rejoicing. No swaying. This country doesn't know how to mourn, Gabe. Let's face it. We just don't."

"Nora . . ."

"Do you know he was in prison for more than a quarter of his life? Twenty-seven years, Gabe. In prison. And we complain when we can't get a table at Poggio."

Her eyes were fixed still on the television screen. Now they were showing the current South African president making the announcement. He was at peace now, the great man was at peace. Nora turned to Gabe and buried her face in the sleeve of his shirt. "I'm just sad, Gabe. I'm just really, really sad."

No way could he tell her. Not now.

CHAPTER 46
ANGELA

Now whenever Edmond Lopez tap-tap-tapped his pencil on his desk Angela concentrated super-hard on *not* turning around. She didn't want to see his smile, lazy or not. She was mortified. She had been mortified since October and now it was December but sometimes her mortification was more pronounced than it was at other times — sometimes she would forget all about it, and be plenty occupied with schoolwork and track and extracurricular activities, and other times it would come rushing back over her like a wave, toppling her until she had sand in her face and little bits of seashells in her mouth. She, Angela Hawthorne, valedictorian (for now, anyway), had put Edmond Lopez to sleep. Maria Ortiz was a seductress, a siren, a real and true beauty, and Angela was a human tranquilizer. *God.*

On the other hand. It was hard not to turn around because she was also trying to avoid eye contact with Ms. Simmons. Just two words, nothing complex, just *See me,* written on the top of the extended essay. But because Angela hadn't seen Ms. Simmons yet — she'd seen her, of course, but she hadn't *seen her* — she wasn't really sure where to rest her eyes. She tried the ceiling, briefly, but she knew that made her look bored and a little bit like a jerk. She tried her lap, her hands, the short story in front of her. Nothing felt right.

How much longer in the class? Twenty minutes.

"All right, then," said Ms. Simmons. "Who has something *cogent* to say about George Orwell and the elephant?"

Tap, tap tap. Angela would never have sex.

"Henrietta?"

"Well," said Henrietta breathlessly, as though she'd just sprinted to class, not been sitting there for twenty-three minutes. "He writes, 'He was breathing very rhythmically with long rattling gasps, his great mound of a side painfully rising and falling.' "

Henrietta wasn't even looking at the story. She had memorized it. Geez.

Angela would go off to college a virgin and return, four years later, a virgin still. She would be the only virgin to graduate from college, ever. Definitely the only Ivy League virgin. She might become famous for it. Edmond Lopez would see her on the *Today* show being interviewed by Savannah Guthrie and he'd say, *Oh yeah, that girl! I'm not surprised. Did I ever tell you about the time . . .*

"But how do you think Orwell's views on imperialism changed after he shot the elephant?" said Ms. Simmons. "If indeed they did at all. Angela?"

Tap, tap tap.

See me.

Angela inhaled and searched her scrambled mind for something to say. Suddenly her eyes were full of unshed tears and she shook her head mutely.

Henrietta raised her hand again. "He writes, 'One could have imagined him thousands of years old.' I think he's comparing the age the dying elephant seems to be to the length of time the British have been imperialist rulers."

Ms. Simmons nodded and called on Olivia Bishop, who said something even more cogent, about the life of the elephant being worth more than the life of the Indian man who had been killed. The *coolie.* Of course you couldn't say things like that these days, totally inappropriate. Olivia made little air quotes around her head when she said the word, just so she wouldn't be accidentally mistaken for a racist.

Time marched on. Edmond's pencil tap-tap-tapped. Angela's virginity stood up and made like it was going to announce itself to the class. Gently, she asked it to sit back down. And finally the bell rang.

She was gathering her things when Ms. Simmons said, "Angela? Come see me briefly before you go." Angela's stomach dropped.

At the front of the room Ms. Simmons said, "Is everything okay with you, Angela?"

"Fine," Angela said. "Absolutely fine." This time she looked Ms. Simmons right in the eye, even though she had to look up to do it. Ms. Simmons had a bunch of inches on Angela. (Who didn't?) Ms. Simmons

461

raised an eyebrow, just one.

All the things Angela couldn't say marched through her mind. *My father is having an affair with the intern. I can't look at Edmond Lopez. I've never liked the flute! I did read the story, I read it carefully. I just wasn't paying attention when you called on me. Because I was thinking about being a virgin. What if Henrietta is smarter than I am? It breaks my heart that it took that elephant half an hour to die. And I am so tired. Just so, so, so, so tired.*

"It's nothing," she said. "Everything is fine."

And then it happened. Suddenly, without even the whisper of a warning, everything seemed unbearable to her: not just the elephant, but Mrs. Fletcher's divorce, and her mom's weird moods, and Maya's struggles in school, and the fact that Frankie was dead. When her mom found out about the intern, what would happen? Would her parents get a divorce, would Cecily and Maya grow up in a *broken home*? Who would Angela stay with when she came home from college? She'd have to have two sets of clothes and an extra toothbrush; it would be exhausting.

So then, like a stupid *baby,* like an idiot, like someone who didn't even deserve to be valedictorian because she couldn't control

462

herself, Angela started crying. Blubbering, really. Nose running, eyes streaming, the whole kit and caboodle, as her grandmother would have said.

"Oh, *Angela,*" said Ms. Simmons, and there was such kindness in her eyes that Angela could see what she must be like with her children, even when they did something wrong. "Angela, I didn't mean to —" She pulled a bunch of tissues from the box on her desk and pushed them into Angela's hand. Angela thought Ms. Simmons might hug her but thank God she didn't, she just pressed her hand firmly to Angela's shoulder and said, "Come here. I've got next period free. I'm going to take you into my office, and you can compose yourself there. There's something I need to talk to you about anyway."

CHAPTER 47
CECILY

"We're *baking*?" said Maya. "Christmas cookies?" She looked like she was going to hemorrhage happiness.

"For real?" asked Cecily. She dropped her backpack, took off her shoes. "We are?" She still hadn't gotten used to coming home with her mom instead of Maddie.

463

"Of course we're baking," said her mom, like this was something that happened regularly. "It's Christmastime, right? Less than two weeks to go. I set this all up before I picked you up so we could get right to it."

Cecily surveyed the kitchen island. Two mounds of dough, one for her and one for Maya. A rolling pin, wax paper. Cookie cutters in the shapes of reindeer and Santa hats and Christmas trees. Plastic containers of sprinkles and Red Hots. Little tins of frosting.

"Aunt Marianne and I used to do this all the time when we were kids, every year. Come here, I'll show you how to roll out the dough. This is the trickiest part. Actually, everybody wash hands first. With soap."

Cecily washed her hands and tried to read the room. Her mom looked slightly less rushed than usual. Not quite calm, but. Not her usual after-school crazed. Maya looked delighted. Angela and her father weren't home.

Okay, this was good. Baking.

Maya was already into the Red Hots. Cecily's mom took the container from her and closed it and said, "Listen, you girls need to get your Santa letters out the door. Have you written them yet?"

Cecily didn't answer. She didn't know

about the Santa letter. There was talk at school and there had been last year too but mostly she didn't listen . . .

Or want to listen. But she hadn't written her letter.

"I need help with mine," said Maya.

Cecily's mom was frowning at the dough she was rolling out. She said, "This is sticking."

"I'll help you," Cecily said to Maya.

"I'm going to put a puppy on my Santa list," said Maya.

"You can't do that," said Cecily. "You won't get it. Santa doesn't bring puppies." (She had thought about the same thing.)

"There," said her mother. "Got it, nice and smooth. This is about how thick you want it. Any thinner and they'll crack in the oven. Girls? Are you looking?"

"Santa can do anything. He's Santa. He brought Olivia a puppy last year."

"Well," said Cecily. "Don't count on it." She didn't know what had gotten into her. She was usually nicer to Maya. She took the rolling pin and started to roll out her ball.

"You just need a little more flour . . . ," said her mother. "Here, let me."

Cecily pulled the rolling pin away. Meanly. Her mother said, "Hey —"

"Got it," said Cecily.

It wasn't the dough. It was . . . a lot of other things. Cecily hadn't gotten used to spending so much time at home instead of at the Seamus O'Malley School. When she was home instead of at dance she felt like someone had vacuumed out her insides and then emptied out the vacuum bag into the garbage so that there was nothing left.

Maybe she should have listened to Angela — maybe she should have kept dancing.

Every once in a while she went into her room and put some music on her iPod, a slip jig or a reel, and danced around a little bit to see how it felt. But it wasn't the same; it wasn't the same without her Irish friends, and without Seamus. Everything was turned upside down. She wanted things to go back to the way they were before the fall.

She couldn't really see the dough anymore, or the rolling pin; her eyes were all blurred up. A big wet tear fell out of her eye and landed in the middle of the dough.

"It's ruined," she said. Her voice sounded weird. "It's all wet, it's ruined." She smashed up the dough and threw it across the kitchen. It stuck for just a few seconds to the wall, like it was trying to decide what to do, and then it fell to the ground.

That felt good. And bad.

"Cecily!"

Her mother was staring at her. Maya was staring at her too, with that sort of triumphant look that little kids get when they aren't the person in the room misbehaving.

"I don't *care,*" said Cecily. That was a lie. She did care that she'd thrown the dough. She cared a lot: she wished she could take it back. She still wanted to bake the cookies. "Anyway," she said. "I miss Maddie. Why'd you fire her?"

Her mother looked startled. "I didn't *fire* her. I told you, she had too much schoolwork. Finals. She needed extra time, and things were slow at work for me, so . . ."

"You fired her," Cecily said in the tiniest whisper she could create. She waited to get in trouble, but when she looked at her mother her mother didn't look mad: she looked sad, like she was going to cry herself. That made Cecily feel worse.

Maya said, "Is she —" And her mom held up her hand to stop Maya from talking.

"Oh, honey, come here."

Into her mom's sleeve, which smelled like perfume and lemons, she said, "It feels wrong, Mom." She didn't mean just the dough. She meant everything: not dancing, and Angela leaving them soon, and Frankie being gone, and not seeing Grandma and

Aunt Marianne at Christmas. And Santa . . .

"What do you mean?"

She hesitated, not sure about the next question. But she really wanted to know. "Is it my fault?"

"Is *what* your fault?"

"That everyone is mad all the time."

"Who?"

"Daddy. Angela. You."

"*Cecily!* My goodness, why would you think something like that? Of course it's not your fault. Why would it be your fault?"

Cecily shrugged.

"I don't know. I was just wondering. Maybe because I messed up at the *feis* . . . or maybe there's another reason . . ."

"Maya?" said her mom. "Run to the laundry room and see if the dryer has stopped."

Maya's expression said, *And miss all this?* But she did as she was told.

"Listen to me, Cecily. Sit down."

Cecily sat. There was a gob of dough on the stool; she peeled it off and put it on the island. Her mom said, "You are ten years old. You are responsible for yourself. You are not responsible for anyone else in this family, for their happiness or their unhappiness or anything else. Do you understand me?"

Cecily nodded, and another one of the big fat tears fell out of her eyes.

"Do you really understand me?"

Cecily nodded again.

"That's better. And you know what? Whatever feels wrong now, it won't always feel wrong. I promise you."

"Are you sure? Are you positive?"

"Positive."

Cecily wanted to believe her. But she didn't, not really.

Chapter 48
Gabe

Friday the thirteenth.

Traffic was deadly, a full stop on the Golden Gate.

NPR on the way home. Kim Jong Un had executed his *own uncle.* Wow. Visa awarded its CEO compensation valued at $10.5 million. Asian stocks fell for a second straight week. A Finnair flight with the number 666 to Helsinki (designation HEL) had an almost full flight. Gabe didn't consider himself superstitious but no way in hell would he have boarded that flight. No way in Helsinki.

Gabe picked up the phone to call home

and check in, then put it down without dialing. His Bluetooth was broken and the cops were real bastards about the tickets at rush hour, plucking off the drivers like cherries from a tree. Must be some kind of quota thing. Gabe had three over the past year, stupid nothing calls, not worth the price tag. It never was.

Man, he was so tired, the NPR voices almost lulled him to sleep. *The Desolation of Smaug* was still trouncing everything else at the box office and they were expecting a killer weekend. Gabe had zero interest in *The Desolation of Smaug*. His brother Michael was a *Hobbit* fan, but Gabe never got into it.

Early to bed, early to rise, was the way they used to do it on the ranch. That was the way to go. Let your body give in to its natural rhythms, the rhythm of the earth. The land. But he never did that anymore. Late to bed, early to rise, that was the way he was playing it, burning the candle at both ends. He'd better watch it. He was no spring chicken anymore.

Finally, traffic moved. Slowly, but it moved. He wound his way toward home.

Pulling into the driveway he saw Angela. What was Angela doing, in the driveway, waiting for him?

He got out of the car and moved toward her, and later, when he replayed it, it seemed like it took him several full minutes to get to her. But of course it didn't.

She was wiping her nose with the sleeve of her sweatshirt, her Harvard sweatshirt, and talking incomprehensibly into it.

"Wait," said Gabe. "*What* happened? What is it?" Fire was his first thought. That didn't make sense. He would have noticed a fire. Or: robbery at knifepoint, Angela the only survivor. Also unlikely, but it happened, sometimes there was a single survivor from a tragedy. "Where's everyone else?"

Angela lifted her face from her sleeve. "*Everyone else?*" She spat the words right at him. He sort of had to duck. "I don't *know* where everyone else is. I'm not talking about everyone else! I'm talking about *me,* Dad. I didn't get *in.* I just got the *email.* I didn't get into Harv—"

The last syllable of the word disappeared into an alarming sort of gulp as Angela's crying began anew.

"*Oh,*" said Gabe. "Oh. Oh, I see." His heart nosedived. He felt dizzy. Anna Fletcher passed in her Infiniti. She waved, but Gabe didn't wave back.

"I'm a failure," said Angela. "My whole *life* I worked for this! My whole life. Maria

471

Ortiz got into Yale. She's *sixth* in the class, Dad. I'm first. And I didn't get into Harvard."

Gabe looked at his daughter's crumpled, tear-soaked face and said, "Come here." He reached for Angela but Angela turned from him and ran back into the house. For a long time he could hear her sobs, long after he could no longer see her.

Chapter 49
Nora

8:15 p.m.

Dear Marianne,
Oh boy. It's official. The world has come to an end. Do I sound facetious? I don't mean to . . .

The embarrassing thing was that Gabe also cried. Not that afternoon, and not in front of Angela (thank God) but later, in the bedroom, in the dark, when he thought Nora was asleep. In fact Nora was asleep, but the crying woke her. She lay for a minute without acknowledging it (she had been sleeping with her face turned away from Gabe), just to make sure she wasn't imagining it.

She wasn't.

He was crying.

This was the man who had stoically brought Frankie to the vet on the day of his euthanasia, not just handing him over to the tech but going into the room with him and holding his gigantic, fluffy head throughout the awfulness, of which he had never spoken to Nora after. She hadn't asked because she knew she couldn't handle the details.

This was the man who had, dry-eyed, tossed the first shovelful of dirt on his father's coffin after it was lowered into the grave in a wooded cemetery in Laramie. Who hadn't cried when Nora made him drink Cabernet and watch *Terms of Endearment* with her on DVD on her thirtieth birthday because she'd never seen it before. This was *Gabe,* who'd been scooped up in the early days of Elpis because he was so shrewd and even-tempered, because he could look at a foundering company and see immediately what the problem was, then set about fixing it with methodical care. He was as unflappable and pragmatic as Barack Obama. He was a stalwart, a rock.

She flipped over, and in the dim light afforded by the moon shining through the skylights she observed her husband of eighteen and a half years lying on his back, his shoulders quaking, tears falling and wetting the gray T-shirt he always wore to bed and which had been washed so many times it was nearly transparent. She loved that shirt, and every time she considered relegating it to the rag bin something stopped her (not just the fact that she did not really have a rag bin); she always folded it lovingly and returned it to the dresser drawer.

Nora said, "Gabe?"

In answer Gabe offered only a sniffle that turned into a snort halfway through.

Nora put a hand on the gray T-shirt in the vicinity of Gabe's shoulder. She said, "It's *one college* she didn't get into. There are hundreds more, millions more!"

Nothing.

Nora sighed. What she wanted to say was "Are you kidding me with this?" She wanted to say, "Pull yourself together." She wanted to point out that there were real tragedies occurring in the world, refugees fleeing war-torn countries in the Middle East and Africa, children going to bed hungry in Appalachia, young girls forced into drug dealing and prostitution just across the bay in Oakland, walking up and down International Boulevard at all hours of the night. Even right here at home was a tragedy big enough to cry about: Nora had lost her job.

But she had to be the calm in the middle of the storm. So what she actually said was, "I know this was important to you. I know you really wanted her to experience what you experienced. I know, we thought they'd accept her. But the truth is, she didn't get in. And just because it meant so much to you, that doesn't mean it's the be all and end all of everything —"

"But," interrupted Gabe, and his voice breaking through the tears was somehow more pathetic than the tears themselves.

"I know," said Nora. She tried to adopt the soothing, maternal tone she used when her children had stomachaches, right before they threw up into the garbage can. "It's hard to see her this upset. I hate it too. Believe me. But it's *life,* Gabe. Kids don't get everything they want. Nobody gets everything they want, that's just how it is."

"But —"

"I mean, no offense, but you don't know if *you* would get into Harvard today."

"Nora."

"Don't get mad that I said that. It's just I'm sure the standards have changed. I read this article online . . . there are six-year-old violin prodigies and thirteen-year-old doctors out there. There's a fourteen-year-old who gave a TED talk, and a four-year-old member of Mensa. How are regular people, even regular super-smart people, supposed to compete with that? It seems hopeless. The whole thing seems really, really hopeless. Honestly, I'm not sure why most people bother."

"Nora."

Okay. Enough was enough. He was still crying. Nora couldn't be in the bed any longer. She swung her legs over the edge. Reflexively, she stepped carefully, in case Frankie was sleeping there. Old habits.

"You know something?" She wasn't in a comforting mood anymore. Suddenly she was livid. She thought of all the people who had died making their way west. Nelson Mandela, ambassador of peace, was dead. Nora had disappointed Arthur Sutton. She could have been arrested. She might lose her license. She had certainly lost her job. Cecily had quit the one thing she loved. Angela had cried herself to sleep. And even if she'd gotten in, so what? That could mean how many more years of the same pressure? Depression rates at the Ivies were just as high, higher sometimes, as they were anywhere else. Nora was a lioness protecting her cubs from harm, and the harm, it turned out, was in their very own den. "You know what? I'm glad she didn't get into Harvard."

She expected an audible explosion but she received only silence. She moved close to the door to see if she could hear any movement from the hallway. Quiet as the grave.

She turned back to the bed. "That's right. I said it. I mean it. I'm glad. I'm glad she doesn't have to go through four more years of keeping up with the best of the best. I am so *tired,* Gabe, of all the stress in this house. I can't stand it another second. I don't want it for her, and I don't want it for us. Do you know that a fifth grader in Cecily's school had to go home last week because she had an anxiety attack before a science test? Eleven years old, Gabe."

"Nora —"

"I don't want Cecily to go through all this. I don't want Maya to. I hope they want to go to art school! Or no school. I look at Angela and her friends and they're all walking around like a bunch of terrified zombies. They don't laugh anymore. They're seventeen years old, eighteen, whatever, and they don't laugh! Have you noticed that? They used to laugh, and now they don't. I laughed when I was seventeen. I laughed *all the time.* I used to worry about what we'd do when Angela was old enough to start going out with boys, sneaking beers. Now I *want* her to be doing that! I wish that's what we were worried about. Gabe. When is the last time you saw Angela smile, a real smile?"

Nothing.

Nora was on a buttered roll; she couldn't stop. Suddenly it was all enormously clear to her. "We did this to Angela, Gabe. *We* are to blame, not anybody else. We saw we had a smart kid, a kid with potential, and what did we do? We pushed her and pushed her, and then we set the bar so high for her, and we never told her it was okay to want something different. We never even introduced the *possibility* of something different. We joke about how she shoved that kid down the slide at Montessori but really we were proud of it, because it showed she had fight in her. And she had plenty of fight in her when she was three. But now she's seventeen, and she's beaten down, and she thinks she's a failure. She's gotten straight As on every single report card since report cards were invented, and she's in there crying herself to sleep. And you know what? It's our fault."

Gabe cleared his throat.

A little voice in Nora's head told her to stop but she kicked the voice to the ground and stomped on it and kept right on going.

"You know what else?"

No answer. Nora forged ahead, like a pioneer making her way west, like Lucy Whipple in the gold rush tale Cecily was reading. "I wish *you'd* never gone to Harvard. I do. I wish you had never gone there so you wouldn't have spent the last *decade and a half* telling her how great it was. I wish you'd never taken her to that football game, setting up these unreasonable expectations. It's your fault, Gabe. I blame you." Even as she said this Nora knew it wasn't entirely true. She was complicit, the Bonnie to Gabe's Clyde. The pride she'd taken in Angela's accomplishments, the way she'd allowed Angela's light to reflect back on her, like she was the moon to Angela's sun. Like it said something about her, about them as a couple, as a family: Look how successful *we* are, to have raised such a successful daughter! Look how smart *we* must be! Good parents, smart parents, doing it right. And she herself, sneaking around in her underutilized yoga pants to pull up an endangered plant because she was too scared to have a mistake — an innocent, honest-to-goodness mistake — revealed. It was sickening.

"Nora!" Gabe's voice was about as sharp as it ever got. He was out of the bed too, facing her across the expanse, a handful of sheet crumpled in his hand. The tear stains on the T-shirt were almost comical. But not quite. Nora blinked at him. "Stop talking. Listen to me. I have to tell you something. Right now, I have to tell you something."

Nora stopped talking; Nora listened.

Gabe looked down at his handful of sheet, his eyes not meeting Nora's. The moon shined weakly upon them: a waning gibbous. He cleared his throat and spoke distinctly. There was no other sound in the room. Even so, she figured she must have misheard. He said it again.

"I didn't go to Harvard."

"Well, that's ridiculous," said Nora. "Of course you went to Harvard. You graduated in 1989."

"Nora," said Gabe. He reached over and switched on his nightstand lamp. In the shadows it cast across the bed his face looked drawn and haggard. He looked seventy. "I didn't. I made it up."

"There's a diploma hanging in the office." She marched down the hall to the office. Both girls' bedroom doors were closed. Cecily and Maya used to sleep with their door open but suddenly they did not. They were growing up. Nora could hear Gabe padding behind her.

She sat in the office chair and Gabe leaned against the doorframe. Nora looked at the diploma. "Look! It has a seal and everything. There's fancy calligraphy, signatures. It's a real diploma." Nora had never even framed hers, never hung it. She didn't know where it was. Her mother might still have it, along with Nora's wedding dress, which she'd paid what Nora thought was an exorbitant sum to have boxed up and "preserved," in case any of Nora and Gabe's (then hypothetical) children wanted to wear it. Her children would never wear her wedding dress: it had a high neck and long lace sleeves, and it screamed *mid-nineties.*

"I made it," said Gabe. "I had a buddy who did that kind of thing, documents and so forth. We made it sort of as a joke, at first. Someone showed him a real one and he worked from that. But it looked real, so I framed it. It's a dead ringer, you'd realize if you saw the real thing." His voice caught on the last word.

"But," said Nora, "your brother Michael calls you Harvard Boy. You know your way around Cambridge." She was talking fast, trying to make him understand. "You used to hang out at the bar featured in *Good Will Hunting*! Of course you went to Harvard."

481

"I didn't. Nora, I didn't. I lied."

"No." She shook her head. "It's impossible. You have all that clothing."

"Stay here," said Gabe. "I'll be right back." He left and returned holding two glasses of the Bulleit, plus the bottle. He handed a glass to Nora. She downed it like it was coconut water. There were two chairs in the office: the desk chair, which Nora had claimed and wasn't giving up, and a straight-backed chair in the corner in which nobody ever sat.

Gabe remained standing. He started talking. While he talked, he shifted his weight back and forth from one foot to the other. Besides the gray T-shirt, he was wearing a pair of forest-green boxer shorts Nora had given him the previous Christmas.

There was an explanation for everything. Gabe held a degree from the University of Wyoming in Laramie. A good solid state school with a ninety-five percent acceptance rate and a giant football stadium. No Harvard. It was okay, it was fine. He excelled at the business classes he took. His professors said he had real talent for understanding the problems companies had and for figuring out how to fix them. Rare in an undergraduate, they said. A ranch boy! He'd never been told before that he was good at something. His parents weren't much for compliments.

After college he moved to Boston, where he took a class at the Harvard Extension School. One class, that's it, not part of any program. A class on the principles of finance that any old joker off the street could register for. They talked all the time about that, he and Nora, about how they lived only a couple of hours apart but had to move clear across the country to meet each other. That's why his brother Michael called him Harvard Boy. He was making fun of Gabe, not complimenting him.

One of his business professors from Wyoming knew a guy who worked at the Boston Consulting Group — that's how Gabe got the internship. He thrived there, but the country was heading toward a recession. They weren't hiring for any full-time positions. So when the internship ended, he went west in that battered, tan Subaru Leone he had when he met Nora.

"Like the gold miners," he said. "Seeking my fortune."

Nora didn't smile. That Subaru had been broken into three different times when Gabe lived in the Mission. The last time it wasn't even worth putting in an insurance claim — they'd simply removed the plates and left it parked on Dolores Street. One day, when they looked for it, it was gone.

Gabe finished his drink and poured more. Finally he sat in the straight-backed chair, on the very edge of it, like he thought he didn't deserve to lean back. As far as Nora was concerned, he didn't. It seemed that now that he'd started talking about it he couldn't stop. "It happened like this. Remember when we met, at that bar in Noe Valley?"

"Of course I do," said Nora. Her words sounded like someone had trimmed them with nail scissors right before they left her mouth.

"I'd been watching you all night."

Despite herself, Nora felt a little rupture of pride. "You had?"

"Of course. It was impossible *not* to watch you. You were so beautiful, you were like some exotic mermaid. You had all that hair. You were laughing so hard with your friend, swinging around your hair —"

"Colleen," said Nora. "My neighbor. I'd never been out with her before. She was hilarious." She smiled at the memory, and then she remembered she was busy finding out that her husband had lied about something major, so she stopped smiling.

Gabe reached out for her hand, but she

pulled it away. She couldn't. "Honestly, I didn't think I'd ever see you again. I thought I'd just talk to you that night, have a good time."

"Why didn't you think you would see me again?" Nearly two decades later, ridiculously, Nora was hurt. "Didn't you want to?"

"Of *course* I wanted to. But I didn't think I would. I thought you were too good for me. You were so pretty, and so confident. I had just moved out here, I was living in that shithole in the Mission, trying to find a job. I was struggling. I couldn't even afford to buy you a drink. I remember that I was really embarrassed about that. So we were talking, and you misheard me, it was really loud in the bar, and you thought I said Harvard."

"I thought you said *Harvard*? And what did you really say?"

"I said 'hard work.'"

"Hard work?"

"About living on a ranch. You said you thought it would be fun to live on a ranch, and I said it was fun sometimes but it was also a lot of hard work, and you said you had gone to the University of Rhode Island, and you called me Ivy League boy, and that's when I realized what you thought I said. My buddy had just made that fake diploma for a joke, because he was working on all kinds of shady stuff, who even knows, but it got in my head that it would be fun to play the part, for just one night."

Nora chewed hard on her lower lip. She tasted blood.

"The thing is, Nora, you should have seen the way your eyes lit up when you thought I said Harvard. You said, 'I think I've heard of it,' really playing it cool, but you were impressed. That had a lot to do with it."

Nora held up her hand like a traffic cop. "Don't you dare," she said. "Don't you dare put this on me."

"It was just for one night, just for fun. You have to believe me."

"But it wasn't," said Nora coldly. "Apparently." Her glass was empty too. Gabe refilled it from the bottle. She felt the same searing warmth she'd experienced at Arthur's house but none of the well-being.

"It turned into more. But I only meant it to be for one night. But I had been applying for jobs all over the place, and something came up at Elpis right after that. Remember, your friend Colleen had a connection there, to one of the founders? She asked for my résumé, she wanted to give it to them. She said they wanted someone with a pedigree.

She said Harvard was a draw for them. So then I was in a bind, because I was halfway into it — and I thought, what the hell? Why not? If it could impress *you* like that . . ."

"*Don't.*"

"So I put it on my résumé, I had to, because of Colleen, because she was there that night. I never thought it would go anywhere, Nora. It was just a joke! They called me for an interview, and I aced it. Like I'd never aced anything in my life. I was on fire."

"I remember," said Nora. "We went out for a drink after, to celebrate."

"That's right. The Little Shamrock. In Inner Sunset."

"I love that place," said Nora softly. "Right across from Golden Gate Park." They hadn't been there for years. It was a great little bar, not in the least bit trendy, older than old-school, with mismatched plush chairs and stacks of board games all over the place. Home to midafternoon alcoholics. She and Gabe had played a rousing game of back-gammon. Gabe beat her.

"I know why I aced it," said Gabe. "Because when I walked in there I walked like a Harvard graduate, and I talked like a Harvard graduate. I was unstoppable. I wasn't faking it! I knew my stuff."

"Did you?"

"Of *course* I did. My whole life isn't a lie, Nora. Just one thing."

"Pretty big thing."

Gabe continued with his story without acknowledging the truth of that. "And they hired me. And, well, obviously, I've been there ever since."

"I just don't understand how it's possible, to fake something like that. In an interview, maybe. But to *me*? In our everyday life? I just don't see it."

Actually she *was* beginning to see.

This was why they'd never been to a college reunion for Gabe; in fact, now that Nora thought about it, they'd never even received information about a college reunion. She'd never given it much thought because she herself did not care about such things. She had never been to any of *her* college reunions.

That's why Michael turned against Gabe. Gabe told him what he'd done, back when he first did it. He thought Michael might be impressed with what he'd gotten away with. But he was disgusted. By then Gabe had started working at Elpis, was dating Nora, carving out his life. The lie was in motion, unstoppable.

"I thought it was because of the high

school girlfriend, what was her name? That Michael stopped talking to you."

"Lauren. No, it wasn't because of Lauren."

Nora had also moved far away from everyone she went to college with. Sure, maybe when they were younger people talked about college, played the do-you-know-Bob-Smith-he-graduated-one-year-later game at dinner parties. But at some point that all stopped. And it would be easy, if one so chose, to perpetuate a lie. At some point where you went to college was just where you went, a four-year chapter in your ancient history book. It didn't really matter.

Except that now, of course, it did.

"Wait," she said. "If you lied about that, what else have you lied about? Did you really write your college application essay about the stillborn calf?"

"Of course I did," said Gabe. He ran his fingers through his hair and held his glass so that it rested on his knee. Gabe had thick, beautiful hair; he looked, truly, not so different from how he'd looked that night at The Little Shamrock, bent over the back-gammon board, elated because his interview at Elpis had gone so well. He still looked good in the cowboy hat he kept on a back shelf of his closet and trotted out every Halloween. "I swear to God, Nora, nothing else. The thing is, yes, I lied to you when I met you, and I lied when I got the job at Elpis. But it doesn't change who I am. It doesn't change anything I've done since then."

"Doesn't it, though?" She felt herself yielding, but then she hardened again.

"No. It doesn't." He put the glass on the floor, straightened, and became the Gabe she knew, capable and confident, partner at Elpis Consulting. (Despite herself she was glad to see he had some fight left.) "Some diploma didn't oversee the last four business turnarounds at Elpis. I did. Didn't buy us this house."

"*I* bought us at least half this house," said Nora.

"True," he said. "You did."

"Thank you."

"Believe me, Nora, I've thought about this a lot. I think about it *all the time.* All the time, especially lately, believe me. What that" — he cleared his throat — *"decision —"*

"Lie," she interjected.

"Fine. What that lie did was open doors for me. The rest of it I did myself. The life we built here, the community we're in, we did that together."

"Bullshit." That didn't sound like her

490

voice, but it was.

He reared back at that as though she'd reached right across the room and struck him. Then he recovered. "And you have to understand — *you have to* — that that's why I wanted this so badly for Angela, Harvard."

"What do you mean?"

"Because I saw for myself what that degree can do for a person. I saw it probably more than people who actually had it, because I knew what it was like on the other end. You know how many times my résumé didn't get picked up because I went to a state school? Too many times to count." Gabe slid off the straight-backed chair and sank down until he was sitting on the floor, his back against the wall, his knees pulled to his chest. He no longer looked capable and confident. He looked old and broken. He covered his face with his hands, and again he began to cry.

Almost — almost! — Nora felt sorry for him. She handed him a tissue from the box on the desk and he blew his nose. The whole scene would have been comical had Nora not been so irate and bewildered.

Gabe gulped and wiped at his nose in what Nora thought was a decidedly unmanly way and went on: "It's not fair. It's just not fair. She's so *smart.* She should

491

have gotten in. I wanted it so badly for her, Nora. So badly. She worked so hard for so long. I wanted her to get in. I wanted all those doors to open for her, the way they did for me."

"Well, she didn't." Nora crossed her arms over her chest.

"I know," said Gabe morosely. "Don't you think I know that?"

Nora gazed at the ceiling. In one corner, where the ceiling met the wall, she could see a crack. That, she knew, would be called out in a home inspection if they ever sold this house. It could signify nothing, or it could signify a legitimate problem. Maybe the house (like their life) was going to crumble around them.

Not everything that caused a life to fall apart measured on the Richter scale.

There was an officious little voice gearing up in the back of her head. *Don't forget to tell him about your job,* said the voice. She ignored it.

"I still don't understand, Gabe. How you could keep something like this going for so long. So long!"

It was easier than he ever would have guessed. Gabe explained how, once he'd fabricated a history for himself, he started to believe it. Taking Angela to the football game when she was small, walking around Cambridge when they went back to New England to see Nora's family. He began to inhabit the lie. He inhaled it! He felt like he'd gone to Harvard: in his mind, he turned into an honest-to-God Harvard graduate. He chose a freshman dorm for himself (Canaday Hall), and an imaginary roommate (William Bell II, from New Canaan, Connecticut, sort of an asshole, definitely a frat boy in training, but he brought a good stereo so that was a bonus). Gabe started to cry again. "It was just a snowball. I couldn't stop it. We had this one great kid, and we bought the house, and then we had another, and then another, and what was I going to do? Go tell the HR department so they could fire me and we could lose it all?"

Then, when it became apparent how bright Angela was, what a future she had ahead of her, well, it seemed like the right thing to do. To groom her for it, to buy her a tiny crimson sweatshirt, to show her what his parents had never been able to or cared to show him, that the world was her oyster. "And then she got obsessed with it, *she* started talking like it was what she really wanted, and when she outgrew the first sweatshirt she wanted another one. I thought it could be my penance, for lying. To help her, to do everything I could to get her something I never had."

"When are you going to tell Angela?"

Nora watched Gabe's mouth crumple in a way that made him look one hundred and four years old, like a man in a nursing home who had to be given soft food with a spoon.

Then quietly he said, "I can't." His mouth resolved into its normal self — the strong jaw, Cecily's jaw — and he shook his head briskly. "No," he said again. "I can't."

"But she put on her application that her father is an alum! Gabe! She *lied* on her application. You don't think they figured that out? You don't think that has something to do with why she didn't get in?" Nora's stomach was all bunched up, and her heart was knocking away inside her rib cage. She hadn't felt like this since Angela made her run the mother/daughter 5K at the middle school a few years ago. It had been a traumatic experience for Nora, trying to keep up with her fleet-footed daughter, who never broke a sweat, never breathed heavily.

Gabe cleared his throat. "I took care of it," he said.

"You *took care of it*? What does that mean?" Gabe sounded like he'd just stepped off the set of *The Sopranos*. All at once he

494

looked like it too: there was something hard and bright and unfamiliar in his eyes. He lowered his voice and said, "I deleted that part. From her application. When I checked it all over for her. Right before she hit *Submit.*"

"You *what*?"

"I had to." He shrugged. "I had no choice."

"But don't you think she should *know*? So she doesn't loathe herself too much, for not measuring up."

The color emptied from Gabe's face. Now he looked one hundred and thirty. "I can't tell her," he said. "What would she think of me?"

"But you can't *not* tell her. If you don't, I will."

"Please don't. Nora, please."

"Then you have to."

He rubbed his eyes again. "I don't know," he said. "I can't figure that out right now."

Nora remembered Angela in that little sweatshirt, the hood pulled up so that her eyes looked even bigger than usual. Moon eyes. "How come they never checked? At Elpis?"

"I don't know. They just didn't. Sometimes companies do background checks and sometimes they don't. Back then, they were new, I don't know. For whatever reason they didn't, they were just looking for talent, trying to get off the ground. I mean, I first put it on my application for a lark, never dreaming I'd get away with it. After the first interview they called me back for a second, and then a third, and they never mentioned background checks. But now, well, I think I'm going to have to tell them. Do you remember the intern we saw at the Slanted Door? Abby Freeman?"

"Christ," she said. Like a locomotive chugging its way toward her from a distant point, here came the understanding. "That's why you acted so weird around her. She knows."

He nodded. "She knows."

The words hung between them like a curtain. Gabe closed his eyes and rubbed his eyelids with the heels of his hands, the way a tired kid would. "It's been eating me up inside. It's all I think about. I have to tell them. I have to hand in my resignation."

She couldn't look at him, but she couldn't look at the diploma either. She looked instead deep into her glass.

The voice spoke to Nora again; it was not just bossy but persistent too. *You also have something to tell, Nora-Bora.*

She cleared her throat and tipped her glass

to her mouth, but it was empty. The bottle next to Gabe was empty too.

Come on, said the voice. *Do it. Tell him.*

"Um," she said. "You can't resign, Gabe. You can't. I lost my job."

This time she talked and Gabe listened. Sometimes he shook his head and sometimes he nodded sympathetically. When she got to the part about the circles of dirt on her knees he winced and took her hand. Another time, on another day, she would love him for that.

But not yet. Right now she was still bewildered.

"What do we do now?" Gabe said when she was done. His voice sounded like it had been cracked open and cooked on the sidewalk. "What are we going to *do*?"

"I don't know," said Nora. It might have been the truest thing she ever said. "I have absolutely no idea."

Eventually they hobbled back to bed like a couple of old ladies, where, amazingly, annoyingly, Gabe could sleep but Nora couldn't. That didn't seem fair to Nora, that she should be the one to lie awake until the wee hours, fuming and worrying. They were like characters in some kind of twisted O. Henry story, where she risked and lost her job to try to save the family, and he tried to save his job but lost the family in the process. Wait, that didn't make sense. How did *The Gift of the Magi* go again? She was too tired to think it through. Her eyes, opened into the darkness, burned, but when she closed them they opened right up again.

For a long time she tried to hate Gabe.

But as soon as she got the hate loaded up and ready to go little snippets of memory would creep in. This was the man who had danced the Charleston with Maya at her Daisy troop's daddy/daughter dance even though neither of them knew how. Who had, just now, held her hand and nodded sympathetically when she told him about the Marin dwarf flax. Who had run out and bought a little pink hat and a bottle of champagne the day Angela was born. Who always kissed her mother hello and who did that funny-awkward half-stand anytime a woman at the dinner table in a restaurant left to use the restroom and who never said no to a board game with the children and who always remembered to scrape down the grill and who told her all the time she was just as pretty as she was the day he married her, which couldn't possibly be true. The man who, just now, had winced when she told him about her mistakes. He'd winced, like it had happened to him!

How could she hate this man?

She couldn't.

And yet. He wasn't who she thought he was, this whole time. All these years!

Was she partly to blame, for being so impressed when she thought Gabe said Harvard, all those years ago?

Yes, said something inside of her.

No, said something else.

It was all so confusing.

To calm down she imagined herself in the land that Betsy and Tacy had inhabited more than one hundred years ago, where mothers baked a lot and fathers came home early from their jobs at the downtown shoe store or the pharmacy and children freely roamed hillsides after school because there was literally *nothing else to do.*

What had ruined that way of life? Nothing much. The automobile. The airplane, the rocket ship, the rocket-propelled grenade. Two world wars. The movies, the television, the iPhone, Google, Wii, 401(k) plans. Terrorism, global warming, property taxes, gluten allergies. Urban sprawl, Instagram, the SAT, childhood obesity, Twitter, parents friending their children on Facebook.

Yes, indeed, it was all so very, *very* confusing. What could they do now? What would *Angela* think? What would she do, once she knew? How would they manage from here?

Nora wanted then what everyone wants in times of duress or general unease; she wanted what soldiers struck down on the battlefield want before they take their last breath. She wanted her mother. She wanted to go home.

But it was the middle of the night on the East Coast, and Nora was the loneliest person in the universe.

CHAPTER 50
GABE

It would have been so much easier if Nora had *made* Gabe tell Angela the truth on Saturday. He wanted to be forced; he wanted to be marched to Angela's door like a POW with a gun to his head, maybe with a blindfold on. But she didn't force him. Instead she *supported* him, in a way that was both touching and infuriating. For much of the day he caught her looking at him with basset hound eyes: loving, sad, all-knowing in a slightly droopy way. Once in the kitchen she squeezed his hand and he had to blink back tears. It was pretty un-manly of him but he couldn't help it.

Around ten in the morning Angela emerged from her room in her running clothes. She spoke to nobody and slipped out the front door, returning an hour later, sweaty and red in the face. Gabe was hiding around the corner like a spy in a 1950s movie, missing only the fedora and the drizzly weather.

"How was the run?" Nora said. She was using a voice that was like a poor imitation of her normal voice. Angela shrugged and took the water Nora offered.

"Sweetie, you know it's not the end of the —"

Gabe saw Angela hold up a hand, palm out, and Nora stopped talking.

Cecily had a sleepover birthday party at night, and Maya was invited along to keep company with the younger sister of the birthday girl. Two down.

"Gabe, don't you think you should —" said Nora once, but Gabe didn't even let her finish the sentence. He shook his head, and she stopped talking.

Around six thirty Angela asked to borrow the car keys. The rule was that she was to say where she was going and when she was coming back anytime she took the car, but she volunteered nothing and neither Gabe nor Nora called her on it.

Three down.

Well, that settled it. Gabe couldn't tell

Angela something if she wasn't there to tell, could he? Nora and Gabe ate pizza in front of an old episode of *Breaking Bad,* neither of them really watching. Gabe felt like a prisoner on death row granted a reprieve for another day.

But the reprieve didn't last long. At eight thirty Angela returned, tossed the car keys on the counter, and made for her room. Nora gave him a look that said, *Now?* and he gave her one that he hoped said, *All in good time.*

After a while he pulled himself up from the couch and started down the hallway as though it had been his idea all along.

How to broach this subject?

President Obama often said, "Look," before he made a point, and that gave him an air of authority.

Look, Angela, there's something I have to tell you.

Actually, come to think of it, it made Obama sound a little bit defensive. Might have something to do with his dismal approval ratings.

Angela? Do you have a minute?

Too formal, that's how he'd approach Doug Maverick at work.

Knock, knock. Who's there? Daddy. Daddy who? Daddy who has something to tell you.

Finally he knocked, waited for the desultory *Who is it?* and opened the door. Angela was lying on her unmade bed, staring at the ceiling. There was an uncharacteristically untidy heap of running clothes on the floor. In the wastebasket next to the bed Gabe saw a mound of Kleenex, but when Angela turned her face toward him Gabe could see that her eyes were dry. The windows were closed even though the evening was relatively mild, and there was a sour odor that didn't seem to be directly related to the running clothes. It smelled like . . . well, at the risk of being overly dramatic, Gabe might say it smelled like disappointment.

Gabe sat in the desk chair and turned it to face the bed.

"How are you doing there, kiddo?" he asked. He hadn't called her *kiddo* for at least four years.

"Okay," said Angela. "I guess. But not really."

Gabe cleared his throat. "You know it's such a crapshoot, who gets in and who doesn't, I should have been more aware of that. I mean, I was *aware* of it, but all along I thought, well, who wouldn't want *you*? Right?" SMILE ALL DAY LONG, said those little Post-its, back when Angela had so much love to give she didn't know what to do with it all. Back when it was spilling right out of her.

Angela pushed herself to a sitting position. First her lips moved with no words coming out, and then they moved again and the words followed: "Did I disappoint you?" The unexpected guilelessness of the question made something tear in his heart. *Now,* he told himself. *Go.*

"Of course you didn't," he said. Deep breath. "In fact, if anything, I disappointed myself."

She looked warily at him. He thought of the night she was born, a full February moon rising over the city. He remembered it like it was last week. It had been such a shock, that the hillock in Nora's stomach had suddenly become an actual person ("Not exactly sudden," Nora would say; labor had lasted sixteen hours . . .), with a real set of lungs and *tears,* actual tears, squeezing out of her big round eyes. She'd seemed downright offended at first, to be forced from the womb like that and into the harsh light of the delivery room, and Gabe had felt his heart expand to take in all of her.

"What do you mean?" she said.

Now or never. Well, he would choose

never, if it was really an option. But it wasn't.

"A long time ago," he said carefully, as though the words themselves might break if he didn't put them down gently, "a long time ago I told a lie, and instead of coming clean with it like I should have I kept it going for a long, long time."

After he told her, there was a silence so heavy it was like a sheath.

The first thing she did was laugh, long and hard. She'd never laughed that hard at an actual joke he'd told. He waited until she'd finished and he held his face in its passive, guilty expression until Angela stopped laughing and looked at him and said, "I'm laughing because it's a joke. You're joking, right?"

He shook his head. "I'm not joking. I wish I was. Were? I wish I were."

It took a minute, maybe more, for that to sink in fully. Finally he said, "Sweetie?"

"I don't even know what to say. I'm *stupefied.*"

"You see, Angela, I —"

"You mean when you walked me around the *campus* . . ."

Gabe gulped. "I was pretending."

"When you bought me all of those stupid sweatshirts, when you told me what it was

505

like looking out at the *Charles River* —"

He swallowed hard. "I was imagining."

"Not imagining."

"No."

"You were lying! *Lying,* all that time. Dad, you were lying!"

Dad. Not Daddy. The beginning of the end.

"Angela, I understand that you're upset, but listen, it doesn't really change any —"

"Are you kidding? You must be kidding. It changes *everything.* Everything." She sat back against the pillows. "Everything you forced me into, pushed me to do. Everything, my whole life. My whole life, which is now completely ruined."

"Oh, now, honey, I don't really think I *forced* —"

She was standing now, and trembling visibly, her face baking-soda-pale.

"Get out."

"Ang—"

"*Dad!* I said, get *out*! Of my *room*! *I don't want to talk to you.* I don't even want to look at you. First the intern, and now *this*? What's next?"

"Wait, *what*?" Gabe said. "The intern? What do you mean, the intern?"

"Like you don't know what I'm talking about." She spat that at him. If words had actual poison, Gabe would be a dead man. "You're sleeping with the intern."

"Angela! I am *not sleeping with the intern.* I would never sleep with that intern. Any intern!" He shuddered, then he looked around for Nora, who would normally step in and say, *Don't talk to your father that way and put your running clothes in the hamper* and who would then restore peace and order to the house. But Nora wasn't there.

"Get *out,*" Angela said again, "of my *room,*" and this time he thought she actually bared her teeth at him. She was glaring at him with all the force of her moon eyes and the message in them was so clear it needed no translation.

He was Dad now, not Daddy. He was a liar and a cheat. He'd done it: the ultimate damage. He'd lost her.

CHAPTER 51
NORA

"Get some hiking clothes on," said Nora. It was Sunday morning. Angela was back in bed, under the covers, the blinds pulled against the light.

"Hiking?"

"That's right. We're going to see the redwoods."

"I've seen the redwoods."

"We're going to see them again." She pulled the comforter off Angela and shook it a little. Angela covered her face with her pillow and said, "Go away! I don't feel like talking to anyone."

"I will not go away. We're going to Muir Woods."

Angela lifted the pillow a fraction of an inch and said, "Who's going?"

"Just the two of us."

"Really? What about everyone else?"

"They're not invited. Get dressed."

Angela said, *"Ugh,"* but she pulled herself out of bed and began opening and closing her dresser drawers. "This is *ridiculous,"* she said. Still, in ten minutes they were in the car.

At the park entrance, Nora paid the admission fee, consulted the map, and said, "We'll do the Ocean View, to Lost Trail."

Angela said, "Sounds appropriate." And rolled her eyes.

"Then we could do Fern Creek to Boot-jack."

"Bootjack's long," said Angela.

"Have you got somewhere to be?"

Angela rolled her eyes again and Nora said, "Well, we'll see how we do."

Nora hiked her backpack onto her shoulders and started walking, leaving it up to Angela to come along or not. If there was one thing she'd learned from all these years of parenting it was that, when given the option, generally the offspring *did* eventually follow, rather than get left behind.

Nora inhaled and exhaled and began to feel some delicate semblance of peace descend upon her. However many times she walked among the redwoods they never failed to impress her with their majesty and strength and their total disregard for the minutiae that kept humans permanently tied up in knots of anxiety. The redwoods didn't care what college you went to or how you got your job or what your SAT scores were or if you ate enough kale or even if you were a good parent or not: they were just standing there, year after year and decade after decade, concentrating utterly on survival. That was it. One job, and they did it consummately. How *cooperative* of them.

They'd been walking for several minutes when Angela said, "I'm so mad, Mom. I'm so mad I could just scream."

"I know," said Nora. She was breathing more heavily than Angela was, naturally. Oh, to be seventeen again! (But not really, actually.) "I'm mad at Harvard too," Nora added. "Not to accept *you,* of all people! I mean, really, it makes me crazy." Of course she knew perfectly well that wasn't what Angela meant. In front of them a man wearing a small child in a backpack paused to look up at one of the trees. A tiny hand emerged from the backpack, pointing.

"Aren't you *mad,* Mom? Dad told me he just told you the day before yesterday. You! He's your *husband*!" Angela's voice was so strident that the hiker with the backpack turned to look at her. You were supposed to be peaceful in the great outdoors. Nora and Angela passed the man with the backpack and Nora gave him a polite, how-do-you-do nod, but inside she was roiling with envy. That child in the backpack looked so small and uncomplicated. Nora wanted to be able to wear her children like an accessory. Had she appreciated it enough, when she could?

She didn't answer Angela's question. A few minutes later Nora paused at an informational sign about the coastal fire road. She stared at it for several seconds, not reading any of it, not really. Her left quad registered a complaint. She really should start going to yoga with Linda. She attempted a halfhearted stretch. Maybe they wouldn't make it all around Bootjack after all. She'd call Linda tomorrow. No, wait, she couldn't call Linda. Arthur had fired her. She felt a spasm of grief as she remembered.

Angela said, "Mom?" and her voice sounded like a little girl's voice, at once full of hope and doubt. "Aren't you mad?"

Nora craned her neck and tried to see the top of the redwoods. She couldn't, not really. She said to Angela, "These have been here for, what? Zillions of years?" What would they do when Angela was out of the house and they didn't have her to tell them all the things they should know but didn't?

Angela snorted. "Six hundred."

Nora ignored the snort and absorbed the correction. "Right. A long time."

"What's your point?" The words were teenager-ish and even a little bit snotty, but behind them Nora sensed curiosity and maybe even some genuine warmth.

"My point is . . ." What was her point, exactly? She herself was furious with Gabe, then right on the heels of that she felt guilty for being furious, and then confusion about feeling guilty. "My point is, if these trees have been here for hundreds of years, and they're probably going to be here for hundreds more, well, it may not seem related, exactly, but don't you think you could go easy on your father?"

"Do *you* plan to go easy on him?"

Nora looked at her feet in their ridiculous hiking boots, which she trotted out only once a year. Softly she said, "I do. For a mistake." She began walking again.

"No," said Angela. "No. It wasn't a mistake, it was a *lie*! He lied to me, my whole entire life! He tried to make me follow him somewhere that he'd never even been. He didn't do that to Cecily, or to Maya, but he did it to me."

Well, yes. That was certainly true. "But."

"But what?" Angela spat the question at Nora.

"Have you never done anything you shouldn't have? I mean, anything that was a little . . . well, a little morally nebulous?"

"I don't know," said Angela staunchly. But when Nora tried to meet her eyes she looked away. "Nothing like what he did."

They came to a steep set of wooden steps and began the ascent. The blood was pounding in Nora's ears. Angela may as well have been walking on a cloud; she wasn't exerting herself at all.

When they reached the top of the steps Nora leaned against the railing and said, "I have. I dropped Maya on her head and I'm sure that's why she can't read."

"You did? No you didn't."

"I did too, when she was a baby. And only Aunt Marianne knows. I never told Daddy. That's the morally ambiguous part. Isn't that awful?"

Angela's eyes, behind her sunglasses, were inscrutable. "Um, *yeah,* that's awful. Why didn't you tell anyone?"

"Because I felt so guilty. I wasn't paying attention to her. I was paying attention to work instead."

"You *dropped* her?"

"Well. I let her fall. Which is just as bad." Even now, the memory unleashed in Nora a great internal shudder.

"That's not why Maya can't read."

"Who knows? Maybe it is . . ." Nora rubbed her finger along the railing. She'd probably get a gigantic splinter. Gabe was really good at removing splinters. Nora was hopeless; she didn't have the patience for it. What if Angela got a splinter? Would she let Gabe remove it? Probably not. Definitely not.

"I thought he was having an affair with the intern. When he told me he had something to say I thought that was it."

"I did too," confessed Nora.

"You did?"

"It crossed my mind." *A hundred times,* she added in her head.

513

"Gross, right?"

"I think she's horrible."

"Same," said Angela. She almost smiled, but Nora could see her catch herself.

"Would you have preferred *that* secret?"

"Yes."

"You would have?"

"Kind of, yeah. That would have been more . . . expected."

And less to do with you, thought Nora. Fair enough. Teenagers were the centers of their own universe; they almost couldn't help that. It had to do with the hormones. It was practically a medical condition.

"I mean, if he really had been an alum, maybe I would have gotten in. Maybe that was the edge I was missing. I can't stop thinking about that."

Angela was right. That was a real possibility.

There was a pause, and then Angela looked down at the railing and said softly, "I *did* do something I shouldn't have this year."

Nora waited. Even the birds — even the redwoods — seemed to be waiting to hear what Angela had to say.

"I took Adderall from Joshua Fletcher."

Nora wasn't sure what she'd expected, but she hadn't expected *that.* "You *what?*"

"I stole Adderall." She pulled an ironic face. "*Addy,* if you prefer to use a nickname. To help me stay awake to study."

Nora remembered the message on Angela's computer. *Anyone know where Addy is?* She'd thought that was a classmate's name, short for Adeline or Addison. Or maybe a teacher. What an idiot Nora was. "And nobody knows? Oh my God, Angela —" Normally her Catholic upbringing did not permit Nora the taking of the Lord's name in vain, but these were special circumstances. Obviously.

"Daddy knows. *Dad.* Mrs. Fletcher knows." Angela drew a deep breath and let it out slowly. "I apologized to her. I guess Joshua knows too, I'm not sure." She started walking along the path and Nora followed her. "She was really nice about it. She hugged me . . . and, well, she was just nice. It made me feel terrible, like I didn't already feel terrible about enough this year."

Angela slowed until Nora caught up and they began walking in tandem. It was better that way, neither of them looking directly at the other. "And nobody told me?" asked Nora. *This isn't about you,* a little voice said. But wasn't it? If it was about her children, then it was about her. That's what parenting was, the good and the bad of it.

"Dad wanted me to tell you, but — I thought you'd get all mad."

"I would! I am! I am all mad!" Nora was livid, absolutely livid. "I'm furious —"

"But I'll never do that again. It was stupid. I won't, Mom, I swear. The pills made me feel terrible and jittery and awful and lose my appetite, I hated them, I don't even think they helped that much . . ."

What had Maya said back in the fall? *Angela's been crying in the afternoons.* And Nora hadn't guessed. She remembered Angela dropping the water glass, bursting into tears, running to her room. She remembered Angela at Thanksgiving dinner, not hungry. She wanted to scream.

This was why Catholics went to confession. You told your sins to a priest, hopefully one you'd never seen before and would never see again, and you were in the clear. You didn't have to tell your mother or your daughter or anyone else. You didn't really even have to go into the details. *I killed a man. I yelled at a child. I lost my temper, I said a swear, I disobeyed my parents.* Nora stole a sideways glance. Angela closed her mouth and then opened it again and for a second she looked like a baby bird trying to capture a worm from its mother, and, just like that, Nora's heart melted a little bit,

516

and then a little bit more.

After a few beats of silence Angela said, "I feel different. Toward Dad. He doesn't seem like the same person, ever since he told me. He seems like a stranger. Is that crazy?"

Well, it wasn't crazy at all — this was the crux of Nora's problem too. So there, under the redwood canopy, she made a decision. Be first. Be better. Be the example. She rooted around inside the ball of anger and resentment and found a small bloom of love. Small, but with the potential to grow. She said, "You know what, honey? You won't always."

"I will. I *will.*" Angela kicked at a chunk of dirt on the trail.

"Not if you don't let yourself."

They had come to a fork in the trails. How perfectly appropriate! Wouldn't Robert Frost (New England by way of San Francisco) just have had a field day with the symbolism. Angela stopped and sighed. "I don't believe you. I want to, I just — don't." Angela shook her head. "I don't want to do Bootjack. Do you?"

"No," said Nora. "Bootjack is *exhausting.* I never wanted to do Bootjack. I want to go home and have a big glass of wine."

"Yeah," said Angela. "Me too. Except for the wine."

They turned back toward the visitor center, toward the parking area, toward home. Nora wanted to look again at her daughter but instead she concentrated on the trail ahead of her.

Such a messy and complicated business. Life. Family. But there was only one way to do it, wasn't there? You just had to keep going, one foot in front of the other.

"You'll get over it, sweetie," said Nora. "People get over worse."

"No," said Angela. "No, I won't. It's too big. It's huge, Mom. I can't get over it, and I won't. I know I won't."

Truly there was nothing to match the righteous anger of a teenager, was there? That feeling of being wronged, there was almost a joy in it. *Look, see? I told you the world had it out for me!*

And after all, maybe Angela knew her own potential for forgiveness better than Nora did. Maybe the damage was too great, and maybe she wouldn't get over it at all.

In no time Cecily was shaking her shoulder. She had overslept! Nora never overslept. She was generally up with the birds, up like a farmer's wife, preparing her charges for their day, packing Cecily's and Maya's lunch boxes, whipping dishes around the kitchen to get breakfast made for whomever would eat it.

Cecily was dressed, ready for school, right down to her backpack and her shoes, which she wasn't supposed to put on until she left the house (realtor's rules, or just another sign of the differences between Nora's generation and her children's; she and Marianne had grown up cheerfully clomping through their 1,800-square-foot Cape in their Stride Rites and their Buster Browns).

Cecily leaned close to Nora and Nora could smell the mint from her toothpaste on her breath. The spot next to Nora in the bed was empty. Gabe was gone too — that offsite.

"Oh geez," said Nora, squinting at the clock. "I totally overslept. I'm sorry, honey. Let me get you some breakfast."

"I'm good," said Cecily. "I made toast. I made some for Maya too."

"Did you?" said Nora. "That's great." She felt prouder than she should have — it was only toast, and Cecily was ten. But in the world of cosseted, twenty-first-century children self-made toast represented some sort of achievement. "Great," she said again. "I'll throw on some clothes, and let's get you two to school. I can give Angela a ride too, if she's running late."

"Angela's gone," said Cecily.

"What do you mean, gone?" said Nora.

Cecily shrugged, "She must have left early. She must have walked to school."

CHAPTER 52
CECILY

Cecily kissed her mother goodbye and watched her drive away from the turn-around.

To be extra-helpful, Cecily brought Maya to her classroom. Then she walked back toward the turnaround and stood in a knot of students until Pinkie dropped out of her mother's Acura.

"Hey," Cecily said. "Come here for a second." She pulled Pinkie over near the shrubs past the kindergarten building. There were kids playing wall ball and four-square on the blacktop, and two teachers on car duty. The car-duty teachers weren't looking at Cecily and Pinkie. It was easy enough to go unnoticed, and to crouch behind the shrubs as though they were looking through their backpacks.

"Do you have your phone?"

"Of course," said Pinkie. "I always have my phone."

"Good." Cecily walked away from the

building, away from the shrubs.

"Where are you going?"

"We have to do it now," said Cecily. "To-day."

"But —" said Pinkie. "*Today?* Now?"

"Now."

"But we're already at school. How will we —"

The first bell rang.

"Follow me," said Cecily. "But act natural."

Second bell.

"But we don't know how to get there!"

"I do, I copied it down last night. We take the 10 and then the Muni. I have it all right here. I have money for us both."

"But. What about school? They'll call our moms."

"We'll call ourselves in sick, once we're away from the school. You can do your mom's voice perfectly now, you know it. Try it."

"I don't want to."

"*Try* it, Pinkie. Say, 'Pinkie's staying home sick with me today.' "

"I don't know . . ."

"*Say* it, Pink."

"Pinkie's staying home sick with me to-day."

"See? Perfect."

"But I'm not sure —"

"I'm doing this either way, Pink, with or without you. Are you coming?"

CHAPTER 53
NORA

Nora found the note while she was tidying up the kitchen. Angela must have laid the note on the counter, but it had slipped to the floor and somehow wedged itself under one of the kitchen stools — that's why she hadn't seen it sooner, and why Cecily hadn't seen it when she was making toast.

Nora recognized the stationery she'd given Angela for her twelfth birthday, with Angela's initials monogrammed along the top and a little butterfly stenciled in the corner. Angela used to go crazy for butterflies; Nora had forgotten all about that. The note was folded, with *Mom* written on the outside. Not *Mom and Dad.* Just *Mom.* It would kill Gabe to know that, later.

CHAPTER 54
GABE

The partners at Elpis liked to hold their off-sites in a suite in downtown hotels. Twice a year, June and December. This time it was the Fairmont on Mason Street. At approximately seven thirty Gabe was crossing the Golden Gate Bridge. The sky was pinkening and purpling, the city coming into view. Far out in the bay Gabe could see Treasure Island, and, closer, Alcatraz. Think of all the people who'd been incarcerated at Alcatraz, they'd learned about it on the guided tour they took out-of-town visitors on. Out-of-town visitors loved Alcatraz. Gabe loved it too. Being at Alcatraz made you realize that whatever you'd done in your life, you probably stacked up okay compared to the guys who used to live there. Al Capone, for example. He'd done bad, bad things. Murder. Multiple murders.

Gabe had never committed murder, not even a single murder.

And even so. From what he'd done there was plenty of collateral damage. Gingerly, like a car accident victim feeling around for bruises, he assessed the past few months. Nora's job: gone. Angela's Harvard application: rejected. His lie: revealed. Well, partly revealed, but if Abby was true to her word soon to be completely revealed.

Nora was exactly correct: he'd pinned his own hopes on Angela, and it wasn't fair or right. It was never right when parents did that, but in Gabe's case it was particularly egregious because his hopes were based on something that had never happened. It wasn't something a good father should do.

He might have ruined Angela. Had he ruined her? He should call and check on her. But his Bluetooth wasn't working, and no way did he need a cell phone ticket on top of all the other shit that was going down. Anyway, she'd be on her way to school by now.

He hated Abby Freeman, really hated her. But in a way he didn't.

Because she'd forced him to face something he would need to face eventually: the fact that long ago he'd set a lie in motion, and that the lie had determined the trajectory of his life and a good part of the lives of his family. Wouldn't it be not only humiliating but downright wrong to allow his lie to be revealed by Abby Freeman when he could more honorably reveal it himself?

Traffic, there was always traffic. He stopped too close to the Nissan in front of him. Then the Nissan jerked ahead a little bit so Gabe did too. He glanced at the clock on the dashboard.

He'd read somewhere that there'd been thirty-six auto fatalities on the Golden Gate Bridge since the 1970s. Sixteen of those were head-on collisions. What a way to go. He tightened his grip on the steering wheel and drove like an old lady. Nothing wrong with old ladies.

What would he tell his daughters to do, if they found themselves in this situation? His funny, quirky, infuriating, completely one-of-a-kind daughters? He'd tell them to be honest, stand tall, right the wrong.

But what would he be, without this identity, without this job? Without the phantom degree that had followed him for two decades? He didn't know, he couldn't know, but he knew it was time to find out.

Traffic eased — no rhyme or reason to it, it just eased — and Gabe stepped on the gas. Then, the red lights of the Nissan. He slammed on the brakes. A screech of tires.

Chapter 55
Angela

Dear Mom,
Don't worry about me. You have to trust me. Do you promise? I'm doing the right thing, for me, and when I've done it I will make sure you know. Do not call the police or the school or any of my friends' parents or my cross-country coach or anyone at all. I'm not kidding.

Please trust me on this. Don't freak out.

Can you do that one thing for me, can you let me go?

That's it. I'm sorry if I disappointed you.

I disappointed myself too.

Love,
Angela

The phone.

Nora was trying not to worry. Like the note said. But she'd been a mother for nearly eighteen years now. She was going to worry. She ignored Angela's instructions, of course. She wasn't going to sit there and *not* call anyone. She called the high school — Angela wasn't in homeroom, hadn't Nora gotten an automated call from the office? No, Nora had *not* gotten an automated call from the office. She wanted to call every single one of Angela's friends, but she didn't have the numbers — they were all stored on Angela's phone. Gabe was unreachable; his phone was off for the offsite.

It was a beautiful early-winter day in the Bay Area, which meant that it was sixty-five degrees and sunny, or would be until the fog rolled in later in the afternoon. No need for so much as a mitten.

The police? The note said not to. But the

note also said not to freak out, and Nora was freaking out. Yes, she had to call the police. She had to. She was reaching for her cell when the home phone rang.

Nobody ever called the home number. She'd threatened to have it disconnected so many times that it was now a standing joke in the Hawthorne family. Because she never had time to do anything she threatened to do.

Mrs. Hawthorne?

Yes. Her hand shaking as she cradled the receiver.

A man's voice, unfamiliar.

Nora hadn't thought her heart could climb any farther up her throat than it had in recent weeks. But it could, it turned out, it could.

Three wishes, rapid fire.

One. Say what you have to say, quickly.

Two. Tell me it's going to be okay.

Three. Let me go back to the beginning and start over.

My name is Sergeant Stephen Campbell, California State Highway Patrol.

Stephen. Such an ordinary name, Nora would think later, for such an extraordinary phone call.

Mrs. Hawthorne?

Yes!

Yes. I'm right here. I can hear you.

Mrs. Hawthorne. I'm in the security office at the Golden Gate Bridge.

The *what*?

Do you know how to get here, Mrs. Hawthorne?

She couldn't say another thing. The room was whirling. She sat down on one of the kitchen stools.

Listen carefully, please. I'm going to tell you how to get here, and I want you to come right away. Do you understand me? We're on the south side of the bridge. From where you are you have to cross the bridge to get to us.

She swallowed, tried to breathe. She watched a hand that didn't seem like hers grasp at the edge of the counter. She watched the fingers try and fail to grip the edge. There was a sharp sound all around her, a high-pitched noise three octaves beyond glass breaking.

Mrs. Hawthorne?

Mmmmmmmph. The only sound she could manage.

I'm going to put your daughter on the phone, just very briefly, before we disconnect. Before you get in your car, Mrs. Hawthorne, which I want you to do right away.

528

CHAPTER 56
GABE

The Fairmont suite must have cost a pretty penny. Twenty-third floor. Wraparound views of the city and the bay. Wet bar. Full stereo system. Two and a half bathrooms. Five grand a night, Gabe guessed, although what did he know of such extravagances, except that he lived among them.

Joe Stone from HR stood at the door of the suite, holding a basket into which each of the partners was supposed to put his or her phone. "Company offsite policy!" said Joe. Joe loved offsites. He got all hopped up on the change of scenery. He usually introduced some touchy-feely get-to-know-your-coworkers game, the sort of game that really worked well only when people had been drinking. Was anybody drinking? Gabe cast a hopeful look at the wet bar. Of course not, it was eight fifteen in the morning. Just carafes of orange juice and cranberry juice, and coffee.

"Give up the phone!" cried Joe merrily. He made a motion like he was going to snatch it out of Gabe's hands, but Gabe was only too happy to comply. His phone had been off all morning. He didn't want to talk to anyone. His heart was still hammering away from the close call on the bridge. He dropped it into the basket. "Ready to brainstorm?" said Joe, gesturing to the plush couches. "Have a coffee first. You look terrible. Rough weekend?"

"Something like that," said Gabe. "Rough drive in." Close call with that Nissan. Team building and brainstorming were the last things in the world he felt like doing. His brain didn't seem like an actual brain anymore, more like a bowl of pudding, unformed and useless.

Do it now, Gabe. Get it over with. Do it now.

Gabe took his coffee and strolled to the windows to check out the panoramic view. Alcatraz and the San Francisco Bay (again), the double mounds of Twin Peaks, the financial district. And now that he was no longer on the Golden Gate he had a spectacular view of the Great Lady herself. Gabe didn't think anyone called the Golden Gate the Great Lady; he wasn't sure if it had any nickname at all. But it should. Maybe he'd get it started.

Now, Gabe. Now is a good time.

But it wasn't a good time; the partners were settling onto the couches and helping themselves to pastries and tropical fruit salad.

"Gabe?" said a voice. "Gabe? You with

us?" Joe Stone was setting up a giant white-board, and Kelsey was passing out legal pads and perfectly sharpened number two pencils. It was time to brainstorm.

Now, Gabe? No, not now. Don't be an idiot.

"Of course," he said. "You bet." In fact he was a million miles away. He was thinking about the ranch, imagining himself there. He could feel the presence of the cattle surrounding him, shaking their heads and lowing; he could see the ranch house in the distance, and behind it the majestic and forgiving Wyoming sky. The biggest sky in the world. Bigger than all of them; bigger than all of this.

At the midmorning break he thought, *Now. Yes.* He pulled aside Joe Stone. "Listen," he said. "When you get a minute. I don't want to interrupt the morning. But maybe during lunch, or after the afternoon session. I'd love to talk to you, one on one."

"Sure thing," said Joe. The lenses of his glasses caught the light so his expression was inscrutable. He clapped Gabe on the back, a friendly, man-to-man gesture, probably no real meaning behind it. "I'm all ears," said Joe. He was already moving on to the next person he needed to speak to,

531

but over his shoulder he said, "I'll come find you in a quiet moment."

CHAPTER 57
NORA

Right away was an understatement. Nora flew to the car and backed out of the driveway so quickly that had something been in her path, well, good luck to that something. She was a warrior. She was a woman and she was a mother. Hear her roar.

Her baby, her Cecily. On the Golden Gate *Bridge.*

The sergeant had put her on the phone but all Nora had heard was crying, then four words.

Mommy, Cecily said. *Mommy, come get me.*

Easy peasy lemon squeezie Cecily. Cecily, falling at the *feis.* Cecily, working so hard on her landmark project. Cecily, the joy draining from her beautiful brown eyes. And Nora hadn't really noticed. She'd been so wrapped up in Angela, and Maya, and *Harvard,* and her own idiotic troubles with the Watkins home and the Marin dwarf flax, that she hadn't noticed. She thought she was on top of things but all along she wasn't

— all along she was watching, was worrying about, *the wrong daughter.*

And this was her penance.

Genie, I take back everything I've ever wished for in my whole life. That crap about putting the kids in mason jars? Forget I ever said that. The wish about wishing I'd never even heard of Harvard? Stupid. Stupid! I didn't mean it, of course. All the way back to the chocolate appliances, the perms, the one time I wished (privately) that Marianne wouldn't get invited to Lisa Reardon's party along with me so I wouldn't have to watch over her. There is only one wish now, there's only ever been one wish that matters. Make Cecily okay. Genie? Are you hearing me? God? Are you out there?

To get to the security office she had to cross the bridge, just as the sergeant had told her. When traffic halted her progress for a minute she could see, on the east side, knots of pedestrians, a couple of runners. *Hey!* Nora wanted to call to all of them. *Hey, guess what? I've been worrying about the wrong child!*

Cecily and Pinkie were spending more time together than ever before this fall. Nora had attributed this to Cecily's quitting Irish dance but really it was more: they were plotting something, they were plotting *this.*

Whatever this was.

Wrong child, wrong child. Nora had been worrying about the wrong child.

It was confusing, pulling off so close to the end of the bridge, and then squeezing into the small parking area that Sergeant Campbell had described. Nora had to ask a bridge patrol officer examining his bicycle where to go, and he answered her nonchalantly, like this was a regular day, a regular situation. Up a few steps, bridge traffic whooshing by just behind her. Another officer at the window of the security office, a voice that didn't feel like hers asking where to go. Then down a corridor. And there was Cecily, sitting on a plastic chair and holding a cup of water. And Pinkie. And Cathy Moynihan.

Sergeant Stephen Campbell wore a tan uniform with a holster. No hat. Nora realized that on the drive over she had been picturing a hat. *Wrong child, wrong child, I've been worrying about the wrong child.* Probably he had one somewhere, he just wasn't wearing it at the moment. There was a gold star above his front left pocket, and a blue patch on his right arm that made Nora think of the Girl Scout patches her mother spent many a painstaking hour stitching to Nora's uniforms. Now they were all iron-on. Ir-

534

relevant fact. The sergeant's tan pants had a blue and gold stripe running down the side. He was clean-cut, with hair going gray, about Nora's age, although he could have been a bit younger or a bit older. Strong, square hands, deep wrinkles around his eyes, the kind common in avid skiers and hikers — people who summered and wintered near Tahoe. *I've been worrying about the wrong child.*

It was unthinkable, all of it.

That Cecily had gotten herself to the Golden Gate, and that Pinkie had too. ("Took the bus," they said later, almost casually, as though they were talking about an after-school activity, like glee club or lacrosse. "Then the 10 and then the Muni.")

It was unthinkable that the school had never called to inquire after their absences.

"They called themselves in sick," said Cathy Moynihan, who somehow, unfairly, had gotten herself there before Nora. Cathy Moynihan looked as ill as Nora felt; her hair was unstyled and partially damp, as though she'd stepped right out of the shower and into the security office. She wore no makeup. Nora noted in a pocket of her mind reserved for incongruous, unimportant thoughts that she had never seen Cathy Moynihan without makeup.

All of it was unthinkable: Cecily and Pinkie standing on the Golden Gate — two ten-year-olds, *by themselves* — until Sergeant Stephen Campbell happened by on his regular bridge patrol, saw something amiss, and pulled over.

"Wait a second," said Nora. She still didn't understand. She hadn't let go of Cecily since she'd arrived. She was kneeling in front of her, holding on now to the sleeve of her turquoise fleece, as though she might take flight without warning. "You were going to *jump*? They were going to jump off the *bridge*?"

"No! No, Mom, *no.*" Cecily looked horrified. "We were helping."

"Helping *what*?" Cathy's voice was carved straight out of ice.

"Whoever needed it," said Pinkie. Her face was dead white; her freckles looked almost black against her skin. Her hand holding her water cup was shaking; some of the water sloshed over the edge and onto her jeans. "We learned about all those people who help people who want to jump. And we thought we could help. We thought we could save someone. And then we'd be . . . and then we'd be heroes."

"Even if we couldn't be heroes, we thought we could do something," said Cecily. "I couldn't do anything at home, I couldn't help *Angela* with *anything* and everybody at home is so stressed out, and I heard you and Daddy fighting the other night and I don't know, I thought I could do something here. Like, where people's problems are sooooo bad."

It's official, thought Nora. *Worst mother in the world, right here. Bring me the award and I'll frame it and hang it in the office. There are no other contenders.*

"But there was nobody to save," said Cecily. "So we stood there for a long time, and waited. And talked about what it would be like, and why people jump. All those people we saw in the movie, and how they thought everything was hopeless . . ." She started to cry. "And it was so scary, looking down like that. Imagining. The water is black if you look straight down. It was so scary, Mom."

"Then I came by," said Sergeant Campbell. "On bridge patrol. We share that with the bridge patrol officers. We all work together. And I stopped, of course. Because one of them was starting to climb over the rail."

Nora's stomach dropped right out of her body. "Which one?"

"Me," said Cecily. And she began to bawl,

the way she used to when she didn't get her way as a little girl — taking deep gulps of air, hyperventilating.

"I brought them here, and called you both. You know the rest."

Nora looked at Cathy but Cathy wasn't meeting her eyes. Nora looked at Cecily. Nora pictured her hiking a leg over the rail of the bridge. Her mind refused to accommodate the image.

"I just wanted to see what it was like," cried Cecily, in between sobs. "I just wanted to see what it felt like."

"I told her not to," said Pinkie. "I told her not to climb over. She couldn't anyway, it's way too high."

"But if you had!" said Nora. "One slip, one mistake, and you would have been dead. Oh my God, Cecily. You would have been *dead.*" She'd been worrying about the wrong child.

"Listen to me," said Sergeant Campbell. He stood in front of the two girls and looked down at them. Nora, who suddenly felt in the way, released her grip on Cecily's sleeve and moved behind her. Sergeant Campbell was stern but you could see that he was ultimately kind, the way Nora knew parents should strive to be. This was a nearly impossible balance to achieve — it was the hardest part about parenting — but Sergeant Campbell made it seem as easy as slipping on a sweater. Look at Pinkie and Cecily, giving him their full attention! "Listen to me, you two. Listen very carefully. We are trained especially to help people like that. You can't just . . . you can't just be a regular person, even a regular person who's trying to do some good, and help anyone in that situation. You just can't. People who consider suicide are desperate, and we have to be really, really careful about what we say to them. Now I understand that you were trying to help. But you scared a lot of people. And you weren't ready to help anyone. You understand?" The girls nodded. Pinkie's braces glinted in the overhead light. They were mute and obedient; they were practically Girl Scouts.

Sergeant Campbell turned his attention then to Nora and Cathy.

"I got kids of my own," he said. "I know how it is, you try to keep up with everything. You can't always. But you got to keep trying."

"You're right," whispered Nora. She wanted to hug Sergeant Campbell. She wanted to lie down in bed and have Sergeant Campbell wrap a giant soft blanket around her and tiptoe out of the room so she could sleep for sixteen hours straight.

But there was nothing to do but the best thing in the world: gather up her child and go home.

In the car Cecily fell asleep. The promised fog hadn't materialized; the bay was as calm and clear as a sheet of glass.

Nora used the rearview mirror to look at Cecily, who slept with her head leaning against the window and her mouth hanging slightly open. The posture reminded Nora of how Cecily used to sleep as a toddler, leaning to one side in her bulletproof car seat.

Poor Cecily. Of course she wasn't immune to the stress in the house: how could she be? No doubt Cecily looked at Angela, even at her parents, and saw the same fate coming down the pike for her. The other members of the Hawthorne family weren't exactly making it look attractive, growing up.

With one hand she dialed Gabe's number again, then Angela's. Again. Neither picked up. When Gabe turned on his phone he'd see sixteen missed calls and seven voice mails from Nora. When Angela turned on hers: probably twenty, twenty-five. Nora had lost count. Where *was* everybody?

When Nora pulled into the driveway she started to wake Cecily. But instead she climbed in the backseat. The back of the Audi was nice, spacious and comfortable, and still clean, the way she had to keep it to drive clients around. Nora allowed a lot of things in her household, but she didn't allow snacking in the car. She moved a piece of Cecily's hair out of her face and Cecily stirred but didn't open her eyes.

One day Cecily would grow up and fall in love and have her heart broken and do stupid things she'd regret and wonderful things she'd remember for the rest of her life; there'd be a time when Nora might not know where Cecily was for days or even weeks at a time or what she was doing, or with whom. She'd get a job (or not); she'd love it (or not); she might get married and have kids of her own or be a single mother or not be a mother at all. She might be a lesbian or an archaeologist (obviously, Nora knew, you could be both of those at once) and she might hurt people and ache with regret or be hurt herself and ache with sadness. She might not always be safe but for now she was, she was right here with Nora, and she was sleeping, and nothing could get to her at this moment.

But where the hell was Angela?

CHAPTER 58
ANGELA

It was official. Angela Hawthorne was the stupidest smart person she knew.

She was stupid in too many ways to count but, okay, she'd give it a try.

Let me count the ways, said Elizabeth Barrett Browning.

Fine, Elizabeth. Ms. Browning, if you prefer. Here we go.

First, she was stupid enough to think she was smart enough to get into Harvard. Which was the biggest mistake, and she'd been making it for *years* now. So sure of herself, so oblivious. Nobody got into Harvard. Well, people did, obviously, probably about eight hundred people had gotten in yesterday, when she'd been rejected, but nobody she knew. You could be valedictorian, you could be the smartest person in your school, you could be the person who worked the hardest and studied the longest and wanted it the most and ran the fastest and fluted the best and all that didn't matter: nothing mattered. *Nothing mattered.*

Because there were so many high schools, and each one of them had a valedictorian, and there were so many families, and each of them had a smartest child. There were cross-country teams everywhere, and each of them had a fastest person. There were so many people who had already gone to Harvard, and *those* people all had children, or at least most of them did, and there wasn't room for all of them to get in. So they did not all get in. Which was not breaking news, because she wasn't *stupid* (see aforementioned), but still. Not everybody could be chosen. And she had not been chosen. So she was smart, sure. But she wasn't smart enough. (*See me,* Ms. Simmons had written on her extended essay.) Angela didn't even want to think about that essay. Of course Ms. Simmons had noticed, and had called her out on it, *of course,* and Angela had cried like a baby in front of her. She definitely didn't want to think about that essay.

Second, she had no backup plan. Not one single backup plan. Every time in the past year, two years, *five* years, she'd started to think about this moment, and what would happen if it *happened,* if she got *rejected,* she hadn't let herself get this far. Her mother had tried to get her to, but Angela had pushed her off with both hands. Ms. Vogel had tried to get her to too, but same deal. Double push.

Rejection. Not an SAT word. But such an

awful word. Ugly and mean. Not *deferred,* as in wait until our regular admission time and we will reconsider your pathetic little application again, when we have not forty-five hundred people you are competing with, but more like thirty-five *thousand* people who all want exactly what you want, and who all think they deserve it as much as you do. Nope: just flat-out, don't-bother-us-again, your application is going right in the trash or the recycling bin or wherever it is we put the real losers.

She must have blown it with that Susan Holloway way worse than she'd thought. That was all bullshit, Susan pretending to like her handshake, to like her honest answer about not having read a book for pleasure since she was a toddler. And for sure she *never* should have asked that question at the end. Susan Holloway had probably flagged her application. There was probably some special red flag, like a dark red, that meant: Stay really far away from this one. That flag meant: Don't even think about it.

Third, she'd blown practically the entire gift certificate Aunt Marianne had given her on this one stupid, pointless, terrifying trip. She'd rented a car from a really shady place far from the airport because it was the only place that would rent to you when you were younger than twenty-five. And she still had to get home. Eventually.

Fourth, here she was, standing outside the Harvard admissions office, waiting for Timothy Valentine, admissions officer for the Northern California region.

I bow to him, she'd told Cecily. *Like he's Mecca.* Well, maybe she should have.

The stupidest smart person in the world, right here. Angela Hawthorne. Allow me to shake your hand because I've been told I have a wonderful grip. Pleased to meet you.

But whatever flaws she had as a Harvard applicant, she was an excellent stalker. Because here he came now.

Timothy Valentine was a tall man, ginger-haired, thin, with a build similar to that of Angela's cross-country coach, Mr. Bradshaw, which meant that he had a slight stoop to his shoulders that owed something to a deficit in upper-body fitness: the curse of the carb-gulping long-distance runner. *Marathoner,* thought Angela. *Does Boston every April, I bet.* How scary could this man be, if he was a marathoner? And yet he scared the crap out of her.

In one hand Angela clutched the printout of the email from Harvard, and in the other the keys to the dubiously obtained rental car.

Timothy Valentine, exiting the *vaunted* halls of 86 Brattle Street, didn't look around to see if anyone might be following him. He didn't walk particularly quickly, though his legs were long enough that Angela had to hurry to keep up with him. He seemed like a man who was out walking a dog, or strolling through a shopping mall. Timothy Valentine didn't seem like a man with the fate of thousands of high school seniors resting on his narrow shoulders.

Timothy Valentine crossed the street and arrived at a burnt-orange Prius with a Patriots sticker in the rear window. *Fortuitously* (SAT word, not that it mattered anymore), Angela had parked just a few spots away. Angela's mother was big into the Patriots. She was always going on about Tom Brady, but in their house she may as well have been speaking to the deaf, because nobody else in the family cared about football. Her father watched tennis and golf, and they all followed the Giants.

Now that she had found Timothy Valentine, Angela noticed things about her surroundings that she hadn't had a chance to notice when she'd arrived at 86 Brattle Street just a short time before, and at Logan before that. The evening felt different here than it did at home — it wasn't just the chilly quality to the air, though that was part of it, but something was different about the sky, too, which Angela, if pressed, would have described as a heaviness. A *gravity.* Angela had once heard her mother, fueled by a couple of glasses of Cabernet, describe to dinner guests what she viewed as the essential difference between the East Coast and the West Coast: the East Coast had been settled by people who were *escaping* something (persecution) and the West Coast by people who were *seeking* something (gold). "I mean, come *on,*" Nora had said. "Doesn't that just say it all, right there? Isn't that the crux of *everything*?"

There had been an early snow in New England, and vestiges of it lingered in the parking lot in the form of dirty ice chunks and ugly piles pushed against light poles. Christmas was only — what? Nine days away.

Timothy Valentine's Prius purred to life. What else was there for Angela to do? She had flown all the way here. She'd forked over a lot of money at Payless Car Rental. (Although, because of her age, she'd actually Paid Way More. She'd Paid a Lot.) Angela climbed into her rented Hyundai

Accent and followed Timothy Valentine into the Cambridge twilight.

She'd always thought San Francisco was difficult to drive in — all those hills! But Cambridge was a real bitch: small side streets giving way to other streets that were bigger but not exactly freeways, which then gave way again to more side streets. Everything seemed to be a one way going the way you wouldn't expect.

In the early evening — *civil twilight,* Angela had heard it called, though there was nothing civil about her current situation — the headlights of the cars coming toward her seemed to merge with the taillights of the cars in front of her into one big soup of red and yellow. Angela took a second to wonder if she needed to get her eyesight checked. But there was no time for lingering thoughts: Timothy Valentine shifted lanes without warning and Angela almost lost him.

He pulled over at a 7-Eleven and Angela slid into a spot where she could see him but that wasn't close enough for him to see her. (This stalking thing was complicated. And exhausting. She hadn't slept on the plane.)

Timothy Valentine emerged from the 7-Eleven with a half gallon of milk and a package of Lay's potato chips. *A family,* thought Angela, about the first item. And: *A vice,* about the second. She watched as Timothy tore into the Lay's with an enthusiasm and delight that almost made Angela like him. Except he had ruined her life, so there was no way she was going to *actually* like him.

He pulled back onto the main road — Route 2, the signs told Angela — and she stuck with him for fifteen minutes, maybe longer, until he turned off of Route 2 and followed a bunch of smaller roads, eventually pulling up in front of a two-story red house. Cute house. A farmhouse without a farm. The house was on a street of homes that were different enough from each other to avoid the cookie-cutter label. Angela looked at it with her mother's appraising eye and thought, *This neighborhood has character.* They were all two stories or more, which was one of the things her mother liked about architecture out here compared to at home. Though she said that only in private, of course. Never in front of the all-powerful Arthur Sutton.

Timothy Valentine pulled into the driveway and Angela parked the illegal Hyundai in front of the house across the street. She watched as the front door to the farmhouse without a farm opened and a golden retriever bounded across the lawn. She heard a voice call, "Daddy!" And then, more quietly, as though its owner had turned toward the bowels of the house, "Daddy's home!" Except for the rapidly diminishing daylight, Angela could have been watching a commercial for life insurance. Timothy Valentine held the half gallon of milk aloft like a prize and turned toward the voice. He reached down and, with his free hand, rubbed the head of the golden retriever.

This is it, thought Angela. *This is my chance.* She closed the door of the Hyundai, looked both ways, and crossed the street. She cleared her throat twice — she hadn't spoken to anyone since the rental car place, so she wasn't sure if her voice still worked — and said, "Mr. Valentine?"

He turned, squinted. His bewildered face was almost funny. He put a hand on the dog's collar — the dog was lunging toward Angela, but in a friendly way — and said, "Can I help you? Do I *know* you?"

"I'm Angela Hawthorne," she said. She extended a hand, which was ignored (out of necessity, she told herself later, because he was trying to control the dog). "I was an early applicant in November. I recently received this email" — she thrust toward him the printout of the rejection — "and I was wondering if I could talk to you for a minute."

"Oh," said Timothy, understanding. "*Oh. I see.* And you came from —"

"California."

"Cali*for*nia?"

"Northern," she said, as if that explained anything. "Marin County. And I just thought if I could talk to you, then maybe —"

Timothy looked with dismay at the dog, who had loosened itself from his grip and was now making a large deposit in the center of the lawn.

"I'm sorry, Miss — ?"

"Hawthorne," Angela supplied, too eagerly.

"Miss Hawthorne. I'm sorry, but the decisions of the committee are very, very carefully thought out. They aren't made by one person acting alone."

"I'm not crazy," she said. "I don't have a weapon or anything, I swear. I'm just . . ." Here she momentarily lost control of her voice; it began to wobble, and she had to pause and take a deep breath. "I'm just *confused.*"

Timothy Valentine sighed and grimaced, not unkindly. Angela had the thought that if they could sit down together, or, better yet,

551

go for a *run* together, if he got to know her, then he would recognize that there had been a mistake, that she should have been accepted. "I don't remember your application specifically, Miss Hawthorne. But I'm going to take a guess that it was loaded with fantastic grades, extracurricular activities, astronomical test scores, varsity sports . . . am I right?"

"Yes," said a tiny voice that Angela didn't recognize as her own. "I have a copy of it right here."

"I don't need to see a copy," he said. "As I said, the decisions of the committee are final. And I'm sure your application was stellar. Nearly every application we receive for the early-action deadline is stellar. So we find ourselves in the fortunate position of being able to choose from the best of the best of the best. And some of the best don't get in."

A small girl bounded out of the house and up to Timothy. She had bright blond hair and a smattering of freckles so perfect they looked like they'd been drawn on. All of this Angela could see because the path leading up to the red house was perfectly lit by a series of small lanterns. *God.* Timothy Valentine had great taste, too. Or his wife did.

The little girl reminded Angela of Maya.

"Let me ask you this, Angela," said Timothy Valentine. The girl leaned against her father and wrapped one arm around his skinny leg. Oh, to be five again! The girl regarded Angela and said, "Who's *that*?"

"Nobody," said Timothy, and Angela tried not to be insulted.

"Do you think," said Timothy Valentine. "Do you think you're the first applicant who's shown up at my office, followed me to the parking lot?"

"Um," said Angela. "I'm guessing no?" *Speak with confidence during the college interview process,* came the voice of Ms. Vogel, college counselor extraordinaire. (*But not extraordinaire enough for me,* thought Angela.)

"You're not even the first one who's followed me home. It's happened to all of us. Harvard applicants do some really crazy things. They send us stuff —"

Maybe Angela should have sent something. "Really? What kind of stuff?"

"You name it. Socks, hats, shirts, arts and crafts, music videos. Hot sauce."

"Hot sauce?"

"But it doesn't make a difference at all, of course."

The girl tugged on her father's pant leg.

553

"Come *in,* Daddy," she said. Angela saw now that one of her front teeth was missing, and that there was a little stump of an adult tooth coming in. That could be an awkward look on some kids, but this girl pulled it off. God, she was cute. Angela would babysit for this girl in a heartbeat.

Timothy crouched down to the girl and said quietly, "I'll be right in, sweetie. Listen, can you take this milk and bring it inside to Mommy? It's heavy, you have to hold it with both hands. Can you do that? And can you bring Bella with you?" At the sound of her name the dog bounded back over to the crew on the front lawn. Timothy kissed his daughter on her sweet little head. Angela felt like she was witnessing something very private and profound, something from which she should look away, and yet she couldn't look away. Not only was Timothy Valentine a dog owner, he was a really nice dad. Both of these things made it hard to hate him. But he had ruined Angela's life, he and the rest of the admissions board, so she would try to hate him anyway.

Timothy Valentine stood up. He let out a small groan and Angela thought, *Tight quads.* He was definitely a runner. He probably ran at lunch, around the Harvard campus, or right out along the Charles.

That's what she would do, if she worked at Harvard. Then, as though there had been no break in their conversation, he continued. "No, you are not the first to follow me home. You wouldn't believe the things people do, both before and after their application is considered."

Timothy Valentine may as well have taken an oversized pin and placed it in the center of Angela's body: everything about her deflated.

"You mean even in my stalking I'm unoriginal?"

"Something like that."

A little stinging behind her eyes: tears ready to jump out. Angela blinked them back. She felt like she had to say what she said next. He was waiting, even though there was a child inside, a dog, probably dinner. Something hearty and New Englandy. (Chowder?) He was waiting patiently on his front lawn in early winter.

"I thought I was special," she said finally. It wasn't a whine, it was a statement.

Timothy cleared his throat and frowned down at his shoes and said, "Do you want to know a secret?"

"Um," said Angela. "Sure?"

"Everybody in your generation, you and all of your peers, you all think you're special. But how can every single one of you be special? It is literally impossible."

Angela's head was staring to hurt. She blinked again, and the backs of her eyes felt hot. It was dark enough that she'd be able to hide the tears if they fell, but still. As a point of pride she'd rather keep them back.

"I thought you were going to tell me a *good* secret," said Angela finally, and Timothy Valentine smiled. So at least there was that.

She looked to the sky, where the darkness was stripping away the remains of the day. It was odd to Angela to look around and see trees everywhere, along the highway, all through the neighborhoods, instead of open sky or mountain ranges or the San Francisco Bay. It felt like the landscape was closing in on you, instead of opening up, but the closing in felt comforting, the way it felt when you were little and your parents leaned in from two opposite sides of the bed to kiss you goodnight. Most of the houses on this street had Christmas decorations up; the lights were just starting to come on.

Timothy Valentine walked over to his mailbox and opened it. He peered inside, and then removed a stack of envelopes, some catalogs. Angela thought that he was signaling to her the end of their conversation, but then he said, "You know who gets into Harvard?"

She shook her head. She didn't know the answer. *(Will this question be on the test, teacher?)* "Nobody?"

"No, not nobody."

"Right," said Angela. "Of course. That wouldn't make sense."

"The students who get into Harvard are something beyond the extraordinary, because unfortunately the extraordinary has become commonplace. We get so many applications from students who are broadly accomplished, but not always deep. We are looking for the deep. The extraordinary and the deep."

Angela said, "I see." She, Henrietta Faulkner, the rest of the Oakville High senior class (except for Maria Ortiz), they were all too broad and not deep enough, every single one of them. All those hours on soccer fields, in field hockey helmets, puzzling over foreign languages and instruments and algebraic equations — they weren't enough. They had all come to nothing. Or, rather, they had come to this: Angela as stalker, Angela as desperate Harvard reject, clutching a rental car key and a printout of an email.

Just to be clear, though, and because she

sensed that she was about to lose Timothy Valentine's attention, she asked, "Are you saying that I did too *much*? That I should have focused on just one thing, all this time? Just one thing?"

Angela thought about the last cross-country meet, and the way she'd let that girl from Novato . . . just . . . very . . . gradually . . . get . . . ahead . . . of . . . her. She thought about taking Joshua Fletcher's pills, and she thought about how she stole Teresa's paper.

See me, in Ms. Simmons's felt tip.

"What I'm saying," said Timothy Valentine, "is that maybe you haven't found your passion yet. Your one, single, driving passion. And that's okay. Many people haven't, at age seventeen, eighteen. But that's the kind of thing that shines through on an application."

Later there would be time for the tears and the heartache and all of the crappy pain that came out when a dream vanished. It would hurt. It might always hurt, but as much as she wanted to blame the pain on someone else she couldn't justifiably do that. Because the worst part was that Harvard didn't know about any of her transgressions — she hadn't been caught, hadn't been turned in or called out or publicly shamed. The truth was in some ways harder to bear. As mad as she was at her father, as much as she wanted to blame his lie for her failure, he hadn't done anything to hurt her. Not on purpose. She simply hadn't stood out; she hadn't made the cut.

A woman appeared in the doorway, backlit by the light in the hallway, and called out, "Tim?" in a slightly impatient way that was familiar to Angela from a decade and three-quarters of being hurried along by adults. Angela could see a staircase. When she was little she wanted to live in a house with a staircase. "Tim? What are you doing out there? We're waiting for you."

Timothy Valentine waved and said, "I'll be right in. Almost done here."

So Angela hadn't found her passion yet. Cecily was almost eight years younger, but she had! Cecily's passion was Irish dance, and Angela had been ready to step squarely on that passion, to grind it right into the ground. *Take up fencing,* she'd told her. *That'll get you into college.* Her mother's passion was real estate. Her father's passion — well, she didn't want to think about her father right now.

Angela refocused her eyes on Timothy Valentine. Behind him the red house had become a blackish blur. The moon was nearly full. Civil twilight was over; night had arrived. The streetlights illuminated the Hyundai, and from far away she could hear the semi-muffled sounds of highway traffic.

All those people with somewhere to go, somewhere to be, a place in the world. Her North Face fleece, which had been bordering on deficient since she'd stepped off the plane, was now officially, exquisitely inadequate. She shivered and crossed her arms. She met Timothy Valentine's gaze full-on. It was over, her long quest. It had ended right here on a suburban lawn in . . .

"What town are we in?" she asked.

"Concord. As in the battles of Lexington and."

Angela nodded. Sure. Lexington and Concord, she knew. She had scored a five the previous year on the APUSH exam. She had nailed it.

"You caught me at a good time, Miss Hawthorne," said Timothy Valentine. He peered at the mail, although there was no way he'd be able to read it in this light. "The other times I've been followed I've been less . . . how shall we say it? Less *amenable* to offering advice. But there are many, many options out there, available to an intelligent, accomplished, lively young person like yourself."

Angela thought, *Lively? Really?* She didn't feel lively. She felt ancient. She imagined the little blond girl building a snowman, sticking a carrot in it for a nose.

The dog barked twice. The door opened again and the woman called, "We have to start without you! Sarah and I are starving."

Sarah. That was a nice name for that child, very New England Puritan. Sarah Valentine, whose father worked in admissions at Harvard and who lived in a farmhouse without a farm. What a lucky little girl.

"Listen," said Timothy Valentine. "I have to go inside now, my family is waiting. Miss Hawthorne? Do you have somewhere to go? I'm assuming there's an adult with you?"

Timothy Valentine was looking at her expectantly, and she wanted (when had she not wanted this? She'd wanted it her whole life . . .) to give the correct answer.

"No," she said. "I mean, yes, yes, definitely. I do have somewhere to go."

CHAPTER 59
MARIANNE

Marianne was thinking about her current case, which she knew she was about to lose. Just the past Friday night she'd gone out for drinks with her friend Jillian at a wine

561

bar on Federal Hill and Marianne told her how sometimes she felt like packing it all in, going to work for a cushy law firm in Providence, getting a nice condo on the river. Or giving up the law altogether! Moving out to California, where her sister lived, where the winters were mild. Not that she could afford to do that, not in a million years. Although Nora would let her have the guest room. Or even Angela's room, once she went off to college.

"Totally," said Jillian. "I totally get it." But Jillian managed a women's clothing store on Thayer Street. She didn't get it, not really. Her biggest problem was when the overprivileged Brown students tried to shoplift.

Marianne was tired of slogging through the snow, tired of witnessing the underbelly of life, day after day after day. You could make a dent, but that was it. "It's like throwing pebbles into the ocean and expecting to create your own personal island," she told Jillian.

Only Monday! Such a long week stretched ahead of her. Christmas was hard for many of her clients: it made them feel even more grim and hopeless than they already felt, which was saying something.

How lucky Marianne was to have her

mother nearby, her sister geographically far but emotionally close. Still, sometimes around Christmas she did allow herself to indulge in a bit of melancholy. If you'd asked her long ago to make a reasonable prediction she would have said that *she* would be the one with the kids and the husband, not Nora. Nora had been the free spirit, driving her car out to California on a whim, dating a bunch of bastards before she met Gabe. Marianne had been the worker, the voice of the little people, the loyal girlfriend through four failed long-term relationships. She was the one who'd stayed behind. She hadn't strayed, hadn't wavered! And yet she was alone, married only to her work.

Her house was small and bordered on shabby; when it rained a lot, water seeped in through the foundation and into the unfinished basement. Marianne had wanted to redo the two bathrooms for about five years now.

A genie grants you three wishes . . .

A new bathroom, just one. The other can wait.

One of those fancy blenders that chops up whole apples and pulverizes greens.

Maybe . . . oh, maybe (was this too embarrassing, to wish for something so childish at age forty-one?), a Christmas surprise.

As she approached the house she could see the Christmas tree, leaning slightly, through the living room window. She'd put the lights on a timer so they would be on when she came home after work. She'd have to straighten the tree in the stand or she'd wake up one morning to find it entirely tipped over.

Strange. There was a car in her driveway, unfamiliar, a Hyundai. She pulled up beside it and a small lithe figure hopped out. It looked like . . . no, that was impossible — her eyes playing tricks on her in the dark. She should put the porch light on a timer too. She didn't know how to do that.

It really looked like . . .

It couldn't be. But it was.

"Hi, Aunt Marianne," said the voice in the semidarkness. "I didn't mean to scare you. It's me. It's Angela."

CHAPTER 60
NORA

The cost for four same-day cross-country tickets on the red-eye this close to Christmas with an open-ended return date was three thousand, two hundred, and sixty-three dollars, but none of the Hawthornes cared.

After Nora talked to Angela, after she talked to Marianne, after she talked to Gabe, who knew nothing of the whole fiasco until he finally had a chance to check his phone from the offsite, Nora booked them. There were only three more days before Christmas break. Missing three days of school wasn't going to kill anyone. She packed what she could of the Christmas presents she'd already purchased (embarrassingly, not much) and figured she'd get the rest at the Providence Place mall.

Up, up, up. Cecily gripped Nora's hand. They were all seasoned cross-country fliers, they went east at least twice a year, and yet Nora was surprised each and every time about how nervous flying made Cecily. Maya didn't care at all; she chattered with her seatmate, a young college student flying home for the holiday. (Booking so last minute, they couldn't secure seats all together, and Maya adamantly wanted the seat two rows back, so she could be "independent.") Cecily had a fear of heights, poor thing. And yet she'd stood on the Golden Gate Bridge, looking down, looking for someone to help. Gabe's eyes were closed. Nora had scored the window seat — Cecily didn't want it, it made her too anxious, and Gabe didn't care either way.

The senior partners at Elpis were going to let Gabe resign without a fuss. Joe Stone was *dead set* against that. He thought they should use Gabe's situation to send a message, loud and clear, to anyone out there who was considering falsifying a résumé. Internally and externally. That meant, according to Gabe, that it would be actual news — an article in the *Chronicle,* who knew what else. There'd be no escaping it. But the senior partners thought he could go quietly, discreetly, tail between his legs.

"Ugh," said Nora loyally. "I never liked that Joe Stone, did you? He always seemed so smarmy."

Nora pressed her forehead against the window. It was pitch-black; she couldn't see a thing beyond the runway. But she'd done this trip in all types of weather, at all different times of day. She knew what was out there. The glorious bay. The Bay Bridge. And far in the distance, the celebrated, magnificent, odious Golden Gate. She loved it, she hated it.

This city, this city she had loved for so long, was tethered really so tenuously by those two long bridges. It had been carved out of nothing, out of the wilderness and the mountains, its fate tied to the fates of the gold diggers, the intrepid explorers, the bold and the fearless and the plucky. She imagined a roll of fog unfurling from the Transamerica building. And they were off.

It took Cecily approximately thirty seconds to fall asleep. When she was definitely out Nora reached across her and tapped Gabe on the shoulder. He opened one eye, and then the other, like a man in a cartoon.

"Listen," she said. "I've been thinking. About staying out there." No answer. She elaborated. "For good, I mean. *Moving,* Gabe. Back home, back to Rhode Island."

Now he sat straight up and wore, for an instant, the expression he wore when he saw a snake. (Wyoming was home to two kinds of venomous rattlesnakes, and when Gabe was in elementary school a fellow third grader had died from a bite.) "Do you mean —" he said hoarsely. He cleared his throat and smoothed his forehead with the palm of his hand. "Do you mean with me, or without me?"

In another row, a baby cried. Nora remembered what that was like, flying across the country with babies. Awful. (Nobody ever said, *I'm afraid you're going to hurt the baby.*) A flight attendant made her way down the aisle, tapping the tops of the seats as she went. The seatbelt sign shut off: no turbulence.

"Of *course* I mean with you."

Gabe sighed and took her hand and closed his eyes again.

"I mean, what have we got to lose, right? I'm fired. You've resigned. Cecily and Maya are young and adaptable. Who knows where Angela is going to end up . . ."

Gabe held up his hand: the universal signal for *Stop talking.* Nora sat back. This seemed unfair. After the day Nora had had. The month she'd had! (The year.) She felt her temper begin to rise; she was about to get her Irish up. Then Gabe opened his eyes and said, "You don't need to keep selling it, realtor of the century. I was thinking the same thing. I'm in."

"You *are*?" She leaned forward. Never in a million years had Nora expected it to be that easy. *Don't sell it,* Arthur Sutton always said, *when it's already sold.* "You're *in*?"

"I am," said Gabe.

"Wow." Nora sat back. She had a whole box of unused arguments in a corner of her mind. "Wow," she said again.

She and Cecily and Gabe and Maya were the reverse gold rushers now. They were heading east to seek their fortune. They were the opposite of the bold and the plucky, and yet it felt plenty brave to Nora, to do this.

"Do you think we could get a puppy? Gabe? I'll take care of it, I'll do all the work, I'll clean up all the accidents, I swear. Gabe?"

This time he didn't answer; he was asleep.

She poked him, but gently. "Gabe?"

Definitely asleep. Maybe once he was really zonked out, totally dead to the world, she'd whisper a story to him. Tell him about the time she let Maya fall on her head.

Chapter 61
Melvin

Melvin Strickland got home before his wife, Carla, even left Kaiser. Sometimes — often — he stayed late at the school, but today, this close to winter break, he didn't. The shortest day of the year, Winter Solstice, his birthday, was only five days away.

As Melvin drove home, as he observed the white outline of the moon on the rise, as he pulled into the garage, as he entered the house, he was thinking about Virginia Woolf. Fifty-nine years old when she'd put those stones in her pockets and walked into the river in Sussex, only three years older than Melvin would be next week. As a child he'd hated having a birthday so close to Christmas, he'd considered it the ultimate swindle, but now he enjoyed it, because often his children came home for the holiday and were home on his birthday, too. The house, so often empty, filled up again with yelling and laughing and texting and little piles of clutter that drove Carla mad but that Melvin cherished as precious signs of young life.

Who knew what Woolf's output would have been had she lived. Perhaps her best writing was ahead of her; perhaps (more likely?) it was behind her. *Orlando, To the Lighthouse, Between the Acts.* So many brilliant works. Melvin thought again of his novel, the satire of the high school writing class. Yes, moving it to the college campus was just the thing to cure it. He would get started over break. He might get started now! Before Carla got home, he might yank the manuscript from where it lay — the desk drawer in his case not proverbial but actual — and give it a good airing.

On the front porch was a cardboard box that Melvin had asked to have delivered from the storage facility where he kept three decades of papers. He was a meticulous labeler, so this was the right box.

He switched on the two lamps in the living room, the low one on the end table and the tall one in the corner. He loved the way a room looked with lamplight. No garish overheads in the Strickland household, except the kitchen and bathrooms.

You have given me the greatest possible happiness, Virginia Woolf had written in her final note to her husband, her suicide note. Was there any greater compliment? He hoped Carla thought the same of him. He did of her.

In his bag was the paper Leslie Simmons had finally brought him, "The Use of Indirect Discourse in Virginia Woolf." A sophisticated topic but not one that couldn't conceivably be thought of separately by two different students. It happened.

Some mild discomfort, a squeezing in the middle of his chest. He sat down in the living room. It passed. He'd make dinner for Carla for when she got home, pour her a glass of wine. His specialty was a Bolognese sauce like the one he and Carla had on their honeymoon in the Italian Alps. His secret ingredient was chicken livers, pulsed in the food processor. Sometimes a touch of veal stock, if he had it in the freezer.

Virginia Woolf, stones in her pockets. Dinner for Carla, a bottle of Pinot Grigio, her favorite, chilled, poured into a glass just before she walked in the door. *The greatest possible happiness.*

But first, the papers. He used the kitchen

scissors to open the box, then removed the folder from his satchel and spread everything out on the kitchen table. If there was one thing Melvin Strickland couldn't abide (and, truth be told, there were many, just ask Carla!), it was plagiarism.

And there it was. Clarissa Dalloway, running into Hugh Whitbread: *They had just come up — unfortunately — to see doctors. Other people came to see pictures; go to the opera; take their daughters out; the Whitbreads came "to see doctors." Times without number Clarissa had visited Evelyn Whitbread in a nursing home. Was Evelyn sick again?* Woolf's use of free indirect discourse here serves a dual purpose . . .

He could go on, he would go on, but truly he didn't need to. *You little shit,* he thought, *you baseball-cap-wearing louse. Plagiarizing. From your own sister. You, sir, I have no use for. I am going to bring you down.*

CHAPTER 62
NORA

Later, after the tears and the recriminations and the reunions and the you-scared-us-to-deaths and the thank-God-you're-okays, they did what people do in Rhode Island in times of joy or sorrow: they went to Newport Creamery.

"I still cannot believe that you used to work here," said Angela. She said the same thing every time they came to Rhode Island.

"I didn't work in this one," said Nora. "The one I worked in is closed now." Nora said that every time too. She studied the menu and felt a pinch of nostalgia for her earnest, freckled high school self, upselling from a cone to a sundae. Even then she could sell anything to anyone.

"Breakfast?" said the waitress. "Coffee?" Her accent was so perfectly Rhode Island that Nora thought about hugging her.

"Ice cream," they all said together, and Nora said, "Five Awful Awfuls."

"Junior, or Outrageous?"

"I don't know if I —" said Angela, but Nora plowed right over her words. "Outrageous," said Nora. "Definitely Outrageous."

When the waitress had gone Nora cleared her throat and said, "Okay, then." She took out a napkin, and a Uni-ball Vision pen from her bag. They'd arrived at Logan Airport at 5:43 that morning and by 6:20 they were in a rented car heading south on 95 toward Rhode Island. She was exhausted — they were all exhausted. But she was also in Organized Mom mode. She said, "Angela. I've spoken to Ms. Vogel, and she had

573

some wonderful suggestions for other schools you might want to look at, for the regular application deadlines. With the Common Application and your recommendation letters already written it won't take too much to pull things together. There really are some lovely schools in the East that you haven't considered yet. Small, close-knit, wonderful liberal arts educations. Mt. Holyoke, Smith, Williams."

Nora paused and picked up the napkin while the waitress delivered the goods.

"This is gigantic!" said Maya delightedly. "I can't believe you're letting me drink this."

Cecily took up her straw with a considerable amount of glee and said, "We didn't even have *breakfast* yet."

Gabe nodded wisely at Nora. "Wonderful schools. Maybe we can take a look at them while we're out here."

"Dad," said Angela, and there were tiny daggers attached to the word. Nora wanted to say, *Don't say it that way. You're breaking his heart.*

"I'm sure you know, Henrietta Faulkner didn't get into Harvard either."

"Believe me, I know," said Angela. "I know."

"I don't think it was so much your application, specifically, as it was —" He choked on the end of the sentence and failed to get it all the way out. Nora handed him a napkin from the dispenser on the table and he covered his mouth with it and blinked rapidly.

Cecily and Maya were tucking into their Awful Awfuls, blissfully unaware, but Angela, who had pushed hers aside and was drinking water, was taking it all in, watching Gabe from over the top of her glass.

Nora wanted to say, "Do something! *Help* him! Make him feel better!" But it wasn't her place. Angela had to come to this on her own.

"Angela," said Gabe.

"You're stressing her out," said Maya around her straw.

"He's not stressing me out. But. I've been thinking a lot about it and —" Here Angela took a deep breath, seemed to gather some inner strength. "And I'm not sure I want to go to college . . ."

Nora said, *"What?"*

Gabe said, *"Huh?"*

Cecily said, "I *knew* she was going to say that."

Angela took her first sip of her Awful Awful and said, "I wasn't done! You interrupted me, you all interrupted me." She continued, "Let me *finish.* I was going to say I'm not

575

sure I want to go to college *next year.* I might want to take some time, figure out where I really want to be. Take a gap year, make sure I land at the right school when it's time."

"Wow, hey," said Gabe. The old Gabe would have said, *Those always turn into a gap decade.* The old Gabe would have said, *Absolutely not.*

Nora said, "I don't know . . ."

"I've already decided," said Angela. "I've completely and totally decided. I thought about it a lot. I've been thinking about it all fall."

"You're valedictorian," said Nora. "It doesn't seem —"

Angela grimaced. "I may not be, when they recalculate. Among other things, I didn't exactly, um, set the world on fire with my last AP English paper. I was so stressed out trying to be perfect that I almost plagiarized."

"Excuse me?" said Nora.

Maya said, "What's plagiarized?" When nobody answered her she shrugged and went back to her Awful Awful.

"*Ugh,* never mind, forget I said anything, I totally didn't. But it wasn't my best, I wrote it at the last minute and it's a big part of our grade."

Nora thought it was wise of Gabe not to enter the fray just then.

"But what would you *do*?" said Gabe. "To be productive?"

"I'm not just going to sit around playing *Minion Rush*. If that's what you're thinking."

"I wasn't," said Gabe.

"That's what *I'd* do with a gap year," said Maya. "I love *Minion Rush*."

"I'm going to volunteer somewhere," Angela said.

"Not a bad idea," said Nora thoughtfully. "I know there are lots of inner-city schools in Boston, and I bet there are some rural programs not too far —"

"Somewhere far away," said Angela. "I'm thinking India." Her look said, *Go ahead, challenge me. I dare you.*

"India?" said Nora.

"Absolutely not," said Gabe.

"Or Belize," said Angela. "But probably India. It's the right thing for me. Mom. It's the right thing. Daddy, I know it is."

Across the restaurant someone dropped silverware, and closer to them the door opened and brought with it a slice of New England winter air. A baby cried. Ordinary, ordinary, all of it was very ordinary. But not to Nora. Later she would look back on that

577

moment and say, *Yes! Right there. That's when it happened. That's when things began to change back to the way they were supposed to be.* Or maybe that moment actually started a day earlier, when Angela boarded a plane to Boston by herself and wrestled her demons to the ground.

Daddy. Could you feel a person brighten from just one word? Nora thought that you could. She had been sipping at her Awful Awful the whole time. It went down even easier than a glass of Cabernet. Easy peasy lemon squeezie. It was the flavor of her youth — the flavor of full-fat, high-calorie hope and optimism. She looked down. It had happened quickly: her glass was already half empty.

Or was it half full? Corny as it was, Nora permitted herself the question.

EPILOGUE

One Year Later

"Come on, Maya," said Nora. "We've got to hurry, or we're going to be late." Cecily was in the car already.

Sometimes Nora caught a glimpse of Maya out of the corner of her eye and thought she was looking at Angela a decade ago. Maya had grown taller and leaner over a summer spent at the beach and in an ocean discovery summer camp, which she attended when she wasn't working with her new reading tutor to prepare for third grade. When, at the end of August, Maya came to Nora and cleared her young throat and read page one, chapter one, of *Betsy-Tacy* to her in a voice as smooth as butter, with real expression, pausing at all the right spots, Nora had to try hard not to bawl.

"It wasn't just me," said the tutor, shrugging modestly. "Something clicked. Things fell into place. That just takes longer for some kids than it does for others. She'll be right on track before you know it."

"Buckle up," said Nora now. "Hurry, hurry."

"I thought you weren't in the business of hurrying us anymore," said Cecily. Maya's seat belt was tangled, so Cecily reached over and helped her.

"Sometimes, I am," said Nora. "Today I am. I don't want to be late."

Traffic wasn't too bad; it was early afternoon still. They'd get socked with it on the way back, though. No doubt.

Very occasionally Nora missed looking out of a car window and seeing the mountains and the valleys and the majestic Pacific, symbols, all of them, of the vastness and promise of a recently discovered world. But most of the time she felt better in the canopy of trees along Interstate 95. Even when they were bare, awaiting the first snow, as they were now. Apparently they were in for quite a winter.

"Do you think Santa is going to bring me an iPhone on Thursday?" asked Maya.

"Absolutely I don't," said Nora. "You're eight years old. You just got out of your car seat. In fact, I can pretty much guarantee it."

"*I* don't have an iPhone," said Cecily.

"And I'm eleven."

"It could happen," said Maya optimistically.

More often than Nora wanted to she dreamed about the Golden Gate Bridge. Sometimes she dreamed she saw a dark shadow falling, falling over the rails. She always woke up before whoever it was hit the bottom. Sometimes she called out, but other times she woke up and lay quietly, while Gabe slept beside her and Ace, the rescue dog they'd adopted in the fall, snorted and shifted and dreamed in his bed under the window. Ace was of unknown origins — there was maybe some shepherd in there, maybe some collie, perhaps a dash of retriever, but not an ounce of Newfie. That was okay. You couldn't go back and repeat the past, even if you tried. It was never the same.

Most Saturday mornings Nora and Marianne and sometimes their mom and usually the girls drove to the beach with giant coffees from TLC Coffee Roasters and let Ace run on the sand. Gabe came occasionally, if he wasn't buried with work. Gabe loved being buried with work. He was working as an independent consultant, making steps toward starting his own firm in Providence. It was tough going, getting clients on his own, but when he got them, he shined. He had a new résumé — a correct résumé — and a strong letter of recommendation from the founding partners at Elpis, who cited "family reasons" as the impetus for Gabe's departure. Joe Stone had cautioned the partners against signing the letter, but they'd gone ahead and done it anyway.

Nora had a stack of ten books on her nightstand and she had read at least two of them in the past three months. Progress! When they'd first moved to Rhode Island she'd made inquiries at a few of the real estate companies in the area, but none were hiring. That was okay too, she decided. She wasn't sure she had it in her anymore — shining a bright light on all the corners of other people's lives, poking around to see what was worth what. Leave that for others. ("You could always sell anything," her mother told her. "Just pick something different to sell. I have a bird-watching friend who has a business selling —" But Nora stopped her. She wasn't ready.)

"How much longer?" asked Maya. Nora glanced at the clock. "Thirty-five minutes," she said. "I hope."

The Hawthorne house in Marin had sold after two days on the market the previous summer. Nora had asked Arthur Sutton to take the listing but he had bequeathed it to Seth, who, truth be told, had done an extraordinary job with the marketing materials. They had their first offer after the open house, and then a small but vehement bidding war ensued. Sally Bentley represented the buyers, go figure, and all went smoothly, with each and every disclosure sheet filled out correctly and filed on time. Nora even disclosed things she knew nobody cared about. She disclosed the heck out of that house. When Loretta Miller filed for divorce and moved in with a woman she'd gone to college with, neither Miller had the energy to bring up Marin dwarf flax. Barry was considering selling.

There was a lovely little Irish dance school not too far away from their new house and every now and then Nora drove Cecily by and parked outside and they watched the dancers through the big glass window and Nora said, "Well?" But Cecily always shook her head. She had taken up soccer. She was a latecomer to the sport — most of the girls in the fifth grade had been playing since the tot league — but after all of those hours and days and years of Irish dancing her footwork was outstanding. She was scrappy, when she cared to be. And she was a fast learner. Her coach thought she had real promise.

"Like, college scholarship promise?" Gabe asked, and Nora had to say, "Stop!"

With their rescue dog, their gap-year-teaching-in-poverty-stricken-India daughter, their modest Rhode Island house, worth a fraction of what their house in California had been worth, you might look at them and think they'd learned to look only outward. Do unto others, and so forth.

But in fact Nora spent an inordinate amount of time going over the events of the past year in her mind, combing them for clues, or looking for some understanding. And every now and then she caught herself doing something she shouldn't, like checking Gabe's email. Just to see if she was missing something. Just a quick little peek. Of course she *trusted* him. But. A spouse was allowed to wonder, sometimes.

One day she spotted an email with the subject heading "Abby Freeman." Her heart constricted. *Don't,* Nora told herself. *This is not meant for you.* With quaking fingers, she clicked it open anyway. It was from Doug Maverick, letting Gabe know (in case he was wondering) that Abby Freeman, soon after being hired for a full-time position at Elpis, had begun sleeping with Joe Stone. Well, who was to say when it had started, really. Could have been during Abby's internship. Doug Maverick called it "a sordid affair, really messy." He didn't give any other details, though Nora really wanted them. Both had been summarily dismissed once the affair was discovered (unfortunately, by Joe Stone's wife). The whole situation was awkward, Doug noted, because typically the HR department did the letting go, but in this case . . . well, anyway. Doug Maverick was going to be on the East Coast just after the New Year, did Gabe want to get together in Boston? Doug had a couple of leads for projects, he'd heard great things about the work Gabe was doing . . .

You shouldn't take joy in other people's misfortunes, Nora told herself sternly. That is not the way you were raised. That's not the way you're raising your children, is it? *Is it?*

Of course it wasn't. She would never. But she couldn't help it. She smiled, and it felt good.

They pulled into the international terminal at Logan and Nora began scouring the area for a parking spot.

Three wishes, Genie.

Bring her back to me.

Bring her back to Gabe.

Go back to the beginning and start again.

The emails were first addressed only to Nora but as time went on she noticed they were addressed to Gabe too and they got more colorful and descriptive the longer Angela stayed away. This may or may not have had something to do with the fact that Gabe had handwritten Angela a long letter in October. Nora didn't know what the letter said, although of course she was *dying* to read it. (It was much more difficult to spy on communication that wasn't electronic. Unfortunately.)

Angela was teaching in a school for the disabled. India was hot and dusty and beautiful and destitute and terrifying and loud and bright and wonderful and overflowing with life — it was like no place she'd ever seen. A majority of the children at the school had prosthetic limbs. Most of them were so full of love and joy that Angela couldn't believe it. Given their circumstances. Given any circumstances! Angela had learned to make chutney and to eat *paneer parathas* and *aloo tikki*. And *dal*. Lots of *dal*. Angela sent a photo of herself in a sari; a photo of herself on an overnight trip to the Taj Mahal, the building rising like a great white ghost behind her; a photo of herself touching an elephant's trunk; a photo of herself with her arm around a tiny

Indian girl named Sakshi who looked seven but was apparently twelve. Sakshi's eyes were *ridiculously* enormous.

"Moon eyes," said Gabe wistfully, looking at the photo.

In November, Angela emailed and wanted to know if her friend Owen from England could come home with her for Christmas. He taught at the same school.

"Of *course,*" wrote back Nora immediately.

"Where will they sleep?" asked Maya now, as they all squinted at the arrivals board in the international terminal.

"Remember?" said Cecily. "You're sleeping in with me, and Angela gets your room. Owen gets the guest room. You'd better not sleepwalk, you know that freaks me out."

"I don't sleepwalk anymore," said Maya.

Nora and the girls found the gate and positioned themselves where they had a good view of the passengers. Four hours from New Delhi to Dubai, then a six-hour layover, then fourteen and a half hours to Boston. They would be exhausted. She checked her phone again; Gabe was coming from a meeting in Boston, and he wasn't sure if he'd make it in time. Nothing yet.

"I see her!" said Cecily, craning her neck. "I *see* her!"

Nora might not have recognized her own daughter if Cecily hadn't pointed her out first. Her hair was pulled back loosely. She had more color in her face than she'd ever had before. She was wearing some sort of complicated cottony number. The planes of her face had softened significantly. And — here was the unfamiliar part — she was glowing. She was positively *glowing.*

"Oooooh," said Maya. "Look at Angela's *boyfriend.* They're holding *hands.*" She bounced up and down on her toes.

They drew closer. Owen was tall and thin and *British* looking, with a serious expression and Harry Potter glasses and an adorable flop of dark hair. As Nora watched he bent down to Angela and said something in her ear and she smiled and pushed against his arm and lingered there in the way you would do only if you were, for lack of a better word, *intimate* with somebody.

Oh! thought Nora. Oh. Oh my. She recalculated. Of course, they were young and in love, of course there was *sex,* but she hadn't expected . . . well, she didn't know how to explain it.

She guessed, when you got down to brass tacks, she hadn't expected to feel like she'd gotten her daughter back and lost her all in the same afternoon.

"Daddy!" cried Maya, and here came Gabe, bounding toward them, his computer bag banging against his hip, his cell phone in his hand.

"Am I too late?" He looked nervous, like a child about to go up and give an oral report in school.

"No," said Nora. She reached for his arm, pulled him toward the little cluster of Hawthornes. "No, you're not too late at all. You are perfect. You are exactly on time."

ACKNOWLEDGMENTS

Eternal thanks go to my wonderful agent and tireless supporter, Elisabeth Weed, and to her assistant, Dana Murphy, as well as Jenny Meyer for handling foreign rights. A bucketful of gratitude is due to my brilliant editor, Melissa Danaczko, and the eagle-eyed Margo Shickmanter, and to everyone at Doubleday for welcoming me into the fold so warmly. Jo-Ellen Truelove O'Dell, the very best high school English teacher out there, shared myriad and juicy details about rigorous high school classes and steered me right when I went wrong. Shiloh Hagen did the same regarding the high-end real estate market in Northern California. Liana McCabe answered my medical questions. Blair Nelson talked to me about the consulting world. Todd Jacobsen deserves belated thanks for what has become years of website help. The community of Danville, California, welcomed my family and me during the year we lived there. I don't know what I'd do without my tiny writers' club, of which fellow author Katie Schickel is the only other member. Newburyport ladies: you know who you are. Margaret Dunn provided a sounding board when I desperately needed one and along with Jennifer Truelove and my sister put oodles of cross-country miles on the minivan and spent many a night with me in shady, dog-friendly motels. My parents, John and Sara Mitchell; my sister, Shannon Mitchell; and my in-laws in the Moore and Destrampe families always provide love, support, and child care where necessary.

Addie, Violet, and Josie, I thank you for growing up in front of my very eyes with intelligence, grace, and humor. You teach me as much as I teach you. And to Brian, for too many things to name — for everything, really — but especially for bringing us back home.

ABOUT THE AUTHOR

Meg Mitchell Moore is the author of the novels *The Arrivals* and *So Far Away.* She worked for several years as a journalist for a variety of publications. She lives in Newburyport, Massachusetts, with her husband and three daughters.